W9-AEB-532

BENEATH THESE STONES

Also by Ann Granger

Mitchell and Markby Crime Novels
Say It With Poison
A Season For Murder
Cold In The Earth
Murder Among Us
Where Old Bones Lie
A Fine Place For Death
Flowers For His Funeral
A Candle For A Corpse
A Touch Of Mortality
A Word After Dying
Call The Dead Again
That Way Murder Lies

Fran Varady Crime Novels
Asking For Trouble
Keeping Bad Company
Running Scared

BENEATH
THESE STONES

Ann Granger

St. Martin's Minotaur 🅼 New York

Library of Congress Cataloging-in-Publication Data

Granger, Ann.
    Beneath these stones / Ann Granger.
        p.   cm.
    ISBN 0-312-24178-X
    1. Mitchell, Meredith (Fictitious character)—Fiction.
2. Markby, Alan (Fictitious character)—Fiction. 3. Villages—
England—Cotswold Hills—Fiction. 4. Police—England—
Cotswold Hills—Fiction. 5. Cotswold Hills (England)—
Fiction. I. Title.
PR6057.R259B46   2000
823'914—dc21   99-88105
                                                                        CIP

First published in Great Britain by Headline Book
Publishing, a division of Hodder Headline PLC

First U.S. Edition: March 2000

10 9 8 7 6 5 4 3 2 1

BENEATH
THESE STONES

CHAPTER ONE

'Sorry to be a bit on the late side,' said George Biddock. 'I had to go and visit my old auntie. She's over ninety, you know. Bit deaf and legs not too good, but wonderful bright.'

'I understand,' said Meredith Mitchell, glancing obviously at her wristwatch. 'Yes, a marvellous age. I did tell you, Mr Biddock, I had to catch a train this morning.'

'Well, off you go then, my duck,' returned George amiably, 'and get your train.' He made catching trains sound like an eccentric hobby. 'I got your little drawing here and all my measurements.' To prove it, he took it from his pocket, much crumpled and with curious marks in blue pencil all over it.

They were standing by the front door of Meredith's end-of-terrace cottage. George sucked his teeth and gazed appraisingly at the frontage in a professional manner as he tucked the plan back in his pocket. Meredith suspected there it would remain until the job was finished. She gazed speculatively at George and wondered whether engaging Mr Biddock to build a small porch had been the right decision.

The builder was a local man. Bamford people, when they heard someone wanted a small job done, invariably advised, 'You need George Biddock for that.'

The idea that someone might not ask George was seen as an affront to local pride. When Meredith had mentioned to her neighbour, Mrs Crouch, that she was thinking of having a small porch added to her modest house, she was, predictably, recommended to get hold of George.

'He'll fix that up for you in no time.' What was more, Mrs Crouch had George's phone number written in wax crayon on a laminated

1

cardboard owl in her kitchen. After that the die was cast. George Biddock it had to be.

So it had come about that Meredith had arranged to arrive late at her Foreign Office desk today in order to wait for George. There were last-minute details to settle before she went off to catch the London train and George set about constructing the porch. He had delivered the wood and some bags of cement the evening before on an elderly rattling truck. The wood lay in unsawn lengths at the side of the path. The cement bags were decently shrouded in a plastic sheet.

The porch had seemed like a very good idea. The hall was draughty. A porch would, Meredith hoped, lead to lower heating bills. Moreover, anyone standing at the front door in inclement weather got wet through. Meredith, after getting soaked while hunting for her key throughout the winter, had decided that enough was enough and come spring, something would have to be done.

George had received the commission with the words, 'Ah, Doris Crouch said you was wanting a rustic porch.' So it was a good job I asked him, thought Meredith, realising bush telegraph had got there before her.

To be fair, he had seemed to know what she was talking about and his price was reasonable. At the same time, she was fully aware it was necessary to get things quite clear at the outset or George would build what he thought was suitable, not what she wanted. But now, for the first time, a real niggle of doubt as to his overall reliability assailed her. It was kind of George to visit an aged aunt. George was on the wrong side of sixty himself and Meredith wasn't surprised to learn Auntie was a nonagenarian. On the other hand, she hoped Auntie wasn't going to prove the standard excuse for late arrival or outright nonappearance. Still, he was here now, a tall gangling figure wearing an ancient suit over a ragged knitted sweater. The jacket sleeves stopped well short of his wrists and his huge gnarled hands dangled in a sinister fashion by his sides. A greasy flat cap crowned his balding head. A stub of pencil protruded from behind one ear, an unlit crushed cigarette from behind the other.

'I'll leave you to it, then,' she said.

'Ah,' said George absently. As far as he was concerned she was dismissed. To hang around now would be to get under his feet was the unspoken hint.

Meredith backed her car out of the garage and prepared to drive to the station. On a last impulse, she lowered the window and called out, 'I gave you my office number, didn't I? You will ring up if there's a problem?'

'Little job like that?' returned George. 'Be a doddle. Off you go. Doris Crouch will have seen me get here and got the kettle on.'

Oh dear. Meredith let the window up again, shutting out George and whatever work practices he observed. She'd hired him and couldn't unhire him. Anyway, she hadn't time to argue.

As it was, being late set an immediate problem. The station car park was full. She had to drive on to a bumpy grass verge at the far end of it and leave the car there. Technically the verge was within the precincts of the car park and covered by her parking permit, but it didn't improve her mood to swing her legs out of the front seat and feel her high heels sink into the mud.

Perhaps getting George along to build a porch really had little to do with wet weather, but a lot to do with Meredith's general feeling of late. Life wasn't going the way she wanted and she told herself she ought to get a grip on things. It all had to do with Alan, of course. Alan and his proposal of marriage. The proposal she'd turned down. A refusal he, in turn, had accepted with a kind of obstinate calm, as if he were sure, in time, she'd change her mind.

Which she was not going to do, she had told herself countless times, whilst travelling, showering, washing up, cleaning her teeth, ostensibly dealing with official business. In fact, in the course of every activity you could name off the top of your head. Such resolve should have left her at peace. It had left her instead in a state of high dissatisfaction. She blamed his attitude for making her feel a worm and belligerent at one and the same time. Hence the decision to brush up her lifestyle.

The porch wasn't the only thing decided on to this end. She'd got far too careless about clothes and general appearance. She'd never been a fashion plate and never would, although she was tall enough to be a professional model. But she was a plain Jane, as she'd been told often during her childhood. 'Lucky Meredith has got a good brain!' some kindly aunt had once said in her hearing. 'Because she's never going to set the world on fire with her face.'

Reflecting on this in adulthood, Meredith thought that it would be very difficult to set anything on fire with your face. The remark hadn't particularly hurt her feelings at the time, and hadn't worried her later. On the other hand, she'd told her reflection in the bedroom mirror only yesterday, there's no excuse for going about looking, as the same aunt would have put it, as if you'd been dragged through a hedge backwards.

Having had a little more time this morning to get ready, therefore, she'd spent it on her appearance. She wore a new rust-coloured business suit and had styled her bobbed brown hair with care. The shoes were fairly new, too, but now both heels were ringed with a mud collar. No time to wipe it off. The train was approaching. Meredith locked the car, hitched up the tight skirt and, briefcase in hand, sprinted at admirable speed in the heels across the car park. She made it through the station entrance and arrived on the platform as the doors of the train hissed open. She jumped on and fell into the nearest seat.

One advantage of travelling later in the day was lack of fellow passengers. Instead of being jammed in a sweating ill-tempered crowd, she had a choice of seats in a carriage only dotted with other travellers. On the opposite side of the aisle a man sat reading his paper, although he took time off from that to have a good stare at her legs. Meredith wriggled the skirt back down as far as it would go, which wasn't very far. Two women conversed further along. A teenager with headphones clamped to his ears twitched and bobbed his head in a world of his own at the far end. She put her briefcase on the seat and searched her bag for a tissue to clean up the shoes. The train doors hissed shut and they moved out of the station. Before it had progressed very far down the line, however, and before picking up any real speed, it slowed again and came to a stop. Meredith, shoe in one hand and tissue in the other, peered out of the window.

They were just short of a disused Victorian viaduct of modest proportions, surrounded by woodland. The embankment rose steeply to either side of the tracks, overgrown with nettles, mostly blackened from the winter frosts but with a few bright green shoots pushing through. There were brambles, and young elderberry seedlings mingled with last year's straggling bare branches of buddleia, that plant that loves to insert itself into unlikely nooks and crannies and has an affinity with railways, often choosing to sprout up in the narrow space between parallel tracks. That was just coming into leaf. Amongst and beyond these, assorted spindly trees and bushes crawled in a tangled mass to the top of the embankment. But right in front . . .

Meredith's heart gave a startled hop. Right opposite, staring her malevolently in the eye, was a large green frog.

Bright emerald in colour, with bulging black eyes and made of some kind of soft furry pile cloth, it dangled from the lowest branch of a nearby birch, apparently caught by an attached strap. Meredith realised it was one of the popular kind of backpack shaped in comic animal form. She couldn't think what it was doing here. It looked clean, dry, undamaged. Brand-new, in fact. Sadly, people did dump their rubbish in the countryside. Supermarket trolleys, old bedsteads and sundry black plastic bags turned up in the unlikeliest spots. But this grotesque creature, with its expression which was both amusing and just a little threatening, didn't qualify as junk. Meredith frowned.

The man across the aisle put down his newspaper and seeing that his travelling companion was staring intently through the window, observed, 'They'll be working on the new track. We were held up yesterday at the same time. They'll let us through in a minute.'

'Yes,' said Meredith absently. At another time she might have fretted at the delay to a day already beginning behind schedule. At this rate, she wouldn't appear at her desk until lunchtime. But distracted by the frog's pop-eyed gaze, she gave the man's words little attention. He shrugged and taking out his mobile phone, began to communicate news of his predicament to anyone who might be interested and probably to several who weren't.

'Hullo, Roger? I'll be in a little late . . .'

She was now able to distinguish the chaotic jungle of growth in better detail as her eyes became accustomed to the shady bank. Further up, there looked to be a kind of path beaten through the vegetation, though who would want to climb down here she couldn't imagine. Unless, of course, intrepid blackberry gatherers had been attracted last autumn to the brambles, undeterred by trains roaring past.

Suddenly, in a movement which gave her quite a jolt, a large black shape lifted from the ground and burst out of the trees to flap away over the viaduct. She stilled her nerves. Just a crow which had been foraging about on the ground. There must be pickings down there for carrion eaters. Dead birds, mice, the remains of a fox's kill, perhaps. Meredith felt a stir of unease nevertheless. It was that frog, those lifeless shiny protuberant eyes, the bizarre nature of the thing. And what the dickens was it doing there at all? She pressed her nose against the window and squinted furiously.

'Hullo, James, I'm stuck in a train . . .'

That man was going to work through his address book. Meredith wrenched her gaze from the frog and finished cleaning up her shoes. She got up and made her way to a rubbish receptacle and got rid of the muddy tissues. When she returned to her seat, the man opposite was disturbing the morning routine of someone called Cathy.

Meredith returned to her study of the frog. Just then, the train lurched into movement and the frog, caught by the movement of air, swayed, giving the impression it waved farewell with its token green plush arms (or front legs, if one wanted to be pedantic).

'Goodbye to you, too,' murmured Meredith unwarily. The man opposite tucked away the phone and glanced across at her. He picked up his paper and retired behind it again. If you travel by train in Britain, he was probably thinking, you're going to meet the occasional potty one. The young woman across the aisle didn't fit the usual pattern of travelling nutter, but you never knew.

Slowly they rocked down the track, beneath the looming arch of the old viaduct, into shadow, out into the sunshine again. The workmen in their fluorescent orange jackets were standing back from the track, leaning on their shovels. They watched the train pass with little interest. It picked up speed and soon they were rattling along, swaying, as the driver tried to make up some of the lost time. The green frog slipped down into the recesses of Meredith's memory and lodged there, temporarily forgotten.

'Sorry to be so late,' Meredith apologised to Gerald with whom she was obliged to share a roomy office. 'Has anyone wanted me?'

'No,' said Gerald cheerfully. 'But since you're here, I'm taking an early lunch. Coming along?'

Meredith thought of the canteen and shook her head. 'I had a late breakfast and I've got an apple and a bag of peanuts in my case.'

'Planning a trip to the zoo? That's the sort of food they feed the chimps.'

'You say the nicest things, Gerald.'

'I need a proper lunch,' he retorted. 'I like a cooked meal in the middle of the day.'

'What's the matter? Doesn't your mother feed you?'

That was an unkind crack and in revenge for the one he'd made about her lunch. Gerald, at the age of thirty-nine, lived with a doting and possessive mother who, it was obvious to all beholders, fed him very well.

'If I don't eat properly,' said Gerald, 'I can't concentrate. I think they've got macaroni cheese down there today!' He trotted away happily.

Meredith opened her case, took out the apple and set it neatly on her desk. Then she sat staring at the telephone. She hadn't seen Alan since the previous weekend and neither had rung the other. That could mean no more than he was busy. She could lift the phone. Lift it now and ring him at Regional HQ. Just a couple of words. Just to say hullo. But a strange reluctance stayed her hand. There had been a subtle change in the nature of her relationship with Alan. An invisible line drawn somewhere in both their minds had been crossed. It could be expressed more simply and brutally: he was a rejected suitor, behaving decently in the circumstances. She was eaten up with guilt because she'd made him unhappy.

Of course, both had declared they could go on as before, until such time as they might discuss the topic again – *A chance would be a fine thing, chum!* said a disagreeable little voice in Meredith's head at this juncture. *Who says he'll ask you again? Why should he? Anyway you don't want him to, do you?* – but it wasn't as simple as that. How could it be?

Meredith moved her gaze to contemplate the apple instead, and wondered what would have become of the human race if Eve had turned down Adam. No, the other way round, if Adam had turned down Eve. Because it was Eve who picked the apple, wasn't it, and tempted poor old weak-willed Adam. Heh! I bet Adam needed no urging. Why was it always the woman's fault? Why should she feel it was *her* fault? Because her refusal had hurt Alan, she told herself. That was something she wouldn't have wanted and had known she couldn't avoid. Obstinate in this as she was in other things, she'd still clung to a decision worked out with much heart-searching and what at the time she'd liked to think was honesty, even courage. As time passed, she was less sure about either of the last two.

'I just don't know if I did the right thing,' she told the apple.

Good job Gerald wasn't here. The merest hint was always enough to set Gerald asking questions. Perhaps Gerald ought to have been a policeman, like Alan. Gerald, once on the scent, wasn't easily shaken off. For that reason, she'd remained doggedly bright and cheery here at work over the last few weeks. Well, she might fool Gerald, but she didn't fool herself. Meredith sighed. She *had* been a fool, she supposed, to imagine that things could just go on as they were. That they, she and Alan, could just go on. Superficially, they had, of course. But there was no denying there was a certain underlying awkwardness between them now.

Meredith pushed aside the apple and with it the vexed topic. She had spent enough time worrying at it like a terrier with some toy. She turned her attention resolutely to her in-tray.

Even as Meredith made her decision to leave calling Alan until later, gypsy Danny Smith was beginning a cautious descent through the wooded cover of the railway embankment to visit his rabbit snares.

Danny was in his early forties, though he looked older. He had travelled the stretch of road running parallel to the railway line for years. All his life, in fact. His parents had travelled this part of the country before him and now he, his wife and children appeared at six-monthly intervals and parked the trailer in the same field on Hazelwood Farm for five or six weeks at a time.

That arrangement also dated back untold years. His parents had camped there with the agreement of old man Franklin and now Danny and his family camped there with the tacit say-so of the old man's son, Hugh. Danny's elder sons, both married with families of their own, travelled other roads and no longer came to the farm. Normally travelling people weren't welcome on private land, but the farmer's family made an exception of the Smiths who, in any case, were not wandering hippies, but true Romanies. Danny carried a traveller's pass to prove it. The pass would have allowed the Smiths on to established gypsy sites, but Danny had little use for those. Even the idea of being organised to that extent filled him with horror and incomprehension.

His married sons, on the other hand, largely at the urging of their wives, seemed to head from one approved site to the next. Danny saw this as a kind of betrayal of their upbringing. The next step would be a house. They would end up rejecting not only their freedom but a way of life which the gypsies had led in Europe since the Middle Ages, when they'd arrived on their long migration from India, preceded, legend had it, by their king on a white horse and with a band playing.

Apart from the freedom, another advantage to pitching camp at Hazelwood was that the farm offered casual labour and a chance to earn a bit of money. Danny did a fair day's work for his reward, cash only, of course, paid daily.

The warren on the bank here dated back centuries, Danny reckoned. Perhaps it had been here nearly as long as the gypsies had. Rabbits, too, had arrived in England only in the early Middle Ages. He knew this because Simon Franklin, who was a scholar, had told him. Then they were a gentleman's meat. Later they became a poor man's dish. Now, few ate them at all, excepting Danny and his kind and older country folk, despite the fact that they were a clean meat and good eating.

Some of the old workings had been abandoned, others were still in use both by rabbits and other creatures taking advantage of the excavations. The indefatigable rabbits tunnelled out fresh passages and added to the subterranean maze. The whole bank was riddled with holes like a Swiss cheese. The tree roots held the earth together. Without them, given a few winter storms, the whole lot would've subsided into a spongy mess.

Rabbits had their ways and Danny knew most of them. Once an animal left its burrow it didn't just run anywhere. It was a territorial little creature and made for its habitual foraging areas travelling by familiar paths. Once you'd worked out where the rabbits ran, you stood a fair chance of catching one or two overnight. Rabbits liked to feed in the early dawn and at twilight. Then, at a hint of danger, they would scamper away, the light-coloured fur on the underside of their tails a warning in the gloom to fellow browsers.

He scrambled and slid down the bank, following the faint track between the clumps of trees and bushes. As he neared the bottom, he could see the bright glitter of the railway line. He'd watched the stationary train from above and waited until it rattled away before making his own move. He was aware that in the eyes of authority he was breaking the law in several ways by being here, but that was not the only reason for his discretion. Like the wild creatures whose ways he knew so well, Danny had an innate dislike of being observed. Sitting up there on a tree stump, he'd wondered what it must be like to be carried around at speed, hurtling towards distant destinations, the passing landscape just a blur. He'd never been on a train. Wouldn't have fancied the idea, sealed up in a tin can and borne along without control. Danny frowned, not at the glitter of track, but at an alien smudge of garish emerald among the natural shades of brown, grey and spring green around him.

He stopped. Now his senses picked up a faint nuance of some recent disturbance. Something out of place. Something wrong. He turned his head from side to side, peering into the undergrowth with his quick dark eyes. He sniffed at the air. All was quiet. But now his skin prickled. Unease had become a physical thing, almost tangible as if he could indeed have stretched out his hand and felt it. Go away. Leave this place, said all these indications taken together.

He almost turned, but it wasn't the first time he'd been here, and the previous evening, when he'd set the snares, there'd been nothing wrong. Perhaps it was the train which had disturbed things, that clanking metal monster from an outside world. Anyway, he was curious about that green object down there.

Danny carried on down the path and approached it. He saw it was some kind of bag swinging from a branch. Right daft-looking thing it was, made out like a frog. He glanced round, still alert for the slightest movement, ears sharpened, seeking the owner of the bag. But there was no one.

He lifted it down. It was heavy, filled with what proved to be books. Danny lifted one out and stared at it puzzled. He wasn't illiterate, but his schooling had been patchy, and he hadn't progressed much beyond the first reading primer. Pretty well any word with more than one syllable floored him. Zilpah, his wife, was a dab hand at the reading so it didn't matter. She was even teaching the kids. He had sent his children to local schools during the longer stays around the area, but the kids hadn't taken to schooling and he didn't blame them. If Zilpah could teach them reading and writing, he didn't see what more a school could do. The reckoning, now – what they called arithmetic – that came natural. If you couldn't add up, you were done for when bargaining. Danny might be slow to make out his letters but when it came to working out the value of a pile of scrap, he had a mind like a calculator.

He opened the book with care and reverence because it was a rare thing in his hands and probably worth money. It had a picture in it of a fellow in a tin suit sat up on a horse. A ruddy strong horse it've needed to be to carry that load. History, that's what it was. As he made to close it up, the front cover fell open and he saw that someone had printed a name inside. Danny's lips moved as he worked it out. Tam-my Frank-lin. Tammy Franklin, Hugh Franklin's little girl. Danny gave a low whistle. He didn't know what the bag was doing here, but it ought to be returned to the farm and he'd take it up there later on that day. He slung it over his shoulder meantime, to join the grimy canvas sack already there, and turned back to the path. He began to pick his way towards the location of the snares.

He had heard the clatter of wings earlier as the crow flew up but now he became aware of another sound, the frantic buzzing of flies in a feeding frenzy. In the countryside, it was the sound of death.

Danny paused, wariness replaced by alarm. Possibly flies had found a rabbit taken in one of his snares. But that wouldn't attract them in such number. Only one thing did that. Blood. Some creature lay dead among the bushes and he didn't for one moment suppose it was a rabbit.

He sidled forward along the faint track between brambles until his eye caught a patch of blue. By now he was fearful and had to fight the overwhelming urge to retreat. Curiosity pressed him on. He moved a little closer, hooked aside a trailing bramble with the stick he carried, and saw at last a sprawled shape lying on a patch of crushed undergrowth and knew then what had attracted the flies.

No ordinary carrion this. It was a body and it was human.

A woman lay there, a woman with long fair hair escaping from some kind of big clasp. She lay on her back with her knees twisted to one side, and wore blue jeans, a green shirt, a pair of low-heeled walking shoes. The front of the green shirt below the breastbone was a seething mass of flies. Danny, revolted, threw his stick at them. They rose in a protesting mass from the blood on which they'd been feasting. He felt nauseous. The desire to flee became overpowering, but reason made him stand where he was while he worked out what would be the best thing to do. This kill was man's work and other men would soon take interest in it.

He must have left footprints as he made his way down the track, so soft after recent rain. When the police came, as they would in due course, they would find those prints and seek out who had made them. Danny's brown eyes flickered over the terrain around and beyond the huddled shape. There was much trampled earth, broken brambles, crushed ground-level plants not only around the body, but leading back in a trail to the road above. That told its own story and Danny frowned. The body had been dragged here.

At this point, Danny felt a brief spurt of relief followed by puzzlement. Having found Tammy's schoolbag, he'd feared for a moment it would prove to be young Tammy lying there. But since this clearly was an adult, what was the bag doing here? He knew he would have to go and report his grisly find. But not the bag. It would be as well not to report the bag but to return it to the child quietly, saying nothing to anyone else. Danny didn't like having anything to do with authority in any form and was reluctant to admit the necessity of doing so now. He would do what he must, but he saw no reason to involve Tammy or Hazelwood Farm.

The coppers, when he told them, might be inclined to disbelieve him. They'd certainly ask a load of questions. Danny steeled himself to approach close enough to look at her face. It was distorted in death but, with sinking heart, he recognised her even so.

He swore softly to himself and wiped the back of his hand nervously across his mouth. This made things doubly difficult. He knew now the farm couldn't be left out of it. The added weight of the bag of books on his shoulders was another complication. His heart felt heavier than the combined bags. He could report the body to the police – or go up to the farm and tell Hugh Franklin the dreadful news. Danny didn't relish that task. But he owed the Franklin family. He owed it to them to tell them himself and not leave something like this to uncaring strangers in uniform.

Heavy-hearted, he turned and set off up the leaf-strewn path.

CHAPTER TWO

Jane Brady tucked a stray strand of long ash-blonde hair behind one ear and hoped the action hadn't betrayed her inner frustration. She stared at the twelve-year-old before her in a way she intended to be firm without being unkind. The girl stared back unblinkingly. Stand-off! thought Jane, and then: Oh, bother it all. What now?

As a teacher she'd always been careful neither to favour nor discriminate against any one pupil. But it was impossible not to take more interest in some children than others. Especially when, as in this case, there was clearly some problem in the background. The trouble was that dealing with Tammy Franklin was like banging your head against a mental brick wall. Tammy wasn't difficult in the usual sense, not an outright rebel. She had never turned up at school with nail varnish, green hair or a line of studs festooning her earlobes. Perhaps, thought Jane now, it would be easier to tackle her if she had. It would at least have provided a focus of objection. But Tammy showed no sign of taking any interest in fashion or other teenage occupations. She was never seen poring over teen magazines. Her school folders bore no pop star stickers. Instead, she was a bright child, if sullen, and a loner. Her mother, Jane knew, had died some twenty months before and her father had remarried within a year of his bereavement. This, Jane was sure, was where the problem was located. She would like to help, but wishing to help didn't extend to letting Tammy get away with things. Nor had good will on Jane's part prevented the two of them becoming locked into this ridiculous tussle as to which of them would look away first.

Jane cut the duel short with, 'Why is it you can't hand in your homework?'

'I haven't got it with me.' Not rude, not truculent, just a bald statement of fact.

'You forgot it? Left it at home?'

'I haven't got it with me.'

Jane gritted her teeth and chanted mentally, *I will not lose my temper.* It was still too cold for the school summer uniform of gingham dress. Tammy wore the winter version of grey skirt, white cotton shirt and red pullover. The shirt hadn't been ironed. Her feet were shod in sensible lace-up shoes which were scuffed and uncleaned. The girls who attended St Clare's were forbidden fashionable trainers as bad for the feet. Luckily, the sort of leather footwear once known as beetle-crushers had also become fashionable and the girls didn't mind clumping round in them. Tammy's appearance, Jane had noticed on more than one occasion, showed signs of indifference or lack of awareness on the part of someone. To call it neglect would be far too strong. Someone, for example, had plaited the girl's long chestnut hair into the single braid which hung down the back of her neck and done it rather well.

Jane considered Tammy's reply. Hadn't got it with her. 'Tammy,' she asked, 'have you *done* your homework? The truth now.'

'No.'

Well, that was the truth all right but Jane felt both baffled and increasingly annoyed.

'Why not?' Jane knew she sounded tetchy. 'Tammy, you know that at St Clare's pupils are expected to do homework. You know your father is paying for you to attend this school and you owe it to him to work hard and—' Jane faltered. The child's face was a pale little mask. 'Why didn't you do it?' she asked more gently.

Now the grey eyes that had been fixed so steadily on her looked away. 'I'll do it tonight.'

That wasn't an answer to Jane's question any more than the earlier response had been. It was another evasion and that meant Jane had touched on something Tammy didn't mean to tell her. If Tammy didn't want to tell you something, you could ask until you were blue in the face.

'Bring it in tomorrow, then, Tammy. Without fail, right?' Jane knew that she was chucking in the towel. Tammy had won today's battle. As the child turned to go, she added, 'Is everything all right at home, Tammy?'

'Yes, thank you, Miss Brady.'

No sooner were the words spoken than Tammy had whisked out of sight.

Had that been, Jane wondered, because Tammy had sensed Jane's next question would have been, is everything all right at school?

St Clare's paid a lot of attention to the matter of personal responsibility. Each year, a senior girl would be assigned a newly arrived first-year pupil. The older girl was meant to keep an eye on her protégée and sniff out any problems which had got by the teachers. The staff, particularly Mrs Davenport, the headmistress, liked to think they didn't have bullying at St Clare's. But there was a pack instinct in children and they were quick to pick out a vulnerable one in their number. Tammy, for all her outward self-possession, was vulnerable. Jane knew it. What was more, this morning there had been a mood in a certain section of the class. An exchanging of glances and giggling – some of it shamefaced. It had centred round the Hayward twins and their little gang. When they weren't glancing at each other, this little group had glanced at Tammy's back. Jane interpreted the signs as meaning they had played some trick. Whether Tammy knew it yet or not was another matter.

The bell rang signalling the end of break. To her annoyance, Jane realised that by keeping back Tammy for a heart-to-heart – entirely unproductive – she had herself missed her mug of coffee. Drat the kid, she thought. Gathering up her armful of files, she hastened off to instruct the third years on the ravages of the Black Death, a subject, she had always found, they relished. Not the stuff about the resulting shortage of labour and rising wages. Just the bits about the boils and the rats.

Danny stood on the edge of the yard at Hazelwood Farm, partly concealed by a parked tractor. He could see Hugh Franklin just a short distance away, tinkering with the engine of his aged Land Rover. Though the two men were much of an age, Hugh had always looked the younger, though not today. Even at this distance, Danny could see his face was lined, his eyes ringed. He'd aged, thought Danny to himself, in the months since his second marriage. A man carrying a burden he didn't know how to ease or set down.

Just beyond the farmer, through the open door of a barn, Danny glimpsed the nose of the smart Volvo which Mrs Franklin had always driven herself round in and would do so no longer. She and Hugh had

had their differences, Danny knew. Hugh was an easy-going chap but Sonia was of a type Danny privately termed 'a tartar'. Even Hugh had been driven to lose his temper and Danny had heard them yelling at one another more than once. Though, to be fair, Sonia had always been pleasant to Danny and his family. He'd felt a bit sorry for her, to be honest. Fish out of water, she'd been, here at Hazelwood. She'd felt trapped, he'd sensed it. He could imagine being trapped in one place must be torment, which was why he'd always avoided it. Perhaps that's why he'd recognised a kindred spirit in Sonia.

Danny stepped out from his hiding place and cleared his throat. At the Land Rover, Hugh's head shot up and he swung round, hope and anxiety in his face.

'Oh, Danny,' he said. 'It's you.' The disappointment in his voice was unmissable. He came towards the visitor, wiping his dirty hands on a rag. 'The old engine's rattling again. Reckon I'll have to invest in a new one. Or a good second-hand one. Know of anyone with one to sell?'

Danny, on his travels, gathered such bits of useful information. Now he shook his head. Hugh had put the question in a forced casual tone. His eyes were searching the roadway beyond Danny. Whatever was on his mind, it wasn't the old vehicle.

Danny felt sick to his stomach. He didn't know what to say, how to say it. Didn't know how to begin. He thought, suppose someone were to come to my trailer and tell me something had happened to Zilpah or one of the kids? Reckon this will be the end of us pitching camp here. Hugh and me, we'll never be able to set eyes on each other ever again without remembering this moment. He felt a welling up of great sadness in his heart, because, after all, the two of them had grown up together. As youngsters, he'd taken Hugh along with him, showing him how to set snares and hunting hares with the gypsy family's pair of lurcher dogs.

'Your missus—' he blurted.

Hugh twitched and flushed. 'Not here just at the moment, I'm afraid. She – she went to see a friend yesterday and has stayed overnight. She'll be back later. I don't know when.'

Danny shook his mop of greying black curls. 'I seen her.'

Hugh stepped forward eagerly. 'Where?' Then, seeing the agony on the gypsy's face, added, 'Oh God, Danny – what's happened? Has Sonia had an accident?'

16

Danny's eyes were fixed on the ground. He couldn't look into the other man's face.

'I don't rightly know what happened to her,' he said as firmly as he could, but his voice was husky. 'But I found her – down near the railway line, lying in the bushes. I went there after my snares.'

There was a long painful silence. Then Hugh said bleakly, 'Show me.'

Danny nodded and turned to lead the way.

When Meredith got home that night there was no sign of George Biddock. There was, however, a paper notice pinned to the front gate. It bore the legend, familiar to hotel visitors the world over, 'Do Not Disturb'.

It wasn't possible, was it, that George was having forty winks somewhere? No, it was too late in the day and he must have gone home. Meredith's eye caught the gleam of wet cement. George had laid the foundation of the porch and it was still soft. This meant she couldn't reach her front door. She had a back door key, but there was a problem in reaching the back door, too.

Being at the end of the terrace, she would have been able to get down one side of the house had the tiny added garage not prevented it. The garage was windowless and had no door into the yard beyond. However, alongside the property ran an alley which turned into another running along the back of the terrace. Meredith set off, briefcase in hand, down the alley and reached the rear wall of her yard. There was a solid gate in that, but it was securely bolted on the other side. There was nothing for it. She had to climb over.

Further down the alley someone had not taken in their wheelie bin from garbage collection day. That was a bit of luck and she was beginning to feel she needed it. Meredith dragged the bin to her wall. She slipped off her shoes and contrived to squeeze them in the briefcase. Somehow, still holding the case, she managed to clamber on to the top of the bin. The short straight skirt again proved a problem. Short enough to attract the wandering eye of the man on the train, but not short enough to allow athletic activity. Meredith had had to hitch it up to her hips and pray no one was watching. She dropped the briefcase over the wall where it landed on paving below, incurably scratching the leather. She then followed it, hauling herself over and dropping down. That didn't do the suit any good. Two large holes had appeared in the knees of her tights. She retrieved her shoes and, as she was slipping them on again, was hailed.

'What on earth are you doing there, Meredith?'

It was Doris Crouch, her next-door neighbour. Her head had appeared looking uncannily as if it rested, disembodied, on the wall between the two back yards. Doris was on the short side, and must be standing on something to be able to look over at all. Her round, snub-nosed face, with its helmet of rigidly permed grey waves and curls, watched Meredith with surprise and disapproval.

Meredith explained the predicament which had led to her mountaineering attempts.

'Does a neat job, George,' said Doris automatically, following this up with, 'If you needed help, why didn't you come round and knock on my door? Barney would've climbed over this wall and unbolted your back gate.'

'Didn't think of it,' confessed Meredith.

'You haven't done those stockings of yours any good,' said Mrs Crouch.

Meredith gave her a conciliatory grimace before going to unbolt the back gate and return the bin to its original location. She was then at last able to reach her own back door and let herself into the kitchen.

'It's your own fault,' she muttered. 'You should have thought of this.' No, it wasn't. It was George Biddock's, who might have mentioned that he'd be blocking off access from the front.

Meredith plugged in the electric kettle and went upstairs to change out of the now not-so-smart suit and into jeans and a sweater. When she came down, she thought again about ringing Alan but at the last moment chickened out and settled with her feet up on the sofa and a mug of hot tea cupped in her hands. Alan, had she but known it, wouldn't have been at home to take her call. He'd set off for the railway embankment.

Alan Markby drew over to the side of the road and parked behind one of the police vehicles. Just ahead of him the road was spanned by an arch of the disused viaduct. On the railway side it emerged from the trees and on the far side it was anchored to the hillside. In the dusk the massive shape loomed threateningly, like a giant disturbed in his slumber by the antlike scurryings of the men at his feet.

SOCO and others had been busy here all day. Emergency lighting had been set up on the bank and gleamed between the branches and bushes so that each twist of a twig or outline of a leaf was a clear-cut silhouette. It transformed the scene into an accomplished piece of artwork and made it look beautiful.

But what was down there wasn't beautiful. Markby sighed. He'd been called out to just such a scene more times than he cared to remember in his professional career and had never got used to it. Many police officers developed a deliberate flippancy. They cracked macabre jokes as they worked around the body. Morgue attendants, Markby knew, were apt to do the same. And who could blame them? They had to cope with daily horror somehow.

He, on the other hand, had kept his instinctive respect for the departed. Perhaps it came from an old-fashioned, Anglican upbringing, to say nothing of an uncle who'd been a priest. Perhaps he was just squeamish. After all these years? he asked himself wryly. Come off it. Then he thought that perhaps, after all, he was just tired of it all. That thought surprised him because he'd never regretted his choice of job and still found something about each new case which caught his attention and made him want to know more. Admittedly it'd been better in the old days, before rise to senior rank had put him behind a desk for most of the time.

How contradictory can anyone get? he mused. One minute I'm regretting being here, the next that I don't get called out as I did once, at all hours of the day and night, in all weathers, regardless of my personal commitments. Make up your mind! he admonished himself. Well, he was here and had better do the necessary. He walked round to the boot of his car with the intention of getting out his gumboots and making a descent on the bank. Before he could do so, however, he was hailed.

'Sir?' Someone was scrabbling up the bank, climbing over the police tape secured around the site. The dark figure which loomed up, blanking out the silhouetted trees, was familiar.

'Hullo, Dave,' Markby said. 'I've just come out to see how you're getting on.'

'Body's been removed,' said Inspector Pearce, ineffectually brushing off his jacket. 'Didn't know you'd—'

'No,' said Markby, abandoning his intent to get out the gumboots. 'I had no desire to see it.' With a touch of humour, he added, 'Your privilege, Dave.'

'Thanks,' said Pearce.

Markby reached into the capacious poacher's pocket inside his waxed jacket and took out a Thermos flask. 'Brought you some coffee.'

Pearce thanked him again, this time with more enthusiasm. Markby waited until he'd drunk a plastic cup of the hot brew before asking, 'Well? What have you got?'

'Female in her thirties. Rigor was beginning to set in when the squad car got to her. By the time the doc had been and the photographers finished, she was stiffening up well. The doc puts time of death provisionally at between nine and ten yesterday evening. We have an identity. Sonia Franklin, wife of Hugh Franklin up at Hazelwood Farm. She'd been stabbed. Post mortem may tell us more. So far there is no sign of a weapon. Searching down there is a nightmare. We'll have to wait for daylight to finish it off properly. In fact, we were just about to pack up here.'

Markby hid a smile at the longing in Pearce's voice. Dave wanted to be off home to his wife, Tessa, and his supper. Lucky Dave. Single men like Markby himself had time on their hands, but it wasn't really a bonus. He asked, 'Who found her?'

'Gippo—' Pearce amended this hastily to, 'A traveller, Danny Smith. He's quite a well-known figure in these parts. We've nothing recorded against him, though he's reckoned a bit of a poacher by some. He turns up with his family twice a year and camps on a field at Hazelwood Farm with permission. Lends a hand around the farm. I don't suppose,' said Pearce with a grin, 'that he's paid a penny in taxes in his life, but that's not our problem, is it?'

'No, thank God. What's his story?' Whatever it was, Markby knew it would have to be carefully checked and that the luckless Smith would automatically be placed on a list of suspects.

'He was walking along here back to his campsite, he says. Just that,' said Pearce.

'Bet you a pound to a penny he was rabbiting,' growled Markby.

Pearce permitted himself a grin. 'Reckon so. But he won't admit it. He may have to, of course, if he can't think of a more convincing innocent explanation. The point is, he recognised her, having seen her often enough and spoken to her at the farm. He went there straight away and told Hugh Franklin. Hugh came down here to see for himself and then called the police. From Smith finding her to Franklin calling in was slightly under an hour, during which time Smith probably removed his snares and traps and generally walked all over the scene,' concluded Pearce gloomily.

'Does Smith say whether he contemplated calling us directly when he found the body? It wasn't on Hazelwood land.' Markby asked the question though he thought he knew the answer. In his experience, relations between the travelling community and the police were often based on mutual distrust. Danny had preferred to pass the job to Hugh Franklin.

'He says, and I'm inclined to believe him, that he thought he should tell her husband first. He's known Hugh and his family all his life and it seemed the right thing to do. He thought Hugh should hear it from a friend rather than from the police. It makes sense to me,' conceded Pearce. 'Travelling folk have their own strict codes of behaviour. Oh, had it not been Sonia – or rather, had Danny not recognised the corpse – he says he would have called us direct, not contacted the farm.'

Markby accepted that. 'Though Smith would've had to contact the farm anyway, I dare say, to get to a telephone. Unless he's got a mobile in that caravan, which I doubt. Hazelwood Farm must be the nearest habitation.'

'I had a look at the map,' Pearce paused mid-speech to slurp the rest of the coffee, 'and it isn't. The neighbouring farm, Cherry Tree, is marginally closer, but I expect Smith wouldn't be as welcome there.'

'The question,' Markby mused, 'is what the dickens the woman was doing out here at that time of night.'

'If she was,' said Pearce, and was forced to explain. 'I know it's early for theories, but I fancy she was killed somewhere else and the body dumped here. There's a newly beaten track from the road edge through the undergrowth to where she was found. Smith showed us the way he climbed down there, or claims he did, and that's further along. Possibly the body was brought by car and carried or dragged down there by the recent track.'

'Tyre tracks?'

Pearce shook his head. 'Chummie could've parked on the road.'

'So, in that case, what about the husband?' It was in any case always the first question, Markby thought resignedly.

'At the moment it's difficult to get any sense out of him. He's acting pretty cut up, as you would expect. He says his wife went out yesterday evening and didn't come back. He doesn't appear to have reported her missing, that's the odd thing, and on the face of it pretty suspicious. I'll have to talk to him again tomorrow when, with luck, he'll be more coherent.'

'Fair enough, wrap it up for tonight, Dave. Do more harm than good rummaging about down there now.' Markby glanced at the illuminated dial of his wristwatch.

Pearce screwed the top back on the Thermos and returned it to its owner. 'Thanks, I needed that. I got called out just as we were sitting down to a nice bit of steak. Tessa wasn't too pleased.'

Tessa, Markby thought grimly, would have to get used to that sort of thing. She was married to a copper. A number of police marriages bit the dust. His had. He hoped Pearce's didn't. He wondered if this clash of interests was one of the things to influence Meredith when she'd turned him down.

He slid into his car and shut the door. In darkness, he sat for a few moments, digesting what he'd been told so far. The significant point appeared to be the rigor mortis and the indication it gave of time of death. Had she not been dead long when found earlier that day, a number of possibilities would have suggested themselves. But if she'd died the previous evening, then it began to look like the usual sort of domestic tragedy.

No, leave it now, he told himself. Leave it till tomorrow.

Markby switched on the ignition. He supposed it was too late now to go back and call round to Meredith's and see if she wanted to go out for a drink. Tomorrow was Friday. He'd call her tomorrow at her office and fix up something for the evening.

Provided, of course, she wanted to go and he hadn't messed up everything with his heartfelt but, it seemed, mistimed or misworded proposal of marriage.

Aloud he said wearily, 'Oh hell.'

CHAPTER THREE

'It's not your fault, Hugh, come on!' Simon Franklin shook the shoulder of the man hunched on the kitchen chair. The other, refusing to be comforted, continued rocking himself back and forth, arms clasped around his body, head lowered. At each movement, the chair legs scraped on the tiled floor.

'It is, it is! It's all my fault, all of it!' The words emerged as a mumble but filled with despair.

Simon straightened up and looked down at the huddled form in a mixture of alarm and exasperation. This wasn't like old Hugh at all. Who'd have thought he'd crack up like this? Had he really cared for Sonia that much?

He went on, in the carefully reasonable tone people adopt when trying to calm others, 'It's natural for you to feel this way, you know. Just as it's natural, even good, to grieve.'

He paused, regretting the inadequacy of the clichés and telling himself he sounded like a blasted agony aunt. But he'd been caught out, not expecting anything like this, not prepared to deal with it. He'd expected Hugh to be distressed, but he hadn't expected him to go so over the top emotionally. He'd never seen him like it, not even when Penny died. In fact, even having known him all his life, he wouldn't have imagined Hugh *could* break up like this. Even as a kid he'd been a phlegmatic, keep-it-to-himself child, rather as young Tammy was now. Yet here was stolid old Hugh, this sunny Friday morning, coming apart at the seams. It made a difficult situation even more difficult. Simon found himself resentful. When he spoke again his tone was brisker.

'There is no way this could be your fault, Hugh,' he repeated. 'You've got to believe that. I wouldn't lie to you, would I? Me?' He put out his hand again and gave the other's shoulder an affectionate tap. 'When did I ever tell you anything other than the plain unvarnished truth?'

Hugh Franklin looked up, his face distorted with pain. He nodded and managed to whisper, 'Yes, I know you'll tell me the truth as you see it, Simon. It's just, you're wrong on this one. It is my fault. It has to be.'

A stranger, looking on at the scene, would have registered that the two men were brothers. A ray of watery morning sun coming through the window above the sink struck the pair of them and brought out the same red highlights in their hair. They had the same grey eyes and pale sandy eyelashes and eyebrows, the same small neat features. Where they differed it was in build and complexion. Hugh, even seated, could be seen to be a man whose life included much physical activity, most of it out of doors. His skin was weathered, his forearms muscular and his hands roughened. He hadn't shaved that morning and gold stubble covered his chin.

Simon, on the other hand, had the pale complexion of a man who spent most of his time within four walls, and the slightly stooped shoulders of the desk worker. The spectacles propped on top of his head added to this impression and now he reached up with a sigh and brought the specs down to rest in their proper place on his nose. They had slightly old-fashioned thick black frames. One side, where the bar looped over the ear, had been amateurishly mended with parcel tape.

'It's a bit early in the day,' he said. 'But you need a drink, old man.'

'No. If I start knocking back the hard stuff, I'll be finished.' Hugh looked up and managed a wan smile.

'No, you won't. Just a dram. Stay there and I'll fetch it.'

Simon made his way out of the kitchen to the family living room. He stood, chewing his lower lip, on the threshold as he stared at the familiar sight. In some ways it had changed little since he and Hugh had been boys. This was the oldest part of the house, its age announced by the thick beams which ran across the ceiling. The house had been extended, remodelled, part knocked down and restored time without number over the centuries. But this room, Simon was confident from his own researches, dated from the mid-fifteen hundreds. It was an untidy, comfortable room with old furniture, much of it from their parents' day and some of it from their grandparents'. Sonia had resented that and, bit by bit, had been making it over. She had freshened it up with pretty curtains and a new wallpaper. She had also brought in that little French console table which looked like a stranded aristocrat amongst the homely chairs and cupboards. Rather as Sonia herself had looked when in this room, poor bitch.

His niece was there now, curled up on the sofa, turning the pages of a book. It looked like a schoolbook. How many times would someone, coming into this room thirty years ago, have discovered him in just such a position, just such an occupation? But never Hugh. Hugh had always been out and about the farm. A true son of the soil, Simon thought wryly.

Snoozing on the sofa beside Tammy was an elderly spaniel. It opened red-rimmed eyes as Simon appeared and, recognising him, promptly closed them again. Tam must be shocked, too, he thought, and no one had time for her. Hugh hadn't, not in the state he was in himself. But then he never had at any stage, so far as Simon had been able to make out. That hadn't been due to cruel indifference, but to long hours, hard work, a sick first wife and many worries.

'All right, Tam?' he asked, and went over to her and put a hand on her shoulder. He felt her freeze beneath his touch and after a second's hesitation, took his hand away. Funny little person that she was. But he felt uneasy and frowned. 'Tammy?'

She looked up, met his gaze briefly, and then turned her eyes back to her book. 'I'm all right.'

'What's that you've got there? History?' He was genuinely interested, being an historian himself.

'I was late getting my homework in. Miss Brady was cross. I haven't got to go to school today because Sonia's dead, so I can do it now.'

He was, despite everything, shocked at the coolness of her tone and by hearing the words 'Sonia's dead' spoken so bluntly.

'Well, don't make yourself do it if you don't want to. No one will be cross, not Miss Brady nor anyone else.' He spoke kindly because he was fond of the child and had always thought she'd seemed fond of him. From the time she was small he'd told her stories culled from his historical studies, tales of knights in armour and adventures in strange lands, of great armies turned to dust and mingled with the sands of the desert. She'd lapped it all up. He'd even entertained a fancy she might make an historian herself one day. He'd told Hugh, 'If the kid wants to go on and study when she's older, I'll chip in with the cost. After all, I've got no one of my own.'

Now her eyes remained fixed on the page. She didn't want to talk to him. She was coping in her own way in her own private world. Simon left her to it and went to the drinks cabinet to pour his brother the promised dram. He poured himself one at the same time because he needed it even if Hugh didn't. Only Hugh *did* need it and any other prop he could get at the moment. Anyone could see that with half an eye. He was going to crack up when the police got here, damn it. It couldn't be long before they were knocking at the door. Simon glanced at his wristwatch and calculated how long he had to coach his brother in some sensible answers to the questions which would come.

Simon took both tumblers of whisky back to the kitchen and splashed water in them. 'Here.' He held one out to his brother. 'I haven't drowned it.'

Hugh took the whisky, hesitated and then drank it down with indecent haste. It was a good malt.

Simon, sipping his, said slowly, 'Look, Hugh, I don't like having to push you, but you know the police will come back today and want to ask a load of questions, most of them personal. You've got to try to pull yourself together, and above all don't, for heaven's sake, start telling the coppers that it's all your fault! They've got literal minds.'

Hugh, still sitting on the wooden chair but straight now, with his legs splayed out before him and the empty tumbler in his leathery hands, shrugged.

'We had a hell of a quarrel, a real cat-and-dog fight, Wednesday evening.'

'That, for a start, you don't need to tell the cops.'

'Yes, I do, because it explains why she didn't come back. She'd done it before, you know, when we'd had a spat – gone off and stayed over with a friend for the night or even taken a room in The Crown in Bamford.'

'What did you quarrel about?' Simon set his own empty tumbler down carefully on the draining board. As he turned towards the window, the light reflected off the lenses in the heavy black frames and it was possible to see how thick they were.

'The usual. She was bored. We didn't go anywhere. We didn't take holidays. I mean, a farmer can't take a holiday, can he? Just because his wife fancies a few days off, even if he'd like to go away himself and lie in the sun. I told her, if she wanted to go away, she could perhaps take a girlfriend. That made her madder. "I've got a husband and I

bloody well want to go on holiday with him, just like any other wife!"
That's what she said, or rather screamed at me.'

'And then she stormed out?'

Hugh hesitated. 'No – we argued some more. I suggested she might
like to take Tammy away somewhere for a week or so. She – she didn't
want to do that.'

So, they'd quarrelled about the child. 'I saw young Tammy in the
living room. She's taking it very calmly.'

Hugh mumbled, 'Yes, she's a good kid. Doesn't kick up a fuss.'

'Might be better if she did. Has she cried for Sonia?'

Hugh hunched his broad shoulders again, this time to indicate he
had no idea.

Getting exasperated, Simon persisted, 'Has she said anything, anything at all?'

'Not a lot. She didn't like Sonia much. Sonia did try, you know. But
Tammy just didn't take a shine to her, I suppose.'

'Perhaps Sonia wasn't the maternal type. You did get hitched very
quickly, you know, after Penny died.'

Hugh looked resentful. 'What was I to do? I had a young daughter.
No, that makes it sound as if I just married Sonia because of Tammy
and that's not true. I did love Penny but it is possible to find love again,
or I thought so, anyway. I fell for Sonia. I thought she cared for me.
She didn't replace Penny – of course she didn't. I'm sure Tammy
understood that. But both Tammy and I had to go on, make our lives
without Penny. Tammy's lived on the farm all her life. You see death in
some form throughout the year on a farm, but you see new life springing
up, too. I did talk it through with her, you know, tried to explain about
death and life. I talked it through with both of them.'

Simon had some doubts about how much discussion had gone on,
but he couldn't contradict his brother. He would particularly have
liked to say, *You didn't discuss it with me! If you had, all this could have
been avoided. I'd have warned you—*

There was a movement by the door and they both swivelled their
heads round. Neither of them had any idea how long the child had been
standing there, listening. Her pale face was as usual expressionless, only
her eyes wary.

She said, 'There's a man walking towards the front door. He hasn't
got a uniform, just ordinary clothes, but I think he's a policeman.'

*   *   *

Pearce had raised his hand to knock at the farmhouse door, but before he could do so it was jerked open from within. A man stood in front of him, blocking entry. He wasn't the man Pearce had come to see, but he bore a close enough resemblance to be a family member. That was normal enough because families pulled together at times like this and naturally, someone, or several people even, had come round to support the widower. Pearce rather hoped he wasn't going to find a roomful of people, all drinking tea and giving their opinions at once. Relatives could, from the police point of view, be a bit of a stumbling block. He couldn't remember how often he'd had to clear a room before he could talk to the person he'd come to see.

Pearce produced his identification and indicated as firmly as he could without being rude that he wished to talk to Mr Hugh Franklin.

'I'm Simon Franklin.' The man in the doorway made no move to admit Pearce, but thrust out a hand. Pearce shook it. 'I'm Hugh's brother, younger brother. Look, I'd like a quick word before you go in.'

That had happened before, too. Pearce, anticipating what was going to be said, said it first. 'I realise this is a very distressing time for you all and especially for Mr Hugh Franklin. I'll do my best not to make things worse but I do have to ask some questions. I'm sure you all want this matter cleared up.' He was aware that he sounded rehearsed and had probably said the words, or a version of them, many times before. He couldn't help that. He wished the bloke would get out of the way. Pearce had a busy day planned, and they were short-handed.

'Yes, of course we do!' Simon sounded affronted. 'I just don't want you to misinterpret anything my brother might say. He's in shock.'

'We make allowances, sir,' said Pearce stolidly. Privately he was thinking, Oh yes? So what are you afraid he might say, then?

Simon seemed to realise he had to let the police into the house at last and unwillingly turned to lead the way. Pearce, following him, took a look around. It was a nice old house. Pearce was himself a countryman by upbringing and a lot of what he saw inspired nostalgia in him. A lot of old furniture, passed on generation to generation. Family photos. Everything a bit dusty, a bit cluttered, a bit in need of a lick of paint. Pearce would've given his eyeteeth to own a house like this, but if ever any such came on the market, amputated from the farmland with which it had been associated, the price always went through the roof.

He found he was being shown into a cluttered living room which smelled pervasively of elderly dog. The dog was a spaniel, which, at the approach of a stranger, slid from its place on a sofa and landed with a thud on the carpet. It walked slowly towards the newcomer, sniffed at his shoes, waggled its stump of a tail and then creaked out. But the child who was there stood her ground and eyed Pearce resentfully.

'Why don't you pop out for a breath of fresh air, Tam?' Simon said.

The child gathered up her book, walked silently past them and disappeared in the wake of the dog.

'Just wait here a tick, will you?' Simon said to Pearce. 'I'll fetch my brother.'

This room, Pearce noted when he was left alone in it, for all its general ramshackle air, bore the stamp of a woman's hand. A woman, it seemed, who had been tackling the job of renovating it. Pearce and his wife, Tessa, had been doing up an old house, their first home. That sort of wallpaper and those fancy curtains, that was the sort of thing Tessa would have chosen and had probably been Mrs Franklin's choice. He sniffed. Simon's remark about fresh air had been apt. There was a distinct lack of it in here.

Clumping footsteps on the old oak boards announced that both brothers were back. Pearce would have preferred to talk to Hugh alone, but Simon was clearly determined to lend his support to his brother. Pearce could understand that. Just so long as Simon didn't keep interrupting. Putting a positive spin on the unavoidable, Pearce could interview both and that would save him time. Kill two birds with one stone was the unfortunate phrase which came to mind. Markby was always telling him to watch out for slips of the tongue of that kind when talking to bereaved and distressed witnesses.

They all sat down, Pearce taking care to avoid the spot on the sofa which would be covered with dog hairs. He made formal condolences to which Hugh listened stony-faced and Simon impatiently.

'I hope your little girl isn't alarmed by the idea of the police,' Pearce added. 'She saw me coming towards the house and skittered from the window.'

'That's just Tammy's way,' said Simon.

Hugh mumbled assent, clasping and unclasping his broad hands.

'She'll be very upset about her mum,' said Pearce with genuine sympathy.

'Not her mother,' said Hugh. The words burst out of him as

if someone had pressed a speech button. He seemed to realise it, straightened up, cleared his throat and made an obvious effort to pull himself together. His brother watched with a nod of encouragement or approval, Pearce wasn't sure which.

'Sonia—' Hugh paused after speaking the dead woman's name. 'Sonia wasn't Tammy's actual mother. That was Penny, my first wife.'

Pearce digested this information rapidly. 'I see. How long were you married to Mrs Sonia Franklin?'

'A little over six months. Getting on for seven, isn't it, Sim?' Hugh turned to his brother.

'Nearer nine,' said Simon pedantically.

Pearce felt a spark of empathy with Hugh. He, Pearce, and Tessa hadn't been married all that long, only just over a year. If he were to lose Tessa now, after so little time . . . Still, it seemed odd Hugh needed to be told by his brother exactly how long he'd been married. Pearce wondered what had happened to the first wife. Death or divorce? He heard a dog bark outside the house and thought: The kid's scuttled off with her pet for consolation. A lonely child often formed a deep attachment to an animal. He wondered how Tammy had got on with her stepmother.

'Why don't you tell me about Wednesday evening?' he suggested. 'Take your time.'

'Wednesday – Wednesday evening, she went out for a walk, that would be about half-past eight. It was the last I saw of her.' Hugh reddened as he spoke, anticipating Pearce's reaction. 'I told you that yesterday!'

'Yes, you did. But you were very upset and I thought, now you'd had time to think it over—'

'I haven't got anything to think over!' Hugh interrupted vehemently. His brother put his hand on his shoulder.

'Right,' said Pearce sceptically. 'So you didn't see her again that night? What about during the night?'

'No.' Hugh twisted in his seat. 'She wasn't here.'

'Where did you think she was?'

'*I don't know!*'

Pearce assembled the known facts in his head as a man might shuffle a deck of cards. 'You're telling me she was missing all night until she was found on Thursday morning?' He couldn't hide his incredulity. 'Weren't you worried?'

'Yes, of course I was.' Hugh threw a look of appeal at his brother.

Simon moved in quickly. 'Sonia was a very independent woman. She often stayed with friends.' He looked meaningfully at his brother.

'And that's what she told you on Wednesday? That she was going to stay with a friend?' Pearce demanded of Hugh, cutting out Simon's contribution. He'd seen the glance and knew what it meant. But Hugh didn't take the lifeline his brother had tried to throw him.

'No, no, she didn't. The truth is,' Hugh ignored the glare directed at him by Simon, 'Sonia and I had a bit of an argument. It wasn't about anything important. It was about holidays. She stormed out.'

'This storming out, that's what you earlier described as going for a walk, is it?'

'She did go for a walk,' Hugh insisted. 'She just went in a bit of a huff, that's all.'

'It was my sister-in-law's habit to go for a walk every evening,' Simon said loudly. 'She said it enabled her to keep fit.'

Pearce still ignored him. 'When she didn't come back, you didn't go to look for her?'

'Yes, of course I did!' Hugh snapped. 'But a farm's a big place to search. She wasn't around here. I rang Simon and he hadn't seen her. I thought she would come back later. Look, I was tired, I'd had a hard day, and I was cross at the way she was behaving. I – I thought, blow her, and went to bed.' Misery oozed from his voice at the last words.

Pearce hardened his heart. 'Had she taken her car?'

Hugh shook his head.

'So she couldn't have gone far?'

Hugh grasped at that eagerly. 'That's what I thought. She must be around somewhere.'

'You didn't think to phone the police?'

'She hadn't taken the car!' Hugh insisted, his voice rising. 'She had to be on the farm. I thought she was playing some silly game.'

Pearce waited a moment to let things cool down. Simon Franklin, who'd been fidgeting, said, 'Sonia was a law unto herself, Inspector.'

Pearce turned his attention to him at last. 'Your brother phoned you to ask if you'd seen his wife. Do you live nearby?'

'About a mile and a half away. I took over a pair of labourers' cottages and knocked them into one. I bought them off the farm; they're my property,' he added.

'You farm together with your brother?'

Both brothers looked at him startled. 'God, no,' said Hugh. 'These days a farm this size only supports one family. No bloody money in farming now. Milk prices down, cash crops competing with foreign imports – no one raises cattle for beef. Got a small dairy herd. Keep a few sheep, sell the lambs . . .' He fell silent.

'So what do you do, Mr Franklin?' Pearce asked Simon.

'I'm a historian. I used to teach – but now I write and lecture.'

'He's been on the telly,' said Hugh unexpectedly.

Pearce, whose television watching was confined to sport, was impressed. But it didn't make him any more satisfied with Hugh's story. 'So when you woke up on Thursday morning and saw Mrs Franklin still hadn't returned, you still didn't think to call the police?'

Hugh shifted uneasily in the sagging armchair. 'I would've done. I was making up my mind what to do when Danny Smith came up to the farm and told me – said he'd found her.'

If things were going to plan, Sergeant Prescott was at this moment talking to Danny Smith. 'I understand Smith camps on your land frequently.'

Both brothers nodded. Hugh replied, 'Depends what you'd call frequent, I suppose. Twice a year. Turns up regular as clockwork.'

'You've no objection to that? Most landowners are wary of travellers on their land.'

'My father,' said Hugh truculently, 'let Danny's father camp there and I let the arrangement stand. I've known Danny all my life. He lends a hand on the farm when he's here. He's a good worker and honest. So don't go trying to pin anything on him.'

'We don't pin things on people!' retaliated Pearce stiffly. He was nettled to see that neither brother appeared to believe this. 'Was Mrs Franklin happy about this arrangement?' he asked.

'Why shouldn't she be?' Hugh sounded genuinely puzzled.

Simon chipped in with, 'Look here, you're barking up the wrong tree. It's not real travellers like the Smiths you've got to worry about. It's these blasted New Age hippies with their ruddy dogs running out of control.'

'You've had New Agers camping on the land recently?'

'Not since last year. We had a bit of a run-in with some then.' That was from Hugh.

Simon took off his spectacles and held them in magisterial manner as one about to instruct a dim pupil. 'There are all kinds of strange characters wandering about the countryside these days, Inspector. Some of them are certainly capable of violence. Things in the country aren't as they were when we were young, and I include you in that, Inspector.'

Pearce, who was thirty-four and put Simon at about thirty-eight, none the less accepted the man's statement. Things had changed quickly. New roads and motorways had opened up the country to an influx of undesirables, the police were more than aware of that. However, true as that might be, it didn't mean one of such new arrivals had killed Sonia Franklin. As for the possible New Agers, he fancied he recognised a red herring when one was trailed under his nose.

Pearce realised there was little more to be gleaned from Hugh at the moment, especially with Simon in attendance. He stood up.

The brothers scrambled to their feet in unison, both looking relieved. 'I'll see you out,' said Simon, taking charge again.

'I'll have to talk to you again,' Pearce warned Hugh.

'I'm always here,' said Hugh in a sour tone. 'Not going anywhere, am I?' He turned his back on his visitor and walked to the window where he stood, hands in pockets, staring out.

Simon touched Pearce's elbow and indicated with an urgent gesture that he should go. Though Pearce had made up his own mind to leave, he didn't like being dismissed like this. He retraced his steps through the hall, Simon at his heels, but at the front door, stopped. Behind him Simon stifled an oath as he nearly cannoned into him.

'There is one thing I'd like to ask *you*, Mr Franklin,' said Pearce briskly.

Simon looked both angry and wary. The wariness put Pearce in mind of the child Tammy. 'Indeed?' said Simon in a voice that, Pearce thought, wasn't merely cold, it had icicles hanging from it.

'Was Mrs Franklin a regular visitor to your place, especially of an evening?'

Simon's face turned a deep unattractive magenta, clashing with his gingery eyebrows and hair. 'Some people, Inspector, might consider that a very offensive question.'

'Oh?' said Pearce. 'I only ask because you said it was a mile and a half from here.'

'I told you Sonia was a good walker!' Simon snarled at him. He looked as if he'd like to shove Pearce physically out of the door. 'When I shared my home with my partner, Sonia'd sometimes pitch up of an evening for a chat and a drink. The women were friends. After Bethan left,' Simon took a deep breath, 'she rather avoided me. Took Bethan's part, I dare say. That's often the case, isn't it? When a couple split up? Their friends range into separate camps. She certainly wasn't there on Wednesday evening.' Simon took off his spectacles again and squinted at Pearce in the poor light of the hallway. 'Know your Kipling, Inspector?'

'Kipling?' Pearce had vague memories of being made to study 'If—'. 'Can't say I do.' It was now his turn to be wary, sensing he was about to be wrong-footed.

Simon gave a dry smile with just a hint of triumph in it. '"When the moon gets up and the night comes, he is the Cat that walks by himself . . . waving his wild tail and walking by his wild lone."'

Seeing Pearce's bemusement, Simon stretched out his hand and tapped his chest with a forefinger. 'Replace "he" with "she", and that, Inspector, is the best description of my sister-in-law anyone will ever give you.'

With that, he did bundle the visitor out, leaving Pearce on the front step, a closed door behind him.

'Smug blighter!' said Pearce to the empty air.

On his return, Pearce gave Markby a lively account of this episode, concluding, 'For my money, the husband did it and the brother suspects he did. Simon Franklin,' added Pearce, 'is a cleverish sort of chap and is counting on being smart enough to get Hugh off the hook.'

'If Hugh Franklin is our man,' said Markby.

Pearce looked amazed. 'It's a straight choice, isn't it? Either the husband's a murderer or he's got no more sense than one of his own perishing cattle. By his account, she was missing for fifteen hours before she was found and he hadn't even phoned a hospital or called the local police. Does that make sense to you?'

'Sometimes our actions don't make sense,' said Markby, adopting the role of devil's advocate, to Pearce's obvious annoyance. 'Perhaps it happened just the way he said. She went out for a walk, fetched up on that lonely road near the old viaduct and was attacked there. Her killer tried to hide the body by dragging it down the embankment.'

Pearce had had a difficult fifteen hours himself. Tessa had still been grumbling that morning about how he'd gone off and left an expensive steak to go cold and rubbery. As if he'd done it by choice. Still, even after a squabble he would still want to know where Tessa was if she'd been missing for as long as Sonia Franklin had. He said as much to Markby. 'He should've been tearing that farm apart when she wasn't in by ten!'

'Unless she'd done it before. The brother seems to have suggested as much. A story as shaky as Hugh's might be a mark of truth. After all, he's had time to think up a better one and he hasn't.'

'Ha!' countered Pearce, leaning forward and looking, Markby thought, rather as if he was about to burst out with '*Treasure, Jim lad!*' 'I've been thinking about that! The story he's telling may take some swallowing, but it's going to be a ruddy hard story to crack! So perhaps he's not so daft!'

'Just keep an open mind, Dave!' advised the superintendent.

Pearce looked hurt.

CHAPTER FOUR

As Pearce had anticipated, Sergeant Steve Prescott was trudging over a heavily rutted field towards a parked trailer. Someone had already interviewed Danny Smith briefly and got his basic story of how he'd found the body. Very basic, since Smith still hadn't come up with a good reason for being on the spot. Prescott's mission was to fill in this and some of the other gaps.

He had no idea how he was going to get on. The first time he'd had anything to do with travellers was when he'd still been in the uniformed branch. There had been a heck of a punch-up at a gypsy wedding. The police had been called in by the manager of the pub which had hired out the room for the celebrations.

'If you don't get here quick,' he'd gasped down the line, 'I won't have a brick left standing!'

That had been an exaggeration, but the mayhem had still been impressive. The room had been filled with rioting bodies. Broken furniture lay everywhere. Eventually some sort of order had been restored and the bride's father, a tiny, wizened nut-brown man, had emerged from the mêlée to be spokesman.

'Don't you worry, officers,' he'd said. 'It's only the young folks being a bit high-spirited.'

'What about the damage?' the luckless landlord had howled. 'There's four or five hundred pounds' worth done!'

At this, the bride's father had retired to confer with a couple of others, and returned holding out a wad of money. ''Tis all there.'

The landlord had counted it. Five hundred pounds in a mixture of tens and twenties.

'No need for the police, then, is it?' the old man had asked. He'd pronounced the word 'polis'. 'The boys will tidy up a bit.'

So that had been that. Prescott and his colleagues had been thanked for attending but it was all sorted out now. No charges.

'Well,' the landlord, happily clasping his cash, had said, 'they paid up. I've had football fans here, wrecked the place, taken them to court and still never got my money.'

Prescott remembered all this with a wry smile as he neared the trailer. The Smiths had settled themselves in for a stay of several weeks. Laundry, of a shining cleanliness which would have impressed the makers of a detergent commercial, was spread over nearby bushes. Some chairs had been set out on the grass near the remains of a fire. A dog was tied by a length of rope to a rusting truck. Of human life there was no sign, but the trailer door was open. The dog, spying an interloper, began to bark, rushing the length of his rope and bouncing at the end of it in an infuriated ball of fur and teeth. Prescott hoped the rope held.

Still no one came but Prescott was pretty sure he was observed. He halted at a polite distance and called out, 'Hullo there. Anyone at home?'

There was the faintest sound behind him and he whirled round. Three children had appeared, it seemed, from out of the ground. The eldest was a boy of perhaps eleven or twelve, the youngest a grimy-faced three-year-old. They stood in a row, ranged according to height, and studied Prescott.

'You a copper?' the boy asked eventually.

'Yes,' said Prescott. 'Your dad anywhere about?'

At this there was a movement from the trailer. Prescott turned back. A woman was clambering down, causing the whole structure to rock. She was vast, but not with the soft rolls of fat a town-dweller might have had. All her flesh was solid, powerful. She made towards Prescott with purposeful step, her shoulders shuddering and the gold chains around her neck glinting in the sun. Her black hair was long, straight and lank, pinned up on either side with a couple of tortoiseshell combs. Her brawny arms swung by her sides and her mountainous bosom quivered with a life of its own. Prescott was himself well-built. But he felt he'd met his match here.

'You want my husband?' Before he could reply, she turned and yelled at the dog, 'Shut up!' The dog immediately lay down and put its nose on its paws. It, too, knew when it was out-ranked.

'If he's around,' said Prescott.

'You go fetch him,' she ordered the boy. He trotted away. 'Cup of tea?' offered Mrs Smith.

'Thank you.' He didn't dare refuse.

'Best sit yourself down then. You kids, don't you go bothering the officer, right?'

Prescott seated himself unhappily on one of the chairs. The remaining two children sat down on the ground a short distance away and stared at him. Mrs Smith was plodding towards the trailer. Her rear view was awesome.

'Hullo,' said Prescott to the children, in an attempt to be friendly.

'You've come about the murder,' said the older of the two, a girl about eight. Not a question, a statement.

'Yes,' said Prescott.

'You caught many murderers?'

'Not many,' he confessed. 'People don't get murdered all the time.' It occurred to him the child might be concerned at the thought of such violence. 'It's very unusual,' he said earnestly. 'And whoever did it, we'll get him. Don't you worry. You're not in any danger.'

'Course I'm not,' said the child scornfully. 'Anyone come round here nights, the dogs'ud have him.'

Failing the dogs, Mrs Smith could probably take care of an intruder.

The trailer creaked and settled on its wheelbase. Mrs Smith was climbing down again. She handed the sergeant tea in a mug painted with roses, and a piece of shop-bought fruit cake containing lurid red cherries on a very pretty antique plate. Lacking a table, Prescott put the plate of cake down on the ground and concentrated on the tea.

Figures were approaching. The child had fetched his father. Accompanying them was a pair of lurcher dogs. Prescott wondered what Smith had been up to, and looking at the dogs, which were panting, guessed running down some form of game. Whatever it was, it had nothing to do with matters in hand. But he was hard-pressed to contain a smile at the sight of Zilpah Smith's partner in life.

Danny was a small, wiry man, a wraith beside his spouse. He was smiling and watching his visitor sharply at the same time. But when Prescott tried to meet his gaze, he found the gypsy's curiously elusive. Smith looked at the sergeant as if he could read his mind. Prescott had no more knowledge of Smith's mind than he'd have had of a wild animal's. In truth, Prescott's eye was as much taken by Danny's coat as by the man himself. The coat seemed way overlarge for the wearer and bulged in a manner which suggested concealed pockets.

Danny shook Prescott's hand and seated himself on another of the chairs. Mrs Smith handed him his tea, this time in a mug decorated with forget-me-nots. The children were shooed away. There was a curious air of gentility about all this. He was being treated as a guest. That, Prescott supposed, was a positive thing. The Smiths weren't acting as if they had anything to hide. On the other hand, that could be a front.

'I already talked to a copper,' said Danny hoarsely. 'Told him what happened, how I found her, like.'

Prescott cleared his throat and set down his mug. 'I'd like to run through it again. Did you know Mrs Franklin well?'

'Seen her several times. She wasn't the first one.'

Prescott looked startled. 'Not the first body?'

Danny looked at him as if the sergeant had betrayed himself as somewhat wanting in the top storey.

'No, not the first Mrs Franklin. There was another one before. Nice lady but always poorly. Then she died. And Hugh, he married the other one. Not but what she was a nice lady, too.'

Prescott attempted to redeem himself by sticking to what he already knew. 'You say you were walking home along the railway embankment yesterday morning.'

'That's it. Just walking. It was a nice enough morning. I told them other coppers.'

'You're going to have to do better than that, you know,' said Prescott cheerfully. 'What were you really doing down there?'

'Nothing. What I told you.'

'Look,' said Prescott, 'we think you were probably poaching. That's an offence but frankly, I couldn't care less and neither could my boss. We're from the Regional Squad serious crimes unit. This is a murder inquiry and that's what we're here for. Not to act as unpaid gamekeepers for the railway company. But from your own point of view, if you can't come up with a good explanation for being on the embankment, you're going to put yourself at the top of our list of suspects.'

That got a reaction. Danny looked alarmed. 'What reason would I have to kill the poor lady? She never did me any harm.'

'Dare say not, Danny, but you've got to see it from our point of view.'

Prescott paused and then asked casually, 'What have you got in your pockets there?'

'Nothing,' returned Danny quickly, 'of any interest to you. And I know the law, too. It's broad daylight and this is private land which I'm on with permission. You can't search me just because you think maybe I've been taking a rabbit or two.'

'Is that what you were doing? Rabbiting? Come on, Smith!' urged Prescott. 'You've got to help yourself.'

Danny thought about it. 'You're not going to be issuing a summons against me?'

'No,' said Prescott, hoping, but fairly sure, his seniors would agree.

'All right, then, I went down to check my snares.' Danny blew on his tea and slurped from the mug.

'Can you tell me when you set them?'

Danny's reply showed an awareness of the Night Poaching Acts. 'Evening before, but early on, before the rabbits came out to feed. It was well before sunset. And I didn't go back to get them till the next morning, which was when I found her.'

'Night', as defined by the Acts, was an hour after sunset to an hour before sunrise. Rabbits, not normally classed as game, might be considered game if taken during the night hours. Prescott sighed. Since Danny clearly knew this, he might be telling the truth or just protecting himself. 'Are you sure?' he asked.

'I'm sure. I'm also sure she wasn't there then, when I set the snares. Wasn't nothing there then.' Here Prescott had the impression that Danny broke off speech a little abruptly.

'What are the snares like?' Prescott asked curiously.

Danny hesitated, then fished one out of an inner pocket. It was a strong wire bent into a running noose, with a hook at the other end to enable it to be secured more easily. Simple but effective. Needless to say it was illegal. Moreover, Danny might have permission to be on Hazelwood land, but the embankment where the snares had been set would be railway land. Danny certainly didn't have any permission from the railway to be there. Poaching, illegal snares, civil offence of trespass . . . Prescott had enough to give him a hold over Smith. On the other hand, he had no wish to antagonise the man or frighten him. He'd just clam up and any information he might have would be lost for ever.

But his train of thought led him to ask, 'Did Mrs Franklin, I mean the dead woman, did she wander around the farm much on her own? Did you see her walking alone ever?'

'Afore she died?' Danny showed an unexpectedly sharp appreciation of language. 'May have done. Come out here once or twice to see Zilpah and the kids, just calling by.'

'You never had any arguments with her? She didn't mind you camping here? I know Mr Franklin allowed it.'

'She didn't mind. Or she never said if she did. I told you, she was a nice enough lady, always friendly, have a cup of tea like you're doing now.' Danny drew attention rather pointedly to the fact that Prescott was enjoying Smith hospitality and was, therefore, under some obligation as a guest to behave himself.

'On Wednesday evening,' Prescott pursued, 'did you happen to see any strange cars or other vehicles parked on the road, top of the embankment, round about where you found the body the next day?'

'Can't say as I did.' Without warning, Danny leaped up, darted past Prescott and snatched up something from the ground. There was a yelp and a scurry of fur.

Prescott realised that he'd forgotten his cake which he'd left on the grass. One of the lurchers had sneaked up as the men talked and stolen the tasty morsel. What happened next startled Prescott even more than Danny's initial sudden move. Smith picked up the pretty plate on which the cake had rested, and in a swift movement, smashed it against the side of the trailer.

'What did you do that for?' Prescott asked.

'Dog ate off it. 'Tis no good no more.'

Prescott sat silently, aware that he was in the presence of an alien culture and a set of values perhaps different to his own, but putting no lesser obligation on the holder. He had a feeling that there was something else which Smith had not chosen to tell him. It could be neither trapped nor bullied out of the man. But he might, if he saw fit, tell Prescott of his own free will, as he'd done about the snares. But not today. Today the courtesies had been exchanged. Prescott had been sized up and, except in his carelessness with the cake, not set a foot wrong, or so he hoped. He should quit while he was ahead – or, at least, even.

He stood up. 'Sorry about the cake. I'm obliged to your wife for the tea. You won't be moving on, will you?'

'I was told we had to stay. Other coppers said so.'

'That's right. We'll have another talk sometime.'

Danny watched him walk away. When he'd gone, Zilpah emerged from the trailer and stood silent, her dark eyes fixed on her man.

'Big feller, ain't he?' observed Danny. 'Take care of himself in a mill, that one.' He meant one of the illegal bare-knuckle contests beloved of travelling folk, on which huge sums of money were wagered. He glanced at Zilpah. 'I gave the bag of books back to the little girl, slipped up to the farm with it while the coppers were all busy by the railway. No point in mentioning it. Can't have anything to do with this.'

At St Clare's, the staff had gathered in an emergency meeting to discuss Tammy Franklin, and specifically the shocking news.

'She won't, of course,' said Mrs Davenport, the headmistress, 'be returning to school until she's had time to come to terms with this. She ought, I feel, to be offered counselling. Possibly the police have something in mind. If not, social services.'

Mrs Davenport was a large lady, dressed perhaps unfortunately in a frock patterned with big yellow and navy squares. She sat on her chair with one leg stretched forward, her plump forearm resting on the wooden armrest. She looked a little like the figure of Britannia.

Jane was impelled to say, 'Tammy doesn't take kindly to strangers. Even a trained counsellor would have a problem.'

There was a silence in the staffroom and during it, Jane became aware that all eyes were trained on her. Mrs Davenport in particular was looking at her thoughtfully. 'Of all the staff, you seem to be the one who's had the most rapport with her, Jane.'

'I've tried,' said Jane. 'I don't know how much success I've had. She's always polite but distant. She's very bright. But she has a way of answering any question with not quite the answer you're looking for. I mean, it's as if she's answering a different question.'

Mrs Davenport inclined majestically in Jane's direction. 'I still wonder, Jane, if you might not be the best person in this situation. Perhaps you could get in contact with the father and suggest you drive out to the farm and chat to Tammy?'

'Oh, I really—' Jane's automatic reaction was horror at the thought of the responsibility. But everyone was looking at her and Mrs Davenport's whole manner suggested this was an offer she couldn't refuse. She had always been Tammy's champion, after all. Put your money where your mouth is! she thought. 'Yes, all right. I'll give it a try,' she agreed unhappily.

'Good,' said Mrs Davenport. 'At least you can report back on what you find. And if you don't feel you're making any progress, we'll have another think about it.'

Which was all very well and good, thought Jane as she drove along the country road at half-past four that Friday afternoon. But she didn't look forward at all to the task and it wasn't just cowardice or a feeling of inadequacy. She also felt she was proposing to intrude on a very sensitive and personal situation. The whole family must be in shock. It wasn't just Tammy who needed to be treated with care. What would she say to the adults? Nothing in her life to date had led her to have even the slightest acquaintance with murder and all that went with it. The thought of such violence used against someone, against a woman, was sickening. Who could have done it? Why had he done it? Where was he? Would he do it again? Was he watching that farm? Would she, Jane, be in any danger . . . ?

Here Jane firmly told herself to watch her imagination. This of all times was a moment to be practical. Even as she thought this, the good resolve was swept away by a totally unconnected matter.

She had reached a cluster of buildings at a bend in the road. It wasn't a village or even a hamlet, just three or four cottages along the roadside and a large stone barn converted into a workshop. She could, should, have driven straight past. But Jane's foot pressed on the brake of its own volition, or so it seemed. She drew up, switched off the engine and sat, debating what to do.

The workshop appeared deserted but its doors were open to the road and that meant Peter was about somewhere. A board above the entrance advertised 'Handcrafted Traditional Furniture'. Jane got out of the car and walked towards it.

She had no right to drop in like this unannounced and, she knew in her heart, unwanted. She didn't know why she was doing it, unless it was to delay by fifteen minutes her arrival at Hazelwood Farm. Yet this visit would be, in its way, as difficult an encounter as any with the Franklin family.

Jane breathed in the smell of the place, the warm scents of fresh-cut wood, aromatic promise of resin, chemical tang of varnish, the over-lying moisture of steam. Beneath her feet the ground was carpeted with sawdust and it had already powdered her shoes. By the entrance stood four completed chairs, a set. Probably an order.

She called, 'Peter?'

He didn't answer but she fancied she could hear the faint noise of a human presence in the partitioned area at the rear, which was his office. She walked towards it and tried again. 'Pete? It's only me, Jane. I was passing and I—'

She had reached the office door. He was there seated at his desk. The desk was covered as it always was with papers and debris, unwashed coffee mugs, unopened post. But he wasn't working. He sat with his head in his hands and his whole attitude one of total despair. She realised he hadn't heard her voice and didn't even now realise she stood beside him.

'Peter?' Jane touched his shoulder.

He stirred as if awoken from a deep drugged sleep and turned his face towards her. She drew in her breath. He looked ghastly. His complexion appeared bleached, his eyes ringed with dark circles, his cheeks sunken. He was unshaven and, from the general look of him, had slept in his clothes.

'Peter? What on earth is wrong? Are you ill?'

'Jane,' he said tonelessly. 'No, I'm all right, I'm fine.'

He wasn't. But what could she do? The way he was looking at her alarmed her. His gaze passed almost through her, as if her presence was of no interest. Which it wasn't to him, she realised with cold shock. He'd wiped her out of his life and her reappearance made no more impression than if she'd come selling charity flags.

Over is over, she reflected bitterly. You tell all your friends and family that you've parted by mutual consent. But it's never really mutual. What it comes down to is that one of you no longer wants the other one. The rejected one has a choice: plead, crack up, try to recover the lost ground or retire from the fray with dignity. Jane had chosen the last. So they'd parted, in the ironic phrase, as friends. But friends don't part. It would have been easier, she realised now, if they'd parted with a terrific row and cut one another off completely. As it was, they were left in an awkward limbo, ex-partners, ex-lovers, ex-friends, still linked by some sort of invisible tie only they were aware of.

Although perhaps she was the only one aware of it. 'I'll make some tea.' That was the British way out of any tight spot and she chose it now.

When she'd brewed up and brought the mug to him, he'd made some sort of effort, left the desk, and was messing around with some strips of pine in the workshop. She set down the mug on the workbench.

'Look, Pete, something's wrong or you're sick. You look like—' She broke off just in time, realising she was about to say 'like death'. But in view of her main errand this afternoon, the phrase was inappropriate. 'Ghastly,' she substituted.

He looked defensive and passed a hand over his hair as if the gesture could make any improvement. 'I've been working a lot. I've got an order to finish, four standard chairs and two carvers.'

'The ones by the door?'

'That's them.' He picked up the tea and bent his head over the mug. The hair at the nape of his neck where it was cropped short was darker than that on the top of his head where it was sun-bleached. The sight sent a pang through Jane, such an ordinary thing and sparking so many memories.

'What are you doing out here, Jane?' He didn't ask because he wanted to know. The tone was too superficial. He was trying to sound normal.

'I've got some business at Hazelwood Farm.'

The tea slopped; Peter swore as hot liquid dribbled over his fingers, and set down the mug hurriedly. 'What business? Why should you be going to Hazelwood?' His eyes, fixed on her, were wild and she felt a brief twinge of fear. He looked as if he were quite out of his mind.

'One of my pupils lives there, Tammy Franklin. Her mother, her stepmother, has been found dead.'

'I know, I heard.' His voice sounded unnatural, forced out. He twisted his hands together. 'I don't understand why you've got to go there.'

'The school has a responsibility for Tammy, to see she's— to see what arrangements have been made for her.' Jane hesitated. 'Peter, have you eaten? I mean, today, at all? If you like, when I've finished at Hazelwood I can come back here and cook something—'

'No, I don't want anything. I can manage. I'll do it myself.' He was shaking his head.

'Pete, you can't. Whatever it is—'

'For God's sake, Jane!' The words burst out of him in a kind of agony.

She stepped back, face burning with misery and embarrassment. 'I'm sorry, I didn't mean to interfere,' she began. Then wounded pride and anger took over. 'All right, I was only trying to help! You don't have to be so damned surly about it! Your problems are nothing to do with me! I was just trying to do a good turn. If you don't need that, fine!'

She marched out. She thought he called after her once, just her name, but she ignored it. She climbed back in her car, slammed the door and struck the heel of her hand on the rim of the driving wheel. 'Ignorant pig!' she muttered as she switched on the ignition. 'He could at least be civil!'

Brought it on yourself, said a voice in her brain. *Shouldn't have gone there.*

'And I won't again!' she replied aloud to the voice.

When she reached Hazelwood Farm, after negotiating a long, badly maintained track, she feared at first she'd come upon another seemingly deserted place. But as soon as she left the sound-insulated bubble of the car, she heard the lowing of cattle from a nearby building which she took to be a milking parlour. Before she knew it, it was followed by a rustling, a stamping of hoofs. Suddenly a man's voice uttered a loud whoop.

The herd burst out of the building. To Jane's appalled eyes, they formed a solid mass of horns and huge steaming bodies, dribbling muzzles and lustrous eyes. Hoofs sank into the mud-smeared surface of the yard as they jostled one another. Bellowing, tossing their heads and swishing tails, they surged towards her.

Jane scrambled back into the car and managed to close the door in the nick of time before she was surrounded. They bumped against the car, one or two pausing to gaze in curiously, their breath misting the windows. The warm odour of manure seeped in. Then at last, blessedly, they had passed by and were streaming through a gate on the far side of the yard into a pasture. She heaved a sigh of relief. She realised then that a man had appeared at the side of the car and was stooping down to look in at her.

Lacking the aplomb she would have liked to show, Jane let down the window.

'Sorry if they gave you a fright,' said the man. 'They wouldn't hurt you. I didn't know you were there.'

'I – I wasn't expecting them.'

His face wore the tolerant look that country people have when they come across hopeless town-dwellers nonplussed by some everyday rural situation. She supposed him about forty, weather-beaten, stockily built, not unhandsome in a well-worn sort of way. She saw now that there were lines of strain in his face and his eyes were sad.

'Mr Franklin?' she ventured.

'That's me. You'll be the lady who rang? Tam's teacher?'

Jane decided it was time to get out of the car. She managed it with some dignity. 'Thank you for allowing me to come, Mr Franklin. I realise what a difficult time this is for you and that you don't want strangers butting in.'

'I've already got them,' he replied with some bitterness. 'Police. Asking questions, trampling all over the place. They've even been down to poor old Danny's caravan. You can see Tammy if you want. But, no disrespect, we can manage. We don't need help, tell the school. She's indoors some place. I'll be along shortly.'

He set off across the yard to close the gate after the herd, then made his way back to the milking shed and disappeared inside.

Jane looked round her. Farm work couldn't be halted whatever else had happened. Animals had to be fed, cows milked, everyday tasks attended to. Jane's forehead puckered in a frown. She had met Sonia Franklin only twice and both times briefly. She had not struck Jane as a countrywoman. She'd have guessed Sonia's stamping ground to be more likely Knightsbridge, if she'd not known better. Jane hadn't given it any particular thought until now. She screwed up her nose in an effort to recall the slender, well-dressed figure, the carefully applied make-up, manicured nails. What on earth had possessed the woman to take on this rustic lifestyle – a life for which she must have been entirely unsuited? What, come to that, had made her settle on Hugh Franklin? He seemed a nice enough man, as far as their fleeting encounter permitted judgement, but a practical man to his fingertips, perhaps even a little of a rough diamond. Nor was there any sign of wealth about the place. Jane supposed any man might fall for a good-looking woman like Sonia. But what had Sonia seen in Hugh?

Jane walked towards the farmhouse. As she reached it, the door opened and Tammy appeared.

'Dad said you were coming.' To Jane's relief, she didn't sound unfriendly, more slightly curious to know what the visitor wanted.

Jane asked, 'May I come in?' and was led through to the sitting room where she was greeted by an old and smelly spaniel.

Tammy, taking her role as hostess seriously, invited her to sit down and offered tea. 'Only don't sit there where Pogo sits. You'll get hairs on your skirt.' Then she whisked out.

Jane sat carefully in an armchair and patted Pogo's head. His long white and brown coat felt slightly tacky to the touch. He sighed wheezily and subsided into a heavy lump on her feet. She looked at her surroundings. A lovely old room in a lovely old, ramshackle, everything-at-the-wrong-angle house. Nice old furniture speaking of a family's history. Oh, and some twee muslin curtains. No prizes for guessing who put those up. Jane mentally ticked herself off for criticising the dead woman's taste.

Tammy was back, carrying a tray on which were balanced a cup and saucer and a plate with biscuits. She put it down on a low table, on top of a pile of newspapers and farming magazines, and gravely handed Jane the cup and saucer. 'Do you take sugar?'

'No, thanks, this is kind of you, Tammy.' Jane tried to ease her feet from beneath Pogo but he was a solid mass pinning them to the spot. An antisocial odour was arising from him. Jane pretended not to have noticed it.

'I'm glad you don't take sugar because I forgot to bring it. You can have a biscuit. That's all there are because no one's gone shopping.'

She sat down and stared at Jane. 'I've done my homework now. Do you want me to give it to you?'

'Oh, Tammy,' said Jane in a surge of pity. 'The last thing anyone's worried about is your homework. That's not why I'm here. We're all very sorry at school about what's happened. I've come to see if I can help in any way, and of course, you won't be coming back to school until you feel you can face it. It's half term next week, of course, but no one will mind if you stay away longer.'

'Sonia wasn't my mother,' the child said. 'She was my stepmother.'

'Yes, I understand that. But you must still be very upset. Especially as – as it was so sudden.'

'A policeman came this morning in ordinary clothes. He didn't have a uniform, I mean. He talked to Dad and Uncle Simon. Another policeman went over to Danny's trailer and talked to him and his wife.'

'Who is Danny?' asked Jane at this second mention since her arrival.

'He's a gypsy, a real Romany. He comes twice a year with his family

– that's his wife, Zilpah, and his children – and camps on one of our fields. He's always done it. Dad says when he was young, Danny's father camped there. Dad and Danny went hunting rabbits together when they were boys. Danny found Sonia's body, you know.'

'I didn't know . . .' Jane said faintly, feeling all this was slipping away from her. She'd only formed the vaguest plan with regard to this encounter, hoping that instinct would guide her. Now she had the feeling that she was being put more and more at a disadvantage. The sensible thing would have been to have a word with one of the investigating officers first, before turning up here totally unprepared. She had no knowledge of even the main elements of the case, other than that a woman was dead through violence.

'Dad didn't kill Sonia.'

Jane sat up with a start. This was something she could meet head-on. The child sat there, white-faced and defiant. 'No one is saying that, Tammy!'

'Then why did the policeman keep asking about the quarrel?'

Jane's sensation of sinking into quicksand increased. This was a murder inquiry and she'd blundered into the middle of it. She had no authority whatsoever for assuring the child no one suspected her father of the crime. For all Jane knew, he might be at the top of the police list of suspects. A warrant might be in the process of being drawn up even as she sat here . . . a car full of stern-faced representatives of the law might be on its way. They'd burst through that door like something on a TV film and—

Jane nearly jumped out of her skin. There was indeed a movement out in the hall, a stamp of feet, a man's voice softly cussing.

'That's Dad coming in for his tea,' said Tammy. 'I'll go and make it. 'Scuse me.'

'Oh,' said Jane faintly. 'Yes, of course.'

She heard a brief murmur of an exchange between father and daughter outside the door and then Mr Franklin came in. He had taken off his gumboots but not replaced them with any indoor shoes. His left big toe protruded through a hole in the end of his sock. The toe of his other sock was cobbled together so inexpertly that he'd evidently either mended it himself or his young daughter had. Apparently oblivious of this, he sat down opposite Jane, his elbows resting on the arms of the chair and his broad hands dangling. He had washed them, she was relieved to see.

'Shift that danged dog,' he said. 'He's stretched out all over your feet. Can't move, can you?'

'No,' confessed Jane. She stooped and gave Pogo an ineffectual shove. Unfortunately this only resulted in another malodorous blast.

'Oy, dog!' ordered Mr Franklin with a sharp whistle.

Pogo raised an ear, opened a bleary eye, and struggled, wheezing, to his feet. 'Go on out of it,' ordered the farmer. 'Go on in the kitchen. See Tam, go on.'

Pogo plodded out obligingly. The word 'kitchen', Jane suspected, had filled him with hope.

Picking her words carefully, Jane said, 'I'm very sorry about what happened to your wife. We all are at school. Though clearly you're managing very well, there must be something I can do to help. At a time like this there always is.'

His gaze moved away from her and she saw the twinge of pain round his mouth. 'Nice of you to offer, Miss Brady, but I don't see as there is, thanks all the same. Like I told you, we're fine.' Unexpectedly, he added drily, 'Doesn't look to me like you've ever done much farmwork!'

'I'm called Jane,' she said. 'And although I might not be any good with livestock, I might be handy doing something else.'

His head twitched back as he stared at her in momentary surprise. 'Oh, yes?' was his only comment.

'Tammy says no one's been shopping.' Hastily Jane added, 'In the circumstances of course ordinary household tasks have been pushed to one side. Tammy and I could make a list of what's needed and do the shopping together. Please don't say you don't need someone to do that. You do. You'll starve otherwise. I shall be free all next week while school's off.'

The man was studying her thoughtfully. 'Fair enough,' he said at last. 'Leave you to sort that one out with Tam, then.'

Encouraged at her progress, Jane ventured to tread on more dangerous ground. 'How is she taking it all? She does seem rather more composed than I'd like. It's a matter of some concern to the school, as I explained on the phone.'

'Don't know as I can rightly tell you. She doesn't say much, it's not her way. Perhaps you don't like that but that's how it is.' There was a trace of obstinacy in his voice. It had been there before in his denial he needed help.

'It's not your way either, I'd guess!' she said. The words slipped out before she could stop them. Jane put a hand to her mouth in dismay.

Thank goodness he didn't appear to have taken offence. He nodded. 'That's right. We never had much to say to one another, Tammy and I.' He raised his head and Jane suddenly found herself the object of a very direct look. 'But it doesn't mean I don't care.'

The words were spoken simply and from the heart. Jane said impulsively, 'Of course you care. And Tammy cares about you.'

To the extent that she's worried the police will arrest you for killing your wife. But you didn't kill your wife, did you? What was the quarrel about? All this last ran through Jane's mind unspoken.

'Tamara, she's called rightly,' Hugh was saying. 'My wife – I'm talking of my first wife, Penny, Tammy's mother – she picked that name. Tamara. She fancied it.'

'I've seen it in the school register,' Jane admitted.

'Penny wanted Tammy to go to your school, St Clare's, so that's why we sent her there.'

Hesitantly, Jane offered, 'If there's a problem with the fees, Mr Franklin, we've had such situations before when there's been an emergency in the family. The school could come to some arrangement to defer payment until later, when things are – are settled.'

'Reckon if I'm to call you Jane, you'd best call me Hugh. I can pay the fees. Don't fret about the school's money. I dare say, looking around here, you think we don't have two halfpennies to rub together, and in the normal way of things, we don't. But Penny's dad, Tam's granddad, he left Penny a bit of cash. She put it by in the building society for Tam's education. Earmarked it, you might say. That's what it's used for. I respect her wish and won't go back on it. I've never touched it for anything else.'

The door creaked. Tammy was back, holding a large mug of steaming tea. Hugh reached over from his chair to take it from her. 'Thanks, love. Jane here thinks you and she might do a bit of shopping.' He turned to Jane, 'If you're going into Bamford with Tam, would you mind popping into the feed merchants' and asking when they mean to send the receipt for that last bill I paid?'

'Not at all,' said Jane faintly.

CHAPTER FIVE

Friday morning had begun for Meredith with a visitor. The cat was back, mewing plaintively outside the kitchen.

'Hullo, Tiger,' she said, opening the back door for him. 'Where have you been?'

He strolled in and rubbed himself around her ankles before going to sit meaningfully in the corner where she always put down his dish. He was technically a stray and had first appeared some months before. He'd been in very poor shape – thin, bedraggled and nervous. Since then his life had obviously taken a turn for the better. She suspected he had established himself in several homes around the neighbourhood and moved from one to the other when fancy took him. Certainly he didn't look as if he'd been suffering any want since she'd last seen him.

Meredith struggled to open a tin of tuna without tipping the brine over her office suit. As she set the cat's breakfast before him she heard a familiar clank and rattle in the street.

She opened the front door to see George Biddock clambering down from his battered truck. She called out a greeting to him as he made his way towards her with his stiff, slightly rolling gait. They met over the new base of the porch.

'Morning, my duck!' returned Mr Biddock. He had either the same or an identical crushed cigarette behind his ear. 'How are you this morning? This all set nice and firm, has it— Bloody hell!'

His amiable tone had abruptly deserted him. Meredith stared down at the cement square at her feet. Diagonally across it, set for ever like a star's handprint, was a line of feline pawmarks.

'Does it matter?' she ventured.

'Them dratted beasts,' said George, 'they do it on purpose, I swear. They see it's new and goes and jumps on it straight off.'

Unfortunately the cat, his tuna finished, chose that moment to stroll up the passageway behind Meredith and sit at her feet. He began to wash off his whiskers with a front paw.

'Him, was it?' asked George, glowering. 'You never said you had a cat. If I'd known I'd have put a plastic sheet over it or something.'

'I'm sorry,' said Meredith. 'But you're going to put tiles on it, aren't you? So it won't show in the end.'

'It's the principle,' said George with dignity. 'I take a pride in a good finish.'

Meredith left him and the cat to sort out their differences as best they could, and set off for work.

Things picked up at lunchtime. Alan rang.

'How are you fixed for this evening? I thought we might go out for a pub meal. They say the new cook at The Red Lion is very good.'

'Sounds great.'

'I'll pick you up a little before seven.'

Both set down their respective phones with feelings of relief of which neither suspected the other.

We're starting over again, thought Meredith ruefully. Which way now?

Daylight was fading as they reached The Red Lion that evening. The pub was situated ten miles out of Bamford but, despite being tucked away on a country road, was well known in the area. Several vehicles were already in the car park. Inside, the lights were on, lending a welcoming glow, and a row of coloured bulbs flickered amongst the wisteria covering the façade. Markby parked beside a dusty green Japanese off-roader in the rear window of which was a sticker reading 'SUPPORT BRITISH FARMERS'.

The pub was an old place, low-ceilinged and cramped. The inner walls bulged unevenly, indicating plaster over local stone. Its relatively small floorspace was already crowded but they managed to get a table by a window. Markby left Meredith there while he went to the bar to get their drinks and obtain a menu. He found a gap between a burly man in a hand-knitted sweater and a tall, thin man with spectacles. The spectacles, Markby noticed, hiding a smile, had been mended with parcel tape.

As he was thinking this, the man turned his head and stared at Markby very directly, as if aware of his amused scrutiny.

'Sorry if I jostled you,' Markby apologised. 'I was just trying to attract the barman's attention.'

The man moved along slightly to give him more room, but still stared at him in a disconcerting manner.

'Two gin and tonics, ice and lemon, and a menu, please,' said Markby to the harassed-looking youth who had come to take his order.

'Copper,' said the man with the mended spectacles.

Oh, dash it, thought Markby. He couldn't go out for a blasted quiet drink without someone recognising him. Did the man know him personally? Or was it just something about him which betrayed his profession?

'Seen you before,' said the man in explanation. 'About a year ago. There was a meeting to discuss the quarry extending its operations. Protesters had been up there and done some damage. Someone pinched some dynamite and everyone got in a stew about terrorists, but it turned out to be kids. You were one of the speakers on the platform.'

'Oh, right. Yes, I do recall the occasion, but I'm afraid I don't recall—'

'My name's Franklin, Simon Franklin.'

'Ah, quite.' Markby made the necessary connection. Sonia Franklin. Murder victim. Pearce's pigeon, not his, thank God. 'Unpleasant business, very sorry, nasty for your family. I'm not dealing with it.' It occurred to him this might be the widower. He'd known the bereaved do stranger things than head for company and prop up a bar. He asked tentatively, 'Your wife?'

'Sister-in-law.' There was a certain ferocity in the way the man said this. He lifted his pint to his lips.

Markby saw a chance for escape and to help things along, the barman brought the drinks and handed over a couple of menus in plastic covers.

'Well, if you'll excuse me,' said Markby hastily, tucking the menus under his arm and scooping up glasses and tonic bottles.

He retreated to the table and Meredith.

'Someone you know? You look a bit cheesed off,' she observed.

'Thanks.' She relieved him of one of the glasses and a tonic bottle.

He set the other down and handed her a menu. 'Rather someone who fancies he knows me. Or knows I'm a policeman.' Lowering his voice, he added, 'Rather tricky: he's a relative of a murder victim, a case Pearce is on at the moment.'

'We can go elsewhere,' she whispered.

'No, he's only having a pint by the look of it. With luck, he'll move on shortly.'

But luck was taking time off. Simon Franklin was bearing down on them, fresh pint glass in hand.

'This,' muttered Markby crossly, 'is definitely out of order!'

'Superintendent Markby, aren't you?' Simon had reached the table and was standing over them. 'I remember now you used to be at Bamford. Someone told me at the meeting you were at Regional HQ now with promotion. Serious crimes squad, that'll be, will it? I suppose that's why they roped you in when they thought they had terrorists on the loose.'

Franklin didn't wait for anyone to confirm or deny any of his deductions. He was ploughing on determinedly to a goal. 'Look, sorry to barge in on your party—' Here he acknowledged Meredith with a nod, but was clearly not sorry enough to have any qualms about spoiling her evening out. 'I wonder if I could just have five minutes' chat?'

'Mr Franklin,' Markby said, knowing he sounded tetchy, 'I'm sympathetic, believe me. But Inspector Pearce is the man you want. And we all need an evening off.'

'Appreciate that. Pearce is the fellow came to see us this morning. Doesn't know his Kipling.'

'Kipling?' Markby refused to ask why Pearce's lack of literary interests should have any bearing on a murder inquiry. 'No idea what his reading habits are,' he said aloud. Well, not quite true. Pearce read the tabloid papers, mainly the sports pages, and occasionally, in the past, had been seen on stake-out passing time with a western.

'I quoted to him from the *Just So Stories*, the Cat.'

Meredith smiled. '"The Cat that walks by himself, and all places are alike to him."'

This got her an approving look. 'Glad to see someone reads the classics.'

'Brought up on those stories,' she confessed. 'And *Kim*, of course.'

'Which you were told, wrongly, was a child's book. It is nothing of the sort. It is a book for adults.'

'Why?' asked Markby, despite himself, knowing that he should be putting a stop to the conversation, not asking questions. 'Not why is it an adult book,' he added hastily, sure that Franklin was about to tell him, 'why quote Kipling to Inspector Pearce?'

'I was trying to explain my sister-in-law's character and why it wasn't so strange that she flounced off and didn't come back.'

Simon appeared to think that the trend of the exchange meant his request for a chat had been accepted and, as Markby had feared he would, pulled out a chair and sat down. He set his pint on the table and leaned forward confidentially.

'Your man Pearce seemed to think it odd, you see, that Hugh hadn't been more concerned. But she was a very independent woman.'

'Independent?' Markby unwisely glanced at Meredith and got a frosty look. 'Look here,' he said. 'I'm aware of the basic facts in the case, but I really can't help you.'

'I just want to explain to you about Sonia, then you can tell your inspector. Trying to explain to him directly doesn't work.'

Markby realised it would be easier to let Simon speak his piece and promise to pass it on to Pearce. Besides, he had to admit to a twinge of curiosity. This man appeared to be some sort of academic. The deceased had been the wife of a local farmer. Markby glanced apologetically at Meredith. But he needn't have worried on her account. Far from it. She was settling down to listen to Simon quite happily. That, also, was a bad omen.

'Five minutes, you said,' he reminded Simon.

'That's all I need. It's like this: when my brother's first wife, Penny, died just under two years ago, he already knew Sonia. She was a friend of Bethan's and had been down to stay at my place.'

'Bethan is your wife?' It was a curious thing, but total strangers often assumed he knew all about them. Did they think the police had supernatural powers?

'She was my partner but we split up. The point I'm making is, that's how Hugh met Sonia. He was very cut up when Penny died, missed her about the place, and he'd got a young daughter to consider. All in all, he was looking for another wife and Sonia was – well – a very attractive woman. I'll be frank, I didn't realise what was in his mind. Old Hugh, he tends to keep things to himself. But he really sprang a surprise on me that time. Not the remarriage so much as his picking Sonia. More particularly, Sonia picking him. But there you are, opposites attract, they say.'

'Was it a good marriage?' Meredith asked that question. She sounded as if she were really interested to know the answer. Markby took another look at her, slightly alarmed.

'Actually, I think it was. Lively, mind you. She could be a bit temperamental, Sonia. But Hugh was devoted to her.'

'What about the little girl? How did she take to her stepmother?' That was Meredith again.

Markby tried to telegraph *Don't encourage the man!* He had a horrible feeling she was becoming hooked. Unfortunately, Meredith's eyes were on Simon, and she didn't see his anguished look.

He sat back in his chair, folded his arms and fixed his stoniest stare on Simon. He'd noticed in the past that women often seemed to like these intellectual-looking chaps and were prepared to hear them out. Possibly their appearance suggested that what they were saying was worth listening to. That, in Markby's experience, wasn't always the case. Meredith, who was normally a shrewd judge of character, appeared mesmerised by Simon Franklin. She was hanging on his every word. Markby had already decided that allowing Simon to sit down was probably a decision he'd regret for a long time. This was going to last a lot longer than five minutes and was in a fair way to wreck the entire evening.

'Tammy? The relationship was taking time to establish, as you'd imagine, but it was coming along,' Simon was assuring Meredith.

He turned back to Markby. 'Look, surely the police can understand that Hugh had had a hard day's work, with another to come the next day. Just for the purpose, the one permanent labourer he employs is laid up with a strained back. It's not inexplicable that he went to bed and left Sonia to come back in her own good time. Of course, on Thursday morning he realised something wasn't right and was debating what to do when Danny Smith came with the news that he'd found her body down by the railway line.'

Meredith started, opened her mouth and closed it again.

Simon was leaning forward to lend emphasis to his words. He fixed Markby with a glittering eye which put the superintendent in mind of the Ancient Mariner. If he remembered rightly, the old salt had stopped one of three. The other two must have scampered off feeling themselves very lucky, leaving their fellow wedding guest trapped by an old bore.

'My brother tried his level best, given his distressed state, to explain this to your inspector, but the fellow really didn't seem to get hold of the fact that Sonia was an individualist. He seemed to think there was something unusual, even sinister about it, but there isn't – wasn't.'

'I'm sure Inspector Pearce won't make a mountain out of a molehill, if that's what you're fearing. But he has to ask questions.'

Meredith was giving him a puzzled look and little wonder. What sort of answer was that? More sharply, he asked Simon, 'Look, spit it out, can't you? If there is any more? We're trying to enjoy ourselves!'

Simon steamed on regardless. 'I told your man Pearce' – Markby managed, just, not to interject that Pearce wasn't his valet – 'we have a lot of odd characters wandering about the countryside these days. I'd warned Sonia to take care, especially when she walked out of an evening. Because she was on Hazelwood land didn't mean others weren't there who had no right to be. She wasn't a countrywoman and she didn't realise it isn't like it seems to be to townies. Even being married to Hugh hadn't really opened her eyes to the reality of country life.' Simon sipped at his pint. 'I tell you, Markby, farming's not like it was. You should see some of the odd characters Hugh has to take on to harvest his cash crops. Last year he grew potatoes. More trouble than they were worth. He ended up employing a bunch of Polish students.'

Who may or may not, thought Markby, have had work permits. He resisted the temptation to bury his head in his hands and groan aloud.

'But no such people are working there at the moment? Or recently?' he asked woodenly.

'What? No. But there're plenty of odd bods around, even so.'

'And you think that she met such an unauthorised stranger and—' Markby broke off and felt a twinge of embarrassment because, after all, they were talking of a family bereavement here as far as Simon was concerned. Not that Simon appeared unduly grief-stricken. Rather, the whole thing had given him a platform to expound his views and he was making the most of it.

'Yes, I do. And if your inspector doesn't go looking for him, he'll be clear out of the county before you can nab him.'

Simon stood up and collected his empty glass. *Hoorah, hoorah!* cried the inner Markby.

'That's all I wanted to say. I appreciate your letting me tell you about it. I feel a lot happier now. Enjoy your evening.'

'Thank you,' said Meredith brightly.

'Feel free!' growled Markby.

They both watched Simon as he strode off, deposited his empty glass on the bar and made his way out. Meredith moved the corner of the dusty velvet curtain over the window by which she sat. It looked out on to the car park. She saw Simon, in the pink glow cast by red light bulbs strung along the exterior of the pub, making his way to the Japanese off-roader.

'He's parked next to you. Or you parked next to him, rather. He really wanted to get all that off his chest, didn't he?'

Markby picked up his gin and tonic and said, 'I'd apologise for that if I didn't know you were hanging on his every word.'

'You can't blame me. I didn't know you had a new murder case.'

'Pearce has,' he corrected. 'I handed it over to him. I'm merely supervising things. He's got Prescott to help him and tomorrow I'll have to rustle up a couple of detective constables. I admit I wish I could do better than that, but we're very short-handed at the moment, and I can't manufacture help out of thin air. A point I'm sure our friend Mr Simon Franklin doesn't appreciate.'

'And she was found near the railway line?' Meredith asked this question with an elaborate casualness. 'Where, exactly? And when?'

'On the embankment, a couple of miles from the farm, Hazelwood Farm, where she lived. The body was hidden in scrub and trees. Chap found it yesterday morning.' Markby opened the menu. 'I came here to eat, not talk shop.'

She put out a hand, closing the menu again. 'Hang on, just one question and then I won't say another word. This place where the body was found, it wasn't near the old viaduct, was it?'

Markby sat back in his chair and studied his companion. One of the things which had come between them in the past was his work. There was no use denying it. His work, basically, had finally pushed over the teetering edifice which had been his marriage to Rachel. His work, certain aspects of it, had proved a bone of contention more than once with Meredith. It wasn't that she didn't respect it or approve in a general sense. It certainly wasn't that she had no interest in it. She had more than once taken far too much interest. But there were aspects of police work she couldn't accept. Things which upset her. Sometimes police officers were themselves upset and found what they were doing hard to take. But a policeman couldn't allow himself to be too sensitive. He had to get at the truth by any lawful means he could, and sometimes the innocent got hurt. That was the particular aspect she found so difficult to swallow and probably never would. But now she was asking about it, asking a specific question. When Meredith did that it was because the answer mattered.

'Why do you want to know?' He put the question quietly.

The gaze of her hazel eyes faltered. She pushed back a troublesome hank of dark brown hair. 'It'll sound daft.'

'Nothing you've ever said to me has sounded silly.'

'Thanks, but there's always a first time and this is probably it. Yesterday morning I caught a later train. George Biddock came to make a start on the porch.'

'How's he getting on?' Markby was sidetracked.

'OK, well, the cat walked on the wet cement. They're working on the tracks, you know. It's caused delays. We'd only just pulled out of Bamford, and just by the viaduct we were stopped for about five minutes. I looked out of the window and there was a large green frog thing hanging on a tree, staring back at me.'

'Frog?' he repeated cautiously.

'Not a real frog. A plush one, a bag, backpack. Teenagers carry them around. I couldn't see anyone nearby. It just seemed so odd, miles from anywhere. It would be a dangerous place for anyone to be anyway, wouldn't it? Right near the bottom of the embankment close to the track.'

'It would,' Markby agreed. 'Though people stray on to the railway for a variety of reasons. They also throw rubbish away in the oddest places, you know.'

'I do know, but this wasn't rubbish. It looked fairly new, clean, in good condition.' She gave an embarrassed laugh. 'I'm not saying this has anything to do with your murder inquiry.'

'Pearce's murder inquiry.'

'You're his boss.'

'The secret of successful management is knowing when to delegate.' He drummed his fingers on the table. 'Tomorrow morning, if you're free, we could drive out to the spot and you could show me. Do you think you could find it? The tree, I mean.'

'Pretty sure. It was just short of the viaduct pillar.'

'Right, then. Now can we leave it?' He reopened the menu. 'The pork in cider sounds nice.'

They weren't, however, to spend the rest of the evening free of the troubles of the Franklin family. It was clear to Markby that his companion had something on her mind. No matter what they talked about, it was as if a part of her attention was elsewhere. By the time they'd got to the coffee, he was forced to give in.

'What is it? You're brooding about something.'

'You don't want to talk about the Franklins,' she said defensively.

'No, I want to talk to you about other things. But since I've only got half your attention, it might be easier if we cleared the decks by getting whatever it is out of the way first.'

She hesitated, picked up one of the mint chocolates which had arrived with the coffee, and carefully unwrapped the silver foil. 'I was thinking how quickly Hugh Franklin remarried after his first wife's death. I realise Simon had an explanation for it. But it was still very quick. It must have been difficult for the child.'

'I don't know how old the daughter is,' Markby said. 'The younger she is, the more understandable his hasty remarriage becomes.'

He let his gaze travel round the crowded room. Although The Red Lion attracted trade from a wide area, it remained the local pub and there was a fair sprinkling of red faces and ancient pullovers. An elderly man had just arrived, weather-beaten to the hue of walnut, a disreputable flat cap on his head, an antique watch chain draped across his old-fashioned waistcoat. He moved with a stiff gait and bent forward at an awkward angle. He was greeted at once by half a dozen voices. 'Hullo, there, Sid. How's the back?'

'No better. I got the wife rubbing it with some stuff the doctor give me. I go about smelling like a bloody chemist's shop.'

'Wintergreen,' said the burly man in the pullover, who was still at the bar. 'That's what you want if you can still get the stuff. My old dad used to swear by wintergreen for man or beast. Aches, sprains, knocks. Cleaned his boots with it, and all.'

A bad back. Hugh Franklin's labourer had a bad back. They were less than a mile, here, from Hazelwood Farm. Simon Franklin drank here. Sid, by deduction, was very likely the absent farmhand. Markby eyed him curiously and as he did, his suspicion was confirmed.

The burly man in the pullover set down his glass. 'Young Simon was in here just a short time back. You've only just missed him.'

Young Simon? Local people would have seen both the Franklin boys grow up. They'd remain 'young' for as long as memory of their parents lasted. Markby, to his annoyance, didn't catch Sid's reply.

'Ah, nasty business,' said the burly man. 'Still, can't say as she didn't have it coming to her.'

Markby almost rose from his seat at this and demanded an explanation. Before he could, however, someone else observed it wasn't right to speak ill of the dead.

The burly man accepted the rebuke and talk turned to football.

'Alan?' That was Meredith, looking at him, eyebrows raised.

'What? Sorry, sidetracked.' He made an effort to return to the topic of their conversation. 'I was just thinking, we shouldn't criticise Hugh. He's got a farm to run. He's only got basic help. He needs a woman to run his home, care for his child.'

'Cook his dinner, darn his socks,' said Meredith with some asperity.

'Yes. It's not the sort of life to appeal to you.' Markby knew he sounded sharp, but he couldn't help it. 'But life's like that in the country.'

'I'm sure,' Meredith said obstinately, the fringe of brown hair falling over her eyes again, 'he could have found a woman who'd be willing to come in daily and housekeep, a local widow or something.'

'Don't be naïve,' Markby told her.

'Ah, sex. Yes, he'd be missing that too.'

Markby leaned his arms on the table and held her gaze. 'Look here, as far as we know, Hugh Franklin was happily married for some years to his first wife. He probably liked being married. He's not the only man to remarry quickly after being widowed. Other people might tut-tut, but it's human. It's the company, the companionship and, all right, it's the sex.'

She didn't answer this, but the question was in her eyes.

'In my case, it's love,' he said. 'I'm not looking for someone to cook my dinner and darn my socks. I know you don't like cooking and I'm willing to bet you don't darn! I don't miss Rachel. We weren't happy and were heartily glad to see the back of one another. I'm not Hugh Franklin. I'm someone who loves you and wants to marry you. It seems to me to be a logical progression. I want to be with you. Us, together.'

Meredith dropped her eyes to the table and began to push around the screwed-up bits of foil. 'I shouldn't have started the discussion about Hugh. I'm sorry.'

He drew a deep breath. 'Damn Simon Franklin! Why did he have to pester us with his troubles during a pleasant evening in the pub?'

Impulsively she put out her hand and took his. 'Forget him. Forget Hugh. Forget – if you can – that we can't seem to agree on something I know means so much to you. Let's go home.'

He smiled. 'My place or yours?'

CHAPTER SIX

'All right, Tam?'

Hugh Franklin paused in the kitchen doorway. His daughter was at the sink, washing up the breakfast dishes. They didn't have a modern stainless-steel sink unit. The farm kitchen still had a venerable porcelain-glazed stone trough of imposing proportions surmounted by a large, unwieldy cold water tap. To wash up, Tammy had almost to stand on tiptoe and struggle to reach down into the sink's cavernous depths. Above the sink the pilot light of a small gas-fired heater hissed gently, its narrow spout bending down gracefully to discharge hot water at the turn of a broken plastic knob. This contraption had been seen at the time it had been installed, more than thirty years before, as the height of domestic convenience. 'No more boiling the kettle every time I want to wash up!' Hugh's mother had said admiringly.

Sonia had felt differently. 'Do you realise how *old* that thing is? It could be dangerous! It could blow up in my face.' Sonia had grumbled about that sink, too. 'For crying out loud, Hugh, it ought to be out in the farmyard! It's big enough for the cattle to drink out of.' A new fitted kitchen, that's what she'd wanted. He hadn't been unsympathetic to her view, but the money hadn't been there for it, it had been as simple as that. 'One day,' he'd promised. A disbelieving snort had greeted this.

'All right, Dad,' said Tammy, stretching for the tap. Her small hands just about managed to grip it and she needed both of them to turn it.

Hugh had begun to cross the kitchen with the intention of helping, but she'd managed it before he could get there. Cold water splashed in and she began to rinse the washed dishes and transfer them carefully to a rack on the wooden draining board which required scrubbing down regularly and had been another of Sonia's numerous dislikes.

Hugh remembered his mother using soda on it. Sonia had used a modern kitchen cleaner and poured a lot of bleach around, all the time grumbling about how unhygienic it was and the damage to her hands, even though she wore rubber gloves.

'I don't know how much longer you think I'm going to carry on with this old-fashioned skivvying!'

Remembering it all and watching his young daughter's doughty struggles, Hugh's feeling, that he was adrift on an ocean without sight of land, increased. Simon insisted what Hugh felt was grief for Sonia. But Hugh knew it wasn't grief he felt when he thought of her, it was guilt. Simon misread the guilt, too, attributing it to Hugh's fear that he'd failed his wife. The truth was, his guilt was due to the relief he felt now she was out of his life, the lifting of the burden from his shoulders. He was deeply ashamed of this but he couldn't deny it. He and Sonia had reached the end of the roller-coaster ride which had been their brief marriage. Unfortunately, the fairground car they rode in had lacked brakes and they'd been destined to hit the buffers with an almighty crash. She had been so angry inside of herself. A deep-rooted seething sullen fury directed at him, the farm, her life. On his part, he'd grown to hate the beauty he'd once admired and had felt he would do anything to silence that accusing, hectoring voice.

Jane's question, how was Tammy taking all this?, had pricked his conscience even more painfully. He didn't know how his daughter felt because he hadn't asked her. He hadn't asked her because he didn't know how to, and that was something he couldn't admit to the schoolteacher. Though probably, he thought wryly, she'd already guessed. He knew he ought at least to try, and he tried now, standing at his daughter's elbow by the old sink.

'I'm sorry about all this, Tam.' It sounded lame but it was the best he could manage. Looking for more words to express his concern was like looking into an empty bucket. He'd never been like Simon, having a way with words, able to conjure them up, it had always seemed to Hugh, with an effortless ease he'd envied even when they were children. Simon, he thought, had always done the talking.

'Not your fault, Dad.' She sounded composed as she always did and he wondered if he only imagined an underlying strain in her voice.

'She did her best, did Sonia,' he went on. 'I know you didn't much like having her around, Tam. But it was difficult for her, too.'

'Then she shouldn't have come here, should she?' Tammy turned her pale little face towards him and he was shocked at the accusation in her eyes.

He floundered. 'I thought you understood. It wasn't that I didn't love your mum. You know that's not so. But life goes on.'

It struck him that he couldn't have chosen a worse phrase. For Sonia, life had come to an abrupt and shocking end.

Tammy had gathered up a tea towel and begun to dry off the crockery, putting it away carefully in the right place, plates stacked here, cups on hooks there, knives and forks into the drawer in separate compartments.

Hugh said awkwardly, 'I thought it'd be a good thing for you, Tammy. I thought, a growing girl like you needed a woman around the house. Someone to talk to. No use talking to me, is it, about clothes and hairdos and so on? Much I know about it!'

'I'd never want to look like Sonia,' Tammy said, her voice filled with disgust. 'All made up and wearing nail polish and everything.'

He felt he ought to defend his late wife. 'She always looked very nice, Tammy, and there's no harm in that.'

But perhaps there had been harm in it after all. Hugh turned his head to look out of the window above the sink to give himself time to sort out what to say next. Tammy's direct grey eyes pierced through flesh and bone, it seemed, to his very soul. He could just walk out and leave the conversation where it was. If he tried to prolong it, very likely he'd only make things worse, as he'd done when arguing with Sonia. But if he walked off, he'd be running away. Run away, he thought ruefully, was what he'd always done in an emotional confrontation. Had that failing in himself contributed to the tragedy? He'd asked himself that question time without number since she'd died. The answer, cruelly, always came back: *Yes!*

He was brought abruptly from these reflections and spared having to find words for his daughter by a surprising sight in the farmyard. A deputation was approaching the farmhouse, comprised of Mr and Mrs Smith and the three youngest Smiths.

It was unusual for them all to come together. When Danny called by the house, he usually came no further than the kitchen door, only occasionally edging in far enough to sit on one of the wooden chairs. Often he carried an old bag made of strips of cloth stitched together and part-filled with bits of firewood he'd collected along the way. Today was different. The Smiths were turned out in their finery.

Danny was squeezed into the suit he'd probably got married in, from the cut of it. Zilpah was resplendent in a tent-like garment fashioned from a purple velvety material which made her look like an advancing Roman emperor. She was bedecked with gold jewellery wherever jewellery might be displayed, from her ears, round her neck, her wrists, on her fingers. The young Smiths were likewise turned out immaculately. The boy's hair had been brushed ruthlessly flat and the girls' hair braided. They wore clean clothes crisply pressed.

'We got company, Tammy,' Hugh said in some awe. 'Danny and his missus have come to call, pay respects most likely. Kids and all. You'd best put the kettle on.' He rubbed his hands over his hair in an ineffectual attempt to smarten himself up and went to the door to greet them.

Since this was a formal call, Hugh ushered his visitors into the sitting room. He felt underdressed in his none-too-clean jeans and old sweater. Even Danny could now be seen to be wearing gold rings on nearly every finger. Pogo, alarmed by the sight of so many people crowding into the room, took himself off, wheezing gustily. The Smiths arranged themselves around the available seating. Zilpah clasped her gold-caparisoned workworn hands in her velvet lap and screwed up her eyes in judgement on the state of the room. Danny cleared his throat.

Hugh waited but instead of speaking, Danny delved into a pocket of his suit jacket, which bulged suspiciously, and produced a half-bottle of whisky. He set this on the coffee table with a diffident glance at Hugh.

'Much obliged,' said Hugh. 'We'll put a drop in our tea.' He remembered the younger visitors and turned to them. 'Why don't you young 'uns nip out to the kitchen? There's cans of Coke and such like in the fridge. Tammy'll show you.'

'Mind your manners!' warned their mother as the children filed past.

'We've come to make our condolences proper,' continued Zilpah, when her brood had departed. 'We're very sorry, Dan and me, for your loss. Mrs Franklin was a very nice lady. It's a shocking business when you can't go for a walk of an evening without something dreadful happening to you. I don't know what the world's coming to. It was never like it when I was a girl. I tell my kids, you watch out. You don't know who's out there.'

Danny cleared his throat again and this time words emerged in a hoarse croak. 'When's the funeral to be?'

'Got to be an inquest first, Monday,' Hugh told him. 'Then, if the police release the – if they let us have Sonia back, we can bury her. I've spoken to the vicar.'

'I gotta go to the inquest,' Danny informed him. He still sounded as if he'd been inhaling woodsmoke from his campfire. 'I might have to say how I found her.'

There was an awkward pause broken when Tammy appeared, staggering under the burden of a tray of tea things. Hugh hastened to relieve his daughter of the load. 'I'll manage this, Tam, you go and talk to the young 'uns.'

With the arrival of tea, there was a subtle rearrangement of roles. Hugh set the tray down on the coffee table. Lubrication of the vocal cords being called for, Danny unscrewed the whisky bottle. Zilpah appointed herself tea-pourer in chief.

'She's managing very well, your little miss,' said Danny.

'Tammy's been terrific,' said Hugh despondently. 'It's not what I'd have wished for her. First her own mother dying and now Sonia gone.'

'Not good to be without your mother,' said Zilpah. 'My mother's still going strong, so's my grandma. Eighty-four is Grandma and had seventeen kids.'

They sipped tea, laced with whisky, in a genteel manner. Mrs Smith kept an eagle eye on her husband, who was having a little difficulty with the best bone china cup unearthed by Tammy. He'd have preferred a mug.

'The police been to see you too, I believe,' Hugh said. 'One of them was here. An inspector, he came yesterday morning. Simon was here with me, thank goodness. I don't think I could've dealt with it on my own.'

'Sergeant came to see us,' said Danny. 'Big feller, weren't he, Zil? Still, pleasant enough bloke for a copper. But you can't trust any of them, Hugh. You watch what you say.'

'That's more or less what Simon's been telling me. Sorry you had to be involved in all this, Danny – and Zilpah.' He met Danny's eye. 'It won't make any difference. You'll always be welcome at Hazelwood.'

'Ah . . .' said Danny, and his gaze shifted away.

Hugh wondered, when this should all be over, if he'd see the Smiths ever again. He hoped so. But would anything ever be the same again? It was at that moment that he fully realised that what was happening was a full-scale murder inquiry and, whatever came out of it, everything would be changed for ever. Somehow, his mind had run only on the immediate things, the inquest, the funeral. But, of course, this coming and going of the police, the questions, this would go on indefinitely . . . until they knew the truth.

'They won't let it go,' he said slowly. 'Police will worry at this like a terrier with a rat.'

Danny nodded and repeated his warning. 'Ah, they're tricky blighters. You watch yourself, Hugh.'

'Watch yourself!' warned Alan Markby at about the same time.

He was descending the embankment, branches and thorny brambles catching at his old green Barbour, his feet sliding away from him on the soft earth. The recent influx of visitors had disturbed things down here. They'd raked aside the brambles and churned up the carpet of leaves. Detritus of all kinds combined in an odd pungent smell. Markby sniffed, trying to identify the component parts. Dogfox. Faecal matter. Putrefaction. Rotting leaves and things mouldering unseen in the bushes. It was the odour of old burial places after rain or of cathedral crypts where dampness crept up the stones to stain the mortar and there was always something powdery about the stale air. *Earth to earth, ashes to ashes, dust to dust.*

Aloud, he quoted, '"Now get you to my lady's chamber, and tell her, let her paint an inch thick, to this favour she must come."'

Meredith, who was following, objected vigorously, 'You don't have to rub it in!'

He turned back and grinned, holding out his hand in an offer of assistance.

'I can manage,' she said starchily, probably keen to make the point she wasn't ready to drop off the twig yet. She slithered down the slope to arrive beside him. She had eventually given in and bought herself a waxed jacket like his, but a dark blue one. 'I am not,' she'd said, 'going round with you looking like twins.'

'No,' he'd said. 'You look like a police officer.'

That hadn't gone down very well, he reflected now. 'Your jacket,' he observed, 'makes mine look even worse than I thought it did.'

'Get yourself a new one.'

'I like this one.' Defensively. 'The new ones smell of wax.'

Meredith sniffed at her sleeve. 'Yes, it does. But yours hasn't got any wax left. You can buy a spray, you know, and redo it.'

'It's all right as it is.' Obstinate, now.

'I didn't say it wasn't. You're the one said it looked awful.'

Markby gazed down at the garment. 'Time was this was standard CID wear. Every copper had one. It kept him warm and dry while he hung about in the cold watching villains and it had plenty of pocket space for his sandwiches.'

'And every crook recognised him immediately,' she retorted.

'Probably. Where did you see this frog thing, then?'

But she hesitated, looking about her. 'Where did they find . . . ?'

'The body? Over here somewhere.' He led the way along a path created by the trampling of many feet. The area in the bushes was easily distinguished. Brambles had been broken down and nettles beaten flat. The damage had revealed the open mouths of the rabbit warren. Pellets of rabbit faeces lay on the ground. Other signs spoke of the recent presence of man. Crushed cigarette packets, spent matches, lengths of blue and white plastic tape caught like bunting on the trees.

'I wish,' Markby said, 'I knew more about this case. I came down here when she was found, but after that I left it to Pearce. He's more than capable, don't get me wrong. But since I seem to be drawn in anyway, I now wish I'd taken an interest at the start.'

Receiving no answer, he turned his head. Meredith was staring, not at the trampled ground, but through the undergrowth and spindly tree trunks down to the tracks below, glittering in the sun.

'Was she killed here, do you know that yet?' she asked quietly.

'That I can tell you. No. Or we don't think so. There was evidence suggesting someone had part carried and part dragged a heavy object down the embankment. Snagged scraps of blue jeans material were recovered and, although the results aren't back from the lab yet, may well prove to match the woman's clothing. Efforts to retrieve tyre tracks from the verge up there,' he pointed up at the road running alongside the embankment, 'were frustrated by the fact that the patrol car first on the scene probably parked on top of them. Then the officers in the car weren't as careful as they might have been. Again, one can't entirely blame them. People do report seeing bodies which turn out to be bundles of rags or old Guy Fawkes dummies. We had a woman come into Bamford station once, in hysterics, to say she'd seen a skeleton in the woods. She had too. A plastic one set up there by some medical students as an April fool joke.'

'So she was lying here dead while I was sitting in the train, staring out the window at the frog.' At this reminder, Meredith turned and set off diagonally through the scrub in the direction of the viaduct. Her haste indicated that the scene of the crime had suddenly become distasteful to her.

Markby, who had followed Meredith, raised his eyes. An ancient road had once rambled across the hills linking scattered villages. The coming of the railway had driven a deep cutting through the land, necessitating the viaduct to carry the road across the gaping wound. The dark grey weathered stones could be glimpsed through the foliage. It spanned the track in a double arch supported by a triplet set of piers. Near where they stood, one massive pier rose from the surrounding brambles. Creeping green fingers clutched at its stone leg as if they would drag it down to some subterranean world. Its great blocks were veiled in moss and marked with the stains left by rivulets of rainwater trickling through the crevices created by crumbling mortar. This first arch spanned the 'up' track and was supported on the other side by the middle arch which stood between the tracks. Another vault spanned the 'down' track to the sister pier on the other side, sinking its stone foot into the parallel embankment. In the tangle of branches on either side of the track, further ivy-covered masonry was dimly discernible.

What a scene of activity this must have been, thought Markby. The navvies toiling to dig out the bed of the track and create the embankment. The engineers supervising the laying of the rails. The builders' labourers swarming up wooden scaffolding as the stone bridge rose from the ground. The sound of strange accents rising on the air as men were brought from far and wide to work on the project. The women who were brought in to cook up the great cauldrons of food, shrieking and squabbling. The drama of accidents as cuttings collapsed or men fell. The fetid tents housing the sick who'd fallen prey to the cholera which stalked the navvies' gangs.

Now it was a forgotten monument to the past. Since those far-off times, new roads had been created and the old one had fallen into disuse, disrepair, and finally had been obliterated by encroaching scrub. Men still worked along here, though. Working on the railway, as they'd done a hundred and fifty years before. Markby could hear voices floating from further down the track and the noise of a generator. The maintenance work which had held up Meredith's train. He frowned, then glanced up at the parapet again. At some point, it had been reinforced with iron rivets linking its stones and covered with a wire mesh.

'It still looks none too safe to me,' he said, pointing to the repairs. 'Worth reporting to whoever is responsible for it. Just think, if one of those blocks fell on to the line. They ought to take the thing down.'

'Bet the Victorian Society wouldn't let them.' Meredith squinted up at it. 'It's possible to get up there, I suppose.'

'Yes, I imagine so. You'd need to go up the hill and find a way through the undergrowth.'

'It reminds me of Sleeping Beauty's castle in the tale,' she said. 'Left to become overgrown and lost in the woods.'

'That's a very romantic notion,' he replied, surprised.

'I've just had an idea which is anything but romantic. Grisly, in fact. Want to hear it?' She glanced at him, eyebrows raised.

'Go ahead. Grisly is more in my experience than romantic.' He hadn't meant that as anything more than a joke. She, however, took it otherwise.

'Sorry,' she said stiffly.

'I didn't mean— Look, just tell me your idea.'

'Why didn't he put the body on the track? I take it he brought it here under cover of dark. A late train travelling along here might well have struck it and then it would've looked like a suicide.'

'He wasn't sure of that. Or he didn't think of it in his panic. Perhaps he was worried about the men working further along, laying the new tracks. I wonder what time the last shift knocks off. Must have a word with Pearce about that too on Monday.' Markby heaved a sigh. He didn't want to upset Dave by behaving as though he were taking over. But, on the other hand, it was his business to know how investigations were going.

Meredith had moved on and was prowling round the tree trunks. 'I think, this one.'

He joined her. They were very near the track here. She could certainly have seen this tree from the train. The viaduct cast a dark shadow which fell just short of it. He glanced at his wristwatch: mid-morning, about the time Meredith's train had passed by. 'Was it in sunshine?' he asked.

'The frog? Yes, it was. It was very bright green and the sun made its black eyes shine. It was a horrid thing, not a bit cute.'

He was examining the surface of the bark carefully, inch by inch. Suddenly he muttered, 'Ah!' From out of his pocket came a plastic bag and a pair of tweezers. As Meredith watched him, he painstakingly removed something from a twig and dropped it into the bag which he then sealed. He brought it back to her.

It was a very small piece of bright green cotton. 'Your frog,' he said.

Meredith's reply was cut short. There was a blare of a horn and a train appeared, rushing down the track towards them. Markby grabbed her arm and pulled her back up the embankment. It swept past in a blast of warm air which tugged at them both. Meredith grabbed a branch to steady herself.

'Come on,' he said. 'The driver will report having seen vandals near the track. We don't want to be arrested.'

Jane took Tammy shopping that afternoon. Tammy had taken her task to heart and a neatly written list of groceries and other household requirements was produced for Jane's inspection. She read it with interest and a touch of surprise. She supposed she'd always believed, as many people do, that farms must be *ipso facto* self-supporting places. But of course, they weren't, not nowadays. Some things they did produce for their own use. Other tasks had long disappeared from the farmhouse kitchen.

'We're right out of bread,' said Tammy. 'And cheese. That's the most important because Dad takes cheese sandwiches with him when he's out working away from the house. So's he doesn't need to come back at lunchtime. We need pickle as well. Mum used to make it herself, but Sonia didn't know how, so we have to buy it. The shop pickle's not as nice as Mum's, but it's better than nothing at all,' she concluded on an old-fashioned note.

Jane smiled. There were no eggs on the list, because the farm did keep hens, enough to keep the family in eggs but not to sell on. 'Because of the salmonella regulations and having to have the flock tested,' explained Tammy. 'It's just not worth the trouble.'

Jane was by now beginning to feel that their roles had been reversed. In school, she'd been the teacher. Today, Tammy was, and very much so. But at least this sense of being in charge had loosened Tammy's tongue.

As for Hugh's part in the shopping expedition, he'd simply handed Jane a blank signed cheque and his cheque card. With responsibility weighing on her shoulders, Jane set off with Tammy. It turned out a surprisingly enjoyable afternoon. Tammy continued to chatter freely about the farm's needs, what her father liked to eat, his pet dislikes. 'He can't stand pressed tongue.' She had a housewife's mind. 'We could take a quarter of ham, but look, the cold roast pork is cheaper; it's on special offer.'

By now a thought had lodged in Jane's head. 'Did your stepmother like shopping?'

'Sonia? She liked shopping for clothes.' Tammy invested the last word with scorn. 'But when she shopped for food she bought a lot of frozen stuff. My mum never bought frozen stuff until right at the end, when she was so ill, you see.'

Jane did see. Tammy had appeared 'different' to the other girls in the school because her life had been different. During the last months of her own mother's illness and during the tenureship – it seemed the most suitable word – of her stepmother, Tammy had been the housekeeper of Hazelwood Farm. She had kept an eye on the store cupboard, reminded Sonia of what was running low, of what her father liked and needed. Had her father realised this? And did he realise how much responsibility was likely to fall on his child's shoulders now there was no woman at Hazelwood? It was a delicate matter but Jane knew that sooner or later she'd have to tackle it with Hugh.

When they got back, and were sitting at the kitchen table, she produced the receipts for Hugh's inspection and tried to explain why they'd spent the sum of money they had. But he didn't appear in the slightest interested, content that the goods needed had been purchased and put away and he'd had no part in it. Jane had laid out the receipts in a row. Hugh glanced at them dismissively.

'All right, then.'

'No, it's not all right,' said Jane energetically. 'Look, this is your money I've spent. I'm trying to show you where it's gone.' Like it or not, the man was going to have to take some interest.

'Gone on food and stuff, I understand that,' returned Hugh infuriatingly.

'But you should know what kind of food, and what basic needs constitute what you call "stuff". You should make a list of items like washing powder, lavatory cleaner, kitchen scourer. Each week, on shopping day, check them down and make sure you're not running out.'

'Good God, woman,' said Hugh, his weather-beaten features creased in shock, 'I haven't got time to do all that. Takes me all my time reckoning what the farm needs.'

'Look,' said Jane, determined not to let this go. If he got away with it now she'd never get him to accept it, not once she started shopping regularly for them, as she would at least for the foreseeable future. 'This really won't do. I know this is a difficult time for you and I don't want to nag. I'm more than happy to lend a hand for a bit, but in the end you're going to have to take more interest in the household side of things. Tammy can't do it. Or she shouldn't do it. She's twelve years old, Hugh.' She hadn't meant to raise the matter so soon, but there it was, spoken.

'Anyone could tell you're a teacher,' said Hugh with a twitch of his eyebrows. 'Given me a right good telling-off, haven't you?'

'I didn't want to do that.' Jane was taken aback. 'I'm sorry if that's how it sounded. You've just lost your wife and for me to grumble at you is unforgivable. I was thinking of Tammy.'

'I think about her too,' he said drily. 'She's my daughter. As for losing my wife, as you put it, it's a funny thing but I think of Penny when you say that. Penny, my first wife, Tammy's mum. Sonia and I – well, it wasn't like you'd call a marriage. It was more like an experience.' His grey eyes narrowed, perhaps in response to the expression on her face. 'That doesn't sound right to you, I expect.'

Flustered, Jane mumbled, 'It's not for me to say.'

'But you've got an opinion. Don't tell me you haven't. Seems to me you've got an opinion about everything else.'

This jibe stung Jane, who retorted, 'I said I was sorry! You don't have to be rude.'

'Was I?' He looked puzzled. 'I thought I was just saying the obvious. The fact is, I do miss Penny. I miss her right now with all this bother. I wish she was here, of course I do, but then if she were, there wouldn't be any bother, would there? Because I'd never have married Sonia. I'm not bad-mouthing Sonia to you. I'm just saying the obvious again.' He pulled a face. 'I'm too quick to say the obvious, it seems. Perhaps I ought to learn a bit of tact.'

Jane suppressed the urge to snap, 'Yes, perhaps you should!' She gazed at him. That was an awful sweater, even allowing for it being one he kept for messy jobs around the farm. It had holes in both elbows and the ribbing round the neck was becoming unravelled. But he had shaved today and really, he was a nice-looking man. In fact, she judged him a nice man anyway, but not good at facing up to certain problems. Like a lot of people, he was entrenched in his own viewpoint. He needed shaking up a bit, she thought. But then, his second wife's death ought to be a shaking enough experience. He was painfully honest about his second marriage. She wondered what the police made of it, of him.

'Better to speak frankly,' she said at last, although she wasn't altogether sure she was right in present circumstances. 'Say what you mean.'

'Right, then I will. I've got a farm to run,' Hugh told her, and that now familiar obstinacy was back in his voice. 'I get up half-past four of a morning, more often than not. I've only got old Sid to help me and he's laid up sick right now. Luckily Danny Smith is passing through and I can call on him. But he only turns up twice a year. Simon will come over and give a hand if I get really stuck. But then, he's got his own work, writing books. Tell me when I've got time to go round the house counting bars of soap.'

'Well,' said Jane, 'that's frank enough, to be sure.'

He gave an odd little sound which might have been a suppressed chuckle. 'You want to have a word with my brother,' he said. 'You ought to tell him how it's best to be frank. Simon is like a cat on hot bricks in case I say the wrong thing to the detectives looking into Sonia's death. But I keep telling him, what can I say but tell them the truth? Just tell them how it was.' Unexpectedly he added, 'I do feel responsible for what happened to her, you know. She was my wife, after all, and I should have looked after her better.'

There was an awkward pause after this, broken when Jane said, 'Tammy was telling me about her Uncle Simon. I hadn't realised he was Simon Franklin who wrote the children's series of life in past times. We've got them in the school library. Most schools have, I should think. We use *Life in a Tudor Family* as a textbook.' In explanation, she added, 'I'm a history teacher myself.'

'I read the odd book now and again, when I get a chance,' Hugh defended himself. 'Raymond Chandler and that sort of thing. We've got books in the house. Got a bookcase of them through there.' He jerked his head in the direction of the sitting room.

Jane had seen them. While waiting for Tammy before their shopping expedition she'd been drawn to the row of book spines as she was to any collection of books. They were as might be expected – venerable paperbacks which had very likely been sitting there since Hugh's father's time, or even his grandfather's: Edmund Crispin's mysteries and a collection of Agatha Christie's; Margaret Irwin's historical sagas. *Billy Bunter of Greyfriars School*, Frank Richards' tale, existed as a well-thumbed hardback. A complete set of *Household Hints* and *Care of the Family*, both dating from early in the century. *Household Hints* told you how to black-lead the stove. *Care of the Family*, she wouldn't be surprised, advised parents to sew young children into cottonwool vests for the winter. Yet Simon Franklin had turned out academic. He must have removed all his books when he settled in his own home.

Hugh put his sunburned hands on the table, the fingers laced. 'Don't think I'm deaf to what you've been trying to tell me. I know it's difficult for young Tam. I'm not blind nor daft, neither. I did try and arrange things better when her own mum died. I knew she needed another mother. As it happened, and conveniently as I thought then, I'd met someone I fancied, so I got married again. But look how that turned out.'

She didn't know how it had turned out, but from the references which had been given, she thought she had a fair idea. A disaster.

'Perhaps you didn't give it enough time,' Jane ventured. 'Both for your own sake and Tammy's. I mean, before you remarried. It's not something to rush into.'

'And perhaps I don't understand much about women. Perhaps I just flattered myself Sonia felt about me the way I felt then about her. It doesn't do to speak ill of the departed and, God rest her soul, I won't speak badly of Sonia, as I said to you just now. She did her best. It wasn't her fault. But we'd come to the end of the line, anyway. Know what I mean?'

'I think so,' Jane said soberly.

'Whatever it was she wanted, it wasn't me, that's it and all about it.' There was deep emotion in his voice for all his studied sang-froid.

'I do understand,' Jane told him, trying to ignore the painful memories his words aroused from their half-slumber. Peter hadn't wanted her in the end. As Hugh said, that was it and all about it. Nothing more to be said.

She realised that Hugh was watching her face. His grey eyes, which his daughter had inherited, were surprisingly sharp. 'Yes,' he said quietly. 'You do understand.'

Jane pushed back her chair with a noisy scrape on the kitchen floor. She snatched up her bag and fumbled in it for her car keys.

'I have to go now. I've got things to do. I hope everything you need is there. Help Tammy to make another list for next weekend and we'll go again.'

She bolted out of the house, not realising, until she'd driven off, that she hadn't said goodbye to Tammy.

CHAPTER SEVEN

'And so you see, Gerald,' said Meredith into the phone on Sunday evening, 'I think I'd better take a few days' leave. I am due some leave, you know. I realise it's short notice but I'm taking the week. I'll ring Personnel in the morning, but I thought I'd let you know first.'

'Sounds fishy to me,' said Gerald, dismissing this sop. In the background the television could be heard. From the sound of galloping hoofs and of clashing blades Meredith guessed Gerald's mother was watching costume drama in some form. She enquired.

'What? Oh yes, she likes the boots and bonnets stuff. Listen here, you're not going off sleuthing again, are you?'

'Don't be silly, Gerald,' said Meredith sternly. 'I told you, I have a builder working here and I really feel I ought to be on hand.'

'Only,' continued Gerald, dismissing this explanation, 'you know what you are for finding bodies and so on. It never happens to me.' He sounded plaintive.

'I haven't found a body, Gerald, Girl Guide's honour.'

'And you've really got an old boy building a porch?'

'I swear.'

Gerald accepted this reluctantly. 'Well, see you next week, then. And if, mind you, this turns into one of your mysteries, I expect to be told all the details!'

'You should get out more, Gerald.' Meredith put down the phone.

She did feel one faint twinge of guilt but dismissed it. If she'd told the absolute truth, that she wanted to attend an inquest, there would have been no holding Gerald back. He'd be on the phone for the whole week, wanting up-to-the-minute information. She felt slightly more guilty at suggesting George Biddock needed to be supervised. But since George didn't know of the excuse she'd given Gerald, it couldn't worry or insult him.

She'd told Alan she intended to attend the inquest on Sonia Franklin. He hadn't seemed surprised but warned her she would probably be wasting her time.

'I can't be there myself,' he said. 'Pearce will be on hand. It'll all be over in minutes, you know. They're bound to adjourn.'

'Satisfy my own curiosity,' said Meredith. 'I've met Simon and I'd like to see Hugh Franklin.'

On Monday, she drew back the curtains to find the windowpanes spotted with drizzling rain. When she opened the back door, the bedraggled cat shot in, sat in front of the one-bar electric fire she'd switched on to warm up the kitchen, and began to lick his fur back into place.

'You're in luck,' she told him. 'You can stay indoors today. I'm going out later but I'll be back some time this afternoon. Don't get under George's feet.'

The cat paused in his ablutions to cast her a jaundiced look.

George arrived a few moments later. 'You not going off to London today, then, my duck?'

'No, I've got some odd jobs to do and I'm taking a week off. It looks like rain all day.'

'Nothing much yet.' He glanced knowingly at the sky. 'Still, don't want that wood getting wet. I might do a bit here, then go on somewhere else and come back tomorrow.'

'Whatever you think best, Mr Biddock.' She suspected the idea of supervision was unwelcome to him.

George removed the inevitable crushed cigarette from behind his ear and contemplated it. Then he put it between his lips, whence it stuck out crookedly, and lit it. Meredith left him puffing serenely as he checked out the work he'd done the previous day. The porch was taking shape fast. She was impressed. She admonished herself for being sceptical about George.

Alan had been right. The inquest on Sonia Franklin wasn't attracting much interest. The large spartan room would have seated forty, but when Meredith took her seat at the back, only the front row of chairs was occupied. She recognised Inspector Pearce. A uniformed officer sat beside him, consulting his notebook. After a gap of two chairs came three more people, two men and a woman. From the back, nothing much could be distinguished about them, but she recognised the mended spectacles which marked out Simon Franklin. The other man, broad shoulders stretching an ancient jacket, must be his brother, Hugh, the bereaved husband. They did, she noticed, have the same reddish hair. As for the woman, she couldn't think who she might be but that *was* red hair!

Beside the woman's mane of bright carrot red, the Franklin brothers looked only sandy-headed. Meredith sat for a few minutes, immobile, fascinated by the sight of it. It was as straight as a yard of pumpwater, as that long-gone aunt might have described it. It shone with health and was beautifully trimmed. When the woman moved her head, which she did very occasionally, to murmur something to Simon, the flaming head of hair brushed the collar of her black suit. Meredith couldn't really see any more of her but the hair and the back of her jacket. She appeared young, but a trim rear view can mislead. Was it possible, wondered Meredith, that she was a relative? Or a solicitor, brought along to advise Hugh Franklin? Suddenly that seemed far more likely. That black legal suit. Yes, Hugh had wisely engaged himself a lawyer.

Without warning, as if she'd suddenly become aware of Meredith's scrutiny, the redhead swivelled in her chair and cast a fierce look down the room. Meredith saw a pale face, the brow hidden by a fringe, and a slash of geranium-red lipstick. Briefly the redhead's gaze rested on her, then the woman turned back to face forwards. Simon leaned towards her and whispered something. She tossed the flame hair in an irritated way, but it wasn't possible to tell whether she made a reply.

Meredith considered her own outfit. Because of the rain, she'd slipped on the Barbour but taken it off on entering the room and draped it over the back of the chair in front. On this dull morning, the place was chilly and a caretaker had thoughtfully switched on the central heating for the benefit of the coroner. As the air warmed, the new-wax smell rising from the Barbour threatened to become obvious. Fortunately there was no one near enough to notice it, or so she hoped. Her shoes, resting on the crossbar of the chair in front beneath the hem of the Barbour, were still mud-stained from her expedition with Alan to the railway embankment. She ought to have cleaned them up. The damp atmosphere outside had probably led to her own hair drooping. And you, she told herself, a woman who promised herself she was going to smarten up! Take herself in hand!

Two more people had come in. One was a small, walnut-skinned man in an old-fashioned suit who took a seat by himself at the front but on the far side of the room. The other was a young woman who was closing up an umbrella as she entered. She saw Meredith and started.

'Meredith?' She came to join her and slid into the free chair alongside. 'What are you doing here?' The words were whispered urgently.

'Curiosity,' whispered Meredith back. 'What about you, Jane?'

'I'm Tammy's teacher. That's Hugh's daughter. I've been helping them out since – since it happened.'

Meredith eyed Jane Brady. Her appearance suggested she might have walked some distance through town to the inquest and Meredith was churlishly cheered by the observation that she wasn't the only one to have suffered from the day's rainy weather. Jane's light-coloured raincoat was patched with dark damp stains, her long ash-blonde hair hung in rat's tails round her face. The closed umbrella, which she'd propped against the free chair beside her, was forming a puddle on the wooden floor. Its owner looked tense and chilled. An aura of unhappiness hung about her. Meredith stopped worrying about her own appearance and wondered what was wrong with Jane. Misery was seeping out of her like the water out of that brolly.

'No school today?' Meredith asked, as the first move in a roundabout approach.

'Half term. Got the week off.' As she spoke, Jane's gaze was fixed on the front row, particularly, Meredith noticed, on the man she'd decided must be Hugh.

She asked Jane if he was and had it confirmed. A thought struck Meredith. 'Is the little girl alone at the farm, since everyone else seems to be here?'

'Oh no. I made sure of that. She's very worried about her father. I rang and asked if they wanted me to drive out there and keep her company. But Hugh said the Haywards at Cherry Tree Farm had offered to have her there for the day. I also teach the Hayward twins. They're in Tammy's class.'

'Good idea for her to be with her friends on a day like this,' Meredith observed.

Jane shifted uneasily in her seat. 'Yes, I suppose so. Though I hadn't thought—' She broke off and changed the subject. 'Do you know who that woman is?'

'Not a clue. Thought she might be some sort of lawyer. Before you came, I was sitting here watching her and she was making me feel like a bag lady.'

Two women had come in as they spoke and proved to be the only two members of the public besides Jane and Meredith. Both were middle-aged, wore practical rainwear including transparent plastic bonnets, and carried shopping bags. Meredith wondered whether they were habitués of inquests, knew the Franklins, or simply wanted a place to sit down and rest their feet. One of them had produced a tube of what appeared to be peppermints and was offering it to her friend. They were settling in.

A door opened in the side of the hall. There was a rustle and the atmosphere sharpened. The tube of peppermints was stuffed away hurriedly. Beside Meredith, Jane had realised that the puddle from her umbrella had formed a mini-lake and that it was too late to do anything about it. She muttered, 'Oh, crikey!' The front row of attendees rose to their feet and the rest of them followed in a ragged sort of way. The coroner had arrived.

It all went as Alan had suggested. Proceedings were brief. The uniformed man reported answering a phone call from someone claiming to be Mr Hugh Franklin. He met Mr Franklin on the road which ran alongside the railway, just before the old viaduct. Mr Franklin had led him to the body of a woman, identified by him as Mrs Sonia Franklin, his wife.

Hugh, his expression set pugnaciously, took the stand. Now she was able to see him properly, Meredith realised the family resemblance between the brothers was strong, yet Hugh had none of Simon's fussy, schoolmasterly way. His complexion was bronzed from a life in the open air and he was of stronger, stockier build than his brother. He gave his account in a few words, standing rigidly to attention, his hands behind his back. The impression he gave was of being at bay, and he lacked any of the fluency with which Simon had bombarded Meredith and Alan in The Red Lion. His manner was, if anything, a touch belligerent, as if he had better things to do than stand here answering a bunch of questions. Watching his fingers clasping and unclasping in the fold of his elderly tweed jacket, Meredith realised he was nervous and the brusqueness a defence.

Jane was watching Hugh, too. She murmured, 'He's not doing very well, is he?' But Meredith couldn't be sure if Jane meant it as an observation to her companion, or was simply thinking aloud.

Meredith was, in any event, inclined to agree with her. In the even more imposing surrounds of a murder trial, if it should later come to that, Hugh's nervousness – and brusqueness – would increase. The poor impression he was making now could only get worse.

Hugh had spoken his piece and returned to his chair. A glance sideways at Jane showed Meredith the other woman's eyes were fixed on the nape of Hugh's neck with a kind of despair.

The small brown man in the antiquated suit turned out to be Danny Smith. He had chanced upon the body whilst 'walking back along the embankment to where I'm camped'. He had gone at once to tell Mr Hugh Franklin because there was a phone at the farm and also because he fancied he'd recognised the dead woman as Hugh's wife.

Evidence was read out on behalf of a medical man, informing them he'd been called to the scene and certified Sonia Franklin as dead. Extensive forensic tests were being carried out but early evidence showed death resulted from a deep upward stab wound to the diaphragm penetrating the heart.

Dave Pearce, sweating slightly now the room had warmed up, announced that the police had begun conducting extensive inquiries.

The coroner, glancing at his wristwatch, adjourned proceedings until a later date to allow the police to complete said inquiries. He then gathered up his papers and left through the side door by which he'd entered. He had the air of a man whose mind was on his lunch.

In the room, the tension and silence were both broken at his departure. The two women with shopping bags fell to whispering together. Pearce and the uniformed man left, conferring. Pearce saw Meredith as he passed and looked surprised before bidding her a polite 'Good morning'. The gypsy, Danny Smith, had slipped out without drawing attention to himself. That left the three people in the front row. They'd all risen to their feet and appeared to be arguing. Then the redhead in the black suit walked swiftly away, exiting through the side door used by the coroner. Simon, after a muttered word to his brother, followed. Hugh was left alone at the front of the room.

'I must go and have a word with him,' Jane said. 'He needs support. Come on, Meredith.'

'I'm not sure I—' began Meredith, torn between a desire to meet Hugh and an unwillingness to be found talking to him by Simon.

Simon knew of her friendship with Alan and he might suspect under-hand methods. But Jane had already reached Hugh and was deep in conversation. Meredith joined them.

'This is Meredith!' Jane introduced her. 'She's interested in crime.'

Hugh looked at Meredith in a way which wasn't particularly friendly. 'Hoping to meet a murderer today?'

Jane gasped and Meredith said firmly, 'It's not the way Jane made it sound. I'm sorry about your wife.'

He shrugged his broad shoulders. One of the buttons on his old tweed jacket had come loose and dangled by a thread. 'This carry-on today wasn't what I expected. Seemed a complete waste of time to me. I thought there'd be some sort of verdict.'

'That'll come when they reconvene,' Meredith said, 'and all the facts are known.'

'And we all have to come back again. Simon was explaining it to me.' He looked around the room. 'I'd better go and find him. Good of you to come along, Jane. Nice to meet you,' he added to Meredith.

When he'd gone, Jane turned to Meredith. 'I'm glad you've met him. What do you think?'

'Of Hugh? I hardly had time to form an opinion,' Meredith returned.

'But you can see what kind of person he is.'

'If I could see anything,' Meredith told her, 'it was that he's a fish out of water in a situation like today's.'

'Exactly!' Jane beamed at her as if she'd given the right answer to a trick question. With a touch of anxiety, she added, 'You haven't got to dash off home, have you?'

Meredith shook her head, wondering where all this was leading. 'No. We could go and find a spot of lunch if you like. There must be a pub round here which does food.'

'Only I do need to talk to somebody and you'd be the best person.'

Meredith wasn't sure she liked the sound of that. 'I'm always prepared to listen,' she replied cautiously. 'But sometimes, you know, people think my relationship with Alan means I can give some sort of inside information. I can't.'

Jane was shaking her head. 'No, no. I wouldn't expect— Look, I know a place. It's not very far.'

'No problem, anyway, I've got my car.'

Jane glanced down at her rain-splashed clothing. 'Perhaps we could find the cloakroom here and I could tidy up before we go.'

The ladies' cloakroom was situated in the bowels of the building, a route which led them down stone steps, clattering past clanking pipes festooned with cobwebs and finally to a door bearing a plaque with an outline of a figure in a skirt. Meredith pushed it open.

Someone had arrived before them. Standing before the spotted mirror affixed to the wall opposite the door stood the redhead, carefully repainting her geranium-red lips. She saw the newcomers reflected behind her and met Meredith's gaze with cool assessment. Jane muttered, 'Excuse me,' and went into the cubicle. The redhead dropped the lipstick case into her purse and turned.

'You were at the inquest. Sitting at the back.' There was something accusatory about her tone and Meredith's hackles rose.

'Yes,' she returned frostily.

Viewed closer to hand the woman wasn't as young as she appeared at a distance. Meredith supposed her pushing forty but with a figure which suggested regular visits to the gym. The suit could now be seen to be not black, but very dark blue. It looked expensive, as did the navy silk scarf printed with flowers the exact colour of her lipstick, draped artistically round her neck and over her shoulder. She wasn't a jewellery wearer, however, having only small pearl studs in her ears and a gold wristwatch. No rings.

'What's your interest?' the woman asked brusquely.

'Private.'

The redhead recognised a personality as strong as her own and a consequent standoff. She thawed slightly. 'My name is Bethan Talbot. I was Sonia's oldest and closest friend. We were at school together.'

'I'm very sorry,' said Meredith. 'My name's Meredith Mitchell.'

Surprisingly this meant something to Ms Talbot. 'You're a friend of James Holland, the vicar here, aren't you? He's mentioned you.' Fortunately, this seemed enough to vouch for Meredith's presence at the inquest. Bethan didn't ask again for an outright explanation. Instead she said crisply, 'He did it, you know.'

'Who?' asked Meredith. 'Did what?'

Bethan drew in an audible impatient breath. 'Don't pretend. We all know Hugh killed Sonia.'

Meredith thought it right to point out police inquiries were only just beginning. That earned another hiss.

'He's not going to get away with it. I mean to make sure he gets his comeuppance if it's the last thing I do.'

That seemed an unfortunate phrase to Meredith. Perhaps we never know what the last thing we'll do might be. She wondered whether Sonia Franklin had realised the last thing she'd do would be to set out for an evening stroll. But by now Meredith was making a connection.

'Are you Simon Franklin's former partner, by any chance?'

'Oh, you know Simon too? Yes. I introduced them, I introduced Sonia to Hugh, I mean. Worst day's work I ever did. Absolute disaster. I don't know what possessed poor Sonia. What did she see in the man? Hugh's not Simon, for goodness' sake. I wish I could have warned Sonia she was hitching herself to an absolute hayseed. She found it out soon enough. I heard all about it. He never read a book, had never set foot in a theatre, never got off that farm for five minutes, wouldn't dream of them taking a holiday. Then there was the kid. I'd have warned her she'd be taking on the kid. I knew that child. She used to spend quite a lot of time with Simon. He lent her books and encouraged her in her studies, which her father certainly would never have done. She wasn't an easy child, sullen. She wouldn't speak two words to me.'

There was a click from the cubicle door and Jane emerged, her formerly pale face now flushed with anger.

'I could hardly avoid hearing all that,' she snapped, 'and I object to every word of it.'

Bethan was unimpressed, merely twitching an eyebrow. 'And who might you be?'

'I'm Jane Brady, Tammy's teacher. I teach her history. She's a very bright child who lost her natural mother not very long ago. Of course she's had some problems and Mrs Sonia Franklin should have realised that. As for Hugh, her father, no one has yet suggested officially he was responsible for his wife's death and there's no reason to suppose it! He's a man with many responsibilities on his shoulders who is trying to do his best. He may not have the gift of the gab,' conceded Jane, 'but he's an honest man. I think it's quite disgusting that you should be making accusations without a shred of evidence. What's more, it's actionable!'

Whew! thought Meredith, that's telling her. She eyed Bethan with interest to see how she took this.

The geranium lips twisted cynically. 'I see he's worked his rustic charm on you! Perhaps you'd better ask yourself what kind of man goes blithely off to bed leaving his wife, whom he knows is upset, wandering around the countryside in the dark? Because if he isn't a killer, he was at least guilty of that. I know he made a token effort and rang Simon, but that was just to cover himself and tell someone she was missing. Simon told him Sonia hadn't been there, so what does Hugh do next? Gets his head down. That has to mean either he couldn't care bloody less or he knew she was dead. When he wakes up the next morning and finds, according to him, she's still missing, he still does sod all about it. He waits to call the police until someone else has found her body.' Bethan slung her purse strap over her shoulder. 'You find that normal? I don't. There are a lot of questions he's going to have to answer a darned sight more convincingly than he has done to date!'

She walked out.

Jane looked at Meredith. 'You see? You see what Tammy's afraid of?'

'Let's find some lunch,' suggested Meredith. 'And you can tell me.'

They ended up in a pub which Meredith didn't know, but which offered parking space, and was claimed by Jane to serve 'quite good food, really'. Meredith, glancing round its bar, decided that it was old without managing to look interesting, something that was quite an achievement. Its low ceiling beams had been painted with black gloss, its walls covered in a scarlet flock wallpaper with a design of fleur-de-lis. A fake log fire glowed in its ancient hearth. If a building could be said to have lost heart, this one had.

'It's popular at lunchtime,' confided Jane, as they squeezed into a corner.

It certainly was that, boasting a clientele of local business people who'd come in for lunch and gobbled their food keeping one eye on their wristwatches. There was a sprinkling of others who looked as if they had no purpose but to exist in this pub. Unlike the businessmen no sense of urgency hung over them. They leaned on the bar, chatted familiarly with the bar staff and appeared able to make one pint last indefinitely.

Meredith settled for the seafood and chips, Jane for the chicken pie, also with chips. Whilst waiting for the food to arrive, she lifted her glass of cider in salute to her companion. 'Cheers, tell me what it's all about.'

'I don't know what it's all about,' Jane said. 'I just know Hugh didn't kill his wife. But poor Tammy is afraid people will think he did, and unfortunately, she's right. In fact, if that dreadful Bethan is anything to go by, the police will be round to charge Hugh within days if not hours!'

'They wouldn't do that without evidence.' Meredith felt she ought to protest.

'Evidence? Who needs it when you've got enough people like Bethan going round saying Hugh did it? Others will start to think he did. Soon no one will believe him innocent.'

That was true enough. Meredith nodded. 'I believe Simon, his brother, shares your fears. Alan and I met him in a pub the other evening and he had quite a lot to say.'

'Oh, you've met him? I haven't, though I saw him at the inquest back there, or I assumed that was him, with Hugh. Do you know, I hadn't realised her uncle *was* Simon Franklin, the historian. Confidentially, Tammy told me that her father bought her Uncle Simon out of his share of the farm.'

'Oh?' Meredith set her glass down. 'When did this happen?'

'Oh, years ago, when their father died. They were left the farm between them. It wasn't doing as well as it should and what with one thing and another, they decided it wouldn't support more than one family. Hugh was married and wanted to stay on the farm. Simon was single and had his eyes on quite a different career. So Hugh bought out Simon.'

'The question being, for how much and how did he raise the cash?'

'That's two questions,' corrected the teacher in Jane, 'and I don't know the answer to either of them. But there's clearly no spare money now. I suspect Hugh ran himself into debt, or at the very least, used all the money he had to buy his brother out. On top of all that, his first wife was sickly and she couldn't have helped round the farm, besides it being an on-going worry for him.'

Their food was approaching, borne aloft by a trim girl in a black skirt and white blouse. 'Fish?' she enquired.

Meredith indicated that was hers. The plates were plumped down.

'Mind, they're hot. Want any sauce? No? Fair enough, enjoy your food.' She hastened off.

Meredith prodded at a lump of batter which when dissected proved to contain something which might once have been a prawn. She speared a chip and bit the end off. To her surprise it was perfectly cooked.

'Surely,' she said, 'your school is private and charges pretty steep fees from what I've heard. How does Hugh have enough money to send his daughter there if he's as broke as you say?'

'Money left by Tammy's maternal grandfather. Hugh told me that himself. Tammy's mother wanted her to attend St Clare's and Hugh is very proud that he's never touched the legacy for any other purpose. That's what I mean about his being an honest man. If anyone deserves a break, it's Hugh. And incidentally, it isn't true that he never reads a book. He denied that to me. The trouble is, I don't think he's read anything published in the last twenty years. He needs someone to suggest an author or two to him.'

'Ah . . .' said Meredith, judging the drift of this and eyeing her companion. 'You?'

'Why not me?' Jane flushed. 'I want to help them both. Hugh cares very much about his daughter and Tammy is devoted to him. But you see, they haven't found a way of communicating it very well to each other.'

'Dangerous ground,' said Meredith, opening another batter shell and finding a square of some unidentifiable white fish. 'You could make things worse.'

'How could things be worse at that farm?' Jane sighed and pushed a piece of chicken round her plate.

'Let me put it another way: you could get hurt yourself. Because people need help doesn't mean they want help. Hugh might think you're interfering.'

'A twelve-year-old girl can't run that household, or shouldn't,' Jane insisted.

Meredith quit the vexed topic for something else. 'Did you ever meet Sonia? Or Hugh before this? Surely they came to the school.'

'Sonia did on a couple of occasions, a parents' evening and an open day. Hugh was too busy, I suppose. All I remember about Sonia was that she was very smartly dressed and appeared bored. I don't mean she wasn't doing her best to ask questions and so on, but I don't think she had the foggiest idea which questions to ask.' Jane abandoned her pie. 'I'm not just being emotional about all this, you know. A teacher does learn to be a judge of character. I don't believe Hugh is a murderer. Besides, Tammy was in the house that evening.'

'Then she might know something you don't,' Meredith said briskly. 'Has anyone questioned her yet?'

'No!' Jane looked shocked.

'Someone will, sooner or later, a kindly policewoman.'

'But they can't do that, can they? Not insist on it?' Jane became even more distressed. 'Tammy couldn't cope with that.' She paused. 'Neither could Hugh, I'm sure of it. He wouldn't want his daughter involved.'

'She *is* involved,' Meredith said unkindly. 'She was a witness to the relationship between her father and stepmother. She was there, Jane, on that farm the evening Sonia died.'

'We don't know,' Jane argued, 'that the murder took place anywhere on the farm. Sonia may have been killed near the railway.'

'I'm not saying she wasn't, but you can't say for certain she was.' Meredith gave up on the seafood, pushing aside her plate. It was unclear whether Jane's chief concern was for father or daughter, but in either case, she was going to have to accept that the police followed procedures in this kind of thing and exceptions weren't likely to be made for the Franklin family. Moreover, her presumption of Hugh's innocence seemed based more on wish than knowledge.

'Look, I'm playing devil's advocate here,' Meredith began. 'Suppose there was a row and Hugh did kill Sonia. No, hang on, let me finish.' She fended off Jane's energetic rebuttal. 'He might not have intended to do it but something happened we don't know about, perhaps a struggle, and suddenly, she's lying dead on the hearthrug. He panics. His daughter mustn't see this dreadful sight. He's got to move the body, hide it away. He puts Sonia in some vehicle and drives her to the embankment. He hasn't time to think rationally. He isn't rational at that moment. You've got to face it, Jane, it isn't just that he has no alibi. The version of events he gave the coroner is full of holes. Any way you look at it he behaved very strangely that evening. You didn't like Bethan and I can't say I took to her, but what she said about Hugh's behaviour was right.'

Jane sat up straight in her chair, tossed back her hair and adopted the sort of attitude sculptors like to give such heroines as Joan of Arc or Boadicea. 'Who of us,' she demanded ringingly, to the startled interest of nearby diners, 'when asked to account for our movements on a particular occasion, could come up with something absolutely logical? Or always makes the right decisions? With hindsight we can see we should have behaved differently. But at the time, especially if we're stressed, we can do really foolish things.'

Meredith debated whether to say the obvious, and decided she might as well, but hopefully without continuing to attract the attention of half the pub.

'Absolutely!' she hissed. 'Hugh was under a lot of stress that evening, tired after a long day's work. His wife wanted to go on a holiday and there was no money for that. She may have objected that there was money for Tammy to attend St Clare's. Jane, you've got to face the possibility he might have done it. Honest, kindly men under stress have killed before now.'

'Hugh didn't,' Jane said stubbornly. 'And I want you to help me prove it, Meredith.'

CHAPTER EIGHT

As Meredith and Jane were making their way towards their pub lunch, Dave Pearce was taking his road back to Regional HQ. There he was greeted with the news that the superintendent wanted to see him.

'He's suddenly taking an interest in the Franklin case,' warned DC Ginny Holding, looking up from the keyboard at which she was composing a report. 'He asked for the file as soon as he got in. Then the post-mortem report turned up and he's got that in there with him, too. Oh, and he asked for some fibres to be sent over to forensics.'

'Cripes,' said Pearce, wondering what he'd over looked and reluctantly giving up all idea of nipping up to the canteen for a spot of lunch himself. He'd thought it odd that the super's girlfriend had been at the inquest. He should have stopped and had a word with her, tried to find out what it was all about.

'He's got that look about him,' continued Holding. She got to her feet. 'Tell you what, you go on in and I'll bring you both some coffee.' She grinned.

Pearce watched her, a tall, athletically built girl with a mop of dark hair, heading for the drinks dispenser. Holding's arrival at HQ had attracted a lot of interest and a good deal of comment. But her admirers' enthusiasm had been tempered by the knowledge that she was Western Region Police Judo Champion (women's section). She had, moreover, an on-going arrangement with a police-dog handler known as 'Snapper' Sykes.

Markby was sitting at his desk, poring over the PM report. He looked up and waved at a chair. 'Ah, Dave. How did you get on?'

'Usual,' returned Pearce cautiously, taking a seat. 'Adjourned.'

'Anyone of interest present?' Murderers were often unable to resist the lure of the inquests on their victims, if only to find out what the police were doing, though more often to congratulate themselves on how clever they were at fooling everyone. This arrogance, Markby had found, often persisted after arrest and even after conviction.

'Miss Mitchell was there with another lady,' said Pearce, fishing unashamedly. 'I was surprised to see her.' He wondered if he was to be told why. He was not.

'Oh yes, she said she'd be going. Both Franklins turn up?'

'Both of them and a woman with them who looked like a solicitor. But she turned out to be Bethan Talbot, formerly an item with Simon Franklin. Also, she's a tax adviser, not a lawyer.'

'An item,' repeated Markby thoughtfully, wondering if that description could be applied to himself and Meredith and deciding that the jury was out on that one.

'She was Sonia's dearest pal and introduced her to Hugh. She's spitting mad and making allegations. Probably,' deduced Pearce, 'got a bad conscience, since she was instrumental in bringing them together.'

'Not her fault if it didn't turn out well. Hugh Franklin and his second wife weren't kids. Consenting adults, if you like. Up to them to sort out their differences.'

'Talbot reckons *he* did. She's sent us two faxes on the subject and made a long phone call which Holding took. I left before she could corner me at the inquest. In any case, I fancy she'd turn her guns on the coroner. She's a lady of strong opinions.'

Markby put down the post-mortem report and leaned back in his chair. 'Ah. Pointing the finger at the husband, is she?'

'He *is* in the frame,' said Pearce. 'I've said so from the first.'

'Yes, you have,' Markby said. 'Don't close your mind to other possibilities, Dave. When you first met him, did you judge him genuinely distressed?'

'Yes,' admitted Pearce grudgingly. 'But he could be a good actor. How many grieving relatives have gone on telly appealing for information to help the police solve a dreadful crime? They cry on camera. They have to be helped away from the microphone. Next thing is, it turns out they're the guilty party.'

Pearce warmed to his theme. 'His story's weak. In fact, it's ruddy unbelievable. He had motive. She'd turned out an expensive lady and a very difficult one. She wanted to spend money he didn't have to spare. She may have thought she was marrying a gentleman farmer and didn't like it when she faced reality. I fancy she didn't get along with the child either. I doubt he could've afforded a divorce.'

'None of us can,' said Markby gloomily as memory returned. He'd never quite worked out why Rachel had ended up with virtually everything and he'd ended up with a camel-saddle stool and a hole in his bank account. Still, that was long past. 'What about the child?' he asked. 'She's twelve and old enough to be interviewed, with a family member or interested adult present, of course. Understandably she'll be distressed and we'll have to take it carefully.'

'Holding's had training in dealing with traumatised witnesses,' said Pearce. 'I was thinking of sending her out there. She'll be sensitive, handle it like walking on eggshells. We are very short-handed, sir.' He thought it worthwhile reminding Markby of this.

'I don't need telling,' said the superintendent crossly. 'I've been trying to get someone on loan from elsewhere, but every station seems short of able-bodied officers at the moment. If they haven't got flu they've wrapped a car round a lamppost. If they haven't done that, they've gone off on honeymoon.' He saw Pearce's eyebrows twitch and moved swiftly on. 'It doesn't help when I can't put enough people out there asking questions. What about the dead woman, for example? How much do we know about her? She arrived in the area on her marriage. Where was she before that?'

'Worked and lived in London,' said Pearce. 'Her husband told me about it when I interviewed him on the day the body was found, although I admit I didn't then realise how short a time they'd been married. It's all in my initial report,' he added reproachfully. 'Her maiden name was Lambert.'

Before Markby could reply, there came a tap at the door and Ginny Holding appeared with the promised coffee. 'Thought you might like a cup,' she said to Markby.

'Oh, Holding. Yes, thanks. Dave wants you to go out to Hazelwood Farm and talk to a twelve-year-old girl. Think you can manage that?' Markby accepted the coffee and put his question at the same time.

'I should think so,' said Holding, giving Pearce a look which said, 'Judas'.

'Do it by the book. She must have an interested adult present, but it might be better if it's not her father. See if you can arrange that.' He smiled. 'When you've done that, as a reward, you can have a trip to London. Find out where Sonia Franklin, née Lambert, worked

97

before her marriage and if anyone at the firm is prepared to chat about her.'

Holding brightened and went out with a bounce in her step.

Markby remembered the post-mortem report, extracted a drawing from it, and tapped it to draw Pearce's attention. 'Cause of death as we supposed, stab wound piercing the heart. The weapon hasn't proved immediately identifiable. That is, we know what it probably *isn't*, which is a kitchen knife. It's a long, thin, double-edged weapon, on the model of a stiletto, but perhaps shorter in the blade. A dagger of some type. Fuller ventured to suggest the weapon may be in need of sharpening or the edges may be damaged – something to do with the way it cut through tissue and muscle. On the other hand, the point was sharp enough to do the job.'

'Dagger, eh?' said Pearce, and surprised Markby considerably by declaiming, '"Is this a dagger which I see before me . . . ?"'

He then blushed deeply at having been caught out in a literary reference and hastily said the English teacher had made them put on a play when he was at school, 'to raise some money for a computer'.

'Were you in this production of the Scottish play?' asked Markby with interest, and carefully avoiding the play's name in deference to any theatrical superstitions Pearce might harbour, unlikely though it seemed.

'I painted scenery,' said Pearce fiercely. 'Catch me poncing about in daft costumes.'

'I see. Was it a mixed school?'

'What? It was Bamford Comprehensive. Oh, we had girls, if that's what you mean. No poor little sod of a third year had to dress up in a long skirt to play Lady Macbeth.'

'Unlike my school,' said Markby, 'where the smallest and most nervous pupils had to be terrorised every year into taking the female roles.'

'Well, that's public school for you,' said Pearce darkly. He didn't expound on this remark.

Markby put away the drawing. 'Fuller draws attention to the fact that she seems to have been in a recent scrap, probably putting up a fight against her attacker. She has long scratches and abrasions to the right side of her face and neck. Also her nail varnish is chipped and one nail broken, as if she dealt it out as well as received it. Two very small fragments of skin have been recovered from beneath her nails and are being studied further. If we're very lucky, we might get a DNA profile from them, but we are not to hold our breath. I quote.'

Pearce uttered a sort of growl.

Markby peered down at the report. 'It says here blue nail varnish. I thought nail varnish was red or pink.'

'Latest fashion,' Pearce informed him. 'Tessa's got a row of bottles on the dressing table, all colours, blue, purple, gold. You name it.'

Markby braced himself for Meredith appearing with gold fingernails and rather hoped she wouldn't.

Pearce had moved on from fashion in make-up and was squinting villainously into the far distance in a way which suggested his imagination was at work. As Dave was not, on the whole, an imaginative person, he tended to put his whole body into the exercise, rubbing his head, fidgeting his feet, huffing and puffing under his breath. Markby again waited with interest. Dave was full of surprises today.

'Right side of face,' said Pearce at last. 'Wouldn't that suggest a left-handed assailant?' He stretched out his right hand. 'See, if I were to clobber you with this hand, I'd strike the left side of your face.'

'Indeed you would. Good point.' Markby sipped at the polystyrene cup holding the coffee, winced, and set it down. 'The body had to be transported to the place it was found. How about the vehicles belonging to the farm?'

Pearce was glad to be ahead on this one. 'We've gone over a Land Rover and a Volvo with absolutely no luck. Both as clean as a whistle as far as we're concerned. The Volvo belonged to Mrs Franklin. He could, I suppose, have stuffed the body in the back of the cab of his tractor, but I shouldn't think it likely, even if there were room. The cab's transparent.'

'How did Franklin take examination of the cars?'

'We told him it was routine. He made as if he accepted that but he's not a fool. He knows he must be number one suspect on our list.'

'He is indeed, but perhaps we should be looking elsewhere.'

Here it comes, thought Pearce resignedly.

'On Thursday morning, Meredith travelled up to London later than usual. Because of work on the line, the train was stopped for a few minutes just short of the old viaduct.'

Pearce began to look interested, less apprehensive and more curious. 'Where Sonia Franklin was found?'

'Just about. Hanging on a branch near the tracks was a bag made of bright green material and designed to look like a frog. A fun article I suppose you'd call it. Meredith saw no sign of its owner. I see no note of it being found by officers at the scene.'

'It wasn't there!' said Pearce promptly.

'No, you could hardly have missed the thing from Meredith's description of it. She took me back to the spot on Saturday morning. I recovered a few emerald-green threads from a tree near the track. I've sent them off to forensics. They may not reveal anything much but what I want to know is, who removed the bag between Meredith seeing it at about eleven in the morning and the first patrol car to arrive on the scene shortly before one?'

'Someone who hid when the train approached and retrieved the bag after it moved off?' Pearce heaved a sigh. 'What about Danny Smith?'

'Smith, indeed. The only person we know to have been there. Since you say Prescott got on so well with the Smiths, you'd better send him out to talk to them again. Take a search warrant for that trailer.'

Markby got up and wandered to a wall map showing the area in detail. He peered closely at it, his fair hair flopping over his eyes, his tall, angular form hunched. Pearce was reminded of a heron waiting patient and still in river shallows. He drank his now tepid coffee whilst the going was good and wondered what was coming next.

'Either the killer was local or he came from outside.' Markby spoke without turning round. 'Simon Franklin favours a tramp. Possible but not probable. If she were walking along that road when she was attacked, it might have been someone in a passing car. In that case, we'll be extremely fortunate to find it, and the body need not necessarily ever have been in it. With me, so far?'

'Yessir,' said Pearce. 'We are trying for witnesses. We're talking to the men working on the line beyond the viaduct. The last shift knocked off about nine thirty that evening. The early shift came on at a little after nine in the morning, after the early commuter trains had gone through. We've interviewed them all and they've nothing to say, other than to vouch for each other. No one walked back along the track to the wooded area of the embankment, not even to answer a call of nature. They've got a Portaloo. No one saw anyone hanging about. Unfortunately the racket from their generator would've blocked any unusual noises. So far, too, none of them has recalled seeing a parked vehicle near the embankment, or noticed headlights of a cruising car. That's not a stretch of road much used after six of an evening.'

'Which would be a good reason for taking the body down there. It would, however, suggest local knowledge and a local person. But the population around there is thin on the ground.' Markby tapped the map. 'Here's Hazelwood Farm and here's Cherry Tree Farm, belonging to a family called Hayward.'

'I haven't got round to talking to the Haywards yet,' said the harassed Pearce. 'I'll get out there tomorrow.'

'The only other settlement nearby is here.' Markby's hand moved across the map. 'At the bend in the road. It doesn't seem to have a name.'

Pearce came to look over his shoulder. 'Oh, that's Fox Corner. That's what the locals call it; it's not a proper name, the sort you'd get on a map. It comes under Cherton, down here.' He pointed. 'Even if it is miles out. My dad told me there used to be a pub there called The Fox. It burned down in the fifties. They razed the ruins to the ground, cleared it all away and left it. But the name stuck.'

'What's there?'

'Few cottages. Some sort of woodwork place. Chap makes furniture. Nothing else. We haven't got round to asking there either,' Pearce admitted. 'I'll try and get someone over there tomorrow, but if I'm going to see the Haywards, Prescott is going to the Smiths' caravan again, Holding may be going to Hazelwood to see the little girl and after that you're sending her off to London—'

'Relax, Dave. I'll do it. Do me good to get out from behind this desk. I fancy a drive in the country.'

From Pearce's stomach came a protesting rumble.

Markby glanced at his watch. 'Keeping you from your pie and chips, Dave. Off you go.'

Ginny Holding was on the phone as Pearce passed her. She put a hand over the mouthpiece and said in a low tone, 'I can see her tomorrow in the company of her Uncle Simon. Today she's with some schoolfriends at another farm.'

'All right for some,' said Pearce, 'trips to London.'

'Obviously the super thinks you're needed here,' she told him tactfully.

'Does he? He seems to be checking up behind every move I make!'

Hunger was making Pearce tetchy. 'He's going out to Fox Corner himself.'

Holding raised her eyebrows expressively.

When Meredith got home there was no sign of George Biddock. She let herself in, made a mug of tea and settled on the sofa with the cat and a road atlas. She'd switched the gasfire on low to warm the chilly room. Spring was late this year.

'I should mind my own business, Tiger,' she said to the cat. He blinked slowly. 'How am I supposed to oblige Jane by ferreting round looking for evidence to clear Hugh – and avoid having Alan hare round here to tell me to keep my fingers out of police business?' The cat yawned, displaying sharp white teeth and a pink tongue. 'You don't care, do you?' she demanded. He curled round in a ball and tucked his nose under his paw.

Meredith opened the road atlas and found the appropriate area. Though smaller than the map Markby and Pearce had studied, it did show local farms including Hazelwood.

Sonia could, Meredith mused, have walked as far as the embankment on her own two feet. She could have been killed there and her body dragged through the bushes down the embankment out of sight. This was the scenario favoured by Jane, because it left Hugh well out of it. But it was a fact that, even now in this day and age of individual mobility, the victim was still most likely to have met his or her fate at the hands of someone close to him/her. So Alan had told her. There was a cruel logic in that. Setting aside cases where the murderer was mentally ill, then the murderer was a person to whom the victim had presented either a personal threat or with whom the murderer was so closely entangled, only the death of the other could set him free. The third motive was financial gain. She didn't know whether Sonia's life had been insured.

But supposing this was one of those cases where the murderer and victim had been totally unacquainted? Or passing acquaintances? Then the long hand of coincidence came in. Sonia, walking along an open and lonely country road, had met with a stranger – or someone only slightly known to her. Known well enough, perhaps, to stop his car and get out to ask her if she wanted a lift. That stranger or quasi-stranger had killed her. Why? Not that such things never happened. Sex or robbery were likely motives on these occasions.

Meredith scratched at her head and heaved a dissatisfied sigh. Supposing that Hugh was telling the truth, why on earth had Sonia chosen, at that time of night, to walk to the railway line? She'd had the whole of Hazelwood Farm to wander over. Nor was an open road a suitable spot for a clandestine meeting. Why not go with what appeared to be the current police theory, that Sonia had been killed elsewhere and her body brought to the embankment? Right, thought Meredith. If we exclude the farmhouse or its immediate area, then we're down to how far Sonia could conveniently have walked. She was distressed when she left the house. 'She went to see someone,' said Meredith aloud. 'She rushed off to see someone to whom she could tell her troubles.' Once that friend would have been Bethan Talbot. But Bethan no longer lived with Simon Franklin and Sonia had been forced to find a confidante elsewhere.

Meredith's finger swept slowly over the map. Sonia could, if she'd wanted to go for a real hike, have gone as far as Cherry Tree Farm, the next holding. Or she could even have got as far as the collection of buildings which Meredith knew were known locally as Fox Corner. That was a distinct possibility. It wasn't more than two miles from Hazelwood by marked road and by cutting across farmland the route was made even shorter. The moon had been very bright last Wednesday night.

Her fingertip tapped the collection of dots representing the habitations at that spot. Since more than one person lived there, the odds that Sonia could've been seen at Fox Corner, on her hypothetical visit, were good.

Meredith finished her tea, switched off the gasfire, left the cat in possession of the sofa, and set off for Fox Corner.

Luckily, when she got there, it had stopped raining. She parked the car under some trees, off the road, and began to walk through the scattered settlement. It had a lonely, desolate air. The wind which ruffled her hair had quite a nip to it. Right at the bend in the road was a large area of wild grasses and thistles growing unevenly over hummocks. It had once been separated from the road by chain-link fencing but this had been broken down or rusted and the uprights collapsed. The impression given was that some large building might once have stood there. A little further on was a pair of cottages. Across the road stood another pair, then a single cottage. Beyond that was a large stone barn with a wooden sign outside. The only other building was a concrete bus shelter. Fox Corner was lucky, she thought, to be on a bus route. Inspection of a yellowed timetable behind a sheet of plastic informed her, however, that the bus ran only twice a day, going from Bamford to Cherton in the early morning and returning in the late afternoon. On its way, it took in Fox Corner and small villages. She wondered how long it would be before it was axed as uneconomic, cutting off the scattered communities completely for all but car owners.

Not so luckily, there was no one about and she had no reasonable excuse for knocking on doors. Meredith walked on until she came to the stone barn. Behind it, not visible until now, was a tiny cottage, its door so low, its windows so minute, it looked like a large Wendy house. Its dimensions might have been adequate for the original inhabitants, stunted by hard work and poor diet. Though hardly if one reflected that a couple probably raised a large family in such a place. As for modern times, it would only suit one person and that only if he or she didn't mind crouching like Quasimodo every time it was necessary to pass through the front door.

Meredith returned her attention to the stone barn, a giant beside the humble dwelling. It had been transformed into a furniture workshop and someone was there. She could hear hammering from within.

She walked through the wide entrance and found herself in a cluttered workshop. Furniture, finished and half-finished, stood around. Lengths of wood were propped against the walls. Benches were covered with tools, wood shavings, tins of varnish. A man with his back to her was working on a nearly completed chair. She cleared her throat and when this didn't work, said loudly, 'Good afternoon!'

He dropped a wooden mallet and spun round. He was youngish, dishevelled, clad in dusty jeans and a checked shirt with rolled-up sleeves. He stared at her wild-eyed, then blurted, 'I didn't hear you come in.'

'I'm sorry,' she apologised. 'I didn't mean to alarm you.'

He made an effort to pull himself together. 'No, you didn't, of course not. I was just engrossed in what I was doing. I'm like that, I'm afraid.'

'So am I rather.' She glanced round. 'I called by because I was wondering, I've got an old-fashioned kitchen and I'd like a cupboard. Just something simple would suit, shelves behind two doors below and two drawers above, sort of Victorian in style. I can't seem to find what

I want in the shops. Would it be possible for you to make me something like that?'

He moved away from his workbench, rubbing his hands on a rag. 'I should think so. But not immediately. I've got another job on.'

'There's no rush.'

He jerked his head towards the back of the workshop. 'My office is back there. I can show you my design book. You can look at it while I just finish off here, if you don't mind.'

He led her to an untidy office and produced a well-thumbed drawing block from a drawer. 'Here, take a look. Back in a tick.'

Meredith sat down in the one chair, put the drawing block on the desk, after pushing aside a mound of paperwork, and turned the top sheet, gradually revealing page after page of meticulously drawn examples. Chairs, tables, cupboards, dressers, a baby cradle, a wine rack, bookshelves. The patterns were all basic, but elegant, without fuss. She hadn't been lying to him altogether. She had searched for a cupboard without finding anything suitable and forgotten about it. But here was one which would be ideal.

She left the block open at the page and sat back to study her surroundings more closely. What a mess this place was in. If he worked here alone, that wasn't surprising. He needed someone to come in a couple of days a week and sort out his office work. But it was unlikely there was anyone in Fox Corner who could be called upon.

Footsteps approached. He was back. 'Find anything?'

Meredith turned the drawing towards him. 'Something like this would be exactly right. How much would it cost?'

'Depends on the wood, but in pine about three hundred, say three thirty to be on the safe side.'

'Three hundred pounds?' She hadn't meant to squawk it out like that.

'That's what it would cost you in a shop in town in that weight of pine, *and* mass-produced, probably badly made. Wood not properly seasoned. From me you'd be getting something individual, quality seasoned wood, stained any shade you like or left natural. Properly waxed finish. No comparison.'

'No, I dare say not. It is nice. Can I think about it?'

'Sure you can. I told you, I couldn't start on it right away, anyway. Take a look at some of the finished stuff while you're here to give yourself some idea of the standard of workmanship. I'm not boasting.' He essayed a faint grin. 'I'm being honest.'

While they'd been talking, Meredith had been able to take a closer look at him. He looked careworn and the grin was a tired one. His cheeks were hollow, grey shadows lurked beneath his eyes. She wondered when he'd last eaten a proper meal. But there was something about him— Memory clicked.

'Forgive me,' she said. 'But haven't we met? I know Jane Brady. Aren't you Peter, who used to be—' Awkward moment. Used to be what?

But he was nodding. 'Yes. Peter Burke. I'm sorry, I don't remember you.'

'I'm Meredith Mitchell. We only met once very briefly. There's no reason why you should remember me.' She'd been slow to put a name to his face because he was so changed from their previous meeting. She recalled a far more hale and hearty sort of man.

'I'm afraid I don't remember you,' he apologised. 'I'm bad with faces and even worse with names. I'm sadly lacking in the social graces despite Jane's best efforts to turn me into a more outgoing sort of animal. Fact is, I'm only happy around furniture, doing something with my hands or designing.' He indicated the workshop. 'This suits me down to the ground. I don't have many neighbours and the ones who are here mind their own business, on the whole. There's one old fellow who hangs around and nearly drives me dotty on occasion, but he's harmless. I call him the ancient monument. Only a couple of buses a day and not much other traffic.'

'How do you advertise your business?'

'Word of mouth. Don't need anything else. I'm on my own here and couldn't take more work than I get anyway.'

Meredith said carefully, 'I had lunch with Jane today, as it happens. In a pub in Bamford.'

'Bet it was The Bugle, red flock paper and nasty replacement beams?'

'That's about it. The food was all right.'

'Jane and I used to go there a lot. She – she dropped in here the other afternoon. I'm afraid she caught me at a bad moment.'

'She was probably on her way to or from Hazelwood Farm. A pupil of hers lives there, Tammy Franklin. Her mother, her stepmother rather, was murdered recently. Terrible thing.'

His gaze slid away from hers. 'Yes,' he said abruptly.

'Do – did – you know the Franklins?'

'I met her, met Sonia.' He spoke unwillingly, then, with a rush, went on, 'She was a charming person, full of life.' He paused and she had the impression that for a moment he'd forgotten she was there. Then he shook his head, dismissing some image. 'She came, like you, to enquire about some kitchen furniture. She wanted to refurbish the kitchen at the farm. I gave her a quote for some chairs and a dresser. Like you, she wanted to think it over.' Naïvely, like a child from whom some illusion has been wrested, he added, 'I can't imagine that she won't come back. When you spoke from the door earlier, when you arrived, I turned and the light was behind you. You're much her build. That's why I was so startled.'

'They'll find who did it,' Meredith said, feeling she ought to offer some comfort and unable to think of any other.

'Do you think so?' he asked, staring at her. 'Do you really think they will?'

Meredith walked slowly away from the barn back towards her parked car. She had thought the situation awkward when she'd driven out here this afternoon. Now it was worse. At Jane's request, she'd undertaken this task, only to find her very first line of enquiry had led her to Jane's ex-partner. Now what? Tell Jane she'd been here? She didn't relish it. Not tell Jane? Even riskier. Jane could well find out anyway.

'Good afternoon, miss!'

The voice, by her ear, made her start. An elderly man in baggy pullover and even baggier corduroy trousers had emerged from one cottage and was leaning on his gate.

'Good afternoon,' said Meredith. She stopped, rightly divining he wanted to pass the time of day.

'Going to buy yourself a new table or summat?' he asked.

'What? Oh yes, a cupboard actually. Perhaps,' she qualified.

'He charges the earth,' said the old man. 'Not but what he does a neat job. He knows his trade. He's a nice feller. He came round and fixed my back door. Didn't charge for that.'

'That was kind of him. Yes, his furniture's very nice. Do many people come out here to buy it?' She was pretty sure by now this was 'the ancient monument'.

'Tidy few.' He gave her a toothless, wicked grin, his crinkled skin scrunching up like crushed crepe paper. 'Tidy few ladies.' At the lechery in his tone she didn't know whether to laugh or be cross.

More than either, she would like to pursue the avenue unexpectedly opened and find out more about Peter Burke's female visitors. But she didn't know how to do it without arousing the monument's suspicions.

'Over there,' she pointed at the area of wild growth, 'it looks as if a building stood there once.'

'It was the pub,' said the old man sadly. 'It burned down 17 April 1954. They sent a fire engine from Cherton and another one from Bamford when the first one couldn't put it out. Flames scorched the paintwork off these windows here behind me. I was a young feller then, of course. I went over to give a hand and help carry out some of the furniture. I managed to stick a bottle of whisky inside my jacket.' He cackled. 'Landlord and his wife got out all right. Bottles of spirits exploded like bombs. They lost all the beer.' He shook his head. 'And they never built it up again, the buggers. Not even though they must've got the insurance. Some said they fired it on purpose for the insurance money. Got nowhere to go for a pint now.' He turned and shuffled back indoors.

Hope you made that bottle of whisky last, then, thought Meredith unkindly. She glanced back at the barn. A 'tidy few' female prospective customers? Or just one in particular?

She drove away slowly, aware the old man was watching her. Where to now? She wasn't far from the scene of the murder. She remembered the old viaduct as it had towered over Alan and herself as they'd searched for the frog backpack. They hadn't taken time to climb up to it and now she wondered what could be seen from up there.

'Only one way to find out,' she told herself.

She reached the roadside below the viaduct in minutes and parked the car in a natural lay-by formed by the entrance to a field barred by a sagging gate. Meredith took bird-watching binoculars from the glove compartment and pushed them into her pocket as she got out. She looked disapprovingly at the ground by her feet. Others had parked here before her and had left their rubbish. She didn't know whether they'd been police personnel or sightseers.

The viaduct loomed just ahead of her. She glanced up at the topmost tier of brickwork. There had to be a way up there. She went to the gate. It was tied with a frayed rope and gave the appearance of not having been opened in years. But there was an old wooden stile affording a way over it, and beyond lay a patch of dried mud imprinted with the traces of solid footwear. Ramblers came this way. Now she saw that someone had attached to the gatepost a disc bearing a painted yellow arrow which pointed upwards, indicating that a public footpath ran straight on across the open land beyond. Was it this path, Meredith wondered, that Sonia had taken on the evening of her death? Had she climbed the gate by means of the stile and arrived here on the road by the viaduct in time to meet her killer? Or was that just all too convenient?

Meredith put a foot on the stile, grasped the top rung of the gate and swung herself over. From here, to gain access to the viaduct was a steep climb up an overgrown hillside. It was treacherous underfoot, with holes and dips disguised by long dry grass. The incline grew steeper, she had to lean forward and grip with her hands. By the time she reached the stonework of the viaduct she was hot, breathless, sweating and her legs ached.

Meredith scrambled over the last few yards and found herself on a stony track, all that remained of the ancient road which had run across the countryside until the railway had arrived to slice it in two. From up here the view was magnificent. Meredith turned a slow full circle, taking it in on all sides. The wind tugged at her hair and stung her cheeks, but the air smelled pure, fresh, untainted by modern life. Above her a dark shape hovered, a bird of prey. Meredith pulled out the binoculars and trained them on it. She thought she identified a sparrowhawk. As she watched, it plunged earthward.

Meredith pushed her hands into her pockets and tramped along the rough track until she found herself passing between grey stone walls and came out on to the viaduct itself.

It was far from the most imposing construction of its type, perhaps only a little more than a very large extended bridge, but she felt as though she stood on the roof of the world. She peered over the edge and found herself looking down on the railway line and the bushes and trees of the embankment. She couldn't see the spot where Sonia's body had been found because of the tangled foliage. As she tried to work out the exact location, Meredith frowned. Below, approaching slowly along the tarmacked road which ran along the embankment, was an elderly Land Rover.

As she watched, it stopped, and a man jumped down from the

driver's seat. Hastily putting the binoculars to her eyes again, she was able to identify Hugh Franklin. He'd changed his clothes. Presumably the ancient jacket he'd worn at the inquest that morning had been intended as 'smart wear'. Now he was wearing a pullover and jeans. He walked across to her car, stared at it for a moment, and then turned and vanished into the embankment thicket. Meredith put the binoculars away. She waited for a few minutes but when Hugh didn't emerge, left her vantage point and began to retrace her path downhill.

Climbing down was nearly as bad as struggling up. By the time she'd reached the gate and stepped back over the stile she fully expected the Land Rover to have gone, but it was still there. She glanced hesitantly at her own parked car, then crossed the road to the embankment.

It was quiet in the thicket and seemed unnaturally still. The ground was sodden underfoot from the morning's rain. She took the only path offered and climbed down cautiously, ears straining for the sound of the other person she knew was in here somewhere. She couldn't pick up a trace of him. Water dripped down her neck from above and when something fell from the trees with a clatter she nearly jumped out of her skin. But it was only a loose branch. She tried to remember the layout of the area from her visit with Alan. The place where Sonia had been found must be to the right. She set off, picking her way at first over nettles and brambles but soon coming upon a freshly beaten path. It debouched into a small trampled clearing, dappled with watery sunlight and still festooned with ragged police tape.

Meredith stopped on the edge of it, puzzled. Somehow, she'd expected to find Hugh here but there still wasn't a sign of him. She began to feel uneasy, not only because she couldn't locate him, but because she didn't know what he was doing or what had brought him here. She moved further into the clearing and thought what a mess had been left behind by the investigation. But in a few months, she supposed, plants would grow over it all and scraps like cardboard would've rotted. The tape, which was plastic, that would prove more enduring. Someone should remove it. She stretched out her hand to the nearest dangling strand.

Without warning, there was a movement behind her, a swish of air and a stick flashed by her shoulder and struck the tape from her hand.

'No, you don't!' growled a male voice. A hand gripped her shoulder painfully and spun her round. She found herself looking into Hugh Franklin's angry face.

For a brief moment he stared at her and then frowned as recognition came to him. To her relief, he released her shoulder. 'You're Jane's friend,' he said. 'You were at the inquest this morning. Is that your car up there by the gate?'

She explained about climbing up to the viaduct and seeing him enter the thicket. Offering bird-watching as a reason for her expedition sounded feeble in her ears but Hugh paid little attention, his mind set on his own explanation for his presence.

'I thought,' he said, 'when I saw the car, another of those ghouls had come out here. Seems murder attracts them. They collect bits and pieces, souvenirs. You wouldn't credit it, would you?'

'Sadly, yes, I would. I know it happens. I'm not a ghoul. I know Jane told you I was interested in crime. But that's because she thought I might be able to help.'

'How? Convince the coppers I didn't kill Sonia? They think I did. Or that one who came out to the farm thinks it. Inspector Pearce, he's called.'

She felt she ought to tell him about Alan. 'Superintendent Markby is a friend of mine.'

'Is he? Well, you'll know how coppers' minds work then!' Hugh paused, then added, 'And has your copper friend told you about murderers returning to the scene of their crimes?'

'He hasn't, but it's an old saying.' She drew a deep breath. 'Is it true?'

'You mean, did I kill Sonia? No, of course I bloody didn't!'

This was expressed with such heartfelt pain that instinctively, she believed him.

She tried not to show her relief but knew she'd failed. 'Thank God for that – for your daughter's sake, and for Jane's. She's totally convinced of your innocence.'

'Is she? That's nice to know, but it isn't her I've got to convince, is it?' he retorted sourly.

'No, but you might at least show a little appreciation!' Meredith snapped.

He looked indignant. 'I appreciate it. She's volunteered to keep an eye on Tammy and me for a bit. Tammy mostly. I meant that plenty of others think I am guilty – and not only the police.'

'If you're thinking of Bethan Talbot you should ignore her,' said Meredith firmly.

Hugh scowled. 'Bethan thinks I didn't do right by Sonia, didn't give her the sort of life she needed. I won't argue with that because it's true, I didn't. But I did what I could and a man can only do that, can't he?'

There was no arguing with that, thought Meredith ruefully, but it did sound complacent. 'This may seem a tactless question,' she said, 'but what kind of life do you think your wife expected, when you married?'

The question seemed to perplex Hugh. 'Blowed if I know. That she'd be a sort of country lady, perhaps. Opening bazaars, going to horse shows, mixing with the county set.'

'Would she have been good at that?'

Hugh stared at her in surprise for a moment. Then he said, 'Probably. She was good at meeting people. She had quite a high-powered job in London, you know, before we married. Public relations. She'd met all kinds of people, celebrities.' He shrugged. 'I guess Hazelwood Farm didn't have much to offer in place of that.' He looked around the clearing again. 'I was thinking, I ought to bring a bunch of flowers down here.'

'It would be a nice gesture,' Meredith agreed.

Hugh glanced sideways at her, a little embarrassed. 'I'm sorry I gave you a fright just now.'

'It doesn't matter. Don't lose heart, for your daughter's sake as well as your own. You've got to hang on, believe it'll all come out right.'

'Sure,' he said heavily. 'Well, I'd better be getting back.'

He nodded a farewell and began to make his way to the top of the bank. Meredith watched him disappear among the straggling trees and, a moment later, heard the Land Rover spring to life and rattle away.

On the heels of this sound came another as with a rattle and roar a train rushed by on the track below.

CHAPTER NINE

'Tuesday, Dave, and the body found last Thursday.'

Pearce, driving slowly, alert for the turning into Cherry Tree Farm, mulled over the conversation he'd had with Markby before he set out. He'd understood the implication of Markby's words. Time was going by since the discovery of Sonia Franklin's body and time mattered in investigations. It was a rule of thumb that if nothing had started to break by the third or fourth day in a murder case, you were in trouble. From then on, the trail would get progressively colder, witnesses' memories ever more unreliable, material evidence more likely to be lost, damaged or destroyed.

'We've been over it all,' he'd protested. 'If he's telling the truth, and she left that farm the way he says she did, then we don't know where she went. If we guess she walked down to the viaduct, we don't why she did it. If she was going to meet someone, we don't know who it was.'

'Well, get out there and find out!' the superintendent had snapped – unjustifiably in Pearce's view. Nor did Dave think much of sending junior officers on away-day fishing trips. The proposal to send Holding to London to check out the firm of Dixon Dubois where, it seemed, the former Sonia Lambert had been employed, rankled.

'Am I or am I not,' muttered Pearce to himself, 'in charge of this investigation? I know he's in overall charge' – by 'he' Pearce referred to Markby – 'but I'm running the day-to-day inquiries and if anyone gets a freebie trip to the big city it ought to be me!'

Pearce was recalled to matters in hand by the appearance ahead of him of the turning to Cherry Tree Farm. It was marked in a way striking enough to cause him to brake and study it. Above a fancy wooden board with the name of the farm in poker-work was a carved horse, head held high, staring out across the landscape. Pearce hadn't thought to enquire what sort of farm Cherry Tree was. He'd assumed something in the same line as Hazelwood. But already, before he set eyes on the place, Pearce realised this was going to be an altogether more prosperous establishment. A stud farm, breeding quality horses, perhaps? He drove on slowly, preparing himself for the unexpected.

Unlike the track leading to Hazelwood, Cherry Tree was reached by a tarmacked lane. Whether this had been laid by the council, Pearce didn't know, but he doubted it. If it had been put down by the owners, it represented a considerable outlay in cost, and normally people didn't pay out that kind of money if they didn't expect, or hope at least, to recover it. To either side of the road, the old dry-stone walls had also been given a drastic facelift, tidied, repaired, reinforced with mortar. The gates stood open. He drove through, parked and, with considerable curiosity, got out of his car.

It looked like a farmyard, certainly. But the sort which appeared in illustrations in children's books or had once been a standard toy in the nursery and now appeared, battered and scratched, in antique shops labelled collectable. In toyshops, the shelf space it might once have occupied was now taken over by the space monster and the muscle-bound action hero. These fantasy newcomers were not more unrealistic than the toy farm. Probably no real working farm had ever looked so pristine in appearance. But Cherry Tree came pretty near. Pearce was ready to bet his pension that whatever kind of farming was done here, it was supplemented by some trade or business involving the public. Cherry Tree Farm was for show.

The house was freshly whitewashed over the original stone, which he privately thought a pity. The wooden window frames and door were painted a sky blue so bright it hurt the eyes. The yard was the tidiest he'd even seen. Nothing so unsightly as a midden. Whatever the animals on Cherry Tree produced in digesting their fodder, the result was well hidden. Nevertheless, there were looseboxes on one side of the yard. Just by them, two young girls sweated industriously at grooming a pair of ponies. Pearce approached them and called out, 'Hullo!'

The girls stopped what they were doing and turned in unison to face him, brushes in hand. The ponies also turned their heads and gazed, ears pricked, at the newcomer with interest. Pearce blinked, affected, he thought for a moment, by double vision. Don't be daft! he told himself. Twins.

Possibly to their parents they weren't exactly identical, but for a stranger distinguishing them would be well-nigh impossible. He supposed them to be the daughters of the farmer and, in that case, classmates of Tammy Franklin. So they'd be about twelve, as she was. They had round freckled faces, curly corn-coloured hair cut short, snub noses, and a daunting air of self-possession. Both wore jodhpurs and boots with tee-shirts. Even the ponies were alike, one dapple-grey, one roan, same size, same type.

'Who are you?' asked the nearer twin. 'Are you enquiring about farm holidays? We're fully booked for most of the summer.'

Ah, that explained the spruce air of the place and the suggestion of extra cash rolling in.

'No,' said Pearce. 'I'm a police officer.'

His questioner was taken aback by that and stood scowling at him and chewing her lower lip. Her sister took up the interrogation.

'You're not in uniform,' she snapped. 'You should have a warrant card and you should show it when introducing yourself. Otherwise, we don't know who you are.'

'Very true,' he admitted. 'Did they teach you that at school?'

'Mummy told us,' said the twin loftily. 'We have to be careful out here, you know. Anyone can come to the door.'

By now thoroughly put in his place, Pearce produced his identification and handed it over. They scrutinised it, glanced at one another and appeared to reach wordless agreement. It was returned to him.

'I suppose it's all right,' said the first twin grudgingly. 'But the photo doesn't look an awful lot like you.'

'Well, they never do, do they?' returned Pearce, adding, 'I'm not in uniform because I'm in the plainclothes branch, CID. Do you know what that is?'

It seemed they did. They watched police drama on TV, they informed him. They listed their preferred programmes rapidly, and consigned to outer darkness the ones they didn't like. Pearce suspected their idea of policework was that of most of the country, which was to say rather more exciting than it was.

Nevertheless, as they detailed their viewing tastes, the twins had moved closer together until now they were shoulder to shoulder. Eventually they fell silent and stared at him in a way which made him uneasy. He'd heard it said that identical twins could communicate with one another without words, a telepathy based on an intuitive understanding. All that spiel about the television, he thought, that was for my benefit! All the time there was a second conversation going on and it was between these two, and not a word of that was spoken. Creepy, really.

'Why have you come to see us?' asked the twin on the left, sounding for the first time slightly uncertain. Pearce was reminded of a dog which, having barked loudly to see off a stranger and finding the stranger had remained, didn't know what to do next.

'Well, I've come to see your mum and dad really,' he told them cheerfully. Lest they should feel left out, he asked, 'What are your names?'

They smiled at him in thinly veiled contempt. They knew perfectly well that even given their names, he would mix them up. He also realised from the earlier reference that they would call their parents 'Mummy and Daddy'. He'd got it wrong again.

The left-hand twin pointed at her sister and said, 'That's Lucy.'

The right-hand twin pointed at the first one and said, 'That's Lynette.'

Though Pearce would have declared it unworthy to take an instant dislike to children, he thought he could very easily make an exception of these two. They must know that by introducing one another instead of each herself, it made things more muddling. They probably played this kind of clever game on all visitors. Heaven help the holidaymakers who landed up at Cherry Tree.

'Is your father around? Or your mother?' Blowed if he was going to talk of mummy and daddy – but he knew better than to repeat 'mum and dad'.

'Daddy's gone to buy a horse,' said Left-Hand Twin. (Lynette?)

'For the summer visitors,' added her sister. 'We offer pony trekking.'

'I see.' Probably cream teas and souvenir postcards as well. 'You must have got other horses, then, besides these two – not counting the one your dad's gone to buy?' He knew he'd descended to a petty, unworthy level of verbal fencing in his use of 'dad', but he was niggled.

'There are five others,' said the same twin. 'They're in the paddock.'

'Mummy,' said Lynette, 'is indoors. Just ring the bell.'

Pearce thanked them and set off towards the house, grateful not to have been sent round to the tradesmen's entrance. By the bright blue door there was a wrought-iron hook for a hanging basket. Window boxes were affixed to the sills. No flowers in them yet, but he was sure that by the time visitors arrived for their farm holidays, Cherry Tree would look a picture. He rang the bell – even that was melodious – and, while he waited, turned to look back at the twins.

They were standing together whispering. He suspected they were having, if not an argument, then a pretty lively discussion. He wondered about what. Probably just about him and what he wanted. He turned back as the door was opened.

Mrs Hayward was a weather-beaten, wire-haired, horsy woman wearing a scruffy bodywarmer over a tartan shirt and the inevitable jodhpurs and boots. 'Were you waiting long?' she demanded in clear, no-nonsense uppercrust tones. 'I was on the phone. Come in.'

He was ushered in smartly without having to announce his purpose or identity. Perhaps she assumed the twins would have already interrogated him. Nevertheless, he offered his identification again.

'Copper, eh?' said Mrs Hayward. 'Not surprised to see you. We were wondering when one of you would turn up. Want a cup of tea or something stronger?'

Pearce declined all refreshment and said he hoped not to take up too much of her time.

'Come about poor Sonia, I dare say. Shocking business. Derry, my husband, isn't here. Gone to look at a nag, probably buy the brute if it's up to specification. It's not easy finding suitable mounts for visitors to ride. They've got to have good manners and good temperament.'

Pearce was not quite sure whether she meant the horses or the visitors.

'Mustn't kick, bite, go on strike or deposit the riders in the mud. Trouble is, the average visitor has only ever ridden a bike before they get here. Derry should be back soon. I suppose you want to talk to him as well? Not that there's anything we can tell you. I had Tammy here yesterday for the day. Because of the inquest, you know. Poor kid. She's a funny little thing. Of course her own mother died, you know that? Nice woman, Penny.'

'What about Sonia Franklin?' Pearce saw an opening and managed to get in a question as Mrs Hayward drew breath. 'Was she a nice woman?'

'Useless,' said Mrs Hayward in a tone of regret rather than criticism.

'I can't say she struck me as having staying power. Mincing round the place in designer wear. No, I never thought she'd stay the course but that doesn't mean I expected, any of us expected, something like this to happen to her. I'd be telling you an untruth if I say I could be doing with her, because I couldn't. And she nearly drove poor Hugh out of his mind, I don't doubt. You may think I'm being unkind, but I speak my mind. She wasn't a bad person, don't misunderstand me, more what you'd call a square peg in a round hole. She was good-hearted in her way. Decently educated. Attractive, I suppose.'

Mrs Hayward rubbed a hand over her own wiry crop of corn-coloured hair, a faded version of her daughters' and streaked with grey. 'Always offering to help. Help do what, for crying out loud? There wasn't anything she *could* do. She didn't know anything about horses, which is where she might have been able to lend a hand. I think myself she was scared of animals. They know it if you're frightened of them. We've got geese round the back here. They chased poor old Sonia all over the yard one day. I had to come out and rescue her. To be honest, I didn't encourage her to come over here. She wasn't above fluttering her eyelashes at Derry. Wasting her time, mind you. Still, none of that's of any interest to you.'

In fact, she was wrong. From the beginning Pearce had been anxious to build up a picture of Sonia Franklin. He wondered whether Mrs Hayward, in talking of Hugh being driven out of his mind by his wife, had realised this mightn't be the most tactful thing to say in the circumstances.

There was the sound of an approaching vehicle. Mrs Hayward peered from the window and announced, 'Derry's back.' He fancied she sounded relieved. Then she scowled. 'He's bought the bay, by the look of it. I hope he hasn't paid too much. I told him, beat them down. Make an offer and if they don't like it, let them take their chances in the sale ring.'

Pearce looked over her shoulder. An off-roader towing a single horsebox had pulled up near the stables. A man got down from the driver's seat and made his way to the back of the horsebox. The twins had abandoned their ponies and were clustered eagerly at his elbow as he let down the ramp. There was a clatter of hoofs, a nervous whinny which drew a response from the ponies. Derry Hayward led a rather smart bay pony with white socks down the ramp.

'What do you think?' asked Mrs Hayward, pursing her thin lips.

'Very nice,' said Pearce cautiously.

'Handsome is as handsome does, but the visitors will like that one. Showy, look good in photographs. It's used to children. Sold because outgrown,' concluded Mrs Hayward. 'The girls will tell my husband you're here.' Pearce sensed that, like the bay pony, he was being passed on.

Derry appeared a few minutes later, a tall, good-looking man with an easy manner and a public-school accent. He extended his hand.

'What can we do for you, Inspector? You're looking into the unfortunate business with Sonia, I suppose.'

'Unfortunate', thought Pearce, wasn't the word he'd have chosen. He eyed Derry Hayward with curiosity as they exchanged handshakes. The man had an urbane manner which contrasted oddly with his wife's forthright ways. He wore a clean sweater over a shirt patterned in tiny check and the sort of trousers which went under the name of cavalry twills. His cap had been pulled nonchalantly over his brow but he took it off now and chucked it on a wooden settle. Antique, decided Pearce of the settle, and genuine. Nothing repro here, unless . . .

He eyed Derry again. It was all a little bit much. When Pearce had been a boy, his grandfather had been wont, at Christmas, to sing an old music-hall song about Gilbert the Filbert, the Colonel of the Knuts. The infant Dave had considered it the height of wit and been reduced to giggles. Then, one year, seeing Grandpa gearing up for his party piece with paper képi from a cracker on his bald head, he'd whispered to an aunt that he hoped Grandpa wasn't going to sing it again. To which his aunt had returned with a sigh, 'Yes, you're growing up, aren't you? Pity.'

At the time, he hadn't understood and felt vaguely insulted. Since then he had realised what she meant and remembered the episode with shame and sadness. Now, looking at Derry, he had an insane impulse to burst out singing it himself.

'Yes, sir, Mrs Franklin,' he said briskly. 'You are by way of neighbours to Hazelwood Farm. You haven't seen any odd characters hanging about lately, have you? Strangers? Undesirables?'

'They mightn't be strange, but as far as I'm concerned they're undesirable,' blurted Mrs Hayward.

Her husband gave her a warning look. 'Belinda means the Smiths, the gypsy family camping on Hazelwood land. They've been coming for years and we've never had any trouble.'

'Make the place untidy, washing all over the bushes, scrap piled up. Not the sort of view visitors want. And he's a poacher. I've chased him off our land a couple of times myself.'

'But never any real problem,' insisted her husband gently.

'Found Sonia's body, didn't he?' demanded his wife. 'You want to ask Smith a bit more about that, Inspector.'

'Did Sonia Franklin ever express any doubts about the Smiths?' Pearce managed to get the conversation back on course. To borrow the horse-world vocabulary beloved of Mrs Hayward herself, one could have described that lady as likely to take the bit between her teeth and bolt.

The Haywards denied this. 'Not to us, anyway,' said Mrs Hayward meaningfully.

'She was in the habit of taking a constitutional stroll of an evening. Did she ever mention to you that she'd met with strangers, fancied she was being followed, anything like that?'

Mrs Hayward shook her head and edged towards the door. 'I'll make the tea, anyway. You'll have a cup, will you, now Derry's here?'

She clearly wanted to be out of the room and leave dealing with the police to her husband. Pearce took pity on her and accepted the tea. She looked relieved, as if his earlier refusal of hospitality had betokened some sinister intent.

His wife out of the way, Derry took over effortlessly. 'This is a very quiet neck of the woods – er – Inspector. We don't go in for much crime.'

'You're fortunate,' said Pearce. 'I mean, to have so few worries on that score. But it doesn't do to be complacent, does it? Perhaps Mrs Franklin thought nothing could happen to her out here.'

'Quite, yes, couldn't agree more. Feel bad about it all. Poor old Hugh.' Derry shook his head. 'Very decent chap. Salt of the earth.'

Mrs Hayward marched back in and handed over mugs of tea.

'Who's that? Hugh? Marvellous chap.' She nodded vigorously. 'Wouldn't hurt a fly.'

Pearce sipped at the tea, which was very weak. 'If I could ask you about your visitors. How do they come to you? I mean, how do they know about you? Advertisement?'

At this, they both shied back in alarm.

'Never advertise in the papers,' said Mrs Hayward. 'God knows who we'd get if we did that. We go on recommendation. You know, word of mouth. People who like it here tell their friends. We're always fully booked. Some come back every year. So I really don't think you could count our visitors as strangers. We look upon them as house guests.' She nodded.

And nothing, thought Pearce uncharitably, so vulgar as trade. 'Did Mrs Franklin meet any of your visitors?'

'Here, I say, steady on!' protested Hayward. 'She may well have come across some of them but that doesn't mean anything. We specialise in family holidays here. We wouldn't accept anyone we thought at all dodgy. Couldn't afford to. Families are easily frightened off. Anyway, the season's not started yet and there are no visitors here at the moment.'

'We're not going to get our names in the papers, are we? Because of this? I hope you're going to be discreet.' This was from Mrs Hayward. 'I told you, we don't publicise and we certainly don't want any *bad* publicity.'

Pearce said he quite understood. He was merely asking them as a matter of routine. The police would be visiting everyone living in the area. The Haywards listened to him and looked more relaxed when he'd finished.

'We really wish we could help,' said Derry in a concerned but firm way which was intended to let Pearce know this interview was over. He drained his mug but his eyes never left the visitor. 'Nobody wants it cleared up more than Belinda and I do. Just as my wife said, it's not the sort of publicity you want if you're running a holiday business, especially one targeting families.'

Perhaps his attitude struck him as showing more commercial acumen than was decent in the circumstances. He hastened to express suitable regret. 'Poor old Sonia. Thoroughly nice woman. We have warned the children to stay close to the house and on no account to separate when exercising the ponies.'

'Very wise, sir. I was about to advise you to keep the children near the house.' He had gained all he was likely to here. Pearce returned his empty mug, thanked them for their time and hospitality, and took himself off.

The twins were fussing round the new pony. They gave no sign of having noticed him pass by, but he was sure they were well aware of him.

As he drove off, he found himself thinking with something like affectionate nostalgia of the run-down confusion of Hazelwood Farm. He knew where he'd rather spend a farm holiday, that was for sure. He hummed Grandpa's party piece under his breath as he turned into the main road.

Watching his departure from the window, Derry Hayward observed to his spouse, 'Golden rule with the constabulary, Belinda old thing: keep your lip buttoned.'

She looked at him in some alarm. 'I didn't say anything to him, Derry. Anyway, he didn't strike me as being awfully bright.'

Ginny Holding, meantime, had arrived at Hazelwood, where she also met with a less-than-enthusiastic reception. She was greeted by Simon Franklin. He held his spectacles in his hand and addressed her from the front doorstep, as she later described it to Markby, like a class of delinquent fourth years.

'Now, I've gone to a lot of trouble to arrange this, Constable.'

'Much obliged to you,' said Holding, thinking, Pompous twit.

'My brother fully understands why you wish to talk to his daughter but I must remind you, the child is in a highly nervous state.'

'Yes, sir. Perhaps if I could see Tammy . . . ?'

'I shall not permit you to harry the child,' said Simon, shaking his spectacles at her.

'Not my intention!' snapped Holding. 'Can we get on with it? I've a very busy day.'

Simon, a natural-born awkward bugger in Holding's view, apparently realised he'd held things up for as long as he could, and led her into the house.

The window was open in the comfortable, untidy sitting room, but there was still a whiff of dog. The animal itself, an aged spaniel, came slowly to greet Holding, sniffing at her shoes and her hand. The child sat on the sofa, feet together, hands folded in lap, stony-faced, her long hair in loose entwining locks. Holding was reminded of the Little Mermaid statue in Copenhagen harbour. She and Robert, a.k.a. Snapper, had taken a cycling holiday in Denmark the previous year.

'Hullo, Tammy,' she said. 'Is this your dog? My boyfriend's a police-dog handler.'

Simon rolled his eyes at the ceiling. Tammy thawed slightly and looked interested. 'That's Pogo,' she told the visitor.

Pogo, hearing his name, thumped his stumpy tail on the ground.

The action served to release a strange odour which Holding did her best to pretend she hadn't noticed. 'If you'd like to come and watch one of the police-dog displays we put on for the public from time to time, I'm sure that could be arranged,' she offered.

Tammy almost smiled. 'That'd be nice.'

Pogo scratched vigorously. Cripes, thought Holding, as the odour got worse.

'No school this week?' She leaned forward informally, her arms resting on her knees.

'Half term.'

'What do you like to do when you've got a holiday?'

'Help Dad.'

Simon was leaning back in his armchair, his eyes still on the ceiling, but his attitude sending out the clear message he was monitoring this conversation and would jump in the moment he felt it necessary.

'When I was a kid,' continued Holding, swivelling her chair so that her back was to Simon, 'I always wished I lived on a farm.'

Tammy returned a faint smile to this observation. 'You have to work very hard on a farm,' she said.

Holding moved in effortlessly. 'I'm sure you do. I expect your dad needs a lot of help and support just now.' Her voice and manner were sympathetic but, behind her, she heard Simon shift restlessly in his chair.

'Dad didn't do it.' The child's grey eyes fixed Holding's defiantly. 'He didn't kill Sonia.'

Simon uttered a series of tuts.

'Don't you worry about that,' Ginny said soothingly. 'Do you remember that evening, last Wednesday?'

It was Tammy's turn to wriggle uneasily. 'You mean when Sonia went out after supper?'

'You saw her go out?' Holding raised her eyebrows.

'Yes, from my bedroom window. She was going for her walk. She always did that after supper.'

'I see.' A thought struck Holding. 'Did she ever take Pogo with her?'

Tammy sat up straight and said indignantly, 'No, never! Pogo is my dog!'

'Yes, of course he is.'

'Sonia didn't like him and he didn't like Sonia.'

I fancy you didn't like Sonia much either, thought Holding. To her relief, Pogo got up and waddled out of the room. 'Did you see Sonia come back from her walk?'

Tammy hesitated. 'No. I'd gone to bed.'

'Do you remember what happened that evening before Sonia went out for her walk?' Holding sensed that Simon, behind her, was about to lodge an objection and headed it off by asking, 'What did you have for supper?'

'Spaghetti.'

'Which Sonia cooked? What about pudding?'

'We don't have pudding. Sonia was on a diet. Dad had cheese and I had a yoghurt. Sonia cooked spaghetti a lot because she didn't like peeling potatoes.'

'Not a job I'm keen on either,' admitted Holding. 'What did you talk about at supper, do you remember?'

'About the farm. Dad asked what I'd done at school. Nothing much. I don't remember anything else.'

'What did Sonia say? Did she ask about school?'

'Only asked me if I'd got any clean socks for the next day. I told you, I can't remember anything else. It was just ordinary talking.'

'Fine, don't worry if you can't remember. What did you do after supper?'

'Washed up.' Tammy tilted her chin. 'Sonia washed and I dried. Then I went upstairs to do my homework. That's when I saw Sonia go out. I did my homework and I went to bed. Nothing else happened.'

Holding smiled encouragingly. 'Did you see which way Sonia went?'

Tammy countered this with, 'The usual way. Across the yard, through the gate on the right.'

'I see. You didn't go downstairs to say good night to your dad? He didn't look in on you later?'

Tammy looked disconcerted and a little annoyed. 'Well, I went down to kiss him good night. Of course I did. I always do.'

'What was he doing when you went downstairs?'

An intake of breath and rustle from Simon.

'Watching telly. Well, he was sort of dozing really. I said good night and he said, "OK, Tam. See you in the morning", or something like that. I bent over his chair and kissed him. He said, "Sleep tight, make sure the bugs don't bite!" That's a joke. Dad always says it.'

'Did you expect him to look in on you later?'

Tammy shook her head. 'He doesn't.' After a moment's hesitation, she added, 'Mum used to, my mum.'

'I see. Before Sonia went out, and after you'd washed up, did you hear your dad and Sonia talking?'

Tammy stared at her. 'No, I was upstairs doing my homework like I told you.'

'Were you never downstairs here in the evenings with your father and stepmother? Don't you watch television?'

'Sometimes,' said Tammy warily.

'What about your father and Sonia? Did they like television or did they talk a lot?'

'Sometimes they watched – and sometimes they talked.' Tammy was growing restless, her eyes flickering nervously towards her uncle.

'I think, Constable,' Simon said loudly, 'you've covered the ground pretty well. That's enough for one day.'

'You've done very well, Tammy,' Holding told her, as she got to her feet. 'You've been very helpful.'

She fancied she saw a flicker of alarm in the child's eyes, which widened. Her lips parted and then snapped shut again. Holding was about to ask if there was anything else, but here came that fusspot uncle, getting in the way of things, as he'd intended to do all along in the name of protecting his niece.

'I'll see you out, Constable.'

'Nice old house this, sir,' observed Holding as she was ushered at a smart pace down the hall.

'Yes,' said Simon. 'Good day, Constable.' The door was shut firmly behind her.

'Now, Tammy, why were you so frightened when I suggested you'd been helpful?' mused Holding aloud as she drew out of the yard. 'Because you'd set yourself to be as unhelpful as possible, I dare say. Now, why should you do that, Tammy?'

In the house, Simon had returned to the sitting room and his niece. 'You did really well, Tammy,' he said approvingly.

Her cool grey gaze rested on him briefly. 'Yes, Uncle Simon.'

Jane Brady was driving towards Hazelwood when she saw Holding's unmarked car pull out of the farm turning ahead. The car passed Jane's, driving in the direction of Bamford.

Now, who was that? Jane asked herself, feeling a twinge of unease.

When she reached the farm, she saw another visitor, a man, standing in the yard by a green off-roader, talking to Hugh. Both looked up as Jane stopped a short way off. She let down the window.

'Is this a bad time to call?' she shouted.

'No,' called Hugh, 'You go on indoors. Tam's there.'

Jane thought she heard the other man say, 'Tammy might not want another . . .' but the last words were lost.

She got out of the car and, as she approached, saw that the stranger was, in fact, Simon Franklin. Close to hand, she was interested to see the ways in which he resembled his brother, although in overall appearance, he was a very different kettle of fish. He was far more slightly built and that, together with the mended spectacles and a certain indoor pallor, gave him a more vulnerable, academic look which contrasted with Hugh's soil-grown independence. Nevertheless, Simon was eyeing her, she fancied, in a hostile way.

Hugh merely nodded and waved a hand at his companion. 'You've met Simon, have you, my brother?'

To say, 'I saw you at the inquest' wouldn't have been tactful. So Jane said, 'I'm very pleased to meet you,' and held out her hand. 'Tammy's told me about her uncle.'

She spoke warmly and sincerely. Even in other circumstances, she would've been interested to meet Simon Franklin.

Simon thawed and shook her hand, though without much enthusiasm. 'You're Miss Brady, then. I've been hearing about you, too, from my niece and from my brother.' He glanced at Hugh. 'It's good of the school to take such a close interest in a pupil.'

'At difficult times like these,' Jane told him, 'we try to help if we can.'

Simon acknowledged this with a half-smile. 'Quite,' he said. 'I'm sure you do.' He then ruined any favourable impression he might have made by adding, 'But then, in an independent school, one would expect that. It all goes to make up what the fees are for, doesn't it?'

This was so gratuitously rude that Jane gasped. 'No, it isn't! It's nothing to do with the fees.'

'Please don't be offended, Miss Brady,' said Simon, which made things worse. 'I wasn't intending to suggest in your case that anything other than Tammy's welfare was on your mind.'

'Jane, she's called,' said Hugh. He'd been listening with some amusement to the exchange. 'Don't upset her, Sim, she'll tell you off good and proper. She's been getting me organised.' He grinned.

Simon cleared his throat and gave his brother a sharp look. 'Yes, well, we can discuss things later. I have to be off, anyway. Nice to have met you, Miss Brady.' Simon opened the driver's door of his vehicle. 'Let me know if you need me again, Hugh.'

'Will do, Sim, and thanks. I'm glad you were there to handle it.'

Simon roared out of the yard. Hugh turned to Jane. 'You don't want to let Simon get you rattled. It's just his way.'

'I had been thinking,' Jane said grimly, 'of asking him to come and talk to the sixth form about his writing. Now I'm not so sure.'

'You ask him. He's good talking about history and books and so on.' Hugh nodded towards the house. 'Tam'll be pleased to see you. We've had another visitor. Left just before you came.'

'I saw the car,' Jane admitted. 'Are you really sure this is a good time for me to be here? I can come back. I feel I drove your brother away.' She grimaced. 'He wasn't very pleased to see me, was he? He doesn't really approve, either of me or my being here.'

'No, stay.' Hugh frowned. 'Sim's not my keeper. I don't need his say-so over who comes here.' He shrugged. 'He's inclined to be overprotective. But really, don't worry about it, he was leaving anyway. He only came over to sit in on a chat between a policewoman and Tammy. That's the woman you saw driving away. She was the plainclothes sort, like the bloke who was here. I didn't much like the idea of her bothering Tammy. Simon said I could refuse. I nearly did.' Hugh scowled again. 'I mean, it's one thing to come bothering me, another to bother Tam, isn't it? But then I thought, well, if Tammy thought she could handle it . . . and she wouldn't be alone. Simon would be there. Seems the police weren't keen on having me there.' Hugh pulled a wry expression.

Jane thought the increased strain was showing in his face. Beneath the tan, his skin was wan. The lines were deeper, his brow furrowed up, she thought, like a boxer dog's. He wore a different pullover today, but, with holes in both elbows, it was in no better shape than the previous one.

'What's up?' asked Hugh, aware of her scrutiny. He glanced at his arms. 'Something with my jersey?'

'Sorry, I was just thinking, I could mend the holes, or try to mend them. I'm not really much good at darning, but I could probably cobble them together somehow.'

'You don't need to do that,' said Hugh, picking at a loose strand of wool at his elbow and making things worse. 'It's only for doing mucky jobs round the place. See, I'm a real farmer, not a boarding-house keeper with a few animals around for show.'

Jane must have looked perplexed because he added in explanation, 'Like Derry Hayward and his wife over at Cherry Tree. That's not farming, that's running a hotel.' He sounded disgusted.

'They do farmhouse B & B, you mean?'

'Pony trekking as well. He takes townies riding over his land. Then he lets them play at a bit of pretend farming, like feeding the poultry. He's got some goats over there. I asked him when he bought them what on earth he meant to do with those. He told me they were really just to keep the children amused. Not his own kids, his visitors' kids. What's he running there, a zoo? Still, I dare say he's doing better at that than I'm doing here,' Hugh acknowledged. 'So I oughtn't to criticise him. Say what you like about Derry, he's never been short of ideas. You want a cup of tea or something?'

'Thank you, I'll go and make it.' Jane suspected he meant her to do this anyway. 'I'm sorry a policewoman came to talk to Tammy but I suppose it was inevitable. Perhaps it was as well you didn't refuse permission, but I hope she wasn't upset. What did the woman ask?'

'According to Simon, she wanted to know what happened that evening – when Sonia was killed. She was fishing to hear whether Tam heard Sonia and me quarrelling, so Simon reckoned. But Tammy didn't let on if she did.'

Hugh squinted across the yard. 'Don't know if she really did hear us. Wouldn't surprise me. We weren't quiet. On the other hand, that old house has walls would stop a runaway truck. Outer walls are nearly three feet thick at the base. Doors are old, solid oak. Sound doesn't travel once you've shut yourself in.'

'Hugh,' Jane asked impetuously, 'what do you remember about that evening? I don't mean what did you tell the police. Not that you won't have told the police everything. I mean what sort of impression do you have in your mind of that evening?'

His broad shoulders hunched in a shrug. 'That it was like any other evening. I came in, washed ready for supper. We ate. Tammy buzzed off upstairs and took Pogo with her. She had homework, you'll know about that. Sonia and I started an argument – and that was pretty normal for us, too. The police want to make out it was something special. But it wasn't. Tell you the truth, I don't think I'm being unfair to Sonia if I tell you she liked to pick a fight. I think she saw it as the evening's entertainment. As usual she accused me of offering her a lifestyle at peasant subsistence level.'

Hugh gave Jane an embarrassed look. 'That's what she called it. She was good at dressing up plain statements in fancy words. I'm not, so I replied, "Bollocks", or something like that. She stormed off out, going for her walk. That was regular, nothing new about that. I watched telly for a bit, but don't ask me what was on because I haven't got a clue. Tammy was busy upstairs with her homework, like I said, so she didn't come down. I was on my own. Can't produce a witness, sorry about that. I was just dog-tired and dozed off.'

Hugh paused and frowned. 'I fancy the telephone rang out in the hall. It woke me. I was going to drag myself out of my chair and answer it, but then it stopped. Tammy must've answered it. Probably one of her friends. She came in a bit later on to say good night to me.'

Hugh considered what he'd said and added, 'That's it, really. I went out to check everything was all right round the yard. I do that every night. I couldn't see Sonia about. Didn't think anything of that much. She'd stayed out late before. But she hadn't taken the car so I thought she'd be back eventually. I came back, turned in, slept like a log. Tammy told the policewoman she saw Sonia leave, by the way. Nice to think there's something supports my story!' Hugh gave a grin but there was no mirth in it. 'Come on, I could do with a cup of something myself.'

He turned and led the way towards the house. Jane followed him, her mind spinning. One thing above all had seized it. Hugh said his daughter went upstairs to do her homework and stayed there all evening. But Tammy *hadn't* done her homework. So what had she been doing? And who had been the mysterious telephone caller?

CHAPTER TEN

Tammy had already seen them talking outside in the yard and was in the kitchen, making the tea. She moved around in a silence broken only by the rattle of crockery and hiss of boiling water, her fingers busy but her eyes resolutely avoiding contact with Jane's. Jane wondered whether it was the visit of the policewoman which had led to this lowering of the social temperature, or something else. Something involving me? she asked herself. There did seem to be a personal element in Tammy's attitude.

'Thanks, love,' said Hugh, and took his mug outside with him. He didn't appear to have noticed anything amiss. Jane thought with some exasperation, well, he wouldn't, would he? He was one of those people one wanted to grab and shake into awareness. But even if such an action were possible – and given his solid build it wasn't – it wouldn't have done any good. She was even beginning to feel a glimmer of Sonia's frustration.

Jane pushed Hugh out of her mind to concentrate on Tammy. She took a seat at the narrow end of the old scrubbed deal table and looked across it at the child. Reluctantly, Tammy perched herself on a stool at the opposite end, as far away from the visitor as was possible without being rude. She showed no more inclination to talk and still scrupulously avoided Jane's gaze. Any rapport they'd built up during the shopping trip seemed to have well and truly vanished. Instead, that invisible brick wall was back, reinforced. It *is* something to do with me, Jane decided. It's not the police. What now? She had to break the barrier somehow, and talking of the recent visit seemed the obvious way, even if the visit wasn't the cause of the problem.

'Was it very unpleasant, Tammy? Talking to the policewoman, I mean. Did she ask a lot of questions?' Jane asked sympathetically.

131

'She wasn't bad,' admitted Tammy in grudging tones. 'She liked dogs. Uncle Simon wouldn't let her ask me lots of questions. It was all right.'

So that confirmed the upset wasn't caused by the visit from the police. Now, what have I done? Jane wondered. She cast her mind back and lit upon a possible cause, albeit a trivial one.

'Tammy,' she said, 'I'm sorry I dashed off without saying goodbye the last time I was here.'

''S all right,' came the mumbled response.

'I would have come over yesterday, but I was told you'd gone to stay with the Haywards for the day.'

Tammy made no reply and twisted her forefinger in a strand of her long hair.

'Did you enjoy the day at the Haywards?'

'Not really. They're not my friends. Mrs Hayward asked me.'

Jane wasn't surprised to hear that. She had never thought Tammy to be one of the Hayward twins' circle. Tammy didn't appear to belong to any circle or to have a particular friend. It was a worrying trait in a twelve-year-old.

Back to square one, thought Jane, wondering how to move the first brick in that wall of reserve between them.

Unexpectedly, that first move came from Tammy, who suddenly asked, 'Have you and Dad had a row?' She lifted her head and stared accusingly at Jane from between curtains of long hair.

Jane was so surprised, she gaped for a moment. 'A quarrel? No, whatever gave you that idea?'

'I thought that was why you left so suddenly last time. I heard you talking in the kitchen. You were telling Dad off. He was saying he hadn't got time to do all the things you wanted him to do. He used to say that to Sonia when she nagged at him to go into town with her or to do something she liked and he didn't.'

'Yes, but—'

Daylight dawned. Hugh's marriage to Sonia had been a disaster. Tammy had watched and listened as the relationship had deteriorated beyond repair. Now the child was unable to draw a distinction between a forthright exchange of views and an outright shouting match based on bitter division. Jane felt a surge of anger at the thought of how much damage had been done to this child – was done to any child – by unthinking, selfish adults. She wondered whether Hugh had any idea what the continual scenes and upsets of his second marriage had done to scramble his young daughter's view.

'We didn't quarrel, Tammy,' she said earnestly. She suppressed the anger which was for Hugh. 'We didn't agree, but that's not the same thing as quarrelling. To be someone's friend doesn't mean agreeing with everything they say. Everyone's got a right to his own opinion. Sometimes you just have to agree to differ.'

Tammy had relaxed somewhat but was cautious. 'I hope you and Dad won't quarrel.'

'I can't promise that. We're human. But if we did, it wouldn't be like Sonia and your dad. They quarrelled a lot, did they?'

'All the time, yelling. Dad never did that before Sonia came. He and my mum never did that. But when Sonia came, Dad changed. He stopped whistling.'

'Whistling?' Jane was startled.

'Yes, when he went out early, first thing in the morning for the milking. I'd still be in bed but I'd hear him. He whistles really well with a proper tune to it. You know, not like some people. Dad used to whistle like some people sing. Then, after Sonia came, he stopped. I'd hear him leave the house and walk across the yard, and the cows lowing and so on. But never any whistling.' Tammy paused. 'It made me feel sad.'

'Because you felt your father was unhappy?'

'I know he was unhappy,' Tammy said fiercely. 'That's why I'm glad she's gone. Perhaps now Dad will go back to being the way he was before she came here. I wish he would. Only, he still isn't whistling, but that's because he's worried about the police and everything.'

Unease gripped Jane. Dad changed, Tammy had said. Her words reminded Jane of Meredith's assertion that honest, kindly men under stress have killed before now. Not Hugh, she'd told Meredith and meant it. She didn't know why she'd been so sure. Was she being foolish? Refusing to face unwanted possibilities? Wanting everything to be all right for Tammy's sake? But why should Hugh not have killed a woman who was making his life and that of his child unbearable? And what of the inconsistencies Jane had already noted in the story Tammy had apparently told the police? Tammy had lied. She'd lied about the homework. If Tammy had lied, it was to protect her father. There could be no other reason.

'Did the policewoman talk to you about your father and Sonia?' she asked quietly.

'About the quarrels?' Tammy tilted her head and considered her answer. 'Well, not straight out. She asked about the evening – that evening, you know. She asked if I heard Dad and Sonia talking after I went upstairs, but I said I didn't.'

'*Said* you didn't? Or really didn't?' Jane had old experience of Tammy's way of splitting hairs.

'Didn't,' said Tammy coldly. 'I didn't hear.'

'You saw her leave the house? That's what you told the policewoman. Your Uncle Simon told your father that.'

'I did see her leave the house, that's true!' Tammy's eyes flashed.

Jane forced herself to put the next question although she dreaded the answer might not be the one she wanted to hear. As casually as possible, she asked it. 'Tammy, did you see Sonia come back?'

Tammy began to shake her head wildly, hair tumbling over her face. Her voice came shrilly from behind the hair veil. 'She didn't – didn't come back!'

'Fine, don't get upset,' Jane soothed. 'Did the constable ask lots of other questions?'

Tammy pushed back the curtains of hair and Jane was startled to see satisfaction in her face. 'She wanted to, but Uncle Simon wouldn't let her.' *So there!* she might have added.

Jane stared down at her cooling tea. The milk had formed a pale skin on the top of it and it was undrinkable. Was she not the only one to realise something wasn't right? Had Simon Franklin also sensed that and decided to step in to protect his niece and also his brother? Tammy was hiding something and doing it very skilfully. However you looked at it, it came back to the matter of the homework. If Tammy hadn't been doing her homework up in her room, what had she been doing? Or—

'Tammy?' Something in Jane's voice must have given the child a hint of what was to come, because her grey eyes froze and her whole facial expression closed down in the way Jane knew only too well. 'Tammy? Were you in your room all evening?'

'Yes! I was—' Tammy broke off abruptly and gave Jane a wild look.

'Not doing your homework, because you hadn't done it the next day, had you?' Jane leaned forward earnestly. 'Look, Tammy, I'm your friend and your dad's friend. You've got to believe it. It's true. I swear it. I want to help. But I can't help if you won't tell me everything. You said you didn't see Sonia come back. But was that because you weren't in your room and you don't know whether she came back or not?'

Tammy said tearfully, 'I know she didn't come back.'

'So when you saw her leave the house after supper for her walk, that was the last time you saw her?'

'I saw her go out. I didn't see her come back.'

They were on the old familiar roundabout again and the child was getting distressed. In a last throw, Jane tried a surprise attack from another quarter. 'What about the phone call? You father told me he heard the phone ring while he was watching television and dozing. He thought you answered it.'

'Oh that,' said Tammy, fixing Jane with a level gaze though her eyes were bright with unshed tears. 'I forgot that. It was a wrong number.'

Beating my head on a brick wall, thought Jane. No point in going on with this. Tammy would get yet more obstinate, probably start to cry and their relationship, already rocky, would collapse.

'OK,' said Jane. 'We won't talk about that any more now.' She saw relief flood Tammy's face. Jane jumped to her feet. 'Come on, action time. We're going to turn out the sitting room.'

'Turn it out?' Tammy looked puzzled. 'I dusted it.'

'You've done really well, but every so often the tidiest place needs a spring-clean. We'll take all the cushions off the sofa and chairs and take them outside. We'll give them a really good thumping and leave them out in the sun. You've got a vacuum cleaner, I suppose?'

'If it's because of Pogo,' said Tammy defiantly, 'he can't help smelling. He's very old.'

'He's a lovely dog, but he does niff a bit. Don't worry, I've got something to take care of that.' Jane reached down into her bag and produced a can which she displayed to Tammy. 'Air freshener.'

Alan Markby stood in front of the map on the wall of his office. It was punctured by coloured drawing pins in a way which suggested a military manoeuvre centred on Hazelwood Farm. He clasped his hands behind his back and let his gaze travel from one coloured dot to another. His expression was glum.

That was how Ginny Holding found her boss when she got back

to Regional HQ. She stood in the doorway and cleared her throat tactfully.

'I thought you might like to know, sir. I went out there and interviewed the kid.'

'Look at this,' said the superintendent without turning round. 'What do you think of this?'

'Very efficient, sir.' She supposed he'd heard her.

Markby turned his head and looked at her suspiciously over his shoulder. 'What does that mean?'

'Well,' Ginny gestured at the map, 'you can see where we all are and what we're doing.'

He walked away from the wall to the further side of his desk where he leaned forward, resting his palms on the Franklin murder file. 'And that gets us where?'

Oh Lor', he's in an awkward mood, thought Holding. 'Dunno,' she said. 'I mean, it's a start.'

'No, it isn't. It's an exercise in self-delusion. If it's got any use at all, it's that we can show it to anyone interested and make it look as if we're making progress. The minute you see someone sticking pins in maps,' Markby continued in rising ire, 'or typing out reports with numbered paragraphs or producing flow charts to illustrate the level of public response, you know it means only one thing.'

'We're stuck,' said Holding, getting the drift of this.

Markby sat down and waved at a chair. 'OK, Ginny, I'll have your report. Let's hope you've got something to move us forward.'

'I don't think I have,' she confessed. She summed up her talk with Tammy. 'The trouble is, I can't talk to the kid on her own. She's got to have an adult there to protect her interests. The uncle is an interfering old— I mean, he's a bit overprotective. I suppose that's to be expected. But if the kid knows anything, I'm never going to get it out of her while Simon Franklin's hovering in the background.'

'And do you think she knows something?' Markby asked.

Without hesitation, she replied, 'Yes.' Seeing that he waited for elaboration, she went on, 'I've no idea what it is or if it's really important. Perhaps it's just mildly interesting or even plain trivial. The thing is, the child thinks it's important and that's why she's keeping it to herself. She swears she saw Sonia Franklin leave the house on the night of the murder. After that she went to bed and had no idea what happened. As long as she sticks to that, we're stymied and the child knows it.'

'She's twelve . . .' protested Markby at this seemingly harsh judgement.

'They've got all their marbles at twelve,' said Ginny in a dire voice. 'It's when they get into their teens and their hormones kick in that they lose interest in anything but themselves. If you can't get any information out of teenagers, it's probably because they haven't noticed anything, even under their noses. They're too busy worrying about their acne or their boyfriends or some pop group. A child like Tammy Franklin, on the other hand, is a gift as a witness if she'll only talk. Twelve-year-olds miss nothing. They might misinterpret what they see, but when it comes to telling you about it, they've got near total recall.'

'I'm inclined to agree with you,' Markby said sadly. 'My niece used to be as bright as a button. But now she's nearly fourteen, she stomps around in great big boots, growling at people, and is letting her hair grow into dreadlocks. Well, you'd better leave it for a week. If we're no further forward then, you can try talking to her again.'

He picked up a piece of paper from his desk and a small booklet. He tendered both. 'Here you go, then. Next job.'

'What?' Ginny asked, taken aback.

'Travel warrant and train timetable. Off you go.'

'To London? What, now? Right away?'

'It isn't to the other end of the earth!' snapped the superintendent. 'All you've got to do is go up there, speak to some personnel officer or other, and come back. I've called the Met to let them know you'll be operating on their turf.'

'Thanks,' said Ginny uncertainly. 'Er, perhaps it ought to be Inspector Pearce? I think he would like—'

'Pearce is needed here. I can't have him taking afternoons off to go to London. Anyway,' Markby hesitated. 'This might call for a bit of finesse. You're the one with the special training in dealing with awkward witnesses.'

'Traumatised witnesses, sir.'

'Well, whatever it is, it ought to enable you to deal with a bunch of PR men!'

'Yes, sir. What about you?' Ginny dared to ask. 'Have you been out to Fox Corner yet to ask around there? Inspector Pearce said you were going to.'

'Not yet,' Markby confessed. 'I was waiting for one of you to come back, hopefully bearing important news. But Dave Pearce hasn't turned up yet and Lord knows what's happened to Prescott. But you don't have to worry about that. Go and catch that train!'

Steve Prescott had already decided he'd drawn the short straw. This time, when he arrived at the site of the Smiths' trailer, he was greeted by the children as an old friend. He felt like a Judas.

'Good morning, Mrs Smith,' he said. 'Danny about?'

Zilpah was sitting on a wooden chair by her trailer, peeling a mountain of potatoes into a bowl of water. She had watched his approach and the children's greeting without any comment other than to shout to the dog to shut up.

'Get your dad,' she ordered now, and a child scurried off obediently. Zilpah waved her knife at Prescott. 'What have you got a long face for, then?'

'I'm sorry to have to disturb you again,' he faltered. 'It's just something's come up . . .'

'Dan told you all he knew.' Her fingers continued to work busily. Another potato plopped into the bowl.

'You're doing enough of those to feed an army,' said Prescott, sidetracked.

'Hugh said we could help ourselves. He's got 'em in a field over there.' She nodded her head of lank hair in the direction. 'He grew a whole lot of 'em last year. Potatoes is good for you,' added Zilpah. 'Anyway, they fill up if nothing else.'

'The thing is,' Prescott feared he was beginning to sound desperate, 'someone's told us about some possible evidence – a bag, a green bag. It's made like a frog.'

A potato splashed into the bowl. Zilpah reached for the next one, watching him, silent.

'You haven't seen a bag like that lying around anywhere out here?' Prescott waved at the fields around them. 'Like as if someone had lost it.'

Zilpah's gaze took in the sweep of the landscape. 'No,' she said simply. 'I don't go walking around much, anyway. I got bad feet.'

Prescott's gaze was drawn to the feet in question. They were stockingless, swollen and thrust into a pair of orthopaedic sandals.

'I can't do nothing about my weight,' said Mrs Smith calmly, adding to the potato pool. 'I was born big. My mother is big. My sisters are all big. At the end, my grandma had got so big they couldn't get her out of her trailer.'

'Really?' asked Prescott, appalled.

That gained him another shake of the potato knife. 'Nothing wrong with being big so long as you feel well with it. My living grandma is never ill. My mum is never ill. My sisters aren't. I'm not. If I was to go on one of them diets, like as not I'd start catching things. Anyway, diets wouldn't work. I'm just big by nature.'

Mrs Smith twisted on the wooden chair which looked hopelessly small beneath her, and pointed out across the fields towards woodlands. 'My dead grandma's buried out there somewhere.'

'I hope no one digs her up, then!' blurted Prescott discourteously. 'We'd have to investigate.'

Zilpah uttered what sounded like 'Pshaw!'

To his relief, Prescott saw Danny approaching.

'All right, Sergeant?' asked Danny amiably, but his gaze was wary.

Prescott repeated his apology for bothering them again and explained his quest for a green bag shaped like a frog.

'Who'd want something like that?' asked Danny. 'Sounds daft to me.'

'Yes, but have you seen anything like it? More to the point, was there a bag like that hanging on a tree on the embankment when you found the body?'

'Never had time to notice,' Danny returned. 'Once I found poor Mrs Franklin, my mind was what you might call all took up with that.'

'A person who found it,' Prescott said carefully, 'might've thought someone else had thrown it away, that no one wanted it. It wouldn't be stealing to take it. It'd just be finding a bit of rubbish someone had chucked out and making good use of it.'

'Totting,' said Danny. 'Zilpah's dad used to do a bit of that, didn't he, Zil?'

'Rag-and-bone man all his life,' said Zilpah. 'I was a dab hand at sorting the rags when I was no older than those kids there.' She indicated her own brood who'd assembled, drawn by the return of Prescott whom they seemed to consider some sort of exotic beast escaped from a menagerie.

'Scrap metal, now,' said Danny. 'That used to be a good business. Bric-a-brac, too. Used to be able to pick up some good stuff – brass, china, odd bit of Sheffield plate. But you don't get the quality items now, not just going round the houses. Them fellows after the antiques has been there before you, and anyway, people take their own rubbish to the local tip. Searching the tip used to be a good way of finding useful stuff but now most places has got some council feller watching over it all from a little hut. Seems like no one can make an honest living.'

All this was getting a long way from a bag shaped like a green frog. But I wasn't, thought Prescott grimly, born yesterday. 'So you haven't got it and you've never seen it. Is that what you're saying?'

'Reckon that's what I said.'

No, thought Prescott, it wasn't what you said. You've told me a dozen things I don't want to know, but that bag is worrying you.

He drew breath with renewed confidence. 'It wouldn't have been stealing to have taken the bag and kept it, but on the other hand, not to hand it over when it might be key evidence in a murder inquiry, that's another matter. The police are very anxious to find that bag.'

'Well, you knows your business, I suppose,' said Danny to this.

'Yes, I do,' returned Prescott. 'And I'm going to have to ask to take a look inside your trailer. Sorry.'

He'd been fully aware what he was asking. The Smiths froze. Zilpah sat with her hands in her lap, still holding the knife. Danny simply stood in front of Prescott. Only the children, who'd retreated to play with the dog which was always tied up, were moving figures in the background.

'That's my home,' said Danny quietly.

Prescott flushed. 'Yes, I appreciate that. Look, I've been sent out to take a look. It won't take a minute.'

''Tisn't a matter of whether it takes you one minute or twenty. It's my home and I've a right to privacy in my home, same as you or anyone else.'

'Look, Danny,' Prescott said, 'let's do this the easy way. I take a look round inside the trailer and then I get on my way. You haven't got anything to hide, have you?'

'I got no green bags in there, made like frogs or anything else.'

'So why not let me just look? I do have a warrant, you know. But I'd rather we kept it friendly.'

'Nothing friendly about forcing your way uninvited into a man's home,' said Danny obstinately.

Prescott put a hand to his inner breast pocket. 'I was hoping you wouldn't insist on it.' He handed it over.

Smith took it but handed it on at once to his wife. She wiped her hands on her skirt and opened it up. They all waited while Zilpah read through it.

She folded it up and handed it back to her husband who returned it to Prescott.

'You won't find nothing,' Zilpah said. 'We've never been in trouble with the law. We mind our own business. Because we don't live in a house and pay them council taxes doesn't mean we've not got the same rights as others. But if you've got to look, then go on.'

Prescott climbed up into the trailer, Danny at his heels. It was, as he'd fully expected it to be, immaculate, a little gem of a place and crowded with every sort of knick-knack and ornament. The walls were lined with decorative plates, each fixed firmly so as not to come loose when the trailer was on the move. Linen was edged with hand-crocheted lace, the velvet cushions hand-smocked. But short of taking it to bits, finding something in it wouldn't be easy. He indicated some overhead lockers and asked for them to be opened. Danny, silent, opened them. Neatly packed-away clothing and linen. No green bag.

Prescott worked his way through family possessions, foodstuffs, clothing, in growing embarrassment, his hands sweating.

'Fair enough,' he said at last to Danny. 'I don't see anything.'

'Not right by my wife,' said Danny. 'Not right looking into all her stores and such. Messing with her clothes.'

'I'm sorry, Danny. It wasn't my idea.'

Feeling the family's combined gaze on him as he walked away towards his parked car, Prescott decided that if any more questioning of the Smiths was to be done, someone else could do it. Ginny Holding could handle it. He hadn't been able to help but feel a touch ashamed at going through their stuff, although he knew that, as a police officer, he ought to have got over qualms of that sort long ago. But his dissatisfaction wasn't merely with having been handed an unpleasant task and being made to look a clumsy oaf. His dissatisfaction came in part from a sense, also born of being a police officer, that he'd missed something. Or to put it another way, that he'd been made a bloody fool of.

Markby, driving slowly along the narrow road towards Fox Corner, was feeling rather more cheerful. He always did as soon as he got out of his office. He'd never been happy at a desk. It had always seemed to him an injustice that, if you did well in the police force, they promptly took you from a job you liked and were good at, and promoted you to a job you didn't want and, as a result, did grudgingly.

It was a nice day. The sky was clear, the roads empty, trees beginning to come into leaf. He braked to avoid colliding with a wood pigeon sitting in the middle of the road. The pigeon took off and insisted on flying at windscreen height directly ahead of him for some yards before turning in its lumbering way and flapping off towards woodland. Here were the first buildings of Fox Corner. Such a small place was it that they were only a stone's throw from the last buildings. He parked and got out.

'Good morning,' he said to an ancient leaning on a gate.

The old man looked him up and down with unconcealed interest. 'You'll be wanting furniture, I suppose?'

'What makes you say that?'

'No other reason anyone comes here.' The old fellow pointed to a stone barn a short way off. 'You'll find him in there. I reckon he must do a tidy business. There's always folk coming out here to see him anyway!' He chuckled hoarsely. It turned into a fit of coughing.

'Wally!' called a voice from within the cottage. 'You want to get back in here and take some of that linctus doctor give you!'

Wally turned and shuffled indoors. Markby walked on to the barn from which there was certainly sound of activity. He glanced up at the sign advertising the furniture workshop and noted, in small print below it, the name Peter Burke. Markby walked through the open doors.

A young man was moving pine planks, stacking them neatly at the rear of the area. He caught sight of Markby as he turned to fetch the next lot, and stopped. 'Yes?' he asked warily.

'Hullo,' returned Markby. 'Sorry to disturb you. You're Peter Burke? Your name's outside on your sign. My name's Markby, as in Superintendent Markby, I'm afraid. Could I have a word?'

'Superintendent?' The young man dusted his hands together and eyed Markby curiously. 'Aren't you a bit high-powered to be footslogging round?'

'They let me out occasionally,' said Markby. 'This is routine and we're very short-handed. We're making inquiries concerning the death of a farmer's wife, Mrs Sonia Franklin.'

Burke nodded. 'Everybody wants to know about that.' He sounded bitter.

'Everybody?' Markby asked suspiciously. 'You've had the press here?'

'Not yet. Had a woman here yesterday, asking, she said, about furniture. I'm not daft. She wanted to know if I'd ever met Sonia and I told her, yes, I had. Sonia'd been here to order new kitchen furniture. She hadn't actually settled on anything so I hadn't started work. Just as well. I suppose they won't want it now.'

'This woman asking questions,' asked Markby with sinking heart. 'Tall? Bobbed brown hair?'

'That's right. Turned out I'd met her before, actually, though I didn't remember her. She's a friend of an ex-girlfriend of mine.' He frowned. 'Don't tell me she's a plainclothes copper. I don't remember Jane having any mates in the police.'

'If we're talking about Meredith Mitchell, no, she's not a police officer,' said Markby.

'That's the name. I did think it odd. Jane's a teacher and most of her chums are, too. You know this Meredith Mitchell, then?'

'Yes, very well. She's not a teacher. She's a – a civil servant.'

To himself Markby was thinking, I should have known when she told me she was going to that inquest, she was going to start ferreting around. But what on earth brought her out here to this place?

'Look, if you've got time, perhaps you could tell me what you told your other visitor?' he suggested.

'That won't take long. You can come in the office – or I live in the little cottage round the back. I'll lock up here and we'll go there.'

Burke's cottage looked to Markby like a Munchkin home. Being tall himself, he stooped awkwardly to get his head under the lintel and then narrowly missed an old beam when he unwisely tried to straighten up inside.

'It gets a tad roomier as you get further in,' said Burke. 'Over there.'

The cottage had no entrance hall or lobby. One walked straight into an open-plan living area. Though it was untidy, the furnishings mostly appeared to have been made by Burke himself and had quality and style. The kitchen area was more cluttered and no one had washed up, Markby guessed, since the previous day.

'What's upstairs?' he asked.

'One bedroom, a shower room and loo. I know it's not much more than a rabbit hutch, but it suits me.'

'You live alone, then?' He didn't expect Burke to deny it. Two people couldn't exist here and stay sane.

Burke was nodding. 'I used to live with Jane in Bamford, but when we split up I moved out here. I already owned the place, had my workshop in the barn. The cottage was derelict but I fixed it up. Want a beer? Or don't you drink on duty?'

'I'd like a beer. Thanks.'

Burke went to the fridge and brought back a bottle of French beer which he opened and handed his guest, and one for himself. He threw himself down on a rug-covered divan under the window, put the beer to his lips, drank deeply, and asked, 'Why is everyone interested in Fox Corner?'

'It's normal, in inquiries of this sort, for us to go knocking on doors. Out here the doors are further apart than usual. Did Sonia Franklin come here often?'

'A few times, don't ask me how many.'

The young man's manner was casual, but then Markby wasn't his first visitor and he'd had time to rehearse what he was going to say. The superintendent felt another niggle of annoyance directed towards Meredith as he looked round the room. Not that she ever set out to interfere as such. But talking to witnesses, especially before the police got to them, was just not on. Supposing, of course, that this young man was some kind of a witness. Well, he was. He'd known the dead woman, she'd been here— Ah, thought Markby. Here, as in the workshop, enquiring about furniture? Or here, in this doll's house?

'Did Mrs Franklin ever come in here?' he asked his host, gesturing at their surroundings.

Burke, beer bottle half raised to his mouth, retorted, 'Isn't that rather a leading question? Why should she come in here? My office is out in the barn.'

'You invited *me* in here,' Markby pointed out. 'She might have expressed interest in seeing the place. It's . . .' he sought for a word, 'quaint.'

'It's very old, you know. Upstairs, when I took down some plaster, I expected to find a beam frame, but I found whole tree branches with wattle and daub between. I reckon this place was originally a shepherd's bothy. You know, just branches thrown together and tied.

Then, later, someone put walls round it and a roof on top. Ought to be a listed building, this.'

'And did Sonia ever go upstairs in the spirit of historical research?'

'You've got a bloody cheek,' Burke said. He put down the empty beer bottle.

'But you were expecting me to ask,' Markby returned. 'And you didn't bring me in here for no reason – or just to give me a talk on medieval home construction.'

Burke gave a short laugh. 'See why they made you a superintendent! Yes, all right. I've had time to think over what I'd say if the police came. At first, I was too upset at the ghastly news to think straight at all. Then I considered just not making matters worse by telling you anything which might upset the Franklin family. Besides, it concerns my private business. You don't have any right to know that. But after that woman Meredith came snooping round–'

Markby raised an eyebrow.

'–I decided that if anyone did come, I'd tell them exactly how it was and let them get on with it. I don't have anything to hide. I'm not going to lie. I'm not ashamed of how I felt and still feel about Sonia.' He stared at his visitor defiantly.

'I see. How did it start? When she came to look at some furniture designs?'

'Yes. She—' Burke hesitated. 'I wouldn't say this to some people and certainly not to some coppers. But you seem reasonably intelligent and not insensitive. Sonia walked into my workshop one morning. It was raining. She had a headscarf on and she pulled it off and shook out her hair. I knew straight away she was the one woman I'd been looking for and never found till then. Sorry, if that sounds corny, but that's the way it was. I thought, that's it. Call it love, call it chemistry, call it what you like. I didn't know who she was, her name, where she came from, what she wanted. I had no way of knowing whether she'd ever be interested in me. None of that made any difference. She was the woman I wanted, would always want. Does any of that make any sense to you or does it sound as if I've been stewing up the magic mushrooms?'

'It makes perfect sense to me,' said Markby soberly.

Burke leaned against the windowsill behind him. 'She was married, of course. Hadn't been married all that long, to a farmer, the chap over at Hazelwood Farm. She wasn't happy. Perhaps I took advantage of that, but if I did, it wasn't because I was selfish. It was because I knew we belonged together.'

'And you started an affair?'

'Yes. I'd have asked her to leave her husband, but I could hardly suggest she move in here!'

Burke put his hands to his face and when he removed them, said, 'Those couple of months were the happiest of my life. She was a wonderful person. When I heard she was dead I thought at first I couldn't go on without her, knowing I'd never see her again. It seemed incredible that she wouldn't turn up, as she did sometimes, at odd moments of the day. I kept believing she must walk in through the door. When whatshername, Meredith, came, well, I was half out of my mind by then and I almost thought Sonia had come back. People talk about having been to hell and back. That's where I've been. Down at the bottom of a great dark pit. And now?' Burke shrugged. 'Now I'm in a sort of limbo. I feel like an observer, like I'm watching myself sit here and talk to you. I'm numb.'

'You're very shocked,' said Markby. 'If you cared for her that much, that's to be expected.'

Burke's mouth twisted mirthlessly. 'And now,' he said, 'you're going to ask me if I killed her.'

'Did you?'

'No. I couldn't have killed anyone so full of life who meant so much to me.'

'Even if she'd tried to break off the affair?'

'Whatever she'd done,' Burke said fiercely. 'But she wasn't trying to put an end to our relationship, far from it. I think she depended on it. It was her lifeline. You've no idea how wretched she was at the farm.'

'When did you last see her?'

Burke's vehemence drained out of him. In a muffled voice, he said, 'The day before – before . . . I saw her on Tuesday.'

'The day before she was murdered?'

'Yes. Do you have to be so blunt?'

'I do,' Markby told him, 'because there mustn't be any misunderstanding regarding what you mean to say and what I think you say. Who told you she died on Wednesday night? In fact, who told you she'd died?'

The other man glared at him. 'If you must know, it was Wally Squires. He's an old boy who lives in one of the cottages just before you get to my workshop. He spends his days leaning on his gate watching the world go by, such as it does here at Fox Corner. Can't blame the old fellow, I suppose. He can't get about much. But he came stomping down here on his stick fast enough to tell me about Sonia.'

Burke looked thoughtful. 'He doesn't miss much, old Wally. He'd seen Sonia come here. He probably guessed we had something more than an interest in kitchen furniture between us. Anyway, he couldn't wait to get down here and tell me.' Burke adopted an enthusiastic but quavering elderly voice. '*They found her in the bushes over by the railway. She'd been there all night, they reckon! What was she doing in them bushes, anyway?*' His voice returned to normal. 'Old brute. Stood there watching me, waiting for my reaction.'

Markby got up and took his empty beer bottle to the kitchen area where he stood it on the cluttered draining board with a collection of others. 'Thanks for this.' He turned. 'I'll send out an officer to take a statement, if that'll be all right with you?'

'You can send someone. I don't know what I've got to say to go in any statement. When I saw her Tuesday she was in very good spirits. She'd been into Bamford to do a bit of shopping and she stopped off here about half eleven on her way home. She didn't stay long.' Burke gave Markby a dry look. 'Not long enough to go upstairs and admire the medieval house construction or anything else. Just to say hullo and have a cup of coffee.'

'So put that in your statement and anything else you may think relevant.'

Burke got up and came with him to the door. As his visitor stooped to get under the lintel, Burke said, 'I did love her. I do still. And if I find he killed her, then you'd better get him in custody quick for his own protection.'

'Who?' Markby turned and looked back into the cottage. Because of the vagaries of its construction, he couldn't see Burke's face, only his body from neck down, on the other side of the door space.

'Hugh Franklin,' Burke's voice said, as it seemed, from out of the wattle-and-daub wall.

CHAPTER ELEVEN

For the cornershop of yesteryear, today read neighbourhood filling station.

Meredith, casting back her mind to a fuzzy, sun-bathed childhood past, remembered her father driving the family car into their village petrol station. It had been run by a portly man in a grubby, oil-stained, blue boilersuit. His name was Mr Perrot, and his fingernails in particular had always fascinated Meredith, so black and dirt-filled they could surely never have been got clean.

Either Mr Perrot or a spindly young man who addressed him as 'Dad' – although apparently, the child Meredith had gathered from listening to adult conversation, there was some doubt about that – dispensed the fuel and took the money. Her father dropped the coins into Mr Perrot's grimy palm from as good a distance as was practical. The garageman would then vanish inside the ramshackle former bungalow behind the pumps which acted both as office premises and general storage area, to re-emerge with the change. Mr Perrot wasn't keen on giving change and always demanded the customer come up with the right money, sulkily declaring he couldn't be expected to return anything bigger than a pound note. He refused to handle cheques. Customers weren't keen on Mr Perrot's pound notes as they inevitably bore the Perrot thumbprint along with the Bank of England's chief cashier's signature. All the customers must have been relieved when the pound note gave way to the pound coin. Mr Perrot had probably viewed that development, as he viewed any proposed alteration to his way of life, with deep suspicion.

Then had come the day when Mr Perrot, under pressure from a spanking new filling station which had opened up only a quarter of a mile away, had modernised. He'd opened up the small front room in the erstwhile bungalow by dint of putting in a door where there'd been a boarded-up bay window. Within he'd installed a counter and an electrically operated till. Behind the counter had been a shelf on which stood a small selection of cigarettes, guarded by Mr Perrot's bottle-blonde daughter-in-law, who was cashier. A selection of motoring necessities filled another shelf beneath which – at suitable times of the year – Mr Perrot stacked sacks of BBQ charcoal. The greatest novelty of all had been a carousel from which dangled packets of boiled sweets. Meredith remembered standing in front of it as her father paid Mrs Perrot junior, fascinated by the colours of the barley sugars, the fruit flavours, the lemon sherbets, the striped mints.

'Come along, you don't want any of those!' her father had always said briskly, marching his young daughter out. It was a decision he'd made on her behalf without reference to her. The child Meredith longed to take down a packet, not to eat, but simply to have – all those wonderful shiny semitransparent shapes like giant marbles, orange, lurid pink, acid yellow. 'Ruin your teeth,' said her father.

Oddly, Mr Perrot had never, as far as anyone knew, set foot in this new-fangled 'shop'. He had retired to a corrugated structure to the rear of the bungalow, there to devote his time to repairs and get himself, presumably, grubbier than ever.

Meredith wondered sadly what had happened to Mr Perrot's independent and idiosyncratic filling station as the years had gone by. Probably it had long gone, or been transformed into something bright, smart and shining, a franchise of some multinational chain.

Looking round her local service station, where she was currently standing, it seemed to be rivalling the nearest supermarket. Cold drinks, soft drinks, hot drinks if you wanted one and a Cornish pasty to go with it, tinned groceries, milk, a delicatessen, newspapers or if you fancied a less depressing read, a selection of paperback romances. Even a stack of wire baskets to put all these things in as the customer shopped in earnest. Mr Perrot could never have coped with all this. But it was useful, no denying it, not only to the modern traveller, but to the modern residential inhabitant for whom the service station was often also the nearest store.

She picked up a carton of milk, a packet of soft rolls and two tins of soup and made her way to the cash desk.

A woman was already there, presenting a credit card to pay for fuel just acquired at one of the pumps to the cheery youth who presided over the till. Mr Perrot would never have recognised credit cards but had almost certainly retired before their appearance. Just as well. Meredith, her arms wrapped round her purchases, took her place behind her. Queuing in orderly manner, she thought, was something built into the British, a gene of some sort. On the other hand, so was refusing to carry a wire basket round the shelves when so few items were involved.

'There you go!' said the cheery youth, handing the bill and credit card back to the woman.

The woman turned, looked mildly surprised and said, 'Hullo. Meredith, isn't it?'

'Bethan!' returned Meredith, startled, adding for want of anything better, 'How are you?'

She'd no idea what chain of circumstances had brought Bethan Talbot here at this time. Sod's law at work again, she thought. Now was a moment, if any, to wish she weren't standing here in jeans and an old cardigan, holding what was obviously her meagre lunch. Bethan was smartly turned out, no business suit this time, but pale fawn slacks and matching polo-neck silk sweater. Sunglasses were perched fashionably atop her head to hold back her neatly groomed hair. Meredith could feel the other woman's critical gaze take in her own dishevelled appearance. She hoped she was wrong in discerning a hint of pity in it.

'Excuse me!' she said robustly, and dumped the tins, milk and bread rolls on the counter.

We're not all fashion plates, are we? Since when did you fill up your car here, Ms Talbot? These last two remarks buzzed furiously in Meredith's head, but remained unasked.

'How're you, then? What have we got here?' asked the cheery youth, letting it be known to all within earshot that Meredith normally did her shopping there. 'Not gone up to the big smoke today? Don't usually see you here until the evening.'

That was another thing about the forecourt shop. It stayed open to all hours, a boon to returning commuters.

'I'm taking a few days' holiday,' said Meredith. Bethan had moved away and was loitering by the ice-cream trough. 'Relaxing!' Meredith said loudly, for Bethan's benefit.

'All right for some!' said the youth. 'Two pounds forty-nine. Do you want a bag for that?'

'I've got one somewhere.' Meredith fished a crumpled plastic carrier from her jeans pocket. If she was on the way to looking like a bag lady in Bethan's eyes, she might as well finish the job.

Bethan was by the exit doors, clearly intent on waylaying Meredith, and there was no getting past her.

'Do you need a lift home with that, Meredith? Or have you got your car?' Her voice was coolly kind. There was no sign of the simmering temper which she'd exhibited after the inquest.

Why not, thought Meredith, just ask whether I've got a car at all? 'Only a five-minute walk, thanks. I can manage.'

The automatic doors hissed open and they both stepped outside. That left little room for a man coming in, who winced as the plastic bag containing Meredith's tins of soup cracked against his knee.

'Surely I can drop you off, anyway? As it happens, running into you is a bit of luck,' insisted Bethan. The man with the sore knee looked as if he felt quite differently.

'Why?' asked Meredith not very politely, though she contrived to give the man an apologetic glance.

'I've been thinking about poor Sonia. I really feel the need to talk to someone.' Bethan's smoothly regular features, framed in tangle-free gleaming wings of hair, eyes painted with the sort of mascara that never ran, gazed into Meredith's. They were about the same height.

Trapped. Meredith put a good face on it. 'Oh, I see. Well, why don't you come back and have a cup of coffee with me?'

'You're sure you've got time to spare?' The hesitation was false but graciously done. Meredith was sure that even if she'd been racing out of there at top speed on her way to an emergency medical appointment, Bethan would still have latched on like a limpet.

'Yes, of course. I'm on leave. You heard me tell the boy at the till, didn't you?' Meredith wasn't into playing silly games this morning, even if Bethan was.

'Right, this way, then.' Bethan swooped across the forecourt, hair glowing in the sunshine like a helmet of golden fire.

Meredith clumped crossly in the wake of the immaculate figure towards a well-polished Mercedes, thinking sourly that the tax advisory business must be going well. She scrambled into the capacious passenger seat and managed to fix the seat belt despite the plastic carrier on her lap with its contents of hard edges and solid shapes. She noticed, as she did so, that her nails needed a file and buff up. Bethan's hand, reaching out to the ignition, displayed beautifully polished coral nails with natural varnish cuticles. Meredith sank into her seat, clasping her plastic carrier to her chest, and gave directions to Station Road.

'What a sweet little porch,' said Bethan, as they drew up before Meredith's end-of-terrace cottage. 'Have you just had it added?'

'Yes, George hasn't finished yet. He's got to tile the floor.' Meredith pushed open the front door and indicated the entry to the sitting room. 'Let me just drop these things in the kitchen. I'll bring the coffee. I don't need any help.'

Bethan hadn't offered any, but was probably just about to. The sitting room wasn't particularly tidy, but the kitchen was worse and Meredith had no intention of letting her see it.

When she got back with the cafetiere and a couple of mugs, Bethan was draped elegantly over the sofa and inspecting her surroundings. 'You really are awfully cosy here.'

Suspecting this meant 'small and cramped', Meredith nevertheless managed a smile and dumped the tray on an occasional table.

'There's nothing worse,' said Bethan unexpectedly, 'than being burdened with someone else's troubles. But you were at the inquest.' Her tone indicated that if Meredith had already shown that much interest, she oughtn't to quibble now.

'I was,' Meredith admitted. 'What's troubling you? I know you're suspicious of Hugh Franklin, but I'm afraid you'll have to kick your heels while the police look into things.'

'Mmm,' said Bethan, cupping her long, tapering fingers round a coffee mug. 'But I've been told you have a long-term thing going with the senior copper in charge of all this. Alan Markby, his name is, so I believe.'

'I know what his name is,' retorted Meredith. 'And yes, he's a friend. I don't know what your informant meant by "a long-term thing". In any case, it doesn't mean I have inside information, or if I had any, I'd pass it on. You're not the first person I've told that. People seem to think I'm in Alan's confidence. I'm not.'

'Good God, no, I wouldn't expect you to tell me *secrets*!' Bethan looked convincingly shocked.

'That's OK, then. Because I don't know any.'

Bethan sighed. 'Have you lived here long in Bamford?'

'Not very long. I rented a place out at Pooks Common before I bought this house. I used to work abroad in the consular service. Now

I'm stuck at a Foreign Office desk and have to commute up to London daily. I need to be near the station.'

'If you get out of the place every day and go to London, that makes Bamford just about bearable, I suppose. I can't stand it here, though I've never actually lived in the town. I rented an office in the centre when Simon and I were together, but we lived out in the sticks in a cottage Simon bought from the farm estate.'

'Where's your office now?' Meredith asked with interest.

'Home and office are both in Cheltenham. I just moved everything, lock, stock and barrel, when Simon and I broke up. Most of my clients stayed loyal. I made it clear I was prepared to drive down and discuss things with them if necessary. That's why I'm here today. Generally it's not necessary. They give me their tax return forms and relevant information. I sort it all out and send it back. Frankly, self-assessment has proved a boon to people like me and I'm not short of work.' Bethan set down her mug. 'I've been wondering about that friend of yours, the teacher. She was at the inquest, too. She went for me because I spoke my mind about Hugh. It struck me she was a bit more interested in him and the daughter than one might expect. She's not sweet on him, is she?'

'Look,' Meredith said exasperated, 'isn't that something you ought to ask her? I only know that Jane is naturally concerned about the welfare of a young pupil.'

Bethan raised a hand. 'Don't get shirty. I'm not gossiping. I'm here for a really serious reason. You see, I introduced Sonia Lambert to Hugh.' She paused. 'Funny, I still can't think of her as Sonia Franklin. Nor can I understand how she came to think of herself in that way. You see, I hadn't expected her to be smitten with him. When she first showed signs of it, I honestly never dreamed she'd got marriage in mind. I thought, you know, it was just a fling. Sonia liked fun. Simon hadn't a clue what was really going on. It knocked both of us back on our heels when they turned up one morning on the doorstep, hand in hand and grinning at us like a pair of Cheshire cats. Hugh wore what I suppose was his best suit. It was probably his only suit. Sonia had a hat swathed in tulle, one she'd worn to Ascot once. The sight of that hat alone made the whole thing look like a prank of some sort. But they asked if we'd like to come and witness them tie the knot at the local register office. They'd fixed it all up without telling anyone a word but they expected us to be witnesses! That would be Sonia's idea of a joke.

She'd do almost anything for a laugh or to surprise someone. She had a low boredom threshold. This time the laugh was on us. Simon and I weren't dressed for the occasion and they hadn't allowed time for us to change. We had to go as we were, Sim in an old tweed jacket and me in jeans and a sweatshirt. We looked more like a fancy-dress parade than a wedding party. Even the registrar looked startled.'

'What about the child?' asked Meredith. 'Was she there?'

'She was waiting in the car, looking miserable, poor little tyke.' Bethan shrugged. 'What can you do in a case like that? Hugh is Sim's brother. Sonia was my oldest friend. We couldn't say, "We don't approve, in fact we think you're both nuts and we're not going to give any support to such a barmy undertaking!" It would have been ridiculously priggish. Anyway, Simon and I were on the point of going our separate ways, so neither of us felt we were in a position to offer advice. I wish I had, though. I wish I'd had the courage to say to Sonia, "Look, a joke is a joke, but this is going too far. Why not wait a month or two and see how you feel then?" I know Simon wishes he'd spoken up, too. But we were both caught completely off balance.'

Something, thought Meredith, I doubt happens to either of you very often. But Bethan had got her thinking. 'If Sonia liked fun so much, I agree, it's odd she should pick on Hugh. But then, people do make odd matches. Sometimes they work. Hugh told me his wife had worked for a PR firm in London. She must have missed that, too.'

'Oh, I don't know about that.' Bethan looked slightly uncomfortable. 'She'd taken redundancy. She was technically out of a job when she met Hugh.'

'I suppose that could make a difference. What's the name of the firm? Would I know it?'

'I doubt it. It's not the biggest. It's called Dixon Dubois. I gather they lost some clients and they found themselves without enough contracts to support all the staff. Someone had to go and on the last in, first out principle, it was Sonia. But she could've found another job. She wasn't unemployable, for crying out loud. Hugh wasn't a last resort in that sense, if that's what you're getting at.'

'I'm not getting at anything,' said Meredith soothingly. Bethan was becoming distinctly irritated. 'But I think you are and that's why you waylaid me in the shop. Why should you be worried about Jane?'

'Isn't it obvious? Don't ask me what Hugh's got.' Bethan looked as puzzled as she sounded. 'As far as I'm concerned he's totally charmless.

But first Sonia, now this Jane person. I wouldn't like to think your friend had committed herself in any way to Hugh. If she has, she's likely to get hurt, and I don't mean just emotionally. Look at what happened to Sonia.'

'Honestly, Bethan,' Meredith told her impatiently, 'you can't go round accusing Hugh like this. You could find yourself in hot water. You're a businesswoman. You don't want to get yourself sued for defamation, or whatever it would be called in court. If Hugh heard what you've been saying about him, he'd hit the roof and I wouldn't blame him. I don't suppose Simon would like it much either, and don't forget the little girl. She'll be the main victim of any vicious gossip.'

Her words were received by Bethan with a dry smile. 'Hugh's heard about it. He's heard it from me. I told him what I thought at the inquest. Hugh won't sue. Believe me, I'm sure of that. He couldn't afford the publicity in the circumstances, partly because of the child, and partly because people living in glasshouses shouldn't throw stones, as they say.'

'If you're taking advantage of Hugh's wish to protect his daughter to give yourself *carte blanche* to insult him, that strikes me as pretty mean. The glasshouses theory applies to you, too, Bethan. At the very least, you're going to feel pretty foolish if the police end up charging someone else with Sonia's murder. Hugh would be within his rights to demand an abject public apology, and don't count on his not going to law.'

Bethan tilted her chin aggressively, something of her former snap and temper creeping back into her manner. 'I didn't speak up when Sonia made a fool of herself over Hugh and I'll have to live with that. Being tactful didn't help then and being sorry doesn't help much now. But I'm not going to stay silent and watch your friend do the same thing. One person on my conscience is enough, thanks.'

'I still think you're taking it too far,' Meredith said as reasonably as she could. 'Look here, Bethan, I recognise you're upset about Sonia and you blame yourself, although it really wasn't your fault. You couldn't have stopped Sonia falling in love with Hugh. But in any case, I think you're worrying about Jane unnecessarily. She's only helping out at the farm because of Tammy. It's half term this week. Next week Jane will be back teaching and she won't have the time to bother about Hazelwood Farm.'

Bethan gathered up her soft leather shoulderbag. 'That's all right then. I hope you're right.' Unexpectedly, she added, 'I suspect you don't like me much, Meredith, but frankly I don't care whether you do or don't. I'm not looking for a fan club. I just don't want to see someone else's life ruined.'

Her honesty, and the fact that however wrongly she might be going about things, Bethan's intentions were good, impelled Meredith to an equal display of generosity. 'I didn't mean to be rude to you, and I'm sorry if I sounded it. Please stay to lunch. I do have other food than tins of soup.'

Bethan laughed. 'Thanks, but I can't. I've got a couple of clients to see this afternoon. Thanks for letting me come and bend your ear.'

'I'll sound Jane out, but I really think you're fretting over nothing. On a totally different subject,' Meredith added as she saw her guest to the door, 'and at the risk of sounding even ruder than I have already, I wonder if I could ask who does your hair. She's given you a fantastic cut. Mine needs doing badly and I'm prepared to travel to get it done by a proper stylist.'

Bethan's pale cheeks flushed. 'Oh, I'm sorry, I can't help. A friend cuts it for me. She's trained and all that, but she doesn't work professionally now. She just does it for a few friends. It helps me because she trims it of an evening when I'm more easily free than during the day.'

She hurried down the front path. Meredith stood in the doorway and raised a hand in farewell salute as the Mercedes glided away up Station Road. After a few minutes thinking it through, she went out to the kitchen, opened up one of the tins of soup, and picked up the phone to punch out the number of Jane Brady's mobile.

'Chef's gone off,' said the barman. 'Can do you a round of sandwiches, if that's any good?'

Markby and Pearce had arrived late at the pub. By the time Pearce had returned from Cherry Tree Farm and Markby from Fox Corner, it had been two o'clock and now it was half-past. They settled for the sandwiches, Markby for ham, Pearce for tuna and sweetcorn, and took their pints to the inglenook fireplace. At least the bar was empty now after the lunchtime rush and having the place to themselves meant they could talk. The barman had deserted his post, possibly to cut the sandwiches himself.

'They know we're coppers here,' said Pearce. 'You could tell by the look on that barman's face as we walked in. What is it about us?'

'Our furrowed brows and lack of fashion sense, Dave.'

'It can be embarrassing,' continued the clearly aggrieved Pearce. 'I mean, Tessa and I have gone out for an evening and as soon as I appear, there's a sort of chill in the air. Even Tessa's mum has noticed it. "I don't know what it is about you, Dave," she said to us the last time we took the old girl out for a drink. "Have you upset any of these people?" What am I supposed to say to that?'

Markby reflected that since Tessa was in her early twenties, her mother was probably about his age. It made Pearce's use of the term 'old girl' quite unjustified, in his view. He wondered how Pearce referred to him when in private company. It was probably better not to know.

Aloud he said, 'Look on the bright side. We're getting our sandwiches.'

Pearce was unconsoled. 'It's either being ignored or being treated like the man who's come to unblock the drain.'

'Ah!' Light dawned on Markby. 'Is this a reference to the interview you conducted this morning at Cherry Tree Farm?'

'Audience,' said Pearce, 'that's what I got. An audience. You should see that place. It's not a farm, it's a theme park.'

The sandwiches arrived. Markby cautiously inspected the filling of his and decided the ham looked rather good. He couldn't feel the same way about the greyish gunge studded with yellow which oozed from Pearce's sandwiches.

'The woman, Mrs Hayward, is as tough as old boots but the real McCoy. You know, county. The kids are weird. He'd like to be thought an officer and a gentleman, but he overdoes it. It's my opinion,' said Pearce indistinctly through a mouthful of the tuna and sweetcorn mush, 'that he was having a bit of a fling with Sonia Franklin.'

'Hayward was?' Markby, who'd been about to sip from his pint, set it down, startled.

'Put money on it. And his wife knows. He's a good-looking sort of bloke, and smooth, you know, when he wants to be.'

Markby thought all this through. 'That,' he said, 'throws a very curious but undeniably interesting light on things.'

'A bit of adultery's not unusual,' pointed out Pearce in a worldly way. 'And it isn't only the townies up to it. Look at the setup there.

Hugh Franklin dresses in the sort of gear you'd think he'd put on a scarecrow. Mrs Hayward is as sexy as a pair of gumboots. Hugh spends his days in the cowshed. Mrs Hayward spends hers mucking out the horses they keep for the pony trekking. That would have left the other two, their respective partners I mean, free to engage in a spot of extramarital nookie. Probably desperate for it.'

He swallowed, picked up his pint and grinned. 'Mrs Hayward didn't encourage Sonia to visit. Sonia wasn't above, she says, batting her eyelashes at Derry. Sonia was wasting her time, says Derry's missus. I bet.'

'Derry being Mr Hayward.'

'Right, only his name is Desmond; I checked. Not got quite the right ring to it, Desmond. Derry, old bean!' declared Pearce, raising his glass in salute. 'Chin-chin!'

Markby laughed. Then he said, 'Why would Mrs Hayward tell you that – about Sonia fancying Derry? Best to keep off the subject, surely.'

Pearce shook his head. 'Putting down her markers and jumping in ahead of gossip. Just in case we heard it anywhere else.'

'Mmm. Well, here's a bit of gossip for you. Only it's rather more reliable than that, and comes straight from the horse's mouth, as it were. Mrs Sonia Franklin was having an affair with Peter Burke, the fellow who makes the handcrafted furniture at Fox Corner. Burke not only admits it, he wants to talk about it.'

Pearce put down his pint. 'Cripes. Got about a bit, didn't she?'

'So it would seem.' Markby pushed aside his plate and empty glass and lowered his voice, though the barman had vanished again. 'So she was two-timing not only her husband, but each of the two men who were her lovers. One of them could've rumbled it and reacted violently. The thing is, which one?'

A little grudgingly, Pearce said, 'Derry's not stupid. He's invested heavily in that place of theirs. My guess is he owes the banks a packet. He's got to make a success of it. He couldn't run it without his wife. Sonia wouldn't have been any substitute for Mrs Hayward when it came to the business. Sonia was scared of geese. He might've rolled in the hay with Sonia but I don't think he'd have let his heart rule his head. I mean, I don't suppose he really cared about her.'

'Suppose *she'd* cared about *him*? From what you say of him, he might appear an attractive proposition to someone like Sonia, unhappy and bored at Hazelwood. Just suppose she was asking him to divorce his wife? Kicking up a fuss? He might want to silence her.'

'He might,' admitted Pearce. 'What about Burke?'

'Burke was in love,' said Markby drily. 'And that always makes a situation very dodgy.' As I should know, he thought.

Pearce, after a pause, observed, 'Gives Hugh Franklin a heck of a motive, too. She was making a real fool of him.'

'He's still head of the list, I admit. But we've got to put both Hayward and Burke on it, too, now.'

'How did Ginny get on at Hazelwood?' Pearce glanced at the empty bar. 'Shall I see if I can find that bloke and get us another pint?'

'Not for me, thanks. I'd – we'd – better get back. Holding was reasonably satisfied with her trip to Hazelwood, given all the circumstances. Simon Franklin sat in on the interview so he could throw the odd spanner in the works.'

Pearce groaned. 'I can imagine it.'

'I think Holding could cope with that. She's less sure she did so well with the child. She thinks Tammy has some kind of information which she's keeping to herself. This is not to say it's important, but as Holding says, the child herself thinks it's important. I've sent Holding off to London this afternoon.' He glanced at his wristwatch. 'She ought to be arriving about now.'

Pearce made a noise which sounded like 'Huh!' and concentrated on the last of his sandwich.

Markby realised this was a touchy subject and returned to the former conversation. 'You say the Haywards have children?'

Pearce nodded. 'Twins. Identical. They're a secretive pair, too, I'd guess. Lots of glances between them and whispering.'

'Little girls do like secrets,' said Markby, 'if my niece is anything to go by. They go into huddles with their chums, or phone them up, and it's all whispers and giggles and shrieks of protest if an adult heaves into view. Do you think the Hayward twins might share Tammy's secret?'

'Wouldn't surprise me,' said Pearce. 'Wouldn't surprise me a bit.'

Jane opened the door of her flat to Meredith at six that evening. She was wearing dusty jeans and a creased tee-shirt. Meredith thought she looked tired and hoped she wasn't taking on too much at Hazelwood Farm.

'Come in,' she invited. 'I'm sorry I couldn't get back earlier. I put a casserole together and left it in the oven for Tammy and Hugh.'

'Did you want to stay and eat with them?' Meredith asked. 'You needn't have come back just on my account.' She kept her voice casual but Jane's words made her even more uneasy. Suppose Bethan were right? Jane seemed to be getting very involved with the Franklins. Tammy had been the person who'd taken Jane to the farm in the first place, but was it now Hugh who occupied her mind?

'Oh, no,' said Jane. 'I was coming back here anyway. They don't need me sitting over them. I think Hugh and his daughter need some time together on their own, just to talk and be friends. I cornered Hugh before I left and told him so. He grumbled about being tired by the evening. I told him it wouldn't do any harm to take half an hour to play a board game, for example. It'd be relaxing for him. They've got Snakes and Ladders,' added Jane, 'Scrabble and Draughts. I looked in the cupboard. They've got a Monopoly board too, but all the little houses and hotels are lost and some of the cards.'

Meredith had to laugh. 'I'm impressed with your thoroughness. Monopoly takes ages to play and is better with more than two people, so perhaps it's as well half the bits and pieces are lost!'

Jane joined in the laughter. 'I was just going to open a bottle of wine. Good idea?'

'Sounds good to me.'

'The thing is,' Jane confided when the wine had been poured, 'I did find Tammy rather upset. You were quite right about the police interviewing her. They'd sent out a woman officer today. I passed her as she was leaving. But Tammy seems to have coped pretty well. It wasn't that interview which had upset her, as it turned out. Her Uncle Simon sat in on proceedings.'

'Somehow,' said Meredith, 'I can imagine him doing that.' She leaned back and surveyed her surroundings. It was the home of a single woman, similar to flats she'd lived in for years before buying the house in Station Road. Lots of books, a sort of comfortable bachelor untidiness, but with much effort gone into making it bright and comfortable. A patterned throw over the armchair, interesting pictures on the walls, a row of houseplants on the windowsill. A photograph of an elderly couple who looked as though they might be Jane's parents. No photos of Jane and none of the man who'd shared this place with her and for a time shared her life. She wondered how much Jane missed Peter Burke. If, indeed, she missed him at all. What had the flat looked like when Peter had lived here? There was no sign of any male presence here now. It was as if Jane had sponged away all traces of him. Sometimes it was easier to do that to a room than it was to do it to your heart.

'Do we know,' she asked, 'what the policewoman had to say to Tammy?'

'Tammy told her she saw Sonia leave the house that evening, which was helpful.'

'Helpful to Hugh,' Meredith said drily.

'Yes.' Jane bridled, then said awkwardly, 'The fact is, I'm pretty sure that there are things Tammy could have told the police, but didn't. I don't know what they are. She won't tell me. She's hiding something.' Jane sighed.

'Something which might makes things difficult for her father?'

'That's the obvious inference. It doesn't have to be the right one. When I tried to talk to her about it, she got upset. The thing is, at some points in our conversation I was sure she was being quite truthful. At others I thought she might be being, well, tactful. All right, fibbing. She denies hearing Sonia and Hugh quarrel, for example. But that might be true. It's an old house with solid walls. I'm sure she's telling the truth about seeing Sonia leave. It's after that . . .' Jane scowled at her wine. 'Whatever she's hiding happened after that.'

They both sat in silence for a while. 'She may have some reason to believe Sonia came back,' Meredith said slowly. 'I don't mean that she saw Sonia return. But she may have heard someone she thought was Sonia.'

'That's possible; I've thought of that.' Jane looked up and fixed Meredith with a direct look. 'But I think it has to do with the phone call.'

Meredith's wine sloshed dangerously near the rim of her glass. 'What phone call? No one's said anything about a call.'

Jane shook her head vigorously. 'Hugh mentioned it, that's how I know. After Sonia left, Hugh dozed in front of the TV. But he was woken by the telephone ringing out in the hall. Then it stopped. He got the impression Tammy answered it.'

'Have you asked Tammy about this?'

'Yes, she says it was a wrong number. I'm sure she's lying about that.

It seems to me,' Jane said reluctantly, 'there can only be one reason for that.'

'The caller was Sonia,' Meredith supplied. 'It's a possibility.'

'It would make sense.' Jane tossed back her long hair. 'Look, this is what I think might have happened. Sonia stormed out in a rage. She walked a long way. Then she calmed down, but it was dark by then, getting cold. She saw a callbox by the road – or perhaps she went into a pub and phoned Hugh to come and pick her up. Tammy took the message but didn't pass it on because Tammy resented Sonia and the way things were between her father and his new wife. Perhaps Tammy thought it would do Sonia good to walk home. Perhaps Sonia did try and walk home and that's when she met her killer. Or perhaps someone offered her a lift. If that's what happened, then Tammy is eaten up with guilt. Getting her to admit it is going to be very difficult.'

'If that's what happened,' Meredith pointed out, 'then it's a sort of alibi for Hugh. Tammy sounds old enough and bright enough to realise that.'

'Oh, I don't know!' Jane threw up her hands in despair. 'But if it wasn't Sonia on the phone, who was it? Why won't Tammy say?'

'Jane . . .' Meredith hesitated. 'I know you want to help the family, but I have to say this. It sounds to me as if you are getting in very deep. I did warn you about that. Giving the child emotional support is one thing. Taking over running their lives is another.'

'I'm not doing that!' Jane snapped indignantly.

'Making casseroles and ordering Hugh to play Snakes and Ladders with his daughter? That all goes well beyond ordinary support.'

Jane's face had reddened. 'I know what you're getting at, Meredith. You think I'm looking for someone who needs me because Peter made it clear he didn't when he dumped me. So what if I am? It's human to want to feel needed.'

'All right, sorry I spoke!' To change the subject, Meredith added, 'I saw Bethan Talbot today.'

Unfortunately, Jane's agitation increased at this news. 'What's she doing still hanging around?'

'Came to Bamford to see some clients. I met her at the filling station. She came and had a coffee with me. She's worried about you, that you may have fallen for Hugh.'

'Bloody cheek!' fumed Jane. 'What's it to do with her?'

Meredith ran both hands through her hair so that it stood out wildly.

'She's got a point, Jane, and don't jump down my throat. I know she's really got it in for Hugh in a big way, but I'm worried about you, too. I'm the last person to give advice on affairs of the heart. But if you can just put your feelings for Hugh on hold until all this is sorted out, it'd be the best thing for all of you.'

Jane sat up straight and glared at her visitor through her fringe of fair hair. 'I'll handle my feelings, thank you. The only help I want from you is in clearing Hugh's name.'

'What if I don't clear Hugh's name? What if I stir up more mud in the pond? I'll tell you what I've learned. Sonia was in the process of ordering some new furniture from Peter, your ex. She used to pop over there to see him.'

'She was? How do you know?' Jane was taken aback. She blinked at Meredith. 'Are you sure?'

'I went out to Fox Corner and talked to him. He told me. The impression I got was he'd really fallen for her. Sorry.'

'He was terribly upset when I saw him . . .' Jane whispered.

'The thing is, how upset does it make you?'

'I'm not jealous,' Jane said quietly. 'I was dreadfully hurt when Pete left. But I've had time since to realise I wasn't ever the most important element in his life. It's rather humiliating, you know, to find yourself playing second fiddle to joinery.' She managed a wan grin. 'I've come to terms with it. I just hope Pete hasn't done anything stupid.' Hastily she added, 'I don't mean harm Sonia. He wouldn't *kill* anyone. He's not a violent person. I just hope he doesn't make any feelings he had for Sonia so obvious that Hugh finds out. That would be a terrible thing. I don't think Hugh could bear it, not with all the strain he's under.'

Jane beat her clenched fists on her knees. 'I'm not surprised someone killed that woman, you know. She should have been putting her energies into building a relationship with Tammy and working out her problems with Hugh, not fooling around with Pete! But, there, perhaps I shouldn't criticise Sonia. I have to say Hugh can be trying. He's obstinate and sometimes doesn't seem to see the blindingly obvious.'

'Even not noticing if his wife was having an affair?'

'I don't know,' Jane said after a moment. 'If he knew, then he's got the sort of motive that'd be a gift to the police, hasn't he?'

They sat in silence as Meredith waited for Jane to come to terms with the unwelcome idea. Eventually, Jane roused herself and said, 'I did find out what had upset Tammy. She thought I'd quarrelled

164

with her dad.' She blushed a burning crimson as she met Meredith's gaze.

Meredith suppressed her annoyance. 'If you're not keen on the man, Jane, you've got to make it clear to him and to his daughter. Otherwise, there will be heartbreak. You do realise that?'

'Yes. I don't know what I feel about Hugh. Other than that I feel he's innocent, even if it's true that Sonia was having an affair with Peter. He loves Tammy and he loves that farm. I think he loved his first wife very much. He's not perfect and he knows it. He needs help. I don't think cooking him the odd meal and doing a bit of shopping is going to make him think I'm keen on him.' Jane looked embarrassed. 'I think he's too modest for that. Anyway, I'm always telling him off. He probably sees me as a battleaxe of a schoolteacher.'

'Do you still want me to go on sleuthing around? Even if I start turning up more unwelcome information?' Meredith asked.

'Even if it leads to Hugh,' Jane told her quietly. 'In the end, the truth must come out. Only the truth can help – really help.'

'It's my experience,' said Meredith, getting to her feet, 'that the truth sometimes causes an awful lot of trouble.'

CHAPTER TWELVE

Danny Smith, hunched over the crackling embers, his strong brown fingers cradling a can of lager, looked up and smiled to himself. A slight figure, jeans-clad and sweatered, was scrambling determinedly over rutted ground towards the trailer. He waited until she reached him before he gave open recognition of her presence.

'Hullo there,' he said affably. 'Come visiting, have you?'

'Sort of.' Tammy was almost out of breath, perspiring from her efforts and her long hair was tangled from a lost battle with the wind gusting strongly across the open land. Before his appraisal she shuffled her muddy boots, delved in her pocket and produced an elastic band with which she managed to secure her unruly locks. She seemed unwilling to meet his eye.

Something's up! thought Danny. He looked over his shoulder and called, 'Zilpah! We got company!'

Tammy sat down on the turf by his feet. She picked up a piece of half-burned wood that had fallen from the fire, and dropped it back in. It spat sparks as the flames caught it.

'Get your fingers dirty,' said Danny severely. 'Burn 'em, too, if you're not careful.'

She drew back her hand from a second piece of wood and rested her arms on her bent knees. 'I've got a message from Dad. He wants to know if you can work for us tomorrow. Sid's lumbago is still bad. Dad says he'd appreciate it if you could come over and lend a hand.'

'Tell him I'll be there early, never fear.' Danny drained the last of his lager. 'How's your dad getting on then? Coppers been pestering again?'

'A policewoman came this morning to talk to me. I don't know if they've been talking to Dad again. I hope they haven't. I wish they'd

167

leave him *alone!*' Her voice rose in frustration and despair. 'I wish they'd leave us all alone! They won't let us have a funeral for Sonia. Why won't they do that?'

'Beats me,' said Danny.

Zilpah had appeared and been listening. She sniffed. 'They should know better than worry a family in mourning. It's disrespectful. They should let you bury the poor woman, too. Then she and you and your dad can all rest easy.' She bent a shrewd eye on her visitor. 'I've got some of that cola stuff, if you want some. Don't know where the kids have got to. Be back soon, most likely.'

'I came to see Danny and you. I don't want any Coke, thank you very much.'

'Not good for you, those fizzy drinks,' said Danny. 'They give you wind.' He put down his empty beer can and picked up another from the pack by his chair. He pulled the ring to open it and there was a satisfying hiss.

'That doesn't, I suppose?' said his wife to him.

'Another thing, I want to say I'm really sorry about the police bothering you.' The words issued from Tammy in a rush. 'Dad told me. He was really angry about it and so am I. Only Dad doesn't know about my frog bag and that you gave it back to me – and he *mustn't* know!'

'Now see here,' Danny said, 'I've always been good friends with your family and I owe the police no favours. I gave the bag back to you on the quiet because I didn't want you mixed up in whatever was going to happen after I found the poor lady.'

Tammy winced at his mention of the discovery.

'It's your business and I don't want to know anything about it, not how the bag got down there by the railway nor anything else,' Danny went on. 'What Zilpah and I don't know, we can't tell. The coppers know about that bag, though— Hey, hey!'

Tammy's face bore such an expression of terror that Danny was stopped in mid-speech and uttered an exclamation of alarm.

'Don't take on! They don't know it was your bag and they don't know I gave it back to you. But somehow or other they know a bag was down there and they want to find it. They were here looking for it this morning, much good it did them. I didn't let on I knew anything about it. You don't have to worry about me and Zil.'

Tammy whispered, 'Thank you.'

Zilpah had lowered her bulk on to the other chair. 'What was the lady police officer like?'

'She was all right but nosy. She asked about the night Sonia died. I didn't tell her anything, only that I saw Sonia leave the house. That *is* true. I watched Sonia go. I could see she was in a rotten temper from the way she went stamping across the yard. The policewoman kept on about it until Uncle Simon stopped her and made her leave, but I'm sure she'll come back.' Tammy sounded despairing. 'I can't go on saying *nothing!*'

'Now, you don't want to get yourself in a fret,' said Zilpah with a glance at her husband. 'Wait and see what happens.'

'I can't wait and see. Jane came today as well. She's my teacher and she's been helping us. I like Jane and I think Dad likes her, but she asks questions, too.' Tammy looked up at them, jaw set. 'I've got to get away from here. I've got to be where people can't ask me things all the time. When you go, can I come with you? I won't be a nuisance,' she added eagerly, 'I can be useful.'

'Why, whatever would your dad do without you?' exclaimed Zilpah, shocked.

'Dad's got Jane now. He'll be all right.'

Zilpah opened her mouth but her husband caught her eye. She closed her mouth again and waited.

'Well, I suppose you could travel along with us,' said Danny. 'Only you won't get much schooling. Seems a pity after all the money your dad's spent sending you to that posh school.'

Tammy dismissed this objection briskly. 'Oh, that's all right. Dad can use the money for the farm.'

'Very likely he can. But that wasn't what your mum wanted, was it? Your dad told me she was very keen on you going to that St Clare's.'

'Mummy didn't know all this was going to happen,' Tammy muttered. She picked up another stick and poked the fire with it.

'You'd have to eat what we eat, and all,' said Danny, swigging from the beer can.

'I eat anything!' Tammy assured them.

'So do we, and that's what I mean,' said Danny. 'Can't be fussy if you live like us. Got to eat what's there.'

Zilpah gave her husband a suspicious look which he ignored.

'Hedgehogs, now,' said Danny. 'A gypsy delicacy is a hedgehog.'

Tammy looked taken aback, but declared she thought she could eat a hedgehog, if need be. 'It's probably very nice,' she added doubtfully.

'They have fleas, do hedgehogs,' continued Danny. 'Never come across a hedge-pig didn't carry a load of fleas on its back. Mind you, they're all killed in the cooking. We eat other things, too, we find up there in the woods.' Rooks flew over them, heading towards their evening roost. 'Them as well,' said Danny.

Zilpah's face was a picture but she pressed her lips together and managed to keep back the emotions clearly fighting for expression.

'Perhaps,' said Tammy less certainly, 'I could just eat potatoes and vegetables, be a vegetarian gypsy.'

'Gets very cold sleeping out in the winter.' Danny turned to another subject. 'Still, we got remedies for aches and chills. Rubbing goosefat on your chest is very good, ain't it, Zil?'

Zilpah uttered a gurgling sound.

'Perhaps you want to think it over, then?' Danny concluded. 'We're not moving on yet. Police won't let us.'

'Yes, I'll think it over,' said Tammy in a small voice. 'Perhaps I ought to get back and tell Dad you'll be at the farm early.'

'That's the ticket,' said Danny. 'Come again.'

Only when Tammy had left did he dare meet his wife's eye.

'Daniel Smith,' said Zilpah ominously, 'I never heard the like! It's a wonder a bolt of lightning didn't strike you where you sat! I never ate a hedgehog in my life and I doubt very much, somehow, you have either! Goosegrease? Where should I get goosegrease to be rubbing on the kids' chests, even if they took sick, which they never do. I hope,' continued Zilpah in rising ire, 'I look after my family proper and don't have them falling ill on me!'

'Little lass is troubled in her mind,' said Danny placidly. 'She don't need anyone turning her away. Just let her think it through herself. She's got sense. She isn't going to leave her dad all on his own.'

Both Smiths sat in silence for a while. Then Zilpah said quietly, 'There's going to be more trouble over at that farm, Dan. I feel it in my bones. You watch out for yourself when you're working there.'

Danny picked a can from his fast diminishing store and handed it to her. 'Here, cheer yourself up. Things will turn out right.'

She took the can but shook her head, her long earrings swinging to and fro. 'It won't come right till a lot more's gone wrong. That you can count on, Daniel Smith.'

When Meredith returned from her visit to Jane that evening, darkness had already settled in. A car was parked before her house, a man sitting in it. Car and the still silhouette were both familiar. She stooped and tapped on the window.

'Why didn't you go in? You've got your key, haven't you?'

'I haven't been here long. You were out and I was deciding what to do.'

Alan climbed out of the car as he spoke. She wondered whether he was lying and the thought made her uneasy. They had never lied to one another. Certainly she'd never lied to him. She believed he'd never lied to her. But lies come in all shapes and sizes, she thought. Little white lies, lies masquerading as politeness, lies to save hurt or embarrassment.

She led the way into the house, switching on the lights as she went and speaking over her shoulder. 'I was over at Jane Brady's place. She's Tammy Franklin's teacher and she's been out at the farm most of the day. Have you eaten?'

'No – we can go out and get something.'

'I've got some pasta.' She turned to face him. 'I don't feel much like going out again.'

'Pasta it is, then,' he returned amiably.

Meredith wasn't deceived. Well, she thought with some exasperation, whatever's on his mind, he'll get round to it in his own good time.

She went into the kitchen and put on a pan of water to cook the pasta. When she came back to the sitting room, bottle of wine and corkscrew in hand, Alan was lounging in a chair, his long legs stretched out in front of him, staring at a blank TV screen. She handed him corkscrew and bottle.

'What have you been doing?'

'Police work,' he said simply. He set about opening the wine and added, head bent over his task and his fair hair flopping forward as it always did, 'Which I have to do according to the rules.'

He paused. That sounded ominous and Meredith wondered if he'd found out about her visit to Fox Corner. If he had, she didn't know how. He cleared that mystery with his next words.

'I had a chat to a furniture maker called Peter Burke. He lives at a spot called Fox Corner. You know it too, I believe. My visit was official. He knew who I was and why I was there.'

So that's it, thought Meredith, bracing herself. 'I haven't been trampling on police turf.' She hadn't meant to sound so defensive. She cleared her throat and tried again. 'I need a kitchen cupboard.'

'Oh? First I've heard of it.'

'Perhaps,' she snapped, 'I don't tell you every trivial detail of my life!' There was a silence and she added, 'Sorry. Hungry. Blood sugar low.'

Alan handed back the opened wine bottle and leaned back in his chair. 'There's no reason why you should tell me every detail. I apologise. I shouldn't have questioned your word.'

Meredith put down the wine and sat in the opposite chair. 'You have a way of putting me in the wrong,' she said. 'I did talk to Peter Burke about Sonia's death, but only generally. He seemed very upset.'

'I'm sure he was very upset,' Alan agreed. 'But by the time I got to him, he'd realised that wasn't perhaps the best thing for him to appear. He'd had time to think out a more suitable reaction. He'd got his speech rehearsed, invited me into his cottage, offered me a beer. It was a good performance.'

'Whereas with me, it was spontaneous. I get the message.'

'He said a woman had been ferreting around, a friend, he said, of his former partner. That will be Jane you've just visited.'

'I didn't seek her out, you know. We met up at the inquest. I hadn't seen her for ages before that. We were only acquaintances, not friends. But she was very anxious about the way things were going. She needed someone to talk to.'

From the kitchen came an impatient rattle and hiss of water hitting a hot surface. Meredith hurried to snatch the lid from the boiling pan and drop in the pasta.

Alan had followed her out, bringing the wine with him, and was looking for glasses in the dresser. 'What's her interest?'

'Strictly speaking, it's Tammy Franklin, Hugh's daughter. Jane teaches her at St Clare's. The school's concerned about the effect of all this on the child. It's half-term holiday this week and Jane has taken to keeping an eye on things at the farm.'

She wasn't about to discuss Jane's possible feelings for Hugh himself, because she wasn't sure of them – and it's Jane's business anyway, she thought virtuously. Her real reason, conscience told her, was because she wanted to keep off the vexed subject of relationships. She took a jar of pasta sauce from her store cupboard and held it up. 'Tomato and mascarpone?'

Alan was at the fridge, rummaging in the salad drawer. 'Want me to make up a salad from this lot?'

'Sure, and there's an avocado in the bowl on the table, just to make it more interesting. Look, Alan, I'm truly sorry if I messed up police inquiries at Fox Corner. But I didn't know, when I went out there, that I'd even meet Peter. I went on spec. I thought, looking at the map, Sonia might have walked there and someone could have seen her. As it turned out, she'd been seen there on several occasions. She was intending to order furniture from Peter.' Meredith hesitated. 'I think they may have been having an affair.'

'They were,' he said calmly. He began to slice cucumber with what seemed to Meredith to be irritating precision. 'He was happy to tell me about it. He struck me as a somewhat volatile but shrewd young man. I thought his feelings for Mrs Franklin were probably genuine.' He paused and amended that to, 'As genuine as they could be for such a self-centred young man.'

'It seemed that way to me, too.' Meredith hesitated. 'Love has led to murder before now, hasn't it?'

'Yes.' Alan looked up, kitchen knife still in hand. 'But I'm not about to go berserk with this.' He gestured with the knife and smiled.

'Perhaps I wouldn't blame you,' Meredith said. 'Though I'm relieved to hear it, of course!'

'I'd appreciate it, though, if you've got any other nuggets of information, if you'd share them.'

'Can't say I have really, except that—' Meredith paused. 'Jane is worried about the child. She thinks maybe the little girl knows something which is worrying her. Something she hasn't told your policewoman and won't tell Jane. It might not necessarily be important.'

He was nodding. 'Yes, Ginny Holding's going to have to talk to the kid again. She realises that. She came to the same conclusion.'

'Apparently there was a phone call to the farm that evening. Tammy took it. She told Jane it was a wrong number. Jane is wondering whether it might have been Sonia. Do you know about that?'

'No. It's interesting and we'll have to look into that, or Holding will.' Markby frowned. 'It's possible the caller was Sonia, I suppose.'

'Jane's theory is that Tammy didn't pass on a message to Hugh that he should drive out and collect her from wherever she was.'

'Perhaps she did pass on the message. Perhaps he did drive out there.' Markby glanced at her. "Perhaps she waited for him down by the viaduct, a place easy to find. 'I'll be waiting by the arch, Hugh," she might have said. So off he went and when he got there they had another blazing row and—'

'And he stabbed her? You mean, he'd taken a knife with him? Wouldn't that make it premeditated murder? I mean, he'd find it hard to explain why he went down there armed with a knife to collect her.'

'Yes, it would. But perhaps he'd had murder on his mind for some weeks, how about that? He couldn't kill her on the farm because of the presence of the little girl. Suddenly an opportunity presents itself. Of her own free will she's taken herself to a lonely spot – and the embankment provides a place to hide her body.'

'No,' said Meredith, after considering this theory for a few moments. She shook her head. 'No, I don't think he did that.'

When she saw he looked questioningly at her, she went on, 'Because his alibi would depend entirely on his daughter. Jane says he loves the child and is an honest man. He wouldn't put that burden on her young shoulders. Nor could he be sure she'd never speak up and tell someone that Sonia rang and Dad went out to fetch her.'

'Good points, both of them. The second is better than the first. Even loving parents ask the unreasonable of their children.'

The pasta knocked at the lid and Meredith extricated a strand with a fork to test it. 'By the way, I also ran into Bethan Talbot again today. That's Simon's former partner. She is one very angry lady.'

Alan tipped his salad into a bowl. 'So long as it doesn't lead her to break the law, I'm afraid Ms Talbot will just have to stew.' He glanced at her. 'As you will, I'm afraid.'

'Meaning?'

'Meaning don't go buttonholing any more witnesses or messing up leads.'

That was pushing it too far. 'I didn't buttonhole Burke!' Meredith said crossly. 'I didn't know he lived there and when I found him, I didn't know he was involved. I've told you I'm sorry if I messed up your inquiry, but I'm blowed if I'm going to grovel!' She waved the fork at him in emphasis. 'I'm supporting Jane, that's what I'm doing. No more, no less.'

'You were snooping.' Before she could object to this word, he shook the salad bowl vigorously, and peering into its depths, went on, 'I don't like this case. I don't like anything about it. Not only are we making far less progress than I'd like, but there's a tension in the air. It's like a build-up to a thunderstorm. Something's about to break out there. I don't know what and I wish I at least knew where!'

'Are you really making no progress at all?' Meredith asked with sympathy.

He hunched his shoulders. 'None I'd call significant. I even sent Ginny Holding up to London this afternoon to make inquiries at the firm which employed Sonia before her marriage.'

'Dixon Dubois?'

He looked his exasperation. 'Now how would you know that?'

'Bethan told me. She also said Sonia had taken redundancy and was technically out of work at the time of her marriage to Hugh.'

He nodded. 'That confirms what Holding was told. She phoned through a report after she'd been to see the people at Dixon Dubois. She'll write it up tomorrow, but she was able to give me the gist of it in minutes. I won't say she got the cold shoulder, but no one there had much to say. None of Sonia's former colleagues knew she'd married. They all expressed themselves shocked at her death. Ginny's impression was that they didn't give a damn.' Markby laughed. 'She said she'd thought you had to tough to be in the police force, but she reckoned PR people were even tougher.'

Meredith was silent for so long that he looked up, puzzled. 'What is it?'

'You might not like this,' she warned. 'It occurs to me that a public relations firm wouldn't like the police walking through the front door and asking questions at any time. I don't suppose for one minute they like the idea of former employees being murdered. I honestly think you were always wasting your time sending DC Holding there. They were never going to speak to her and they'd be experts at fobbing her off.'

'You may well be right,' he admitted. 'Dave Pearce would certainly agree with you. When I told Dave that Holding had drawn a blank he had great difficulty hiding a smirk.'

Meredith cleared her throat. 'Whereas I—'

'No! I don't believe this. What was I saying just now about messing about in police investigations? You're proposing to hare up to London and nose around this PR firm, aren't you?'

'Hold on,' she said reasonably. 'Just now you were annoyed because I'd got to Peter Burke before the police, and tipped him off about the interest that would be taken in him. Fair enough. I agree I was out of order there. But this time, the police will have been there before me. I'm not going to mess anything up. Holding had no luck. I might do better.'

'Why should you?' he asked. 'If they wouldn't talk to Holding, who was there officially, they sure as heck won't talk to you who has no business there at all. Besides which, they may smell a rat if you turn up asking about Sonia so soon after the police – and there's probably nothing to learn.'

'You underestimate me. Let me try. It can't do any harm. What's more, I don't think you can stop me, though naturally I'd rather have your agreement.'

'Spare me the cant at least! It's unworthy of you. You don't care whether I object or not.' Alan heaved a sigh. 'All right, you pop along to Dixon Dubois but be very careful. Under no circumstances are you to give the impression that you have any kind of semiofficial status. What's more, if you get into any trouble, you can get yourself out of it. Don't count on me.'

'Thank you,' said Meredith meekly. 'That's all I wanted to hear.'

'Derry! *Derry! Wake up!*'

Derry Hayward stirred and mumbled, 'Whazzamarrar, Belinda?'

He was acting the part of a man roused from slumber. The truth was he hadn't slept a wink. That damn copper snooping round here with his questions. Belinda was stupid to think he hadn't been very bright. God alone knew what she'd said to him before he himself had got home.

He opened his eyes. His wife was a dark shape looming over his bed. He'd already heard her get out of hers and pad towards him. They'd had twin beds all their married lives, even when newlyweds, and if that hadn't been a pointer to the way things were going to go, Derry didn't know what had. At least, in those far-off days, if she got out of her bed and crept over to his, she'd had something other on her mind than some piffling grumble or other, which is what she no doubt had roused him for now. But it had been a long time since passion had sent either of them scuttling across the intervening floor space. Give her her due, Belinda was a brick. She worked hard round the place and had an utterly reliable business sense. And of course the money was hers. He'd never had a bean. They'd managed all right together as a couple, even without the passion, until Sonia had turned up. Derry uttered up silent curses. Now he was in a dashed tight corner. He must have been mad.

Aloud he repeated, 'What's wrong?'

'There's someone creeping round the stables.'

She sounded adamant but he argued. 'Oh, come on, old girl. You've been dreaming.'

'Don't be such an ass, Derry. I first heard the horses about ten minutes ago, moving about and snickering. I thought it might just be the new animal, slow to settle in. But then, when it kept on, I got up and looked out. The security lights have come on and I swear I saw someone standing by the corner of the stable block, a man.'

Derry sighed and sat up, swinging his legs out of the bed and reaching for his dressing gown which lay across the duvet at the foot. 'OK, I'll go and take a look.'

'Take a weapon with you. It's probably rustlers. It comes of moving that horse today. Someone noticed. Probably someone working where you bought the brute tipped the wink to some mates. They're in the area, you know, thieves. Other people have lost animals.'

'The security lights have come on before and it's only been a fox,' said Derry obstinately, tying his belt.

'This wasn't a bloody fox. It'd got two legs. Besides, if it were a fox, the geese would be raising merry hell. Take the shotgun, Derry.'

'I haven't got any blasted cartridges for it!' he protested. 'And even if had, if I fired the damn thing, the police would nab me for assault with a dangerous weapon.'

'Don't be so *tiresome*, Derry! The intruders don't know it's unloaded. I'm going to phone the police.'

'Not yet!' he ordered. 'Let me check it out first. We can do without more coppers round the place!'

Feeling a fool, he left the house in his dressing gown, his pyjama legs tucked into gumboots, and carrying an unloaded shotgun. It was an old weapon and had belonged to his late father-in-law. He, personally, had never fired the thing. He doubted it could safely be fired after all these years.

He'd left the front door ajar. He hadn't a key and standing out here yelling up at Belinda to let him in again would waken the kids. There wouldn't be anyone out here. He hadn't heard anything and he'd been lying awake. His mind had been running on other matters, of course.

It returned to his main preoccupation now. Nobody knew he'd made a fool of himself over Sonia. He'd misread the signs there, all right. He could've sworn she'd been giving him the glad eye. Then, without warning, she'd changed her tune and started playing hard to get. Set up a squawk when he tried to take what he thought was being offered. She was one of those bloody women who liked to tease and didn't come across, and he'd told her so! It wasn't his fault. He hadn't realised what she was like, that's all. Tell you what, Derry old son, it makes a chap appreciate Belinda. At least she's steady.

He stomped glumly towards the stable block. Belinda had probably suspected, but she hadn't said anything. No more had he. They were pretending it hadn't happened. Well, blast it, nothing did happen! Just as well. In the country, you'd as little chance of keeping a secret as you had of hiding an elephant. He wouldn't have wanted to fall out with old Hugh. Damn fine chap, Hugh. Old-fashioned ideas about farming, though, that was Hugh's problem. Not, of course, that they wanted a rival B & B opening up in the district. No, the problem was that bloody copper who'd come snooping round. The police were always suspecting people of the worst. He wished he knew what Belinda had said to him.

It was a clear night. Even without the security lights he could see straight across the yard, through the gates, down the approach road. The gates were safely shut, he noticed. If rustlers were about, they'd have opened the gates, for a start. He looked beyond them down the road. There was no horsebox parked there. If anyone was intent on stealing the horses, what were they going to do? Ride them away? Lead them for miles? The sound of hoofs on tarmac would be almost certain to be heard on the quiet night air. As it was, Belinda, who'd got hearing like a bat, had heard – or thought she'd heard – the horses moving in their stalls.

'It'll be the bay,' he muttered. 'It's in a strange stable and it's restless. It's upset the others.'

He had reached the stable block. He broke the shotgun and hung it over his arm as he tried the stable doors. None had been opened. He unbolted the top half of one door and pulled it outward and open. He whistled softly into the warm, acrid-smelling darkness. An answering snicker came from within and one of the ponies appeared in the gloom, curious as to why he was disturbing it at this time of night. It poked its head over the door and nudged him with its soft muzzle.

'All right, old fellow,' he said, smoothing its neck. 'You're not the only one who's been got out of bed!'

He persuaded it back into its box and shut up the door again. So much for that. Derry turned and began to trudge back towards the house. Behind him, the security lights went out. There! he thought as he was plunged into darkness. Must've been a fox.

He reached the door of the house, put out his hand and pushed it open wide. It swung inwards. Derry stepped into the hall and as he did, became aware of a dark figure standing at the foot of the stairs.

'Belinda? You haven't called the police, I hope, because there's nothing—'

He was not to complete his sentence. The figure leaped towards him, arm raised, and something hard, cold and heavy smashed into Derry's forehead. He went down like a ninepin. The shotgun fell on to the tiled hall floor with a clatter and the little table on which the phone stood crashed over.

'Derry? Derry!' His wife was running down the stairs, shrieking his name, but he didn't hear her.

CHAPTER THIRTEEN

The news that Derry Hayward had been attacked, had undergone emergency surgery and was currently in intensive care reached Regional HQ a little before midday.

Fuming at the delay, Markby demanded, 'Why weren't we told at once?'

'Bamford were dealing with it at local level,' explained Pearce. 'They're putting it down to an incident with rustlers. They didn't know we had any interest in Hayward until someone thought, as this was the second serious attack in a week in the area and we were dealing with the first and fatal one, we ought to be told.'

'Glad someone at Bamford's got a few brain cells working!' snarled Markby. He thumped his fist on his desk. 'Damn it, I knew something was going to break but I didn't foresee this. Why Hayward?'

'Might be rustlers. Mrs Hayward apparently thinks so,' Pearce ventured.

That got short shrift. 'I don't believe in coincidences, Dave. Besides, think about it. If you were a horse rustler, would you target a farm in an area which has been crawling with police for the past week? Come on, we're wasting more time here. Let's get over to that hospital.'

Despite the urgency expressed to Pearce, Markby had to admit to himself, as the nurse led them down the corridor, that he didn't actually like hospitals much and entered them reluctantly. They were more friendly places than they'd been in his childhood. He remembered being incarcerated in order to have his tonsils removed. The nurses had then appeared to his infant judgement as dragons. Nowadays he saw them as angels of mercy. Sadly overworked angels capable of human failings, perhaps, but that added to rather than detracted from them in his mind. Doing a job when things are going well, he knew from his own experience, doesn't call for more than ordinary competence. It's when things go wrong and the pressure's on that true professionalism gets a chance to shine out. It was this, and the dedication of the nursing profession it highlighted, that he admired most.

The nurse marching briskly along ahead of them was diminutive. Her rubber soles squeaked on the polished floor surface as they wended their way between the constant stream of traffic: people walking, people being pushed along in wheelchairs, patients being transported flat out on trolleys.

At last the traffic thinned, they passed through yet more fire doors, turned a corner and found themselves in a seating area. Two walls were lined with wooden-armed but soft-seated chairs.

'Here we are!' said the nurse brightly.

'Thought we'd never get here,' muttered Pearce at Markby's shoulder.

The only occupants of the waiting area were a wiry woman with faded corn-coloured hair, sitting rigidly upright, her face frozen in an attitude of despair, and two little girls, twins. They sat opposite her, swinging their legs and fidgeting about. They kept their eyes on their mother, but neither, it seemed, was venturing to speak, not even to one another. The whole family was clearly in deep shock.

Poor little souls, thought Markby compassionately of the twins. He walked up to the woman. 'Mrs Hayward? I'm Superintendent Markby. I believe you've met Inspector Pearce.'

She raised her head and stared up at him dully. 'Yes,' she said. She held an empty coffee-stained polystyrene beaker in her hands.

Yes, she remembered Pearce? Yes, she was simply acknowledging that he'd spoken? He couldn't tell. He took one of the vacant seats beside her.

'Very sorry to hear the bad news, Mrs Hayward,' said Pearce to her. 'What's the latest on your husband?'

'They say I'll be able to see him soon. He was over two hours in theatre.' She stirred and made an effort, putting the polystyrene beaker on the vacant chair at the other side of her. 'We'd just bought a new horse. You remember, you were there when he brought it home. They must have been after that.'

'You mean rustlers?' Markby asked.

'Couldn't be anyone else. Other stables have been targeted. I heard them. I saw them – well, one of them, anyway.'

Markby leaned closer. 'You can give a description?'

She signalled a negative with her hand. 'No, too dark. It was at night, confound it. The security lighting had come on but the figure I saw was by the edge of the stable block, just a silhouette.'

'The security lighting – it's the sort which is triggered by someone passing through a beam?'

'Anything passing through it,' Mrs Hayward said. 'Foxes have triggered it before now, and Derry thought—' She stopped abruptly, fished in the pocket of her well-worn Barbour and brought out a man's handkerchief. They waited while she blew her nose noisily. 'Derry thought it was a fox last night. But I knew it wasn't. The geese know when there's a fox around. Nothing gets past geese. The best watchdogs in the world.'

'But they didn't cackle last night, signifying intruders?'

She considered that and shook her head. 'They're penned up round the back. Stables are in the front. But a fox, he'd make for the fowls, wouldn't he?'

They were getting well off the subject here, Markby reflected. 'But it wasn't a fox,' he said firmly, dragging them back to the main theme. 'It was at least one man. Tell me what happened after you woke your husband with the news.'

'Derry went out to check. I made him take the old shotgun though it wasn't loaded. We've got a licence for it somewhere. Don't know that I could lay my hand on it straight away, but we do have a licence. No ammunition, though.' She was waving both hands now in a desultory fashion. 'Daddy used to fire the thing. It was Daddy's.'

'So he went out into the yard,' prompted Markby.

'What? That's right. And he must have left the front door open. He didn't believe me, you see, about it being an intruder. The rustler must have seen him, slipped round behind him and come into the house. Derry was gone a long time so I got a bit worried. I started to come downstairs and as I did, Derry came back. He walked through the front door into the hall. He started to call out something to me but then—' She shook her head. 'It was so fast. He – I mean the rustler – he must have been at the bottom of the stairs. If Derry hadn't come back then, I'd have walked into him. He – he attacked Derry and then he – fled.'

'Did you hear a car, Mrs Hayward?'

She shook her head again. 'But I wasn't listening, I was kneeling over Derry. I thought he—' She remembered her children, silent and listening. 'I thought, you know, at first, that was it. Then I called an ambulance.'

'It doesn't seem odd to you, Mrs Hayward,' Markby asked gently, 'that a rustler, someone bent on stealing a horse, should come into the house?'

'A thief is a thief!' she retorted with unexpected ferocity. 'He saw his chance. He thought we'd have something he could grab, a picture or something.' She met his gaze belligerently. 'It was nothing to do with that bloody woman if that's what you're working round to! It was a rustler! A dirty little common or garden sneak thief!'

The nurse was back. 'You can see your husband for a few minutes now, Mrs Hayward.'

Belinda Hayward got to her feet. The twins looked up expectantly. 'Stay here,' she said to them. 'Won't be long.'

'The surgeon will be along in a moment to have a word with you, Superintendent,' the nurse said to Markby.

When she'd led Mrs Hayward away, Markby walked across to the silent twins. 'Hullo,' he said, smiling down at them. 'Don't worry about your daddy. They'll take good care of him here.'

They stared solemnly back at him. One of them was chewing a fingernail. In front of them was a low table with magazines on it. Markby sat on the table and leaned his hands on his knees.

'Neither of you heard anything last night?'

They stopped swinging their legs. One of them, not the nail-worrier, said, 'We heard Mummy screaming.'

'Yes. I meant, before that?'

'We didn't hear anything,' said the nail-biter.

Markby stood up and moved away out of earshot, followed by Pearce. 'What do you make of it?' he asked in a low voice.

'She knows it wasn't a rustler,' whispered back Pearce immediately. 'It is something to do with Sonia but she's covering up. When I went out there to interview them, they couldn't wait to get me off the premises, and it wasn't just because I had the wrong sort of accent. There's something they don't want us to know and I told you before what I reckoned it was.'

'Hmm. Get Ginny out to Hazelwood to talk to the child there again. I'll tackle these two . . .' he glanced towards the twins, 'but not now, later. I'll go and see Franklin and ask if Ginny can talk to his daughter alone. He mightn't agree, of course, and we can't insist. Well, I can, if I think there's imminent danger of disruption to the peace. I'd say the attack on Hayward justifies me in fearing a repetition, wouldn't you?'

'Superintendent?' The surgeon, disconcertingly youthful-looking, had appeared. He held out his hand.

Markby shook it. 'Thanks for seeing us. What are his chances?'

'Only fifty-fifty at the moment. He's a youngish man, very fit, and that's good. I wouldn't want to be overoptimistic, mind you.'

'If he pulls through,' Pearce asked with some concern, 'will he be paralysed or anything like that?'

'At this stage I really couldn't say. Memory, of course, will be the thing he'll have difficulty with, at least in the short term. That, I imagine, is what will affect your inquiries most.' The surgeon raised an eyebrow.

'He's not likely to remember what happened, you mean?' asked Markby with sinking heart.

'I think I can safely say, if he does regain consciousness, his mind will be a complete blank with regard to the whole incident.' The surgeon looked apologetic. 'Sorry to deliver such a downer, but better you're prepared.'

'Quite. Thank you. Could you hazard a guess as to what kind of weapon was used in the attack?'

'Heavy, small striking head, something like a hammer?' The surgeon glanced at the clock on the wall above Pearce's head. 'I'd like to have a word with his wife.'

They let him go.

'Poor old Gilbert,' said Pearce sadly.

'Who's Gilbert?' Markby stared at him in surprise.

'Sorry, just a—' He managed to stop short of saying 'just a joke'. Nothing funny about it. 'Doesn't matter,' he said.

At midday, as Markby and Pearce were entering the hospital, Meredith had just taken a seat across the desk from the personnel officer of Dixon Dubois. She'd found Sonia's late employers without too much difficulty. They were situated near Marble Arch in what must be very expensive offices. The PO looked expensive, too, a leggy blonde in a slate-grey business suit and pearls. She was so well groomed in every respect that Meredith found it hard not to feel like a bag lady, even though she had taken pains herself to look presentable and had thought, before she got in here, that she didn't look too bad. The personnel officer had just discovered that Meredith wasn't after a job, but information. Her manner, which had been cool at the outset, now plummeted several degrees.

'There's absolutely nothing I can do for you,' she said briskly, adding in a pointed way, 'And I am very busy. I'm on my own here, you know.' She meant, presumably, in her own department. The rest of Dixon Dubois was buzzing away nicely elsewhere.

She wasn't, however, able to point to any actual proof of activity. There was a small wooden marker on her desk labelled 'Anthea', but very little else. Any work piling up was doing it out of sight.

Meredith, conscious of her own in-tray filling up in her absence, smiled benignly at her in a way intended to let the woman know her bluff hadn't worked. 'I only need to take up a few minutes of your time, Anthea. It's about the late Mrs Sonia Franklin. She worked here as Sonia Lambert.'

'Yes, I know!' was the tart retort. Anthea was niggled that her claim to be overworked hadn't impressed. 'The police have already been here. God knows why. I mean, we were all dreadfully shocked at the news. Murdered!' She shuddered theatrically. 'But, I mean, we can't help.'

'She didn't have any close friends among her colleagues?'

'No. Of course, we're a friendly firm—'

I bet, thought Meredith.

'But we all have private lives. Besides, we've had quite a turnover of staff this last eighteen months. There's no one I could possibly suggest you talk to.'

Meredith picked up on the turnover of staff. 'Were many people made redundant?'

'What?' Anthea gaped. She touched her lower lip with pearlised pink-polished nails.

'Sonia Lambert was made redundant, wasn't she? How many other people went at the same time?'

Anthea rallied. 'That's not a matter I can discuss. It's company business. You might,' she added, 'be from a rival outfit, for all I know.'

'I showed you my official pass. You know what I do for a living.' Anthea had been interested in the Foreign Office pass and her curiosity had got Meredith into this office. Now Anthea was trying to get her out again. Meredith felt her spine tingle. Somehow, she didn't know how, she'd touched on a sore point. Something about Sonia's redundancy?

'Look,' said Anthea, 'I don't know what your interest is—'

'I'll tell you,' said Meredith. 'A friend of mine is helping Sonia's husband look after his daughter. That's Sonia's stepdaughter. I'm concerned for my friend. I want to know about that household.'

Jane wouldn't like her saying any of this. If anything, Meredith knew she'd borrowed an attitude from Bethan. Still, needs must.

'But I can't tell you anything about the husband,' Anthea pointed out. She looked at her wristwatch, a neat little gold affair.

'You can tell me about the wife.'

'No, I can't!' Anthea was getting restless. 'I really think you should go—'

'How about Dixon or Dubois?' Meredith cut into the intended dismissal. 'If they exist. Can I talk to either of them?'

Anthea's agitation increased. 'They exist but you can't talk to either of them. Mr Dixon is on a business trip to the States. Mr Dubois saw the policewoman who came and I simply couldn't trouble him again.'

'Let him decide that,' suggested Meredith.

'He's in a meeting!' snapped Anthea.

'How do you know? You aren't his secretary. Ring his secretary and ask if he can make five minutes during the day for me. I can wait.'

Anthea decided to call up reinforcements. 'If you don't go, I'll have security put you out.'

'Is that the old chap dozing in the cubbyhole by the front door?' Meredith took a chance. 'Look here, I think this reluctance of yours to talk about Sonia has to do with the terms of her redundancy.'

Bingo! Anthea turned white, then red. 'Absolutely not!' Her words lacked conviction but they did hold desperation.

'And I want to talk to Mr Dubois!'

'You can't!' Anthea was almost pleading now. 'I couldn't let you bother him about this again. It would be too cruel.' She saw Meredith's expression. 'Listen, it's almost my lunch hour. There's a little fast-food place just a block down. I'll meet you there in twenty minutes. I'll try and explain as best I can without— There are things I can't tell you, and whatever I do tell you I shall have to ask you to be discreet about.'

Meredith got to her feet. 'All right. I'll see you in twenty minutes. But if you don't turn up, I'll be back. And if I don't get to see your Mr Dubois here, I'll find him somewhere else.'

That was threatening something she mightn't be able to achieve, but it worked on Anthea.

'I'll be there in twenty minutes. Look, just go, can't you? I don't want anyone to see you.'

The fast-food café was small, with red-topped Formica tables and a limited menu. Meredith bought a polystyrene tub of fish goujons and retired to a table by the window so that she could watch for Anthea. To give her her due, Anthea wasn't late. She bustled in, greeted the young man behind the counter as an old acquaintance and, armed with an identical polystyrene tub of batter-coated shapes, swooped down on Meredith.

'Look here, can't we sit over in the corner? Any bloody person from the office could walk past and see us here.'

They removed themselves to a far corner. Anthea, taking no chances, seated herself with her back to the room. She jabbed a plastic fork into her carton.

'Fish goujons,' said Meredith.

'Chicken goujons,' said Anthea.

'They don't look any different.'

'You've got sauce tartare with yours,' pointed out Anthea. 'I've got mayonnaise.'

So much for preliminary discussion of haute cuisine. 'What went on?' asked Meredith bluntly. 'Why did Sonia get the boot?'

'Redundancy,' corrected Anthea.

'The boot in velvet. The poor woman's dead. She can't sue. You can tell me.'

'It doesn't just concern her, Sonia, does it?' Anthea set down her fork and prepared to reveal some secret. 'It's just between us, right?'

'I might have to tell the police.' It was only fair to warn Anthea.

'Police?' Anthea squawked and looked anxiously over her shoulder.

'I'd do it discreetly if it was necessary. I've got a friend in the force. He's a superintendent.'

Anthea appeared reassured by the rank. 'Well, all right, tell your friend if you must. But don't go telling any old plod.' She drew a deep breath. 'Sonia was an absolute pain in the neck. She caused so much trouble, you wouldn't credit it.'

'What sort of trouble?'

'Men,' said Anthea crossly. 'Well, specifically one man.'

'Dubois?' Meredith made a shrewd guess.

'Shh! Don't say his name out loud like that! It wasn't his fault, poor man, he was totally innocent. He's happily married, for goodness' sake. Sonia pestered the life out of him. First of all, she kept finding excuses to go into his office. Then she started buying him funny little cards. Then it was aftershave. At Christmas it was cufflinks. She kept suggesting dinner at her place. He didn't know what to do. You should have seen the way she zoomed in on him at the Christmas party. It was downright embarrassing. The poor man was desperate. She had to go.'

'It sounds as though he had a case for sexual harassment. Why not just terminate her contract?'

'And have her claim unfair dismissal? It's the sort of case which gets in the tabloid press. The firm couldn't have that. Besides, you know how people's minds work. No smoke without fire, that sort of thing. He preferred his wife not to know about it. As it happened, business was slack so redundancy made sense. She got a generous golden handshake.'

'She was paid off, you mean?' Meredith said.

'She was made redundant by mutual agreement,' Anthea insisted, tight-lipped. 'The offer finally made her realise she was wasting her time. She was devastated but she'd brought the whole thing on herself. It's just plain stupid to chuck away a good job over an office crush.' She sat back in her chair. 'Are you going to tell this police chum of yours? It can't have anything to do with her death.'

'I'll probably tell him the basic fact – that she stirred up trouble. But he won't use it unless it's relevant. He's very discreet,' Meredith promised.

'Good!' Anthea got to her feet. 'I hope this is the end of it. We don't want any more visits. Honestly, that woman, still causing trouble even when she's dead!'

Anthea's heels clicked briskly across the tiled floor on her way out.

Meredith walked thoughtfully towards Marble Arch tube station. She was so engrossed in turning over the possibilities of the information Anthea had given her that she didn't realise, until the last moment, that a familiar figure was approaching from the opposite direction.

It was Gerald, hastening along the Oxford Street pavement, clutching a green M&S bag, obviously also heading for the tube.

Meredith scuttled back and into the foyer of the Cumberland Hotel in the nick of time. Gerald had presumably popped out in his lunch break to do some shopping. He was the last person she wanted to meet. She'd have to wait here for a while and make sure he was out of the way.

It gave her an opportunity to call up Alan on her mobile. But she was out of luck. He wasn't in the building, she was told. Neither was Inspector Pearce. Did she wish to speak to DC Holding?

'No,' said Meredith. She had made Anthea a promise, after all. 'I'll contact the superintendent some other time.'

And when she did, it would be to tell him that the Sonia described to her today was a far cry from the fun-loving, anything-for-a-lark Sonia described to her by Bethan. Sonia Lambert, if Anthea's account was anything to go by, had been a neurotic, unhappy woman desperate for male approval. Rejected by the man on whom she'd fixed her sights, Fate had led Sonia to meet Hugh Franklin, a widower, a lonely man looking for another wife. What had Jane said? It's normal to want to feel needed. Dubois hadn't needed Sonia, but Hugh apparently had. Poor mixed-up Sonia had rushed into marriage only to discover very soon that it wasn't the answer to her problems at all.

Meredith wondered how much Bethan knew of the history behind Sonia's redundancy. Given the long, close friendship between the women, Bethan must at least have had an inkling.

'Causing trouble,' repeated Meredith beneath her breath, 'even when she's dead.' Poor Sonia.

CHAPTER FOURTEEN

Hazelwood Farm was busy when Markby got to it that afternoon. The old man, Sid, was back at work, stiffly making his way across the yard, and there was a small, dark man who cast a swift glance at Markby and then somehow melted into the background. Markby hid a smile. The gypsy, Danny Smith.

The third person in the yard came to meet him. 'You'll be another copper?'

Hugh Franklin didn't sound so much resentful as resigned. Markby studied the man briefly. First impressions were often important, but that didn't mean they couldn't mislead. Hugh looked as if he might be a reliable, straightforward sort of chap. He wore a disreputable pullover – though one which looked as if someone recently had made an attempt to mend it – grubby corduroys and muddy gumboots. But then murderers seldom looked like murderers. They came in all guises.

Markby introduced himself and saw Hugh's eyebrows twitch.

'We're getting the top brass, are we, now?'

'I wouldn't call myself that,' Markby demurred. 'Is there somewhere we could have a quiet chat?'

Hugh glanced at the house behind them. 'We can go indoors, I suppose. Only I'd have to take my boots off and Tam's there. Or we can go over there and sit in the barn.'

The barn in question was an open-fronted one storing baled hay, ancient farm implements, a clutter of odds and ends. Hugh sat on a haybale and indicated Markby should take a similar seat.

'So, what is it now, eh?' Hugh placed his broad hands on his knees and stared up at his visitor from beneath his eyebrows, head slightly lowered. Markby thought, amused, that Hugh had adopted the manner of one of his own cattle faced with something suspicious.

'You heard your neighbour, Mr Hayward, met with an accident.'

'As I heard, it was no accident. Someone bashed the poor bloke on the head and near beat his brains out.' Hugh delivered this comment in a matter-of-fact way.

'He suffered head injuries, certainly, but we hope he'll recover. Who told you?'

'She did, Belinda. Rang me up from the hospital while he was in theatre. Rustlers, she reckoned, after the horses they got over there. We do get rustlers round here, you know. It isn't only in the Wild West.' He took one hand from his knee to scratch the back of his head. 'Wonder if Sim knows about Derry. Perhaps I ought to give him a call.'

'I do know about rustlers,' said Markby. 'We'll be recommending Mrs Hayward to have her animals freeze-branded. That would stop them being sold at open sale with no questions asked.'

Hugh laughed without mirth. 'You'd be surprised. But you're not here to talk about rustlers, I suppose.'

'No,' Markby admitted. Somewhere to the rear of the haybales something fell, then scuttled away.

Hugh, who'd seen his visitor's attention taken by the sound, said, 'Only a rat.'

'Get a lot of them?'

'Not so many as in my dad's time when we were mixed farming. Dad used to put the terriers in here, clear the barn out from time to time. All we've got is an old spaniel belongs to my daughter. The only way he'd kill a rat would be if he sat on it.'

Markby, glad that the topic of Tammy had been so neatly introduced, picked up on it. 'One of my officers came out and had a talk to your daughter recently.'

Hugh looked at him warily. 'And wants to talk to her again, you're going to tell me, I dare say.'

'Yes, actually, but what made you say that?'

'Because,' said Hugh, 'it seems to me you fellows never make do with talking to anyone once. You keep on and on. Doing your job, I suppose, and never mind if it gets in the way of other people doing theirs!'

'I'm sorry for the inconvenience,' Markby said, adding with a touch of curiosity, 'But we are investigating your wife's death.'

'I know that. Are you any closer to finding out who killed her?'

'We'll keep at it until we do,' Markby told him, adding, 'And the more help we get, the quicker it's likely to be.'

Hugh gave a snort which might have meant anything and fell to studying the ground between his gumbooted feet. 'Whether you find him or whether you don't, it's never going to go away, is it?' he observed unexpectedly.

'No, I don't suppose it will. Coming to terms with murder is never easy.'

Hugh sighed. 'I've been thinking about Sonia a lot, about all the stupid quarrels we had, where we went wrong and if anything could've been done to make it right for us.'

'And what conclusion have you reached?' Markby asked him. 'If you have.'

Hugh leaned back again the haybale behind him. 'That girlfriend of yours, she asked me what I thought Sonia expected from being married to me.'

'Did she, indeed?' Markby exclaimed. He thought of Meredith, to whom he'd more or less given *carte blanche* to ferret around at Dixon Dubois, and felt a pang of conscience. 'What did you tell her?'

'I had to tell her I really didn't know. But it made me think I should have asked Sonia herself before we tied the knot. Perhaps she should have asked me some more questions. Either way, neither of us thought it through properly. You see, Sonia and me, we were in the same boat at the time we met. I'd lost Penny and I didn't know what to do. I was sort of floating about aimlessly. I mean, I was running the farm and the rest of it,' said Hugh more brusquely. 'Farms don't run themselves! But it was like I couldn't see down the road ahead, know what I mean?'

Markby nodded.

'Sonia, she was at a loose end, too. She'd never been married, had a couple of relationships which hadn't lasted, hadn't got any family. She'd had a good job in London, but had got made redundant recently and was working part time. She was pretty fed up and wanted a change. We both thought, somehow, we could start over fresh together. We were wrong,' Hugh concluded simply, adding, 'It's no use pointing the finger of blame. 'Tisn't easy, being married, at the best of times, anyhow.'

'No, it isn't,' said Markby. 'Or I never found it so.'

'Ah,' said Hugh, a slow grin breaking out on his tanned cheeks. 'You've been through it, have you? Married now?'

'No,' Markby said, unable to keep a note of regret from his voice.

'Like to be?' Hugh asked shrewdly.

'Yes, I would.'

'There you go, then,' said Hugh. 'Hope springs eternal, they say, don't they? I wanted to be married again, after Penny.'

'And now, after Sonia?'

'It's a bit soon to be talking about that, isn't it?' Hugh replied, evading the straight answer.

'My problem,' said Markby slowly, 'is that I have to ask questions. It's the nature of my work. Any questions I ask the bereaved appear tactless, to say the least. Some are downright hurtful. It can't be helped.'

He paused and saw that Hugh was watching him with a clear, intelligent gaze. 'Go on,' Hugh said. 'Ask your question.'

'You knew your wife was dissatisfied with her life here. Did you ever think she might have sought out a shoulder to cry on elsewhere?'

Hugh leaned back again, resting his head on the haybale behind him. His eyes were sad but his lips were twisted in wry amusement. 'Running around with someone else, you mean? Wouldn't that give me a motive?'

Markby said nothing.

'Pah!' Hugh said suddenly. 'Of course I thought it. She was always going off on those long walks of hers. Driving off during the day, going shopping, she said. Never brought much shopping home.' Hugh shrugged. 'I even speculated a bit who it might be. I thought, well, there's old Derry – who's lying in a hospital bed now, poor bloke. Except Belinda would kill anyone who messed around with—' Hugh broke off and reddened. 'Hell. I didn't mean that. Figure of speech. And I didn't bash his head in either, in case you're thinking that. He's been my neighbour a few years.'

Markby nodded but still said nothing.

'And then there was a young fellow at Fox Corner who makes furniture,' Hugh went on. 'She was very keen to order some chairs from him and kept going over there to look at designs.' Again Hugh snorted. 'I'll tell you the plain truth, Superintendent, since that's what you want. I wouldn't have minded if she'd left me and gone off with someone else. I'd got to that stage. It might have been the answer

194

to the problem, after all. I don't mean I'd have wanted her busting up anyone else's marriage. But someone like that furniture chap? I honestly wouldn't have tried to stop her. Does that give me more or less of a motive?'

'I don't know, but thank you for being open about it. It is for the best.' Markby paused. 'If I could talk for a moment about your daughter. DC Holding, who came out to see her, thought that Tammy had something on her mind, something she was reluctant to speak about. Do you have any idea what that might be?'

'I expect she heard us yelling at one another that evening, Sonia and me,' said Hugh, 'but doesn't want to say so. She's trying to shield me.' He frowned. 'But that's not right and I'll tell her, she's got to tell it all, whatever it is.'

'I don't mean for anyone to nag the child or make her feel she's done something wrong,' Markby said hastily. 'What I was wondering was, whether you'd object to DC Holding having a few words with your daughter on her own? Tammy might find it easier to speak to Holding, just on a one-to-one basis. Of course, as a juvenile, Tammy oughtn't to be interviewed without an interested adult present. And if she did say anything new to Holding, and Holding thought it relevant to our inquiries, the interview would stop right there and an adult be called in. Or you could ask for your solicitor to be there.' Markby gave a wry grimace. 'We have to be mindful of the rules of evidence these days. All the usual ones apply. And there's no question of forcing Tammy to agree to an unaccompanied interview and absolutely none of her being asked to sign anything.'

'I get the message,' said Hugh. 'I don't see how it could do any harm.'

'Right,' said Markby in relief. 'I'll set it up.'

'You did what?' Simon Franklin's voice rose in a wail of dismay. 'Did I hear you right? You've agreed to let that policewoman come back and quiz Tammy without an adult present?'

They were sitting in Simon's study. Hugh's eyes had been surveying the ranked bookshelves as if he hadn't seen them before. Now he dragged his gaze from them and said, 'I've nothing to hide.' He sounded more surprised than defiant, as if his brother's reaction had taken him unawares.

'That's not the point! For God's sake, this Markby fellow was chancing his luck and you let him get away with it. I must say, I'm sorry to hear it was Markby. I've met him and I'd have thought he'd behave better. Just shows you can't trust any policeman, even a senior chap like that. He had no right to ask any such thing. Thought he'd blind you with his rank, I suppose. It's the sort of thing which ought to be reported to the chief constable.'

'Hold on,' said Hugh peaceably, 'he didn't insist. He just said he thought Tammy might find it easier. He said, of course, Tammy would be asked if she agreed. If I objected, or if I wanted a solicitor there, then all the usual rules of evidence would apply, whatever they are,' concluded Hugh wryly.

Simon pounced on this admission. 'You see? You don't even know where you stand in law on this! You shouldn't have agreed, Hugh.'

'Well, I have,' said his brother obstinately. 'Tammy says she doesn't mind.'

'My niece is a twelve-year-old child and not able to make up her own mind on this matter!' fumed Simon.

'She might only be twelve,' pointed out Tammy's father, 'but she's able to make up her mind all right.'

Simon uttered an exclamation of disgust and got to his feet. Hugh watched him pace up and down for a few moments, then said, 'What's she going to say, Sim? I told you, I've got nothing to hide. Mind you, I sometimes wonder whether you believe that.'

Simon, who'd reached the far end of the room in his perambulations, swung round on his heel. 'What's that? Of course I believe it!'

'So why all the fuss?' Hugh's furrowed brow betokened his bewilderment at his brother's attitude.

Simon took off his spectacles and held them by the mended side of the frame. 'You are a babe in the woods, brother of mine. You always were. You think you only have to be honest and people will be honest with you. You think because you've a clear conscience the police won't be able to put words in Tammy's head.'

'She won't be asked to sign anything, Sim. He told me that. Look, I'm not daft,' added Hugh, aggrieved at the lack of faith expressed in his judgement. 'And it seemed to me it'd look a lot fishier to the police if I refused their request than if I agreed to it.' His eyes returned to the bookshelves. 'Course, I'm not a brainbox like you.'

'It's not a question of being a brainbox, as you put it—' Simon broke off and gave an exasperated sigh.

'Anyway,' said Hugh, 'I really dropped by to tell you about Derry Hayward, in case you hadn't heard.'

'Hadn't heard what?' snapped Simon.

'Some joker stove his head in last night. Seems he went to investigate an intruder at his stable block.'

Simon paled. 'He's dead?'

'No, poor bloke's not dead, but he's not doing too well either. They've got him over at the hospital. Touch and go, it was, when they took him in, or so I heard. They were still operating on him when I last spoke to Belinda. It's a bad business.'

'Who the hell . . . ?' muttered Simon. He looked shaken. 'Hayward? Why the dickens Hayward?' He shook his head. 'Look, I agree, it's a rotten business, but it could help us. It proves what I've been telling the police all along. In fact I told that chap Markby himself, face to face. All kinds of ruffians are roaming the countryside these days. Now perhaps they'll believe me.'

'Belinda thinks it was rustlers.'

'Belinda Hayward thinks of nothing but those damn nags they've got over there,' retorted Simon. 'Still, she might be right on this occasion, I suppose. You take care, too, do you hear? Someone might come prowling round your place. Think of your daughter's safety if you won't think of your own. Start locking doors. Take some kind of weapon with you when you go out last thing at night round the yard.'

'What am I going to do if I meet someone, then?' Hugh asked sarcastically. 'Bash him on the head like Derry's attacker? The police already have me marked down for Sonia's death. It'd look really good, wouldn't it, if I presented them with another body? As it is, they're probably wondering if I went over to Cherry Tree and had a go at Hayward, even though I told Markby I didn't.'

'Why?' Simon stared at him in horror. 'Why should it even be suggested that you did?'

'Markby thinks Sonia was having an affair.'

'Look here,' Simon's face was puce with suppressed anger, 'what's that bloody copper been saying to you? Can't you see what their game is? They're encouraging you to dig a hole so you can fall right in it. But if you sit tight and say nothing, they can't do a thing about it. Not a thing. Remember that! And remember what I've been trying to tell you all along: just tell them what you have to. Don't give them any little opening they can use to build a case. You didn't kill Sonia!'

'That's right, I didn't,' said Hugh. 'And an innocent man never got sent down, eh?' He got to his feet. 'Don't you worry about me and Tam. You ought to be more worried, out here on your own now Bethan's gone.' He paused and asked curiously, 'Do you miss her, Simon?'

His brother pursed his lips and thought about it. 'Sometimes, naturally. At the moment I've got a lot of work on and it doesn't give me time to be lonely. Rather, I'm glad to be able to get on without interruptions.'

'Oh, the new book.' Hugh wandered to Simon's desk and peered down at the computer and sheaf of papers. 'What's this, then?' He picked up a small object from the desk and turned, holding it up. 'Doesn't look as if it's much good to me. Better chuck it out.'

'That,' Simon said, a smile breaking out on his face for the first time, 'is a late-sixteenth-century shoe buckle.'

'Really?' Hugh turned the object over in his hand. 'Bless me. Thought it looked as if it'd seen better days.' He replaced the object with care. 'You've done well, Sim. Better than me, at any road.'

'I do all right,' Simon told him awkwardly. 'I make a living, at any rate. I'll never be a rich man. Is the farm in trouble? I mean, financially how are you placed? I could, if necessary, raise a couple of grand. I couldn't do more than that, I'm afraid.'

'Thanks for the offer but I'll sink or swim on my own.' Hugh smiled. 'At the moment, I'm just about keeping afloat. I'd be better off, I dare say, if there hadn't been so many other things taking my time and attention. Poor Penny. Then this business with Sonia. I'm sure the farm can be made to do better. I need a business plan,' said Hugh unexpectedly.

Simon blinked and didn't hide his surprise. 'This is new talk for you, old chap!'

'Perhaps I need to get myself a few new ideas,' Hugh retorted. 'Well, I'd best get on back home. I'll leave Tam here for a bit, if that's OK with you? She's playing out in the orchard on that old swing you rigged up for her when she was a tot.'

'What? Oh yes, leave her here. I'll run her back to the farm later.' Simon accompanied his brother to his Land Rover and put a staying hand on his arm as he was about to haul himself into the driver's seat.

'Reconsider, Hugh, that's all I ask. No matter what you've told Markby, you can change your mind.'

'I'll think about it,' his brother told him. 'Perhaps I'll have a word with Jane. She's got her head screwed on the right way.'

'No, not the Brady woman!' returned Simon vehemently. 'She's an interfering schoolteacher. She's not family. I am! Listen to me, can't you?'

He watched the Land Rover rattle away, then turned and made his way to what his brother had referred to as 'the orchard'.

It had once been productive, but no one had pruned or cared for the trees in years. Their twisted, gnarled trunks reached out, neighbour touching neighbour, as if in some kind of weird dance. In the autumn there would be apples here, but small, wasp-infested, pecked by birds, attacked by various forms of blight. They'd fall to the ground and be left there to rot. Now the trees were only just in leaf.

Simon's feet crunched over the brown, shrivelled remains of last year's fallers as he approached the swing. Tammy sat on it pushing herself back and forth with her toe. The seat hung too near to the ground for her now so that her feet scuffed along the earth. She couldn't have been more than four when he'd constructed it and her little legs then had dangled from it endearingly.

Sod it, thought Simon. Sod the whole wretched, lousy business. Was there never to be an end to it? Was there an afterlife? If there was, was Sonia somewhere now enjoying a macabre joke at everyone's expense?

Simon glanced up at the branch to which twin ropes secured the swing. Long exposure to the elements had led to the ropes looking distinctly the worse for wear.

'I don't know how safe that is now, Tammy,' he said doubtfully.

'It's all right, Uncle Simon. I'm just sitting on it.'

He leaned against the tree trunk, arms folded. 'About this police-woman, Tammy—'

'That's all right, too,' she interrupted.

'You can ask for your father or me to be there. It might be better if I were there, Tammy.'

The swing creaked as she pushed her foot into the ground. The ropes made a grating noise where they were wound round the branch and the branch itself groaned.

'You don't have to worry about me, Uncle Simon.' His niece's pale grey eyes locked on to his and he blinked nervously. 'It'll be all right.'

In the following silence, a bird fluttered up in the branches of the apple tree, a blackbird watching them with his fierce yellow-rimmed eye. The scene was deceptively peaceful. A bit, thought Simon, like one of those Impressionist paintings of the artist's family, all lounging about enjoying themselves *en plein air*. The dappled pattern of shadow on the long grass in today's pale sunshine. The child with her long hair. Himself appearing as one of those hangers-on of bohemian society. A writer, but not the right sort of writer. An historian, not a poet or a dramatist. As an historian, he was one who wrote for children. Yet what did he know about the mind of a child?

The question, when he was able to bring himself to put it, was dredged up out of the depths of his being, like a magician pulling silk scarves endlessly from his mouth.

'What do you know, Tammy? What is it that you can't tell the police?'

She avoided his eye, gazing down at her feet. As it was half term she wore the trainers banned at school. Simon thought they looked hot, clumsy things. But then he didn't understand children, did he? He might once have thought he understood this one, but he didn't. He feared her. That was the worst of it. He feared what would happen when those childish lips parted and out came, not a string of brightly coloured silk scarves, but something so unspeakably awful that he would give anything to be able to stuff it back in again, silence it, still it at birth.

Her voice a whisper, she said, 'I saw.'

He asked, his voice almost as quiet, his heart leaden, 'Whom did you see, Tammy? Was it Sonia?'

She looked up then. She looked frightened, confused. She shook her head, then stopped in mid-shake and nodded. 'Sort of.'

Oh God, he thought. This is worse than I ever thought anything could be. 'When you saw her, Tammy, was she alive – or dead?'

He knew what the answer was going to be, but he still waited with that dread fascination with which as a child he'd watched the magician.

'I think she must have been dead.' The words might have been little more than a rustle in the branches. 'Because she was being carried.'

So that was it. Now it was spoken, he was surprised at the surge of relief he felt. Because now the way ahead was clear. Now he knew what had to be done. He almost felt a kind of imprimatur had been stamped on it.

'I see,' he said calmly. 'Where were you?'

'I was down on the embankment.'

His calm cracked. 'What the hell were you doing there, at that time of night?'

She looked up, seeming bewildered. 'I went to get my frog bag.'

'Your what?' He didn't know what she was on about. She explained it for him.

'I take my homework and stuff to school in it. The Hayward twins took it off me and dropped it over the old viaduct and it caught in a branch. I couldn't do my homework without it, so I went out to see if I could get it.'

'And you saw?' he said, all expression dulled in his voice.

'Yes, Uncle Simon. I saw you and the other man.'

CHAPTER FIFTEEN

Markby pulled into the side of the road just below the turning to Hazelwood Farm and put through a call to base. He was hoping Pearce might be there, but he was told the inspector was out. Miss Mitchell, however, had been trying to call him.

'Do you know where from?' he asked. 'I mean, from London?'

'I think so, sir. She wouldn't speak to anyone else.'

'I'll see to it,' he said. He sat for a moment in thought and then got out of the car. The wind whipped across the rolling countryside and rustled the leaves on the trees above his head. It was damp beneath his feet, a mulch of mud and dead vegetation. Inevitably, too, a battered fizzy drinks can tossed from a passing car. He kicked it irritably into the ditch. Then he took out his mobile phone and punched in Meredith's number.

'Hullo?' He heard her voice, sounding furtive. In the background was a rattle and muted roar.

'Are you on a train?' he guessed.

'I'm on my way back. I tried to call you before I left.'

She still sounded furtive. Markby smiled. There are those who are gung ho about making and taking calls from mobile phones while sitting in trains, and those who are more sensitive to the glares of fellow passengers.

'Is it something I need to know now? I've just called on Hugh Franklin and I'm on my way back to my desk.'

'That redundancy package,' Meredith muttered into the phone. He could just about hear her.

'What?'

'I'm on the train!' Louder, more forceful. 'I can't shout. She had to go.'

'Go? Who? Sonia? From Dixon Dubois?'

'Office politics, if you like.'

Silently Markby cursed that this conversation was being conducted, at Meredith's end, in a crowded carriage. In a commuter train the word 'redundancy' would have anyone within earshot hanging on every word.

'What sort? Clash of personalities? Shenanigans?'

'Yes, the last.'

'Someone chasing her round the office?'

'No, the other way around.'

'*What?*'

'I'm ringing off. See you this evening, OK?'

He found himself looking at a silent handset. He tucked the mobile away and digested the information. It made sense. Sonia had left London under a cloud. She'd found a hideaway in the country, but was bored there. So she'd begun playing games she'd played before – if 'games' was the right word. Perhaps she'd needed the affairs, needed to believe she could have anyone she fancied. Poor self-image? wondered Markby. Sense of inadequacy or failure? Desperation to prove something without really knowing what that thing was? He'd met both men and women like that before. Philandering men who'd let good marriages go to the wall because they had to play around, show their mates they could still pull the birds. That quiet little woman, he remembered the case at Bamford, married to a respectable man, nice house, plenty of money. Only when two of her lovers had fought it out in the front drive, resulting in a neighbour calling the police, had the truth come out. She'd been running what she'd like to call a sex therapy business at home in the afternoons. Rocked house prices on the entire estate.

Cherry Tree Farm wasn't far from here. Pearce's description, embellished with much critical detail, had made him curious to see the real thing. Why not drive there now, take a look at the place? It was the scene of the assault on Derry Hayward. He wanted to see the layout for himself, get a picture in his head. According to his wife's version of events, given to Markby and Pearce at the hospital, Hayward's walk to the stable had taken long enough for the attacker, under cover of darkness, to slip round behind him and get into the house itself. The local police, called by Mrs Hayward, would have all this in their report and Pearce would be following it up. But Markby admitted to himself that old habits died hard. He couldn't, with the best efforts, remain stuck behind a desk receiving reports from officers. He had to be there, see, smell, touch, pick up his own impressions.

Besides, he knew Belinda Hayward was wrong. The unwelcome visitor had been neither rustler nor common or garden thief, as she'd termed it. He'd targeted neither horse in the stable nor antique knick-knack in the house. His target had always been Derry himself and Markby had a pretty shrewd idea who the assailant had been, too.

He smiled as he turned into the neat track leading to the farm, passing the nameplate with the carved horse. It was certainly a different setup to Hazelwood! His first sight of the farm buildings confirmed this. It looked like a picture off a calendar. He'd anticipated finding the place deserted and being free to wander round on his own. But in this he was disappointed. Though the police had left the scene, Mrs Hayward had returned from the hospital and was decanting her twins from a Range Rover.

'Oh, it's you, the other policeman,' she greeted him as he got out of his car and came over to her. 'I had to bring these two home. Time for their tea. I'll go back and visit Derry again this evening.'

Markby followed her into the house where they fetched up in the kitchen. It was large, untidy and pleasant. Something about the style of its pine furniture rang a bell. He asked whether any of it had been made by Peter Burke.

'Most of it,' said Mrs Hayward as she plugged in an electric kettle. 'Burke's a very good craftsman and his prices are reasonable. It gives the place the right look; it's what visitors expect to see. Sad thing really, poor Sonia always admired it. She talked of asking Burke to make some for the kitchen at Hazelwood. I don't know if she ever did anything about that.'

She turned her attention to the fridge, which was festooned with cartoon figure magnets.

'Listen, you two,' she addressed her daughters. 'It's chicken nuggets or hamburgers, which?'

The twins opted for hamburgers. Mrs Hayward grabbed a packet from the freezer compartment and shook the meat patties out on to the grill pan. 'Open the window!' she commanded Markby. 'These things smell the place out.'

Markby did as he was bid and, as the kettle had switched itself off, busied himself making the tea.

'This is a difficult time for you,' he observed. 'Will you be able to manage here on your own?'

'Have to, won't I?' she retorted. 'I might phone my sister to come over and give a hand. I've got visitors booked in for next week.' Abruptly, she added, 'Derry will pull through. He'll be as right as rain, but of course, he won't be able to do much around the place for a few weeks.'

'The doctors . . . ?' Markby paused awkwardly. It wasn't quite what the surgeon had told him and Pearce.

'I don't need doctors telling me. I know. I know Derry. He's tough and he's a fighter.' Mrs Hayward split the bread rolls for the hamburgers with efficiency.

So are you, thought Markby with some admiration. He watched her flip over the patties on the grill, organise her daughters into washing their hands, set out teacups for herself and Markby and pour out strawberry-flavoured milk for the children.

'It's the only way they'll drink it,' she said of this last item. 'I believe in children drinking milk. They need the calcium. I don't believe in fizzy drinks.'

The children were settled at last and he and Mrs Hayward seated themselves at one end of the long pine table. At the other end, the twins busied themselves with their hamburgers, though they kept a wary eye on the visitor.

'Your daughters,' said Markby, 'they're in the same class at St Clare's as Tammy Franklin, I believe.'

'That's right,' said Mrs Hayward, moodily stirring her tea. 'Funny kid. I had her over here for the day when they held the inquest.'

'In what way do you mean "funny"?' Markby asked her.

She scratched at her wire-mop of hair. 'Very quiet. Secretive, I'd call it. Lost her mum, of course. Her real mother, that is. Sonia wasn't what I'd call much of a substitute.'

Markby guessed the late Mrs Sonia Franklin could have done nothing right in Belinda Hayward's eyes. He glanced at the twins. 'Mind if I ask them a couple of questions? As we're sitting here, anyway.'

'Ask away,' said Mrs Hayward, mildly surprised. To her daughters, she ordered, 'Speak up, you two.'

'Don't worry,' said Markby to the understandably alarmed twins, smiling. 'You're friends of Tammy's, are you?'

206

One of them muttered, 'Know her at school.'

'That's Lynette,' said Mrs Hayward. 'The other one is Lucy. Actually, she's called Lucinda. We thought of calling her Belinda, same as me, but it doesn't do to have two people with the same name under one roof, does it? Even Lucinda sounds a bit like Belinda when you yell it out, so we call her Lucy.'

'I've got a niece called Emma,' said Markby, as Mrs Hayward concluded this involved explanation. 'She and her friends, they sometimes have secrets. It's a sort of game. Would you and Tammy Franklin have a secret, by any chance?'

The twins were looking even more alarmed. Their mother said, 'Come on! Cat got your tongues?'

Without warning, Lucy burst into tears. Lynette turned on her sibling furiously. 'Stop it!' she ordered. 'Stop that, Luce!'

'Good God, what's going on?' exclaimed their mother. 'Stop snivelling, Lucy, do. Now then, what have you two been up to? No beating about the bush now! Let's be having it.'

Markby reflected that if one of his officers interrogated a juvenile in this manner, defence would call it bullying. The twins were, presumably, used to their mother's style. Lucy scrambled away from the table to fetch a tissue from a pack on the dresser and returned, sniffing, but tear-free. Lynette, a chip off the maternal block in Markby's opinion, sat rigidly in her chair and fixed the visitor with a hostile gaze.

'It was a joke,' she said. 'We didn't mean any harm. We didn't know Sonia was going to be murdered.'

'Hey, what's this?' demanded their mother. She turned to Markby. 'Ought I to have a solicitor here?'

'If you choose. But I don't think your daughters have been indulging in homicide. I think they mean they wouldn't have played some sort of trick on Tammy if they'd known what was about to happen at Hazelwood. Is that it, girls?'

They were both nodding furiously.

'Right,' said their parent, 'what sort of trick was this?'

Lynette appointed herself spokeswoman. 'Tammy's got a bag she carries her schoolbooks in. It's made like a frog, a green one.'

Markby, his cup half raised to his lips, froze. The frog bag. They'd never tracked it down. He should have guessed.

'We all get off the school bus together.' Lynette was addressing him. 'Tammy, Lucy and me. We ran off with her frog bag. It was just a joke.

We'd have brought it back, but Tammy got into a temper and walked off, going back to Hazelwood. So Lucy and I were left with the bag.'

She stopped and looked guiltily at her mother, who said, 'You didn't bring it home here. Where is it?'

'We – we took it over to the old viaduct and threw it over the edge. It landed in the trees on the embankment.' Lynette had the grace to mumble, eyes cast down.

'Both of you,' burst out their mother, 'will write letters of apology to Tammy this very evening, you hear?'

Lucy spoke up in joint defence. 'We told her where it was. We rang Hazelwood Farm that evening and told Tammy where she could find it.'

'That evening, which day are you talking about?' Markby asked them.

'Wednesday,' said Lynette. 'But we didn't know that on Thursday they'd find Sonia dead and all this would happen.'

Markby set down his cup. 'You'll have to excuse me, Mrs Hayward. Thank you for the tea and thank you, girls, for telling me this.'

'It's important, is it?' asked Mrs Hayward in unusually subdued manner. 'I mean, it has to do with Sonia's murder in some way?'

'I think it does, though not in any way your daughters could've anticipated.' He smiled encouragingly. 'Don't be too hard on them. Kids play silly jokes on one another.'

'They've been told to stay away from the railway and that includes the old viaduct,' Mrs Hayward returned sharply. 'I hope this hasn't held up your inquiries.'

'I think rather it's just helped them along! I hope all goes well with your husband.'

'Just one damn thing after another, isn't it?' she said.

Markby drove back to Hazelwood, his mind busy with arranging the facts in order, his brain buzzing. Forget the assault on Derry Hayward. That had nearly led him well off down the wrong track. The phone call, that was the pivotal point of it all. Not from Sonia, but from one of the Hayward twins, telling Tammy where to find her schoolbag. Tammy had gone upstairs ostensibly to do her homework, but she couldn't do it because she hadn't her books. Downstairs, Hugh and Sonia had been quarrelling, but Sonia had stormed out and Hugh was dozing in front of the TV. So Tammy had slipped out of the house and made her way to the embankment.

'And there,' murmured Markby, 'she was a witness.'

But why did she not want to speak up? Because the person she had seen was someone she knew and wanted to protect. Not her father who was back at the farm asleep in front of a television set. There was only one other person it could have been. Her uncle, Simon Franklin.

Simon, so keen to insist to Markby that the killer had been a stranger of some sort. Simon, who'd made sure to be present when his brother was interviewed and sat in on the interview with his niece. Simon, monitoring the investigation as it went along, ready to head it off if it turned in his direction.

It had turned there now. He'd have to pick the man up for questioning, but first, he had to warn Hugh to keep his daughter safe at Hazelwood.

'She's not here,' said Hugh.

'What?' Markby gazed at him in disbelief. 'Where is she?'

They stood at the gateway to the farmyard. The old dog, the spaniel with the antisocial habits about which Holding had entertained them all, was sniffing about round their feet. To Markby, that meant the child couldn't be anywhere on the farm. If she were, she'd have the dog with her.

'Oh, she's not gone far,' said Hugh. 'I drove over to Simon's to tell him about Derry Hayward. Tam came along with me. She's still there. Simon will bring her back later.'

Markby tried to control his obvious alarm. 'Where is your brother's house?'

'Follow the road round.' Hugh made a wide gesture westwards like the mariner in the painting *The Boyhood of Raleigh.* 'Turn off at Sprocketts Lane. Can't miss it. It's the only house down there.'

'How far would it be across the fields?'

'Not far to anyone who knows the way. In your case, you'd be quicker driving. Won't take you more than a couple of minutes.' Hugh was getting curious. 'What's the problem?'

Markby could hardly reply, I think your brother's a murderer. He said, 'I just wanted to ask her something. I've been over at Cherry Tree.'

'Derry going on all right, is he?'

'As well as can be expected.' Markby got back into his car, waved a farewell hand and sped away, leaving a perplexed Hugh leaning on the five-bar gate.

He found the house without difficulty. It was of stone under a thatched roof and had once been a pair of labourer's cottages. Knocked into one, they made a roomy and attractive dwelling. Simon's off-roader was parked in the driveway. Markby got out of his car and crunched over the gravel path to the front door.

The sound of his approach brought no curious face to a window. He lifted the heavy iron knocker and struck it twice against the door. As he waited, he studied the knocker, which was in the form of a female hand in a seventeenth-century-style sleeve, holding a ball. He remembered seeing similar pieces in France, on the doors of old houses, but never in England. He wondered whether Simon had brought it home from a foreign trip.

Clearly he was going to get no answer here. Markby made his way round to the back and tried again. Still no answer. Hesitantly he tried the back door handle. At the touch of his hand, the door swung open.

He stepped into the kitchen and called out, 'Anyone at home?'

His voice echoed in the way that only happens in an empty house. Nevertheless he checked out the remaining downstairs rooms rapidly. In one of them, Simon's study, the desk supported a computer, switched off, and was covered in papers, which seemed to be notes and drafts relating to some historical material. On top of these lay a couple of battered and bent belt or shoe buckles. They had a historic look to them. Simon must be working on another slice of life in times gone by. But where was the man himself and more to the point, where was his niece? But they couldn't have gone far. They must be on the property somewhere.

Markby went outside again and scrutinised the landscape. At the end of the untidy garden was a stone wall with a door in it. Beyond that was what looked like an orchard. He set off.

The door was ajar, and as he pushed it open he heard voices, a child's laughter. A surge of relief flooded over him. He was in an old orchard, all right, sadly neglected, but still flourishing in a wild way. He made his way through the long grass towards the sound of the voices.

He came upon them at the far end of the orchard under an old apple tree. A swing had been fixed up. Tammy sat on it and her uncle pushed. The swing flew ever higher and the child shrieked, caught between laughter and the thrill of fear. Above her the bough of the old tree creaked and bent under the strain.

But it was the man who held Markby's attention. Simon Franklin faced him but hadn't seen him. Markby didn't think the man saw anything. His features were a mask, his eyes glazed like those of a man in a trance, and on that pale countenance Markby read a dreadful resolve.

He shouted, '*Franklin!*'

He saw astonishment in the white face, eyes opening wide, mouth parting, then recognition and finally a kind of horrified awareness. Simon Franklin's hands loosed the ropes and fell back by his sides. He stepped away from the swing which, without the momentum he'd provided, slowed and narrowed its arc. Tammy's feet dragged along the ground. She stopped swinging but remained on the wooden seat, still holding the ropes to either side of her at shoulder level, staring at Markby.

He walked over to them. 'Hullo,' he said to her. 'I'm Superintendent Markby.' To her uncle he said, 'I don't think that swing looks very safe, do you, Franklin?'

Franklin blinked. His eyes, which had seemed unfocused, steadied their gaze. Some colour returned to his cheeks and the awful frozen set of his features thawed into humanity. He moistened his lips. 'No, perhaps you're right.' He glanced nervously upwards towards the branch.

'We need to have a talk,' Markby said. 'Perhaps we could drop off the little girl at her home and carry on into Bamford?'

'Am I being arrested?' Simon sounded bewildered.

'No,' Markby said. 'You're accompanying me voluntarily.' He thought he understood the man's bewilderment, directed not at what was happening to him now, but what he'd been about to do moments earlier.

'Voluntarily?' repeated Simon. 'So that's what they call it.' He stretched out a hand and touched his niece's head. 'Come on, Tammy. Time to go home.'

CHAPTER SIXTEEN

In the cramped, spartan setting of the interview room at Bamford Police Station, Simon Franklin looked oddly at home. Perhaps, thought Markby, it was his academic appearance which gave him the air of a monk in his cell. A cell was where Markby hoped to see him eventually, but he had no illusion as to how difficult that would be.

They'd been joined by Pearce, who'd hastened over and who began the interview.

'Would you like to tell us again about your relationship with your sister-in-law, Mrs Sonia Franklin?'

'There's nothing to tell.' Simon removed his glasses and held them by the mended frame in the professional way he had. 'I had met her before her marriage to my brother as she was a friend of my former partner. After their marriage, I saw her often, naturally. I think I got along with her well enough. We had no quarrels, anyway. I considered her a family member.'

'You told me, when we spoke before,' Pearce went on, 'that she sometimes visited your house during her evening walks.'

'Yes, frequently during the time my partner lived there. The women were friends and I defy even you to read something into that! I believe I also told you that after Bethan left, Sonia's evening visits became rare.'

'This afternoon your brother and your niece visited you. Did you have some conversation with your niece, after your brother left?'

'Of course I did!' Simon snapped. 'Look, my niece is a twelve-year-old child, for goodness' sake. I don't see why she had to be dragged into this. She's been through enough over the last couple of years.'

Markby stirred in his chair. 'Mr Franklin, what were your intentions this afternoon when I came upon you with your niece in the orchard?'

Flushing, Simon retorted, 'You came upon, as you put it, a harmless scene of family amusement. I was pushing her on the old swing. You saw so yourself.'

'I did. I also saw that the swing was in very poor condition. The ropes were frayed and rotted. The branch to which they were attached was unequal to the strain. Hadn't you noticed that?'

'I suppose I should have done,' Simon told him. 'But I didn't.'

'We shall be talking to your niece again.'

'You may well put ideas into her head, words into her mouth, but I shall strenuously contest any accusations you may care to make. My relationship with my sister-in-law was entirely above board. I resent your implication that it was anything else. I know nothing about her death.'

'Earlier today,' Markby continued, 'I paid a visit to Cherry Tree Farm where I spoke to the children of Mrs Hayward, in her presence.'

'In her presence!' interrupted Simon sarcastically. 'I'm surprised you didn't try to speak to them alone, as you told my brother you wished to speak to my niece. A highly irregular procedure and I trust my objection to it will remain on this tape.'

'They told me,' Markby was undeterred, 'that on Wednesday afternoon, the day Mrs Franklin died, they played a practical joke on your niece. They took her schoolbag, which is made in the shape of a frog, and dropped it over the viaduct. It landed in the trees on the embankment. Later that evening they phoned Hazelwood and told Tammy where she could find it. I think your niece made her way to the embankment later to fetch the bag.'

'This is fantasy. Has she said so?'

'Not yet,' Markby admitted. 'But I believe she will be ready to tell her story now. She's about to be interviewed.'

Simon sniffed. 'Well, even if she was there, which would surprise me, I was *not*, either on the embankment or anywhere near the place, if that's what you're leading up to.' Simon paused. 'This frog bag, is this the one your minion was looking for when he searched the Smiths' caravan?'

'You know about that?' Pearce asked, surprised.

Simon turned his attention to him. 'Why shouldn't I? The Smiths were both very upset. They're a respectable family. But I've read in the press how the police harass travellers. No doubt you consider them fair game.'

He turned back to Markby, continuing, before either man had had a chance to deny this accusation, 'It seems to me this story you've concocted doesn't hold water. If my niece went to collect her satchel, why were you asking the Smiths about it? Was it still there when Danny found Sonia's body? If it was, how do you know my niece went there to collect it and why didn't she take it home with her if she did?'

'Because,' Markby said, 'she saw something which frightened her so much, she ran home, forgetting the bag.'

'This is a complete house of cards.' Simon leaned back in his chair. 'And I decline to answer any more questions about it. If you insist on holding me here, then I must ask for my solicitor.'

Markby signalled to Pearce to switch off the tape recorder. He waited until this had been done, Pearce having first recorded the fact that the interview had ended and the time. Markby got to his feet.

'We will be holding you here. You can make a phone call to your solicitor. When he gets here, we'll talk again. I think you were intending to engineer an accident to your niece on that swing this afternoon. You were on that embankment on Wednesday night and she saw you. You know it. You knew we were planning to talk to her again. You were determined to prevent that.'

Simon Franklin replaced his spectacles on his nose. 'Prove it,' he said calmly.

'We're going to have a dickens of a job,' said Pearce when the two police officers had left the interview room. 'He's a cool beggar. Even if the kid says she saw him, it hangs on that identification. It was dark, she was scared . . . a defence lawyer would get it chucked out of court.'

'I don't need to be told that!' Markby said irritably. 'But we can only proceed one step at a time. First we need that child's story. I'm as sure as I've ever been of anything that he meant harm to her this afternoon and I arrived in the nick of time. Perhaps he wasn't in his right mind at the time. Scared out of his wits because he'd just learned she'd seen him, I suspect. But he had murder in mind!'

Pearce still looked unhappy. 'What about Hayward? Did he try and kill him, too?'

'Hayward? No, he had no reason to attack Hayward. I'm fairly sure I know who attacked Hayward but that's going to be another tricky thing to prove. First things first, Dave. We need Tammy Franklin's story.'

'You want me to tell them all of it, Dad?'

'All of it, love,' Hugh said quietly. 'Whatever it is, if it's the truth, it's got to be told, even if it hurts. So you take your time and you tell Mr Markby here all about it.' He paused. 'You tell *me* all about it, even if it's got to do with Uncle Simon.'

Markby and Holding were seated in the farm's family sitting room. Pogo had been excluded but could be heard faintly whining from the direction of the kitchen where he'd been incarcerated. It seemed to Markby that Hugh Franklin had undergone a transformation in the bare twenty-four hours since he'd last talked with him. The farmer was pale beneath his tan and his lined face gave him the appearance of a man who had been ill. But his manner was calm. He'd steeled himself to hear the worst.

'I know,' Markby said gently to the child, 'that the Hayward girls took your frog backpack with your schoolbooks in it, and threw it from the old viaduct. They've told us so themselves. According to them, they telephoned you later that evening, to tell you where it was. Is that right?'

'Yes, they did.' There was a spark of anger in Tammy's eyes and her cheeks were flushed. She gave Markby a quick assessing look, then blurted, 'I don't like the Haywards. I never have. They aren't friends of mine at school. I'm sorry their dad is in hospital, but it doesn't make me like them. Lynette took the bag off me as we got off the school bus. She and her sister kept throwing it to one another. They wanted to make me run about trying to catch it but I wasn't going to play their silly game. I walked off and left them.'

'But it was a nuisance,' Markby said, 'because you couldn't do your homework.'

Tammy calmed down slightly and nodded. 'It wasn't my fault but I didn't want to tell anyone at home about it because I'm not a telltale. For the same reason, I didn't tell Miss Brady at school when she asked where my homework was.'

'If those Hayward kids have been giving you trouble, you should've told me, Tam,' Hugh said angrily. 'I'd have put a stop to that double-quick.'

'I didn't want to bother you, Dad. You'd got your own things to worry about, the farm and – and Sonia.'

Hugh hunched his broad shoulders and released a deep sigh. 'Yes, I know. But none of that is anything you should be worrying your head about, love.'

'Well, I couldn't help—' Here Tammy broke off and flushed crimson.

'You heard Sonia and me yelling at one another, I suppose.' Hugh sounded depressed. 'I can't say we tried to keep our voices down when we had a barney. I see now what Jane's been getting at. I put too much on your shoulders, didn't I? I didn't mean it. Did you hear us on Wednesday evening, too?'

Markby frowned. 'I'd rather you didn't lead, Mr Franklin.'

Tammy glowered at him and pointedly addressed her reply to her father. 'Yes, Dad. I did. I sat upstairs with Pogo and saw Sonia go for her walk. A bit later on the phone went and it was Lynette, I think. It's nearly as hard to tell them apart on the phone as it is to do it when you look at them. She told me where the bag was. She didn't tell me because she was sorry. She told me because she thought she'd get into trouble, and her sister, too. So I thought, I could go and get it. I'd take Pogo. It wasn't raining or anything and the moon was very bright. You could see really clearly. But I took a torch.'

Tammy stopped speaking for a moment, pursed her lips and frowned. 'I wasn't scared out on my own. Not while I was on our land. It was a bit spooky when I got to the viaduct. It took me a lot longer to get there than I thought it would because Pogo walks very slowly and he kept stopping to sniff at things. I thought I'd lost him once and I was worried. I called and called him and at last he came. I had brought his lead with me but I hadn't used it till then. After that, after the scare when I thought he'd wandered off, I clipped the lead on. We got to the road all right. I started climbing down the embankment but I hadn't got far when I heard a car coming. I switched off the torch because I didn't want anyone to see me. I thought the car would go by, but it stopped, on the road right by me.'

'What kind of car was it?' asked Holding.

'A big one. I don't know makes of cars. I'm almost sure it wasn't a Volvo like Sonia's. I know it wasn't a Land Rover like Dad's. It wasn't Uncle Simon's, either. I crouched down behind some bushes and held on to Pogo's muzzle. But he's not a barky sort of dog, anyway. Then I had an awful shock.'

The last words were mumbled. She looked down and then quickly, furtively, up at her father as if afraid that what she was about to say might anger him.

'All right, sweetheart,' he said. 'We can guess. You saw—'

'Mr Franklin,' interrupted Markby again. 'Please! She must use her own words. She must tell us herself what she saw. You mustn't put ideas in her head.'

Tammy sat up straight and glared at him. 'I saw Uncle Simon,' she said quickly, 'So you needn't snap my dad's head off. They opened the doors of the car and the light went on inside and I saw it was Uncle Simon on the side nearest the embankment. I was really surprised because it wasn't his car, like I told you.'

'They?' Markby asked.

'There were two people. I couldn't see the other man so well. He was very thin and had very short, flat sort of hair. He was a bit bald, I think. They went to the back of the car and opened the boot.'

At this point Tammy's equanimity deserted her. The interview was interrupted for some fifteen minutes until, fortified by a fizzy drink, she resumed her story.

'They took something out of the boot.' She stared down at her hands. She was still gripping the plastic straw she'd used for the drink and she began to bend it at different points along its length until she could join the two ends to form a ragged circle. 'They had a job to get it out. It was big. I thought at first it was a sack and perhaps they were going to chuck some rubbish down the embankment. I was a bit surprised Uncle Simon would do something like that. When people dump their rubbish on farmland the farmer has to clear it up and sometimes has to pay for it to be taken away, so Uncle Simon wouldn't just chuck something away in the countryside. At least, I thought he wouldn't have. They sort of staggered away from the car and I could see they were carrying something between them not like a sack, something all limp, and it was like a body. The arms were dangling. Uncle Simon held the shoulders and the other man the feet. Uncle Simon started muttering and grumbling about the weight but the other man didn't say anything. They carried and dragged it between them down the embankment until Uncle Simon said, "That's far enough!" Then they dropped it and went back up the embankment to the car. They drove off.'

'In all this time,' Markby asked, 'you're sure the other man didn't speak?'

'He was puffing, really out of breath. I don't think he had any left for speaking.'

There was a silence during which Hugh put his hand over his eyes and Tammy stared at her feet.

'What did you do next, Tammy?' Ginny Holding took up the questioning in response to a glance from her boss.

'When they'd gone, I took Pogo and went to see what it was . . . I still thought it must be some sort of rubbish and the arms were my imagination. I shone the torch on it . . .' Tammy's voice almost died away. 'And I saw Sonia. Her eyes were open, but glassy and blank. She stared up at me but she didn't blink. Her mouth was open, too; I could see her bottom teeth. She was lying twisted, just as they'd dropped her. Her eyes were the worst because they sort of popped at me and hadn't any expression at all. I knew she must be dead. I was frightened. I forgot about my frog bag and ran home. I made Pogo run with me, poor old thing. He was wheezing dreadfully when we got back. Dad was asleep in front of the TV. I went upstairs, cleaned myself up and decided I wouldn't say anything. You see, I' – Tammy raised her face, imprinted with misery and guilt – 'I wasn't sorry she was dead. That's awful, isn't it? That's a sin, like Father Holland says.'

Hugh took his hand from his eyes and held out his arms to his child. She scrambled from her chair and ran into them.

'Now, you're not to think like that,' came Hugh's voice, muffled by Tammy's hair. 'We can't help what we feel about people and that's a fact. If anyone did wrong it was me because I brought Sonia here so quickly after your mum died. I should've talked to you about it more. I was stupid and it's all my fault, if anyone's.'

Holding switched off the tape and sat silently, watching. Markby shifted in his chair and sighed.

Hugh said, 'Are you going to arrest my brother?'

'We're holding him for further questioning,' Markby said evasively.

'I don't understand it,' Hugh said, bewildered. 'Who was the other bloke?'

'Much as I'd like to charge him,' said Alan Markby to Meredith, over the remains of his steak, 'I've got absolutely nothing to go on except the word of a frightened child. It was night. There was moonlight but down by the embankment it was dark because of the trees and the old viaduct throwing its shadow. She was already very upset and nervous, out on her own with just her dog, and she'd had a scare when she thought the dog had wandered off. Suddenly there was a car and she was even more frightened. She hid. What she saw, she saw through gaps in the undergrowth. One would be hard put to find a situation in which she'd be more confused and liable to jump to conclusions. She says she saw her Uncle Simon. He says she didn't. She didn't recognise the car. She didn't recognise the other man.'

He sat back in his chair and shrugged resignedly. 'I can't prove he was on that embankment. He has no alibi but then, probably no one else in his present situation would. He's living on his own, working on a new book. He was in his cottage planning out the new *magnum opus* all Wednesday evening, says he. No one called. No one rang. I saw his work in progress myself. I can't break his story as it stands at the moment.'

Meredith poured them both more wine. 'Do you think it's possible Tammy is mistaken?'

He shook his head. 'No. I might have said differently if I hadn't seen him with her in that orchard. If I hadn't seen his face. He meant there to be an accident with that swing. Even if she hadn't been killed by the fall when the ropes snapped or the branch broke, a quick blow to the head with a piece of wood such as there are any number of lengths lying around there, and she would be dead. Very difficult to show that the blow wasn't caused by striking the ground or crashing up against a tree trunk. I dare say he was hardly in his right mind at the time. It's my guess he was scared witless by having just learned that she'd seen him dispose of her stepmother's body. All he wanted to do was silence her. But so far that's only my opinion. I've no evidence to back it. There were no other witnesses to that scene. Defence will say I misread it entirely. I don't believe I did, but I can't prove it. The most anyone can say without fear of contradiction is that Simon was stupid to allow his niece to use an unsafe swing.'

'I see.' Meredith got up and went to the door. 'All this must be very hard for Hugh to accept.'

'The poor chap's in a real stew. He says he believes his daughter's account, but in his heart I'm sure he'd give anything for her to be wrong. This is his brother and we're saying he killed Hugh's wife.'

He supposed Meredith could hear him. She'd gone into the kitchen and he was talking into thin air. She had heard him. As she returned with the cheese and crackers, she said, 'I can't see Simon having an affair with Sonia. He wouldn't be that stupid.'

'Remember what that personnel officer told you in London? Even if she hadn't succeeded in seducing him Sonia might still have created a lot of trouble and Simon couldn't pay her off with a redundancy package.'

'I still think that, given the rocky state of their marriage, she couldn't have been certain Hugh would take her word against his brother's. All Simon would have had to do would be to tell her to get lost, basically. He didn't have to kill her, Alan.'

'You're telling me I've got the wrong man? What about Tammy's testimony?'

'I'm saying there's something missing. Tammy saw two people disposing of Sonia's body. One of them she identified as her uncle.'

Markby speared a piece of Brie moodily. 'Ah, the mystery man. It's the weakest point in the child's testimony and as long as we can't identify him, a doubt is cast on her identification of Simon. And disposing of a body isn't the same as murder. I may be able to place Simon at the embankment, but I can't tie him to the attack on Sonia. He isn't even left-handed, for goodness' sake.'

'What's that got to do with it?' Meredith asked in surprise.

Markby explained Pearce's theory. 'The abrasions are all to the right-hand side of her face and neck. It doesn't prove a left-handed assailant, but it does suggest it.' He paused, struck by the expression on his companion's face. 'What's up?'

She raised a hand. 'Hang on, don't interrupt for a sec. I'm seeing things.'

Markby glanced worriedly at the wine. She made another impatient gesture with her hand. 'I mean, there's a picture in my mind. Listen. After the inquest, Jane and I went to the ladies' lavatory in the courthouse. We walked in and Bethan Talbot was there, standing in front of the mirror, making up her face. She was painting her lips. We came up behind her.'

Meredith got to her feet and walked to a nearby mirror. 'Look, demonstration. Pretend this teaspoon is a lipstick in a case. You stand where I was standing, behind Bethan, and looking at her reflection in the mirror. That's what I saw, not her face but her *reflected* face.' Meredith mimed painting her lips. 'See? I'm right-handed, so the reflection looks wrong. But the reflection of Bethan looked as if she was painting her lips with her right hand. Which means,' Meredith turned, 'that she was using her left. Bethan Talbot is left-handed.'

Markby thought it over, then shook his head. 'Tammy knows Bethan. Tammy didn't see Bethan or any woman with Simon that night. She saw a thin, youngish man with very short hair, possibly balding.'

Meredith was staring at him thoughtfully and he invited, 'Go on. What is it?'

'I might be wrong.'

'Tell me, anyway.'

She told him and he said, 'How am I going to find that out?'

'I've got an idea about that, too. But I don't know whether I should suggest it. After all,' Meredith smiled at him benignly, 'I wouldn't wish to interfere in police investigations.'

'Cut the sarcasm,' Markby told her. 'Let's hear your idea.'

'Nice place. I wouldn't mind living somewhere like this,' observed Meredith. They were in Cheltenham, standing on the pavement before the house in which Bethan Talbot lived, and looking up at the façade.

'I've never fancied living in a flat,' said Markby. 'Which is why I never have, I suppose.'

'Haven't you?' Meredith considered this. 'I've lived in dozens of flats. Having such a peripatetic lifestyle for so many years, I've more or less had to. It's only since I've been back in England that's it's been worth investing in a house. There's nothing wrong with a decent flat but I really meant, when I said live somewhere like this, live in all of it. You know, have a house like this.'

The building, as so many in the centre of that attractive city, was late-Georgian. Its frontage was whitewashed, its tall windows spaced geometrically, a flight of steps ran up to its black-painted front door beneath a Grecian portico. Another twisting flight led down to a basement. A list of names by individual bells indicated this gracious dwelling was now subdivided into flats, as Markby had remarked.

'Wouldn't it be a bit big?' he asked.

'Are you being awkward on purpose or what? Fat chance I've ever got of owning a house like this. I just said—'

He was peering at the list of names by the bell pushes. 'She's not here, she must live in the basement.'

They clattered down the twisting steps and found themselves in the subterranean hollow. The tiny flagged space in the basement well had been given the courtyard treatment. The walls had been whitewashed and had plant holders affixed to them. Tubs of flowers had been set strategically on the paving, there was even a young wisteria climbing up the wall. The window beside the door had been enhanced by a pair of louvred shutters in traditional Mediterranean style.

'She's made a good job of it,' said Markby approvingly, inspecting the wisteria.

By the bell push was a card bearing Bethan's name and occupation.

'Works from home,' said Meredith, pushing the bell. 'There's a lot to be said for that. Perhaps I could find something I could do from home.' She glanced at him. 'I didn't mean just sit there and look after you.'

'Perish the thought. I never suggested that. I wouldn't expect you to give up your job. I'm not looking for a blasted housekeeper! I've told you that I don't know how many times. I asked you to marry me because—'

Perhaps fortunately, the door was pulled open at that moment. Bethan appeared to view. She was dressed in tight designer jeans, a figure-hugging blue jerseyknit top with a scoop neck and a short-sleeved black cardigan. Large gold hoops dangled from her ears and gleamed through the strands of bright red hair.

'Meredith?' she exclaimed, taken aback and losing for a moment her usual self-assurance. She looked at Markby questioningly.

'Hope you don't mind us dropping in unannounced,' said Meredith cheerfully. 'I've brought Alan with me, Alan Markby who's in charge of the investigation into Sonia's death. You spoke about him to me and I thought you might like to meet him.'

Bethan looked unsure about this, but rallied. 'Oh, how nice – nice to meet you.' She held out her hand. Markby shook it. 'Er, I suppose you ought to come in.'

It wasn't the most gracious of invitations, but her visitors beamed at her. She turned and led the way. Behind her back, Meredith gave Markby a thumbs-up sign and mouthed, 'So far, so good.'

He looked a bit unhappy, she thought. This wasn't the way he liked doing police work. Deep down, she felt a bit uneasy herself at acting the role of Trojan horse. But she'd promised Jane to do her best for Hugh. Nor could Bethan be counted as any sort of friend – and this was a case of murder.

The room into which Bethan took them was the one with the window on to the basement. To Meredith's surprise, at the other end French windows gave on to a patio with garden furniture. She hadn't realised the building was constructed on a slope. There was very little furniture in the room, which was a large one, only the basics and all that very plain. There were four white leather seats, heavily padded but without any arms or sides to them which meant they could be pushed together to make a sofa or stand singly, and a low table with beautifully inlaid modern marquetry. At the far end of the room by the patio doors a work station had been created with drawers and shelves and a desk with a computer. It stood aloofly apart from the domestic area of the room. On the polished parquet lay a single small rug which Meredith judged to be Persian and antique.

To Meredith's mind the general effect, whilst elegant, was also clinical and uninviting. She didn't think Bethan was so hard up she couldn't afford a bit more furniture, a few cushions and some wall-to-wall carpeting. This look was Bethan's choice and had probably been created by some expensive interior designer. The only thing which could be counted as an ornament was an original modern oil on the wall. It had probably cost a horrendous amount. Sorting out other people's taxes must pay. Meredith thought the room unnaturally tidy. Not even a magazine lying on the table or a pair of shoes kicked off in the corner. Not like my place, she thought.

'What a nice room,' she said aloud, duplicitously, to Bethan.

Bethan's eyebrows twitched. 'When I split with Simon, I left him all the furniture, even the stuff I'd paid for, except for the work station there.' She indicated her desk. 'I wasn't being generous to Sim. The furniture had been bought for the cottage and suited it. I bought new for this place. The rug and painting came from the cottage but they were mine before I ever met Sim.'

She folded her arms. She hadn't asked them to sit down and remained standing herself. 'I'd like to think you've come to tell me you've arrested Hugh. But I suppose you're going to say he's complained that I've been making accusations about him. Well, I have. What's more, I shall continue to do so.' She addressed these remarks belligerently to Markby.

'Neither of those things,' he told her. 'But we have interviewed Mr Simon Franklin.'

'I know that,' she said dismissively. 'His solicitor rang me. You're really grasping at straws, aren't you? Of course the kid didn't see him. I'm not saying she made it up, although kids do have unhealthy imaginations and that kid is a weird one. She just *thought* she saw Sim. She didn't, that's all there is to it.'

Meredith, who'd been studying Bethan's appearance, spoke. 'That's a nasty scratch on your neck.'

Bethan flushed and her hand moved automatically to the long, now-fading red line which ran from the point of her jaw to her collarbone. The scoop-necked top she wore today let it, and a second abrasion beneath it, be seen clearly. She tugged the sides of the black cardigan together.

'A neighbour's cat,' she said defiantly. 'I was trying to be friendly but it's one of these highly strung pedigree animals.'

'Bad luck,' said Meredith sympathetically. 'I've got a cat. Well, a share in a cat. He's got several homes. He was wild but now he seems to have sorted himself out. Cats are practical animals. He comes to see me when he feels like it.' She wandered to the far end of the room and looked out on to the patio. 'This is handy. Get the sun much?'

'In the morning,' Bethan said, letting her irritation show. Meredith's move had put her near the work station and a neat stack of folders perilously near the edge of the desk. A bunch of keys lay atop them.

'That means you can have breakfast out there,' said Meredith conversationally. 'But it's a pity not to have the evening sun, I'd have thought. You know, when you could take friends out there for a drink.' She turned suddenly, her hip collided with the stack of folders and they tumbled to the ground in confusion. The keys fell with them and hit the parquet with a clatter.

'Oh, for—' Bethan swooped down the room like an avenging fury. 'Can't you watch what you're doing? Those are clients' papers and now you've muddled them up!' She crouched down and began to grab at the loose sheets.

'I'm really sorry,' said Meredith contritely, dropping down on her heels and making to help.

'For God's sake, leave it alone!' snapped Bethan. 'You're making things worse!' She scooped up the keys and stuffed them in her jeans pocket.

'You're left-handed,' observed Meredith.

'So bloody what?' muttered Bethan. 'Look, just get out of the way, will you?'

Meredith obligingly got to her feet and put her hand on the edge of the desk. The remaining folders there, not dislodged by her first movement, now showered to the floor, striking Bethan on the head and spreading all around her. Bethan screeched. Meredith, all apologies, stooped over her, and this time contrived to brush against the crown of Bethan's red hair. Bethan dropped the papers she'd gathered up and clapped a hand to her head. She glowered up at Meredith.

'Don't touch me!'

'Sorry,' said Meredith. 'Clumsy of me. It's a wig, is it? It's a good one.'

Bethan rose to her feet. 'Get out of my flat. You – and him!' She spun round, pointing at Markby, fairly spitting out the words.

Neither of her visitors moved. 'Is it a wig?' asked Meredith with the same innocent curiosity.

Bethan turned back slowly to face her and said with forced calm, 'I'm not prolonging this conversation by one second. I don't know what you think you're doing here. I don't know why you brought along your police chum, but unless he's got a warrant in the pocket of that disgusting old Barbour, you can both leave right now.'

'We won't outstay our welcome,' said Markby. A look of relief spread over Bethan's face but was wiped off instantly when he added, 'Perhaps, instead, you'd like to come to the local station here? Then we can have a proper chat in the interview room. Meredith won't mind pottering round the shops while we talk things over.'

Meredith blinked at the 'pottering round the shops'. Bethan, after a brief silence when she gawped at Markby in shock, lost all presence of mind.

'No, I won't bloody well come with you! You've no authority to behave like this! Damn cheek, I've never come across anything like it in my entire life. Turning up unexpected and uninvited on my doorstop, invading my home, wrecking a week's work and even asking me personal and very hurtful questions about my hair!' She spluttered to a halt.

'Good Lord, is it a wig, then?' Markby asked, looking and sounding, Meredith informed him afterwards, remarkably like Bertie Wooster.

This amiable tactlessness succeeded in further exasperating Bethan who shouted, 'If I tell you, will you go away?' Before he could answer, she went on, 'If you must know, I've suffered from alopecia since childhood. It's nothing to do with illness, it's genetic. By the time I was sixteen I needed to wear a wig. Now you know that, I hope you're satisfied. Is there anything else you want?' she concluded sarcastically.

'Yes,' said Markby. 'I'd like to borrow your car for a day and have a forensic team look it over.'

Bethan seized a paperweight from the desk and flung it at him. Her aim was good and he ducked in the nick of time. The paperweight whizzed by his ear and struck the oil painting dead centre. The canvas split.

Both her visitors turned their heads to look at the damage and the moment's distraction was enough. There was a rush of fresh cool air. Meredith swung back to see the patio door closing and a last glimpse of Bethan before she disappeared from sight over the rear wall.

Markby uttered a grunt of annoyance. 'That's a pity.'

Meredith, appalled by the loss of their quarry, thought that the understatement of the week. She dashed out on to the patio in pursuit and scrambled up the brick wall over which Bethan had vanished. Thankfully she was wearing jeans today, and managed the manoeuvre rather more athletically than when scaling her own back fence on the day George had put wet cement down by the front door. On the other side of this wall was a long, well-tended and empty garden belonging to a house in the parallel street.

Astride the wall, she had a good view into adjoining gardens on both sides, but it was impossible to tell even which way Bethan had gone. Meredith muttered, 'Drat!' Alan had come out of the house and was standing on the patio beside her, his head at the level of her knee. 'No sign of her,' she told him.

'Get down from there,' he said. 'You're wasting your time. Of course there's no sign of her. She knows the layout of the block like the back of her hand. There's no point in you and me floundering after her like a couple of Keystone Cops. I'll put out a call.'

'Aren't you worried?' Meredith looked down at him from her perch in amazement. He was standing there with his hands in his pockets taking it all still with that inappropriate calm.

'Where's she going to go?' He took a hand from a pocket to help her down. When she'd regained terra firma and dusted herself off, he went on, 'Everything she's got is here.' He indicated the flat behind them. 'Her business, possessions, the lot. We'll either pick her up or, more likely in my view, when she's calmed down she'll come in herself with her solicitor. She's a lady with a quick temper but she's not a fool.'

There was a distant roar of an engine as a car left at speed.

'There she goes,' said Meredith. 'I hope you're right.'

CHAPTER SEVENTEEN

'No, she hasn't turned up yet,' Alan told Meredith when she rang him on Monday while Gerald was out of the office. 'But today or tomorrow she'll show up with her solicitor in tow and her story honed to perfection. Trust me.'

'Is it my imagination,' Meredith asked him, 'or do you sound slightly less certain of that than you did last week in Cheltenham?'

His voice became pained. 'She won't have consulted her legal adviser over the weekend. She'll have holed up somewhere and gone to see him today. Have a little faith in my professional judgement.'

'Have you had a psychiatrist on the case? All respect to your professional judgement and all the rest of it, but perhaps you should consider you may be wrong, as Oliver Cromwell more or less said to someone or other.'

'He wrote it, not said it, in a letter to the Church of Scotland. His actual words were, "I beseech you, in the bowels of Christ, think it possible you may be mistaken."'

'Oh, well! If we're going to swap quotations, didn't Cromwell also say, "Necessity hath no law"? Bethan's in dire straits and she isn't going to play the game according to your rules! I still think you should be out there looking for her.'

'We are looking for her. Don't keep worrying about it. All the usual procedures are in place. But she's not a professional villain who's disappeared into the underworld. When it comes to being on the run, she's an amateur.'

'Somehow, amateur isn't the word which leaps to my mind when I think of Bethan,' Meredith informed him. 'We shouldn't have taken our eyes off her in that flat. Still, lucky she missed you with that paperweight, I suppose.'

'Thank you. Pity she hit that expensive-looking daub on the wall.'

'Where's Simon? Is he back in his cottage? You have checked that out, I suppose?'

'Look here,' Alan's voice came irritated down the line, 'now you're treating us like a bunch of amateurs. We're keeping tabs on Simon but so far there's no sign she's tried to contact him.'

'Gerald's coming back,' Meredith said quickly. 'I've got to hang up.'

'When will I see you? Can't we have dinner during the week?'

'I'll call you. I don't know what time I'll be getting home tonight or tomorrow. I'm catching up on the work which piled up while I was away last week.'

She dropped the phone back into its cradle as Gerald ambled through the door.

'Not quick enough,' said Gerald. 'And you look furtive. You're up to something. It's you and that copper you hang out with. You're sleuthing again. You might tell me something – even a hint.'

'Not a chance, Gerry.' She relented at his obvious disappointment. 'When it's all over, then I'll tell you.'

'Then I'll read it for myself in the papers,' he said crossly.

Alan Markby replaced the phone and drummed his fingers on his desk. Despite the airy confidence with which he'd assured Meredith everything was in hand, he knew it wasn't. Nor had Meredith been fooled. Bethan Talbot was a loose cannon. They had to pick her up soon. That was to say, if she didn't come in of her own accord, something he still thought she would. The question was, when?

In the meantime, there was the matter of Derry Hayward and he could deal with that.

'I'm going out!' he informed Ginny Holding as he passed her in the corridor. 'Fox Corner.'

'Yessir!' she said, startled, in the wake of his briskly disappearing figure.

The drive to Fox Corner was a short one and in every other circumstance, a pleasant one. But Markby wasn't in the mood for it. He had an awkward confrontation ahead of him.

Peter Burke had customers, a middle-aged couple. They were inspecting a pine dresser. Markby, who had slipped in through the open door of the barn and was lurking in a shadowy corner, gathered from snatches of conversation that there was a problem with a finished order. The wife dithered in front of the piece and the husband stood by glumly with his hands in his pockets waiting for her to make up her mind.

'It's very pale,' she was saying. 'It's a lot paler than I expected.'

'It will darken naturally with time,' said Burke patiently. He'd betrayed by a twitch of his features that he'd seen Markby enter. But he gave no other acknowledgement. He picked up a square of polished pine, continuing to talk to his customers.

'This piece started off the same colour as your dresser. Over two years it's already darkened considerably, as you can see. In another year it'll be even darker.'

'I'm not sure,' said the wife.

'Make your mind up, Muriel,' urged the husband.

Since it seemed likely Muriel was going to quibble for some time longer, Markby went outside again and sat on a pine bench by the main entrance. Burke would know the superintendent hadn't left. He might be acting unconcerned, but with any luck, he'd be sweating.

The sun shone down on the road. The elderly man Markby had met on his previous visit hobbled from his cottage and made his way past, stick tapping. He paused to assess with rheumy eyes the seated man before greeting him. Markby returned his 'Good morning'. He wondered, as the old chap tapped his way onward, whether he remembered him, and where he was going now. Just for a constitutional, he supposed, just down the road and back again. A tiny world bordered by the limits of this meagre community. He watched with mild interest. The old fellow had paused by a broken-down chain-link fence and was contemplating, for no obvious reason, a pile of overgrown rubble on the other side.

The middle-aged couple were leaving. 'Well, I just hope it's going to be all right,' said the wife.

'I'm sure it will be, Muriel,' replied her husband in the voice of one who knew he would get the blame if it wasn't.

They drove away. Burke came out of the barn and looked down at Markby. 'Didn't expect to see you again,' he said.

'Didn't you?' Markby asked him.

Burke shrugged. 'One of your chaps came out and took my statement – about me and Sonia. I thought that'd be it.'

'I thought we might have a talk,' Markby said.

'I've nothing to add to the statement.'

'You know we took in Simon Franklin for questioning?'

Burke nodded and shrugged. 'It was on the local news. It didn't surprise me. I was sure one of the Franklins must have done it.'

'No,' contradicted Markby in conversational tone, 'you weren't. You thought Derry Hayward had killed her.'

There was a silence. 'Why,' asked Burke at last, 'should I think that?' He took a seat beside Markby on the bench, conceding that he couldn't get rid of his visitor quickly.

'Because Hayward, like you, had been having an affair with her. You decided that he killed her out of jealousy when she threw him over for you.'

'That's not how it was! There was no affair with Hayward. Sonia was in love with me.' Burke's voice had risen, become more shrill. He seemed aware of it and made a conscious effort to pull himself together. He glanced up the road but there was still no one in sight but the distant figure of the old man. 'You're barking up the wrong tree, you know,' he said carefully. 'I told you when you came before, I thought it was Hugh.'

'Indeed you did tell me. You were very careful to threaten Hugh, because you intended to take your own revenge on Derry Hayward. Pity you got the wrong man.'

Burke leaned towards him, flushed with anger and gripping his hands together.

'She told me about Hayward,' Burke said fiercely. 'He pestered her. You can see why he did. Sonia was beautiful and lively. Hayward's wife is an old boot. But she told him she wasn't interested. He wouldn't take no for an answer. She was worried about him. She told me so. She was scared of him.'

Markby considered this version of events. It might even be true. But unfortunately Sonia's reputation weighed against her. Like crying 'Wolf!', Markby thought.

He said gently, 'She had a certain reputation in London for chasing after married men, you know.'

Burke's features darkened further. 'That's a filthy lie!'

'She had to leave her job because of it.'

'Now I know you're lying! She was made redundant because business fell off!' Burke shouted.

Markby's tone remained reasonable. 'I put it to you, you didn't know her very well and she may not have always told you the truth.' It was a cruel thing to say but he knew he had the man who'd attacked Derry and intended to kill him. There was no excuse for that. He remembered his old Bamford case of the little housewife with her afternoon brothel. Sex with tea and biscuits. Sonia had been a complex woman. They'd never know the complete truth about her.

As if he could read his mind, Burke burst out, 'What do you know about it, about her? She was dead before you ever heard of her. All you know is what people have told you, lies and gossip! She was a wonderful woman. She loved me, I tell you!'

'All right,' Markby said briskly. 'You loved her and believed she loved you. You believed she was being pestered by Hayward. When she was killed you took it into your head that Hayward had killed her in a fit of jealous rage. You were determined he wouldn't get away with it. You set out to administer your own justice.'

Burke chewed his lower lip and glared at his visitor. He'd realised his error in claiming he'd believed Sonia was in fear of Hayward. Now he was working out his best line of defence. Markby had a fair idea what it would be.

'The only time I ever met Derry Hayward was when I delivered some kitchen furniture to his house. He was never here in my workshop. His wife was; she came and chose the furniture. But my one and only encounter with Hayward was in his own office at that farm of his, when he wrote me out a cheque.' Burke was angry and defiant but there was a touch of smugness, too, in his voice, and the dogged tone of the rehearsed denial.

Markby sighed and studied him silently until Burke grew restless. Blanket denial was always a good ploy. Simon Franklin had used it. Burke was going down the same road. It was all too familiar. Markby wished he had a pound for every time he'd heard different voices uttering different denials, but always with that sullen, stubborn tone.

'And you won't prove otherwise,' Burke concluded. His head tilted back against the wall of the barn, and he turned his face up at the sky in the manner of a sunbather.

Markby received the challenge with equanimity. 'Don't bet on that. Give us time.' Arrogance would bring down Burke, if anything did. He was one of those who couldn't resist taunting the police.

Burke allowed himself a thin smile. 'Unless you find the weapon, I can't see you making much progress. And you won't – not here.' He turned his head to look at Markby. 'You can seal the place up right now, if you want, send in a search team. Go ahead. Dig up my garden. Not that I've got a garden, just a plot of rough ground. You might even do me a favour if you do dig it over.' He got to his feet. 'I wish you luck, Superintendent.'

When he'd gone back inside, Markby got to his feet. He couldn't pretend not to be angered by the curt dismissal. The old man was still down the road, stationary in front of the chain-link fence. Seeking to calm his own feelings, Markby walked down there to join him.

'Pub used to stand there!' said the old man as Markby came up. He raised his stick and pointed at the grassy mounds. 'It burned down 17 April 1954. I helped rescue the spirits in the bar. The bottles were exploding like bombs. They never rebuilt the place, the buggers.'

'Seems a shame,' said Markby in commiseration. The pub was often the centre of social life in small communities. In many places, it was the only public facility left. Take it away and you had nothing.

The old man gave Markby a squinting sidelong look. 'You going to buy a bit of the lad's furniture, then?'

'No,' said Markby. 'Not today.'

The old man gave a wicked chuckle. 'I know who you are,' he said. 'You're a copper. I always recognise you fellows.'

'It seems people do,' said Markby with regret.

'Going to arrest young Burke?'

'No,' Markby said.

The old man poked at a clump of grass with his stick. 'Him and that feller what farms over at Cherry Tree, Hayward, his name is. They had a real old falling-out, you know about that?'

Markby, who'd half turned away, froze and turned back. 'What about it?'

The old man was delighted to be able to tell the copper something he didn't know. He chortled happily. 'They had a real old ding-dong of a row out here in the road. I was out for my walk and I saw 'em. I'd stopped to watch Mr Hayward because he was riding a horse and you don't see the horses about so much these days. I like horses. Mr Hayward come clip-clopping up behind me and says good morning to me, very civil. Mr Hayward is a gentleman. Then he rode on and just when he got level with the barn there, where young chap has his workshop, out dashes the carpenter and grabs the bridle. "I want a word with you!" he shouts.'

He chuckled at the memory. 'Mr Hayward took a swipe at him with his riding whip and told him he was a fool and to let go of the bridle. Horse was stamping and rearing up. Young Burke nearly got clobbered with a hoof so he had to let go of the bridle but he still stood there, yelling, "You're a bloody murderer. You won't get away with it. I'll make sure of that!"'

At this point Wally's memories caused him such excitement he nearly choked. When he'd spluttered for a moment, he resumed his account. 'Mr Hayward, he swung the horse round so that it knocked against Burke and the young fellow fell to the ground. "Let that teach you a lesson!" says Mr Hayward. Burke, he was swearing and cussing. He reached up and grabbed Mr Hayward's boot and pulled him out of the saddle. Then they threw a few punches in the road. Burke got the worst of that, too. The horse had come trotting up by me and I got hold of the reins. Mr Hayward come over to me and said, "Thank you!" and then he give me a fiver. Because Mr Hayward's a gent. Then he said to me, there was no need to go telling anyone about this ridiculous episode. That's what he called it. So I never told anyone, till now. That same night, someone tried to knock Hayward's brains out. Some say it was rustlers. I ain't so sure.'

The old man spat to one side. 'If you ask me that woman was the cause of it all. She was always calling by this place, reckoning she was interested in furniture. I knew her, too. She was married to the chap who farms at Hazelwood. But she wasn't no better than she should be. It wasn't furniture she was after. He doesn't keep his work in that little cottage place of his either, and that's where they always went off to when she came by.' The old man raised his stick to emphasise his last point. 'If you ask me, she was what they call a *femmy fatal*.'

'He had motive. He believed Hayward had killed her. And despite having told me he'd only met Hayward once, at the farm, he quarrelled with him outside his own workshop and was heard, by Wally Squires, to threaten him,' Markby said to Pearce. 'But unless a witness places him at the scene of the attack, we'll find it difficult to prove anything, and Burke knows it. He's been smart enough to get rid of the weapon. I could see that in his face. He offered to let me seal the barn there and then. Cheeky blighter.'

'So, he's laughing at us,' Pearce grumbled.

'Mocking us, perhaps, but he's not laughing. He was genuinely in love with the woman.'

'Wonder how she felt about him,' wondered Pearce.

'If you mean, was she in love, almost certainly not. I'd put my last penny on it. I think what happened was, she was unhappy at Hazelwood and was looking for a man who'd make a fuss of her and generally treat her the way she thought she ought to be treated. She may have first thought Derry Hayward might be that man, but I reckon she soon realised that Belinda was prowling suspiciously around and the game wasn't worth the candle. So Derry got the push and she moved on to Burke, a good-looking young man without any inconvenient ties. Burke proved the adoring swain, but in the long term? Come on, can you imagine Sonia, the woman who showed no liking for the simple life at the farm, planning to spend the rest of her life with a man who hammers bits of wood together all day long?'

Pearce chuckled.

'In the end, our chief problem,' Markby went on, 'is that we'll get no help from Hayward and his wife on this. They'll want to deny any connection between Derry and Sonia. They're terrified of bad publicity for their business. They want Derry's attackers believed to be rustlers. You won't shake them on that.'

'I rang the hospital to ask about old Gilbert,' said Pearce. 'He's making good progress, you'll be pleased to hear.' Hastily he added, 'I mean Hayward.'

'I wish,' Markby said, 'you'd explain why you call him Gilbert. The fellow's name is Desmond.'

'Doesn't matter . . .' said Pearce, edging out of the office. 'Sort of what you'd call a private joke.'

CHAPTER EIGHTEEN

Daylight had faded by the time Meredith got home that evening. As she put the car in its lean-to garage the street lighting flickered into life. Key in hand, she made her way up the path to the beckoning shelter of George Biddock's rustic porch with its pointed roof and solid wood sides broken by insets of open latticework. Home, she thought. She'd never tire of walking up to her own front door.

She stepped into the porch's shadows and froze. For a second, disbelief numbed any other feeling. Then waves of nausea surged over her as the reality forced itself on her. The front door stood ajar and the frosted glass panel it contained was broken.

She still couldn't move. Meredith stared at it, willing it not to be so. Horribly it was so. Someone had smashed a hole, put a hand through and opened the door. Anyone who leaves a house empty all day runs the risk of it being broken into, but this, she knew instinctively, wasn't anything so simple as a burglary. Pull yourself together, she told herself. Come on, you've got to cope with this.

With the jerky movement of an automaton, she put out a hand and pushed at the open door. It creaked open with a rustle as it passed over the shards of broken glass on the coir mat just over the threshold. The gloom inside revealed little but it seemed to her a malevolent atmosphere seeped out, the imprint of her visitor.

She called, 'Bethan?' There was no reply. Meredith put her hand through the gap and pressed the light switch. As the yellow glare flooded the hall, she gasped.

The entire hall area was smeared with red paint – walls, carpet, telephone table. The phone itself lay broken on the floor. More red paint trailed up the stair carpet. Across the hall mirror, written in geranium-red lipstick, was the message, 'Bitch. You don't play dirty tricks on me and get away with it.' Meredith pulled her mobile phone from her bag and called the police.

At first she intended to wait for them where she was in the hall, though she was pretty sure the house was empty, that no Bethan lurked behind a door, weapon in hand. If she had done, she'd have heard the phone call and run for it. There was another reason for Meredith's hesitation, a simple dread of seeing what her visitor had done to the rest of the place.

'You've got to look!' she told herself. She tried the sitting room first and found a nightmare scene of paint-streaked carpet, walls daubed with obscene graffiti, broken ornaments, slashed cushions and curtains. Something powerful smelling, Meredith suspected paint stripper or some other industrial fluid, had been poured over the television. Books had been tumbled from their shelves and disembowelled. Unravelled video and cassette tapes were draped like Christmas decorations around the place. A fire had been lit in the grate and still smouldered with the remains of all Meredith's private correspondence and personal papers. In a malicious joke, she was sure, Meredith's charred passport had been propped on the mantelpiece.

Feeling sick to her stomach, she went into the kitchen where the devastation was, if anything, worse. Flour, tea and coffee covered the floor. Water had been poured on to the granules and the result was a muddy lake. The fridge door hung open and the contents had been flung down and trampled underfoot. Every cupboard was opened and the contents of those given similar treatment. The electric wall clock had been wrenched out and hung face down from its twisted wires.

Meredith slowly climbed the wrecked stairway, trying to avoid stepping in wet paint, to find chaos in the bathroom and both bedrooms. In her bedroom, Bethan had wreaked a special vengeance. Drawers and wardrobe stood open and Meredith's clothes were heaped on the floor. She stooped and picked up a jacket. The sleeves had been cut off. Knowing what she'd find, she picked up and dropped half a dozen other items, all cut about and ruined.

Meredith heard a car door slam outside. The police had arrived.

'She's trashed the place,' Meredith said bitterly to Alan who had arrived some thirty minutes after the two local uniformed constables. 'Completely and thoroughly. She must have taken her time. She's broken all the glass and china, and look at that!' She pointed to the ruined television set. 'She even got hold of my clothes and cut them into ribbons. I haven't got a thing but what I stand up in!'

'I'm sorry,' Alan said, looking round him with dismay. 'Will the insurance pay up?'

'I'll have to get in touch with them. I don't know. It isn't just the money value. I've worked hard on this place! I did the decorating. I hunted down the furniture. She's levered the cupboard doors off their hinges and used my own tools to do it! She's read my correspondence and, in every way possible, invaded my private space. I'll have to get replacements for my birth certificate, passport, insurance papers, everything you can think of. I feel – defiled. The house is defiled. Right now, I don't think I want to live here any more, even when it's fixed up.'

He put his arm round her shoulder. 'Come over to my place tonight, anyway.'

'Yes, I will. Thanks. But I'm not moving in with you indefinitely! Tomorrow I'll book myself into The Crown.'

'As bad as that, eh?' he said in a wry attempt at humour.

'Yes, as bad as that.' She leaned her head briefly on his chest. 'Oh, Alan.'

'Come on, where's that fighting spirit?'

'It's sitting in the corner of the ring wondering what hit it. Did you see? She stuck parcel tape over the glass panel in the door before she broke it so it didn't fall down with a noise.'

'Very professional,' he observed.

'I told you she wasn't an amateur.' Meredith moved away from his supporting arm and gestured angrily towards the hall. 'She could do it, break in during broad daylight, because of that dratted rustic porch! It provided excellent cover. No one could see what she was doing. Not even Doris Crouch next door, who doesn't miss much. Even I didn't see the front door was ajar until I got into the porch. Anyone just passing by wouldn't have noticed a thing.'

'Didn't Doris and Barney hear any noise while she was breaking things up?'

'Doris says she thought she heard a bit of a rumble, as if I was shifting furniture around again. They're both slightly deaf and Doris has the television going all the time full blast. She knew I'd been home all last week and she thought I'd extended my time off. Well, there you have it . . .' Meredith glowered at the wreckage around them. 'Or not, as the case may be!'

'She's come into my office,' Alan told her, 'as I thought she would, with her lawyer in tow. She showed up about four o'clock. She must have come in as soon as she finished taking her revenge on you.'

'They took my fingerprints for elimination,' Meredith said. 'They got loads of others. Some of them are probably hers. She must have left some. Not that I personally need any more proof than I've got. You've seen the message on the hall mirror?'

He nodded. 'We'll secure the place for you tonight.'

'It's OK. George is on his way over to put on a padlock.'

He dropped a kiss on her forehead. 'I've got to get back to work. If her lawyer has finished going over her statement with a fine-tooth comb, I hope we can get her to sign it. Simon Franklin has decided he wants to talk, too. It'll be interesting,' added Markby, 'to see whether they tell exactly the same story.'

Simon had been both voluble and indignant on hearing of Bethan's arrest. 'It wasn't my damn fault! It was those two wretched women. I just got caught up in it. What was I supposed to do?'

'Why don't you tell us what you did do?' Pearce had suggested.

Simon glared at him, then at the empty cup on the table in the interview room, and finally at Markby, who sat quietly nearby.

'I'm not at all sure about your methods,' he challenged. 'I don't think sending your girlfriend in as *agent provocateur* is in the police manual.'

'We were paying a social call,' said Markby urbanely.

Simon snorted. He leaned back and stared appraisingly at Markby. 'Look here, can't we discuss this in a civilised fashion?'

'It's not a civilised matter,' Markby replied coldly.

'No, of course . . . I didn't mean . . .' Simon removed his spectacles and blinked. 'I meant, if I co-operate fully, then my part in it – which is entirely that of innocent bystander – perhaps that could be treated, well, leniently? As it should be.'

'I am not cutting any deals,' Markby snapped. 'You should in any case co-operate fully. It's your duty as a citizen and in your own best interest.'

Simon seized on the last words eagerly. 'That's what I mean. It will be in my interest? If I help you, it's only fair you help me.'

'Your co-operation will be taken into account,' Markby told him in a tired voice. 'I'm promising nothing.'

Simon turned this over in his mind and decided that he wasn't going to extract any fuller reassurance. 'Very well,' he said pettishly. 'The fact is, just before all this happened, Bethan and I had been discussing getting together again. We kept it quiet until we'd decided. One reason for that was to avoid getting quizzed by Hugh or by Sonia – or by our other acquaintances.

'On that night, that Wednesday, Bethan was at the cottage. We put her car in my garage in case anyone should call by, and left my car on the drive. We didn't want it known, as I said, that she was there. She was upstairs when Sonia turned up. I was in my study, working. It was typical of Sonia to arrive without notice and just assume I would have time to sit and listen to her complain about Hugh. It's always the same if you work at home, Bethan will tell you. People just assume somehow that you're available and they can ring you up about the village fête. On that particular evening, not only was I keen to get rid of Sonia on my own account, but the longer she stayed, the more chance there was she'd hear Bethan moving about upstairs. On the other hand, if I tried to hurry her out too obviously, she might get suspicious. She was like that, damned neurotic.

'In the event, she sat herself down, clearly meaning to stay for at least an hour. She began to grumble and whinge in her usual way. It was a bit of a chilly evening and I had lit a couple of logs in the grate. It made the room look nice, cosy. Sonia sat huddled over the fire, looking miserable. She said how much nicer it was in my cottage than the farmhouse. She'd been trying to do something to the house but Hugh wouldn't spend any money. I pointed out Hugh didn't have too much spare money. She said that wasn't her fault. It was no reason to expect her to live in a slum. That was a wild exaggeration. I know the farmhouse is shabby, but it isn't a slum. Still, I suppose she was used to something better, or at least smarter. I felt a bit sorry for the silly woman, but what could I do? I gave her a sherry and tried to explain that I was in the middle of a very difficult chapter and it really wasn't a good moment for her to be there.'

Here Simon paused, took off his spectacles, and blinked. 'And then, the most extraordinary thing happened. Sonia started on a different tack and a brand-new one. She said she'd never really cared much for Hugh. She'd really been keen on me, but Bethan and I had been together at the time so she'd settled for Hugh. Now Bethan and I were parted, and she and Hugh clearly couldn't go on much longer living under the same roof, how about she move in with me? She appreciated my work. She could be very helpful to me, she said.

'I don't mind telling you, I was completely gobsmacked. I sat there staring at her, couldn't believe my ears. I was more than ever convinced she was potty. She'd always struck me as unstable. I asked her if she'd really thought about what she was saying. Hugh was my brother. She could hardly walk away from his bed and climb into mine.

'Oh, nonsense, was her reply. It happened all the time. Not *this* time, I told her, and made it clear that there was no way she was ever moving in with me.

'She wouldn't take no for an answer. She argued on, dismissing every objection and putting forward a lot of crackpot ideas. I'd be able to work undisturbed because she'd take care of everything. What's more, she had experience in publicity. That was true, she had worked for some publicity company or other for a while. I needed a higher profile than I'd got, she said. I needed to break out of the school textbook market and make it into the world of the mainstream novel. She went on and on, using every cliché of business-speak you could think of and completely rewriting my life, each plan barmier than the one before.'

Simon sat back and stared meditatively at his questioners. 'I tried reason. I told her I was doing all right in the school textbook market, thanks very much, and anyway, I had been reliably informed that historical fiction doesn't sell so well these days. I didn't want her advice either on what I should be writing or on how to get my face in the Sunday supplements. I suggested that she go home, make it up with Hugh, and we'd forget all about it.

'She took that very badly. She asked me point-blank, didn't I find her attractive? I told her equally bluntly, no, I didn't. I thought she was selfish, bad-tempered, overpainted, stupid and totally round the twist to boot.' Simon's face creased in an expression of self-righteous shock. 'Do you know, she went for me!'

'Perhaps that wasn't surprising,' said Pearce, who'd been standing by listening with increasing astonishment. 'If you said all that.'

Simon was unimpressed. 'I told her the truth. If she didn't want to hear it, she shouldn't have put herself in that situation. Of course, I knew she'd be angry. But I didn't think she'd attack me, did I? She knocked my glasses off and broke the frame.' Simon indicated the mended frame. 'And then Bethan came in. She'd been listening on the staircase. She shouted out, "What the hell do you think you're doing, Sonia?" and then, blow me, the next thing, they were going at it hammer and tongs. They'd both got nails like talons and they were starting to inflict some damage on one another. So I tried to get between them and that's when Sonia snatched off Bethan's wig and threw it in the fire.'

Simon stopped speaking. Beads of sweat had broken out on his forehead and he fumbled for a handkerchief to mop them away. With shaking voice, he went on, 'I have a collection of historical knick-knacks, I suppose you'd call them. Some people might call them antiques. I think of them more as work aids. I've used them for illustrations in my books when writing about costume and that sort of thing. Some of them were lying on my desk and among them was a Toledo dagger, early 1600s. It was the sort of thing an Elizabethan gallant would have worn, along with his sword. They were violent times. The dagger didn't have great value. It wasn't in the best condition. During all the fracas, I'd forgotten it. But as the wig crackled and burned, smelling dreadful, Bethan snatched up the dagger. She was in such a rage – she's got a temper but, my God, I'd never seen her like that before. She shouted, "You bloody well won't play the tricks here you played in London!" Whatever that meant. All I know is that Bethan lunged out—'

Simon grew distressed again and began to polish his lenses with unnecessary vigour. 'Good God, I couldn't believe it. She stabbed Sonia. Bethan stabbed her.' He put down his glasses. 'Do you think I could have another cup of tea?'

A little later, when he'd drunk the tea, he went on with his story. 'At first I was going to call an ambulance. But as I went to the phone, Bethan called out that I shouldn't bother. Sonia was dead. I was horrified, panic-stricken. I went back to the body, tried to find vital signs, couldn't. The old dagger, after three hundred and fifty years or so, had done the job it had been fashioned to do. It had killed. I didn't know what to do. We decided to move the body. Bethan was for putting her on the railway line. I refused to agree to that. It would be bad enough for Hugh, called on to identify her when she was eventually found, without her being chopped up by a train. Besides, I couldn't be sure a post mortem wouldn't find a stab wound, even if a train struck her. We put her in Bethan's car because it has a boot. You can see through the windows of my off-roader, see anything large carried inside. We left her on the embankment,' finished Simon.

'And we went back and cleaned up the study. Bethan went back to Cheltenham. It would have been all right if she'd stayed there.'

He heaved an exasperated sigh. 'But no, she had to come back to the inquest, draw attention to herself, accuse Hugh in a stupid attempt to divert suspicion – suspicion which she was bringing on herself by her own actions and involving me.'

'But it wouldn't have been all right, would it?' Markby pointed out. 'Because your niece had seen you carrying Sonia's body at the embankment.'

Simon looked dejected. 'Yes, I'm truly sorry about that. But if that had been the only thing linking me to the wretched business, I think I could've talked Tam round, you know, persuaded her she'd been mistaken.'

'That wasn't the impression I got when I saw you with her in the orchard,' Markby told him sharply. 'Or you've a very odd idea of persuasion.'

'I was beside myself!' Simon protested. 'It was a nightmare! Look, I wouldn't have allowed you to arrest old Hugh, you know. I was furious with Bethan for trying to pin it all on him. I'd have spoken up if you'd arrested my brother.'

Bethan's story differed in her account of the striking of the blow. According to her, Sonia had picked up the dagger and threatened Simon. Simon, in trying to disarm her, had inflicted the fatal wound.

On being told her fingerprints had been found in Meredith's house, she said calmly, 'Well, they would be, wouldn't they? She invited me in for coffee once.'

When it was pointed out the prints were all over the wrecked furniture and broken phone, and the writing on the mirror could be identified as hers, Bethan smiled.

'If Simon's account is right,' Markby said to Meredith, later that week in the expensive hotel restaurant to which he'd taken her 'to cheer her up', 'Bethan deliberately picked up the dagger and stabbed Sonia. That's murder. She is a violent woman as we both know. We've found traces of Sonia's blue nail varnish in the boot of Bethan's car, and of Sonia's blood. Bethan had cleaned the car out but it's difficult to remove all traces. There are also traces on the clutch pedal of the red paint she used to daub your house. It has proved possible to match the genetic information taken from skin scrapings beneath Sonia's nails to Bethan. One way and another, she's going to have to pull out all the stops to talk herself out of this one! The papers have all gone to the Crown Prosecution Service. My guess is they'll be charged jointly, but it's not up to me. My job's done.'

'Did Simon destroy the dagger?'

'No, actually. He says he realises he ought to have done. Bethan ordered him to break it up with a hammer and scatter the fragments but he couldn't bring himself to do it. It had survived over three hundred years. He couldn't, he says, just smash it into bits. He buried it in his garden. We've dug it up.'

'This place is Elizabethan, or even a bit earlier,' said Meredith, looking round the restaurant.

'And doesn't the management want us to know it! I wish they wouldn't tart these old places up so much. Why must we have red velvet chairs with gold fringes?'

'The designers told the owners that was historic.' She pointed at an indifferent reproduction of Queen Elizabeth the First in the so-called Armada portrait, which hung nearby. 'She's supposed to have lodged here for one night during one of her royal progresses around the country. You can sleep in her bedroom.'

'Not in her bed? That's the claim these places usually make. I must say, if Good Queen Bess really did sleep in all the places she is supposed to have done, she certainly got around a bit on these royal jaunts.' He picked up the menu. 'Do you fancy the Tudor game pie?'

'Not really,' said Meredith. 'Not after what you've just been telling me. I think I might go for the vegetarian option.'

CHAPTER NINETEEN

Hugh was in the yard when Jane drove her car through the open gate in the evening. Starlings were settling for the night in the venerable oak which spread its branches over the barn roof. As she switched off the engine and opened the door, she could hear them squabbling noisily over the best roosts. Every few moments, another dark swarm of birds joined the existing colony until the tree threatened to become the most overcrowded hotel around. The oak presided over Hazelwood Farm like a guardian, Jane fancied. It had doubtless witnessed other dramas than the one played out here recently and would probably witness more in years to come.

Hugh was tinkering with the Land Rover again so that she could only see a decapitated three-quarters of him. He emerged as she came up to him, and turned, wiping his hands on a piece of oily rag. He was wearing his usual grubby jeans and disreputable pullover. Behind him in the open barn she glimpsed the Volvo gathering dust. At the moment a chicken was perched on its roof.

'Hi,' she said, pushing her hands into her jacket pockets.

'Hullo,' he returned. 'Didn't think we'd see you here again.'

Startled, Jane asked, 'Whyever not?'

He gave an odd half-smile and turned back to his decrepit vehicle. 'See this?' He rapped the side of it with a spanner. 'It's had its day. It's done us well – but it's finished.' He indicated the Volvo. 'When all this is over, cleared up, I'm going to sell that car and buy a new Land Rover, or a newish one, anyway. Sonia wouldn't appreciate that so, wherever she is, I hope she doesn't know of it.'

'Are you trying to tell me,' Jane asked, 'that I'm not needed at Hazelwood any more?'

He looked at her in surprise and then in some embarrassment. 'I didn't say that. I just said, I thought you wouldn't come again. I'd have tidied myself up a bit if I'd known.'

'Well, I have come again,' said Jane firmly. 'I'm glad to hear you're thinking of tidying yourself up. It's not before time. If you want to sell that Volvo, you'd better keep the chickens off it.'

He looked over his shoulder towards the barn. 'Right, I'll throw a tarpaulin over it.'

Jane asked, 'Why did you think I wouldn't come?'

He shrugged. 'You never know how people are going to behave, do you? Since Simon's arrest – and Bethan's – I've been getting a few odd looks and remarks. It's because it's turned out a family matter. People think there was a lot more going on here than there was. They started gossiping when Sonia died. Now they're going at it twice as bad. A family with a murder in it, you see, makes people curious, nervous, but sympathetic. On the other hand, a family with a *murderer* in it – that shocks them rigid. That's a whole different kettle of fish. That's a scandal. Not a thing you live down, a murderer in the family.'

'I'm very sorry about your brother,' said Jane.

'I don't blame him,' he said quickly. 'He panicked and decided to help Bethan hide the body. But he didn't strike the blow, did he? Or the police don't seem to think he did.'

'And you?' Jane asked. 'You prefer not to think he did?'

'If you like, yes, I do prefer it.' He gave that wry smile again. 'We see what we want to see, don't we? And believe what we want to believe?'

'Yes, we do,' Jane said. Like choosing to believe Peter had loved her when, really, he probably never had. 'I understand it's a very difficult situation for you and for Tammy. If, as you indicate, people are turning their backs on you now, and spreading vile gossip, then that makes it worse. You have to ignore it, that's all I can say to you. The people who are doing it aren't worth bothering about. But I'm sorry you thought I was so shallow.'

'You've got that wrong!' he protested, looking alarmed. 'That's not what I thought at all. You're a hundred and ten per cent, you are,' he added unexpectedly, and smiled at her.

'Oh,' said Jane, feeling a tide of red rise up her throat and invade her cheeks. 'Thank you. The people you say are gossiping, they'll get bored eventually and want to talk about something else.'

Hugh nodded. 'Perhaps. But they won't forget. Country people have long memories.'

'You're going to have to come to terms with that, Hugh,' she told him earnestly.

'I dare say I will. I'm glad you've turned up again, anyway. Tammy will be pleased!' he added quickly as if he feared he might be paying her too many compliments. He hit the Land Rover again with the spanner for no obvious reason.

Jane laughed and picked a stray strand of blonde hair from her forehead. 'I'll keep coming, then. Who knows, I might even get used to the cows.'

Now it was Hugh's turn to laugh, the first time she'd heard him. 'As a matter of fact,' he said. 'I've got another reason I'm glad to see you.'

'Yes?' Jane hoped she didn't sound as nervous as she felt.

'I've made myself a business plan. Don't look at me like that. No need to shy off. I'd like you to take a look at it.'

'All right.' She didn't know whether to be relieved or regretful. 'But I don't know anything about farming.'

'No, but you've got your head screwed on the right way. I'd value your opinion.'

'Oh, I see,' said Jane. 'Then I'd better take a look at it. I'll go in the house and put the kettle on.'

As she walked towards the farmhouse, she heard, behind her, Hugh whistling softly and tunefully to himself.

The evening had turned chill and Markby had lit the log fire in the hearth. It crackled up cheerily, sending shadows dancing around the walls and investing everything with a rosy glow. Still squatting on his heels before the grate, he turned his head to look across at Meredith, sitting on the old sofa with her back against one arm and her feet on the cushions.

'You didn't really mean it, did you?' he asked. 'About moving into The Crown until your place is fixed up?'

'It'll take ages to fix my house up again. I can't just land on you indefinitely,' she said.

He couldn't see her face because she had bent it over the sherry glass in her hand and her thick mop of dark brown hair had fallen forward. He could see the tip of her nose and that was that.

'You can land on me, as you put it, for as long as you like. You'll hate being at The Crown.'

'Yes, I know I shall.'

'Being here with me can't be that bad, can it?' he asked wryly.

She looked up then, tossing back the inconvenient locks of hair. 'No, of course it isn't! It's not that!'

'I wish you'd tell me what it was, then. Because it's got me flummoxed.' After a moment he added, 'You will want to move back into your house, you know, once it's been cleaned up and redecorated. I accept that. I don't like it much, but I accept it.'

'I suppose I shall, but it won't ever be the same.'

'Suffering martyrdom at The Crown meantime won't improve the situation.' She didn't answer and although he couldn't see her properly, he fancied her resolve to stay at the hotel was weakening. 'Why don't you,' he suggested, 'stay on here for the few weeks it'll take to get your place straight? It's got to make better sense.'

She looked up and across to him. 'Until my place is fixed up?'

'Until your place is back to its shining self.'

'It wasn't ever shining.' She looked thoughtful. 'I hadn't got it quite right, you know. Now Bethan's wrecked the lot, it does give me a chance to start again from scratch. All right, I accept. I'd hate The Crown. I'll move in here for a few weeks. Though it's only until my place is ready, you know.'

'Absolutely,' he said. 'Goes without saying. But I'll open a bottle of wine.'